MINUS

by LISA NAFFZIGER

IRON
CIRCUS
COMICS
™

strange and amazing

inquiry@ironcircus.com   www.ironcircus.com

publisher, editor
C. Spike Trotman

book designer
Matt Sheridan

proofreader
Abby Lehrke

print technician
Rhiannon Rasmussen-Silverstein

published by
Iron Circus Comics
329 West 18th Street, Suite 604
Chicago, IL 60616

ironcircus.com

first edition: June 2019

print book ISBN: 978-1-945820-32-8

10 9 8 7 6 5 4 3 2 1

printed in China

MINUS

Names: Naffziger, Lisa, author.
Title: Minus / by Lisa Naffziger.
Description: [Chicago, Illinois] : Iron Circus Comics, [2019]
Identifiers: ISBN 9781945820328
Subjects: LCSH: Teenagers--Comic books, strips, etc. | College students--Comic
     books, strips, etc. | Missing persons--Comic books, strips, etc. | Autonomy
     (Psychology)--Comic books, strips, etc. | LCGFT: Graphic novels.
Classification: LCC PN6727.N34 M56 2019 | DDC 741.5973 [Fic]--dc23

CHAPTER 1

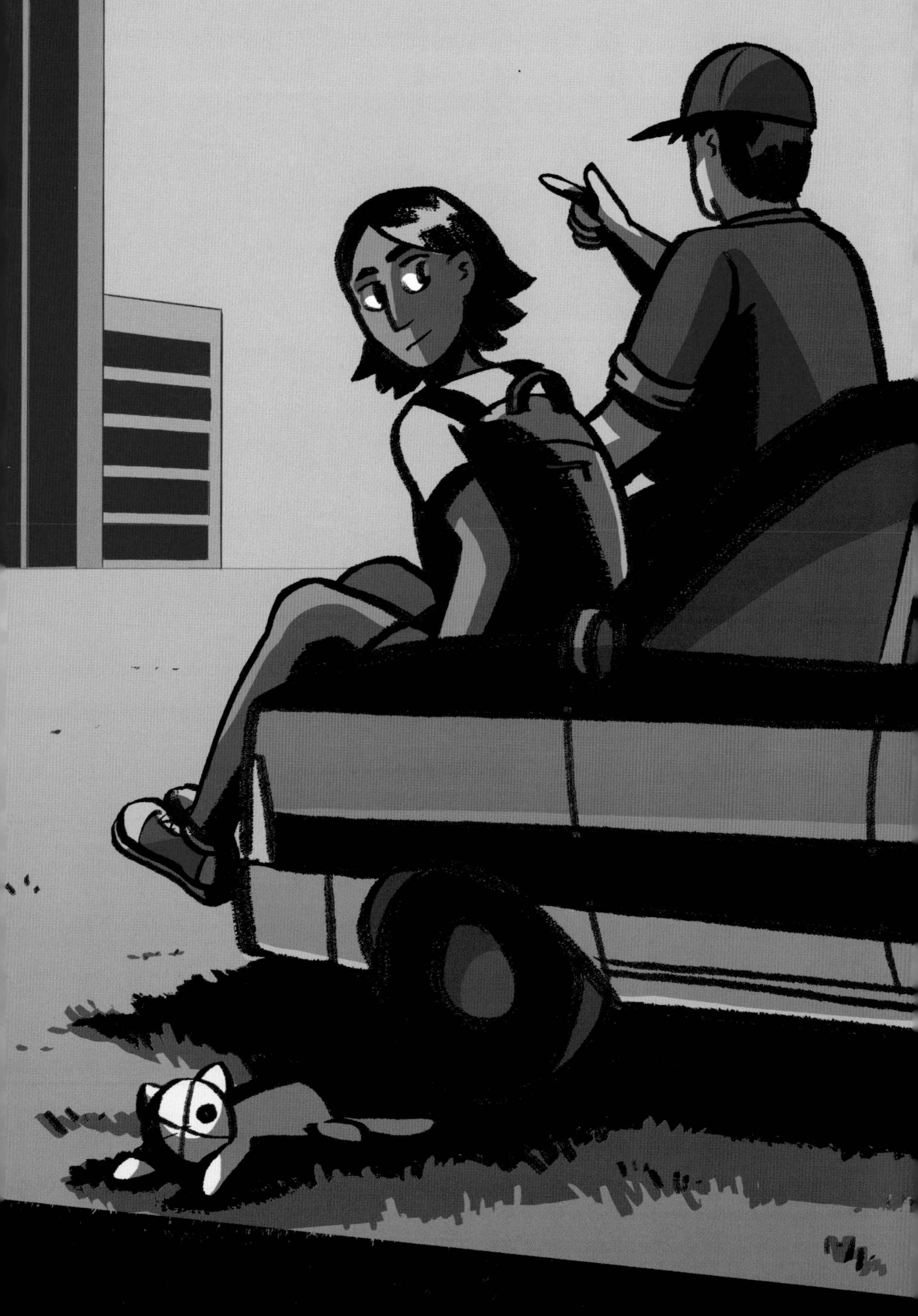

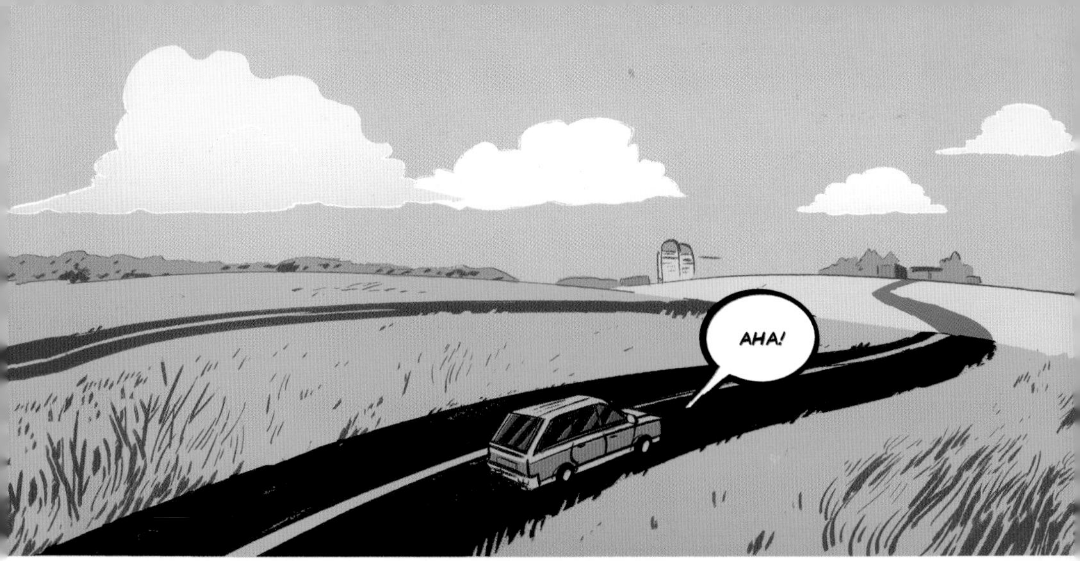
AHA!

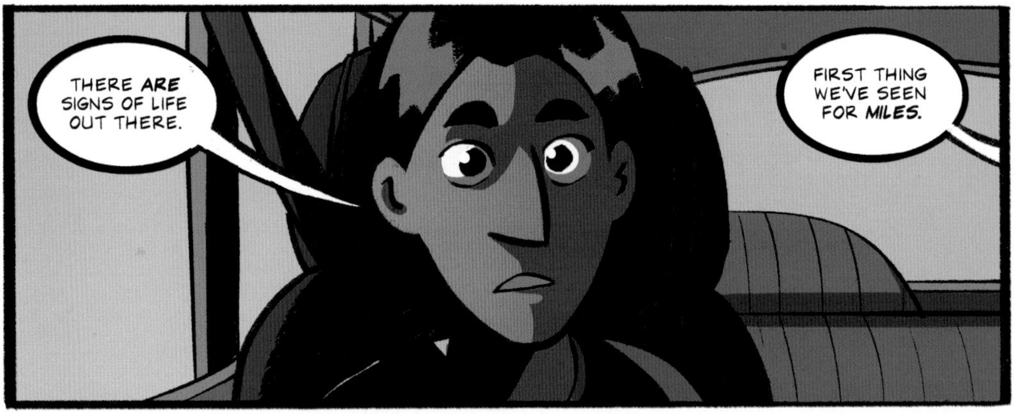
THERE ARE SIGNS OF LIFE OUT THERE.
FIRST THING WE'VE SEEN FOR MILES.

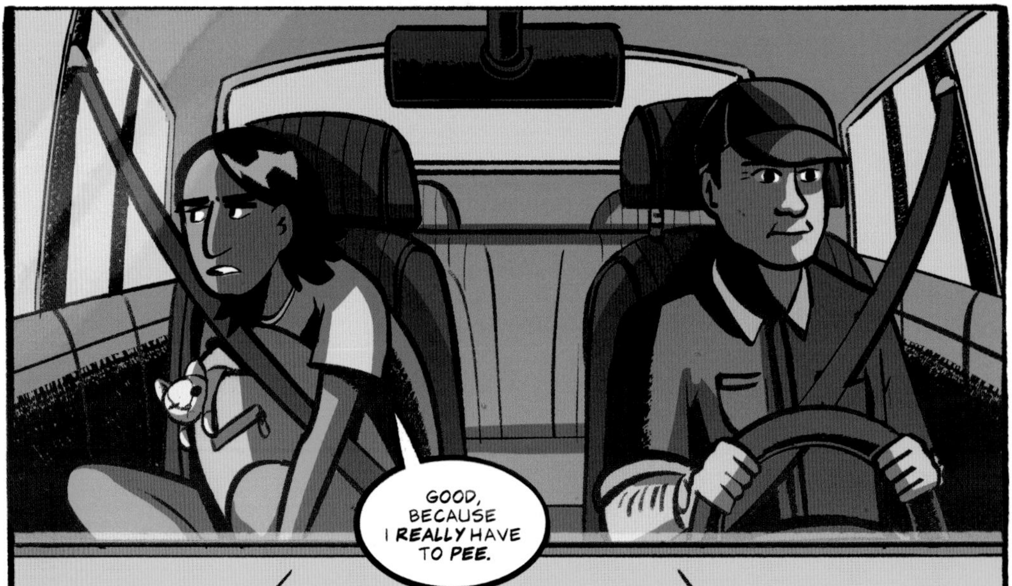
GOOD, BECAUSE I REALLY HAVE TO PEE.

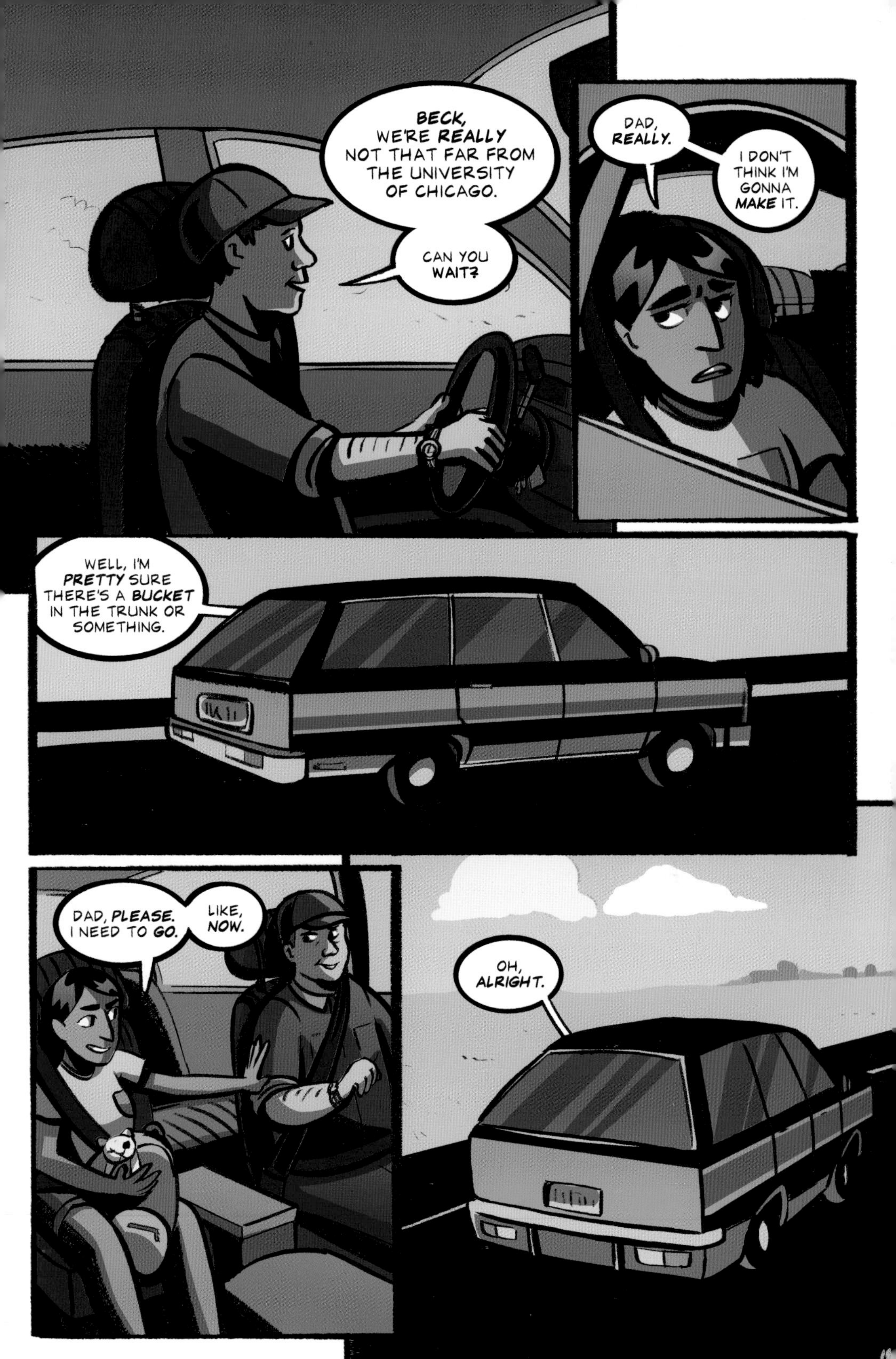
BECK, WE'RE REALLY NOT THAT FAR FROM THE UNIVERSITY OF CHICAGO.
CAN YOU WAIT?
DAD, REALLY.
I DON'T THINK I'M GONNA MAKE IT.
WELL, I'M PRETTY SURE THERE'S A BUCKET IN THE TRUNK OR SOMETHING.
DAD, PLEASE. I NEED TO GO.
LIKE, NOW.
OH, ALRIGHT.

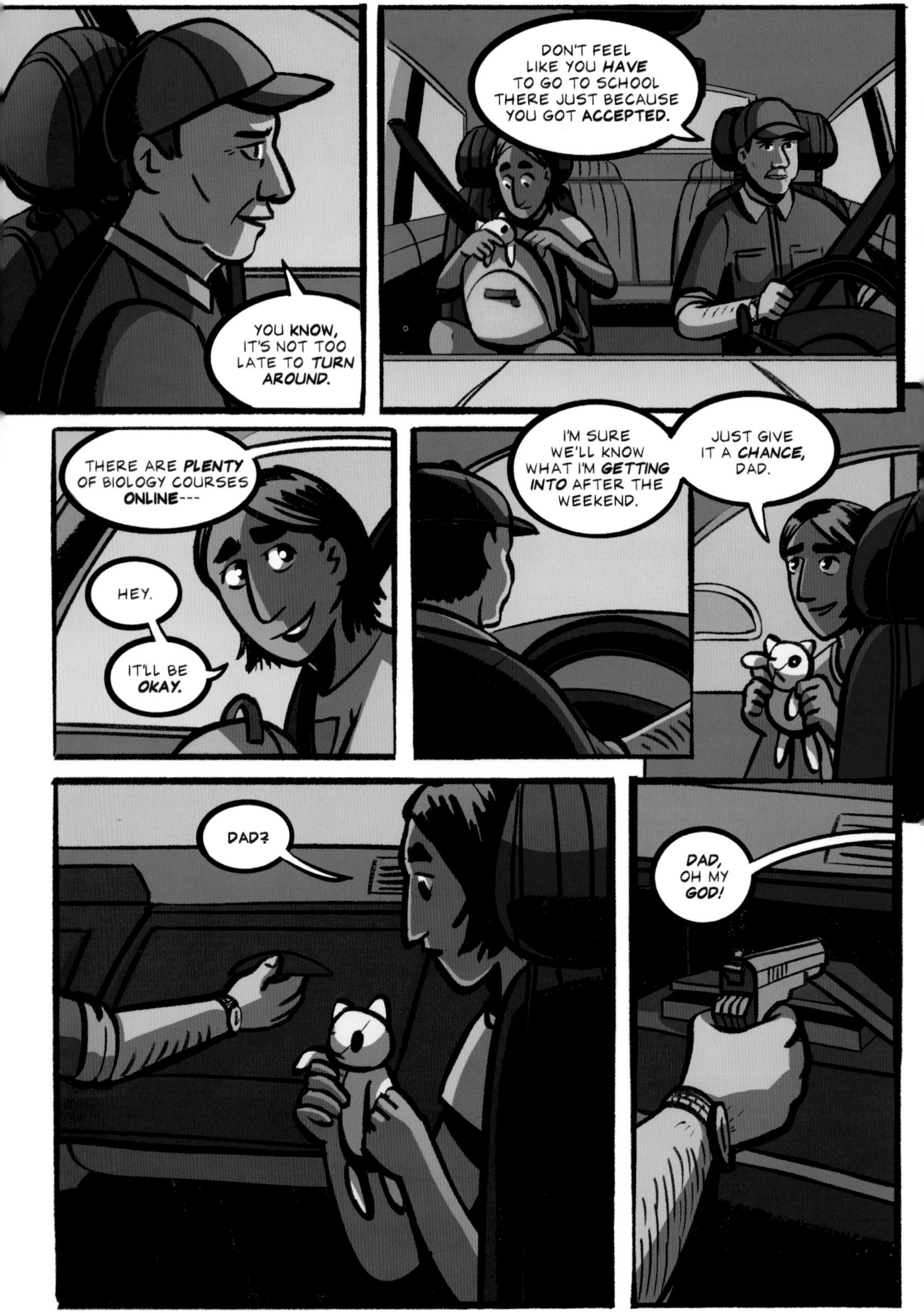
YOU KNOW, IT'S NOT TOO LATE TO TURN AROUND.
DON'T FEEL LIKE YOU HAVE TO GO TO SCHOOL THERE JUST BECAUSE YOU GOT ACCEPTED.
THERE ARE PLENTY OF BIOLOGY COURSES ONLINE---
HEY.
IT'LL BE OKAY.
I'M SURE WE'LL KNOW WHAT I'M GETTING INTO AFTER THE WEEKEND.
JUST GIVE IT A CHANCE, DAD.
DAD?
DAD, OH MY GOD!

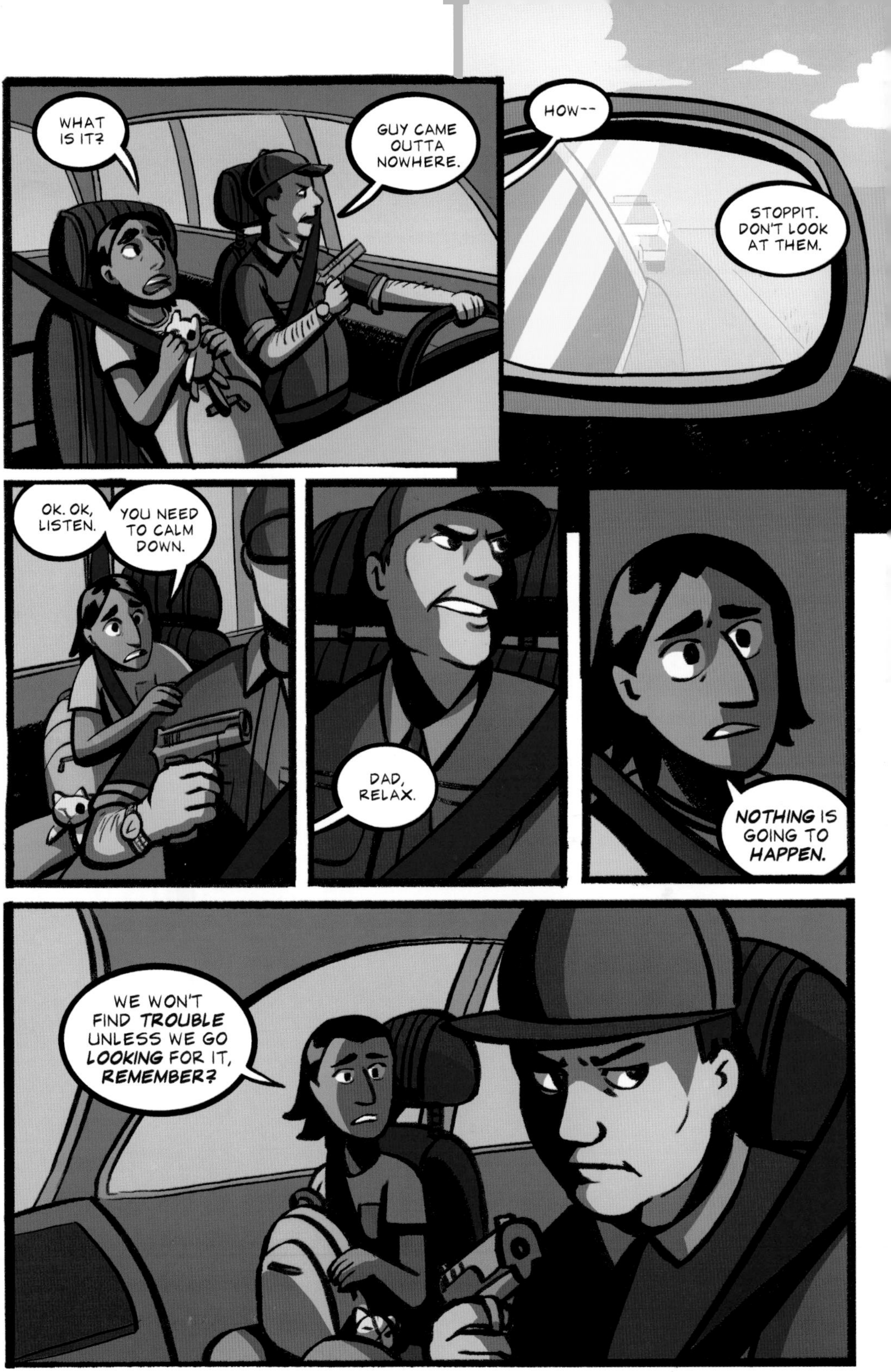
WHAT IS IT?
GUY CAME OUTTA NOWHERE.
HOW--
STOPPIT. DON'T LOOK AT THEM.
OK. OK, LISTEN.
YOU NEED TO CALM DOWN.
DAD, RELAX.
NOTHING IS GOING TO HAPPEN.
WE WON'T FIND TROUBLE UNLESS WE GO LOOKING FOR IT, REMEMBER?

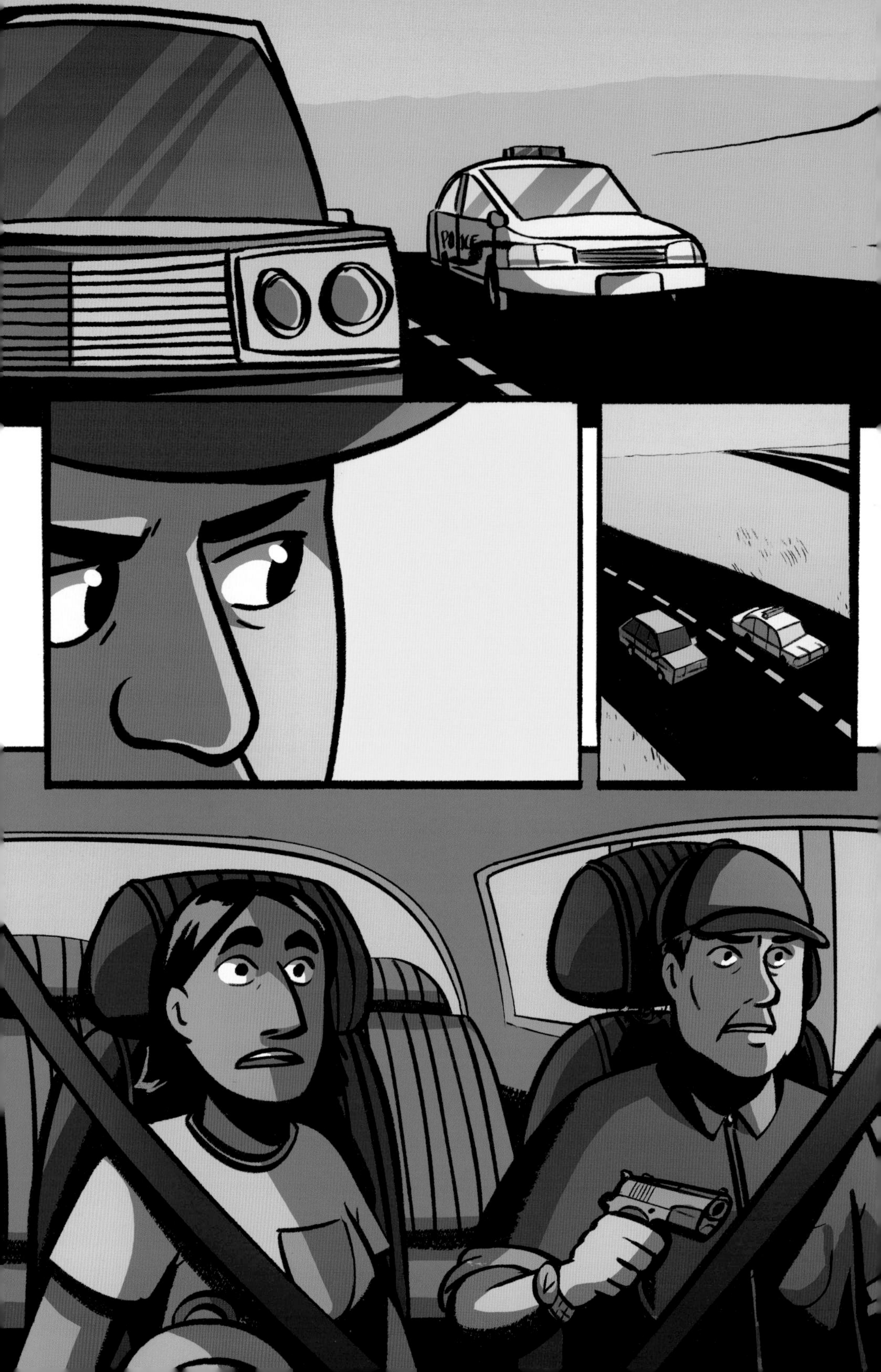

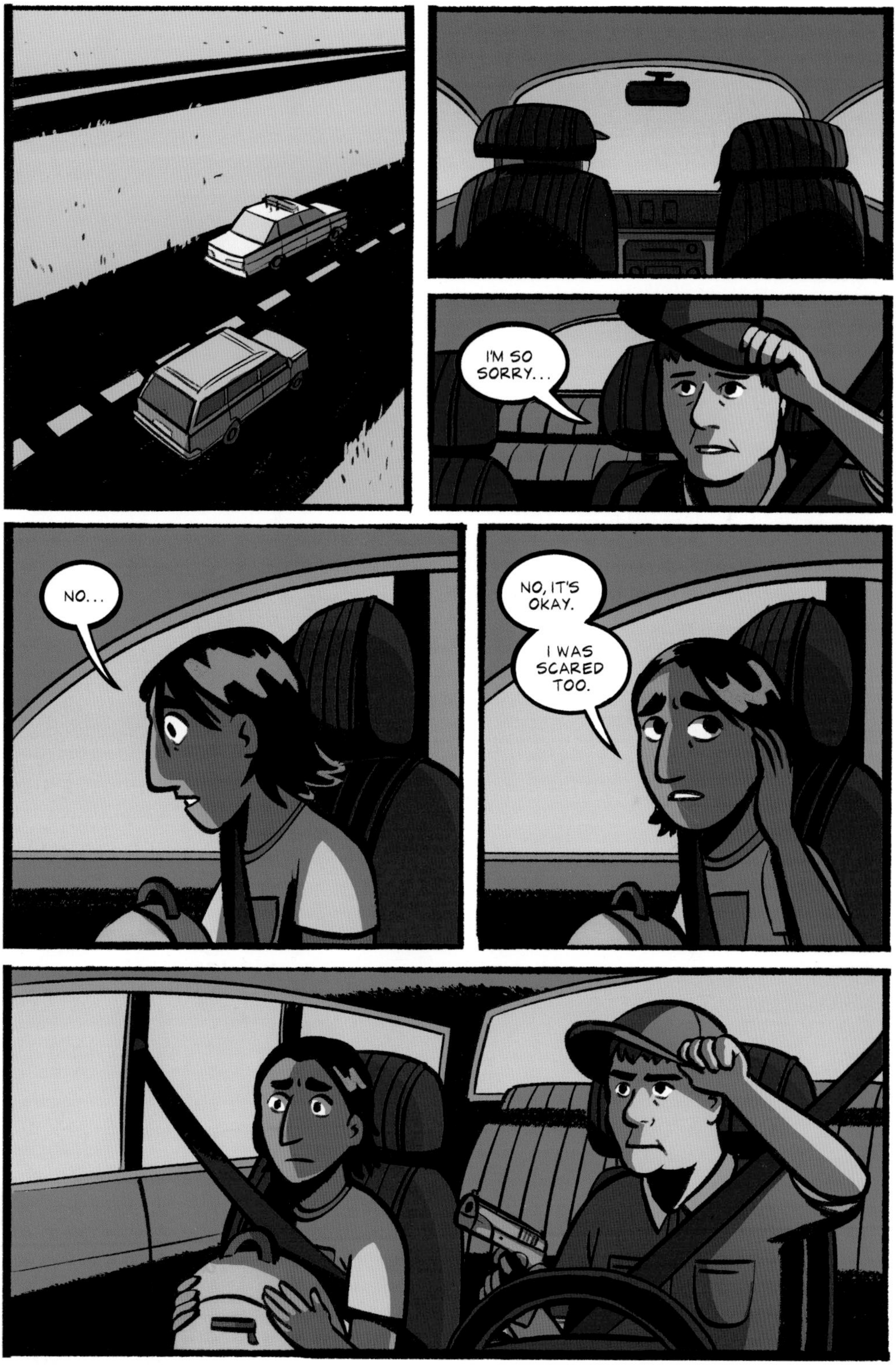
I'M SO SORRY...
NO...
NO, IT'S OKAY.
I WAS SCARED TOO.

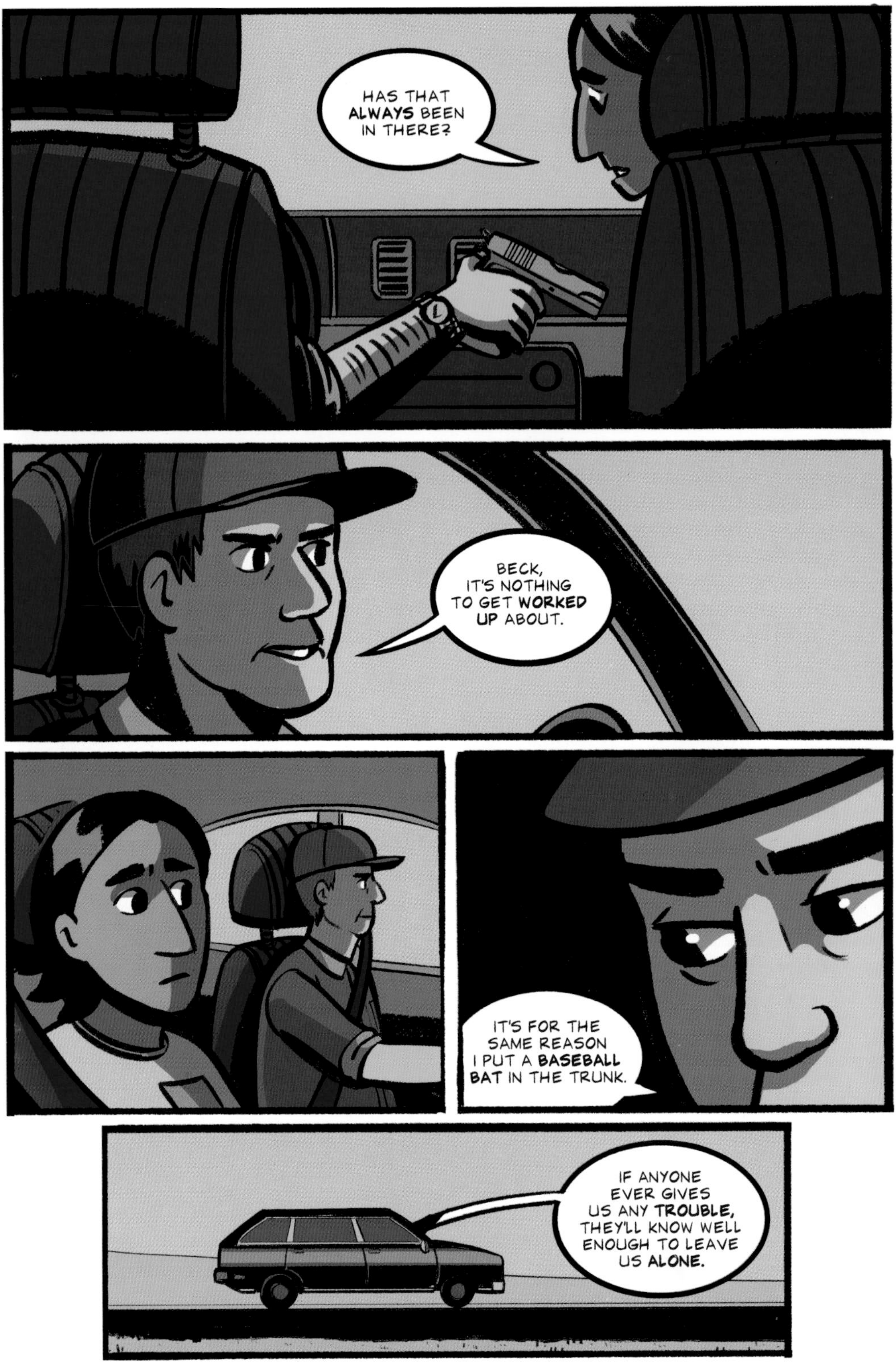
HAS THAT ALWAYS BEEN IN THERE?
BECK, IT'S NOTHING TO GET WORKED UP ABOUT.
IT'S FOR THE SAME REASON I PUT A BASEBALL BAT IN THE TRUNK.
IF ANYONE EVER GIVES US ANY TROUBLE, THEY'LL KNOW WELL ENOUGH TO LEAVE US ALONE.

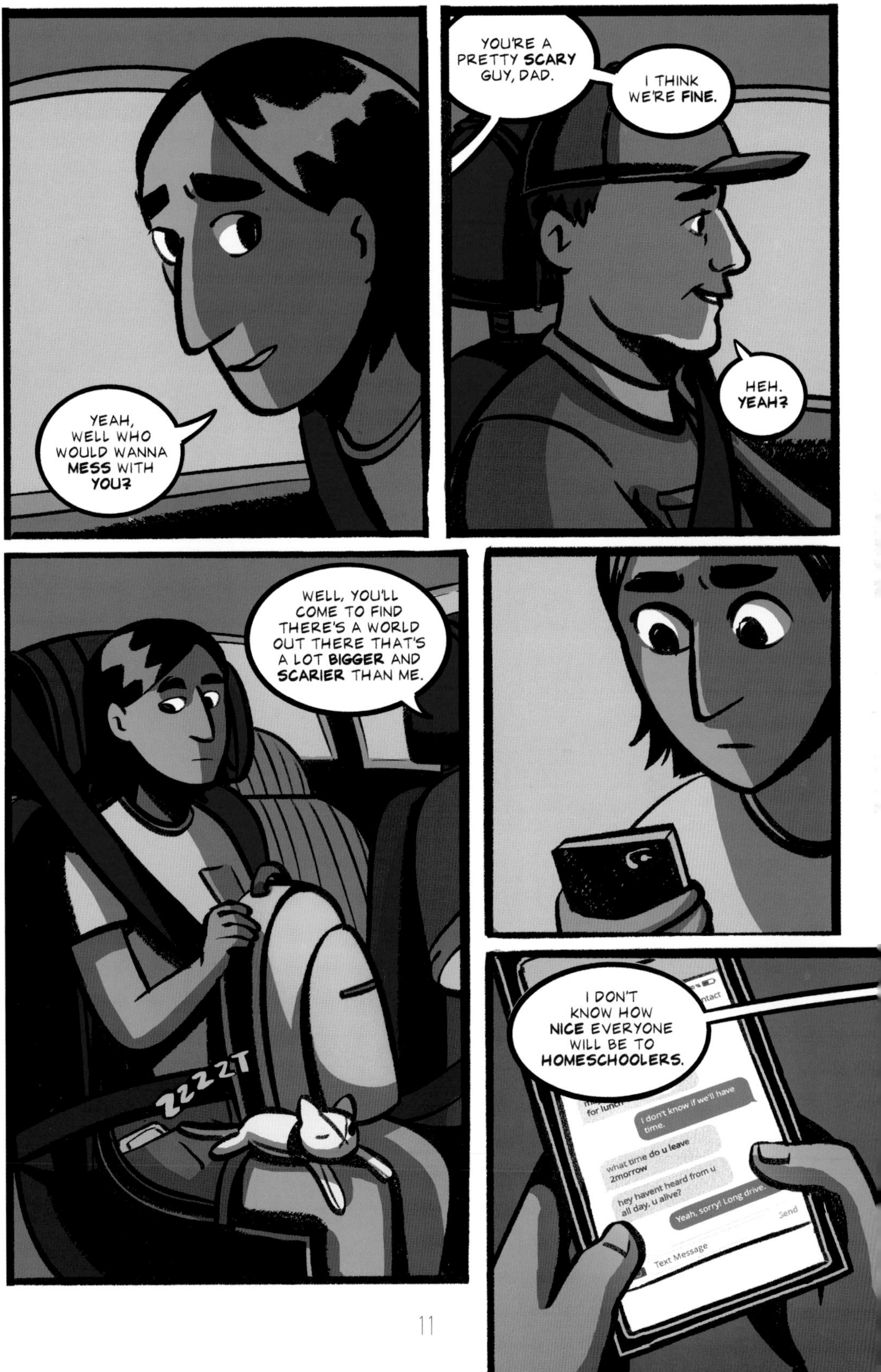
YEAH, WELL WHO WOULD WANNA MESS WITH YOU?
YOU'RE A PRETTY SCARY GUY, DAD.
I THINK WE'RE FINE.
HEH. YEAH?
WELL, YOU'LL COME TO FIND THERE'S A WORLD OUT THERE THAT'S A LOT BIGGER AND SCARIER THAN ME.
ZZZZT
I DON'T KNOW HOW NICE EVERYONE WILL BE TO HOMESCHOOLERS.
I don't know if we'll have time.
what time do u leave 2morrow
hey havent heard from u all day. u alive?
Yeah, sorry! Long drive.
Send
Text Message

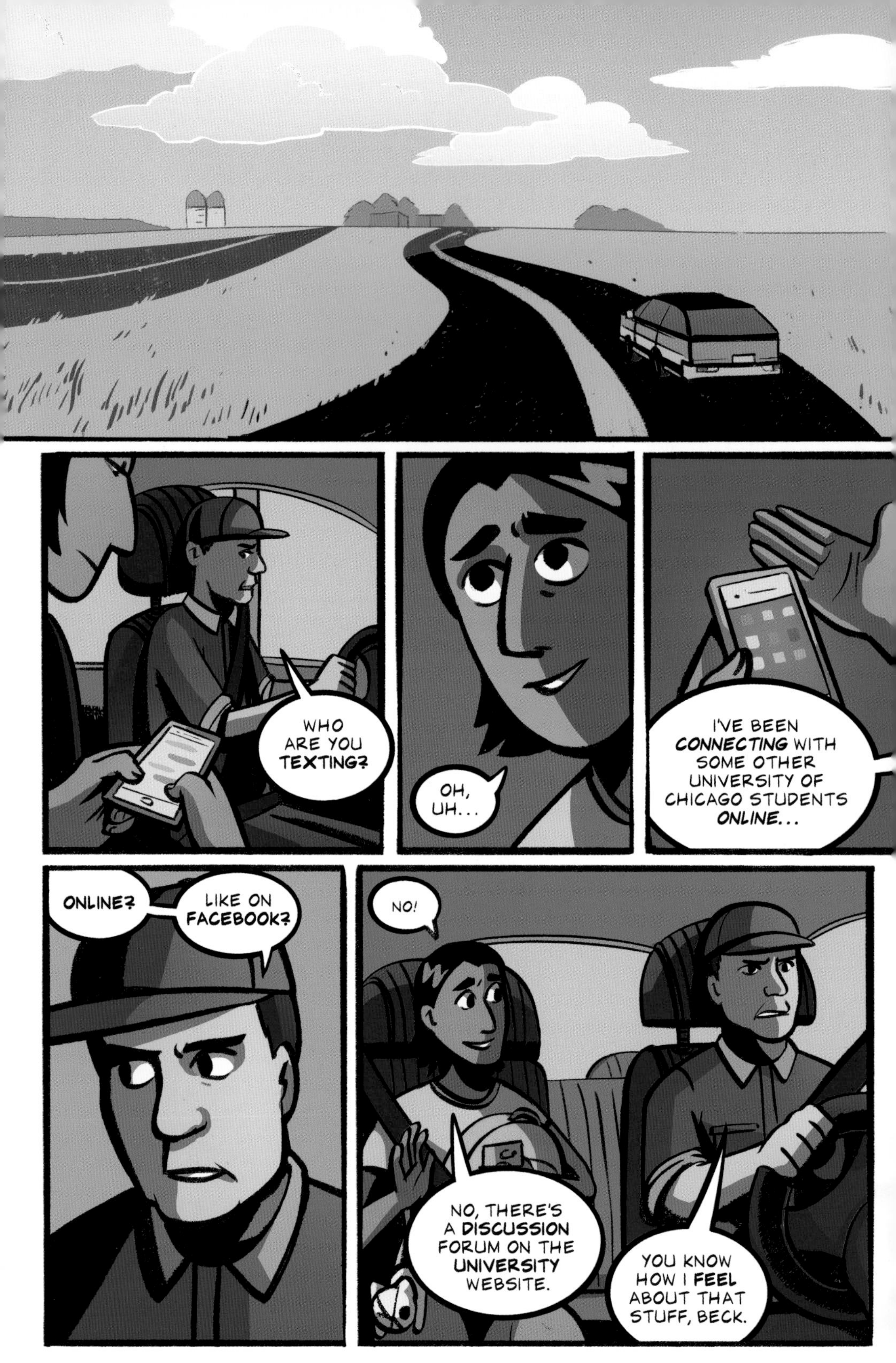
WHO ARE YOU TEXTING?
OH, UH...
I'VE BEEN CONNECTING WITH SOME OTHER UNIVERSITY OF CHICAGO STUDENTS ONLINE...
ONLINE?
LIKE ON FACEBOOK?
NO!
NO, THERE'S A DISCUSSION FORUM ON THE UNIVERSITY WEBSITE.
YOU KNOW HOW I FEEL ABOUT THAT STUFF, BECK.

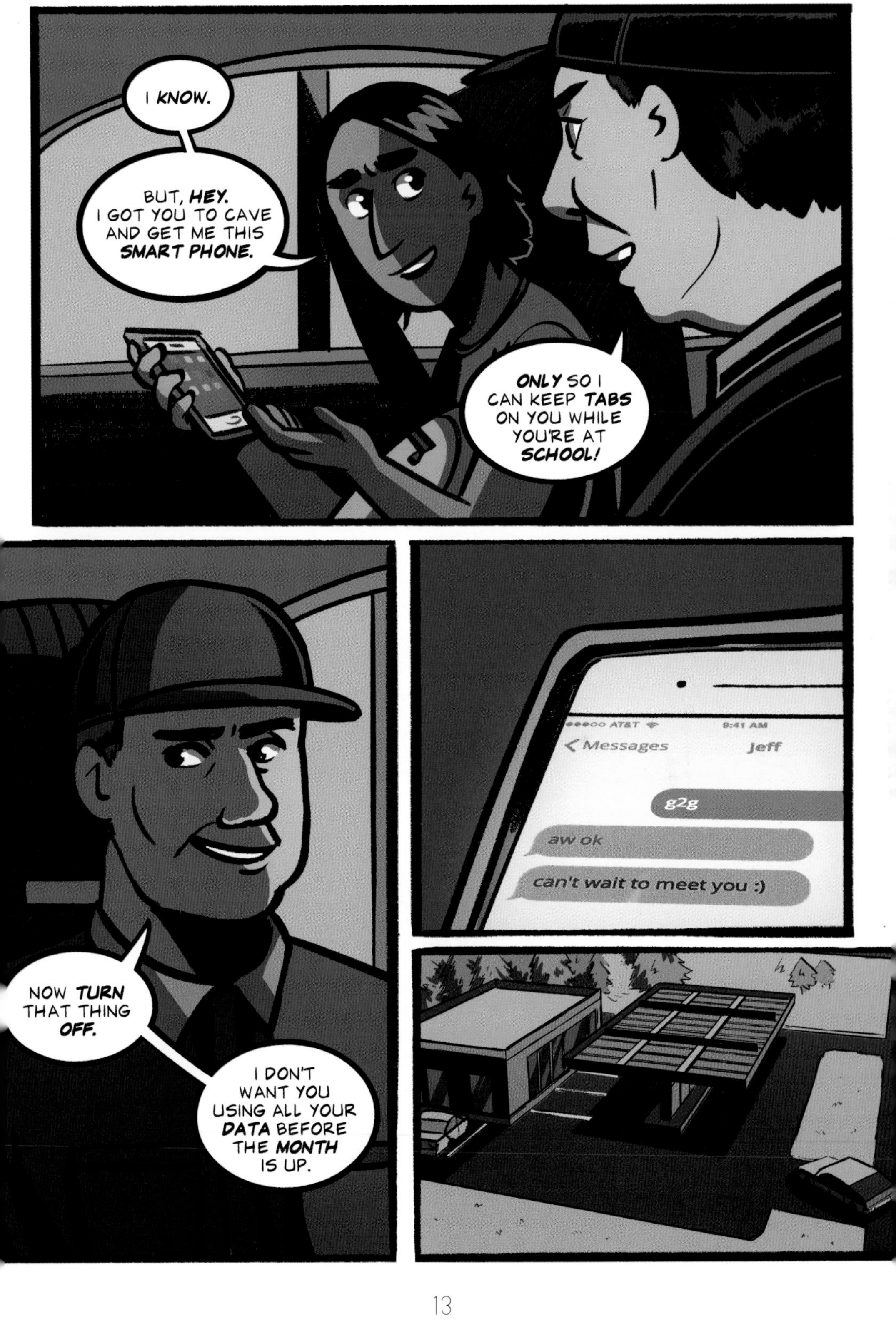

I KNOW.
BUT, HEY. I GOT YOU TO CAVE AND GET ME THIS SMART PHONE.
ONLY SO I CAN KEEP TABS ON YOU WHILE YOU'RE AT SCHOOL!
NOW TURN THAT THING OFF.
I DON'T WANT YOU USING ALL YOUR DATA BEFORE THE MONTH IS UP.
●●●○○ AT&T
9:41 AM
< Messages
Jeff
g2g
aw ok
can't wait to meet you :)

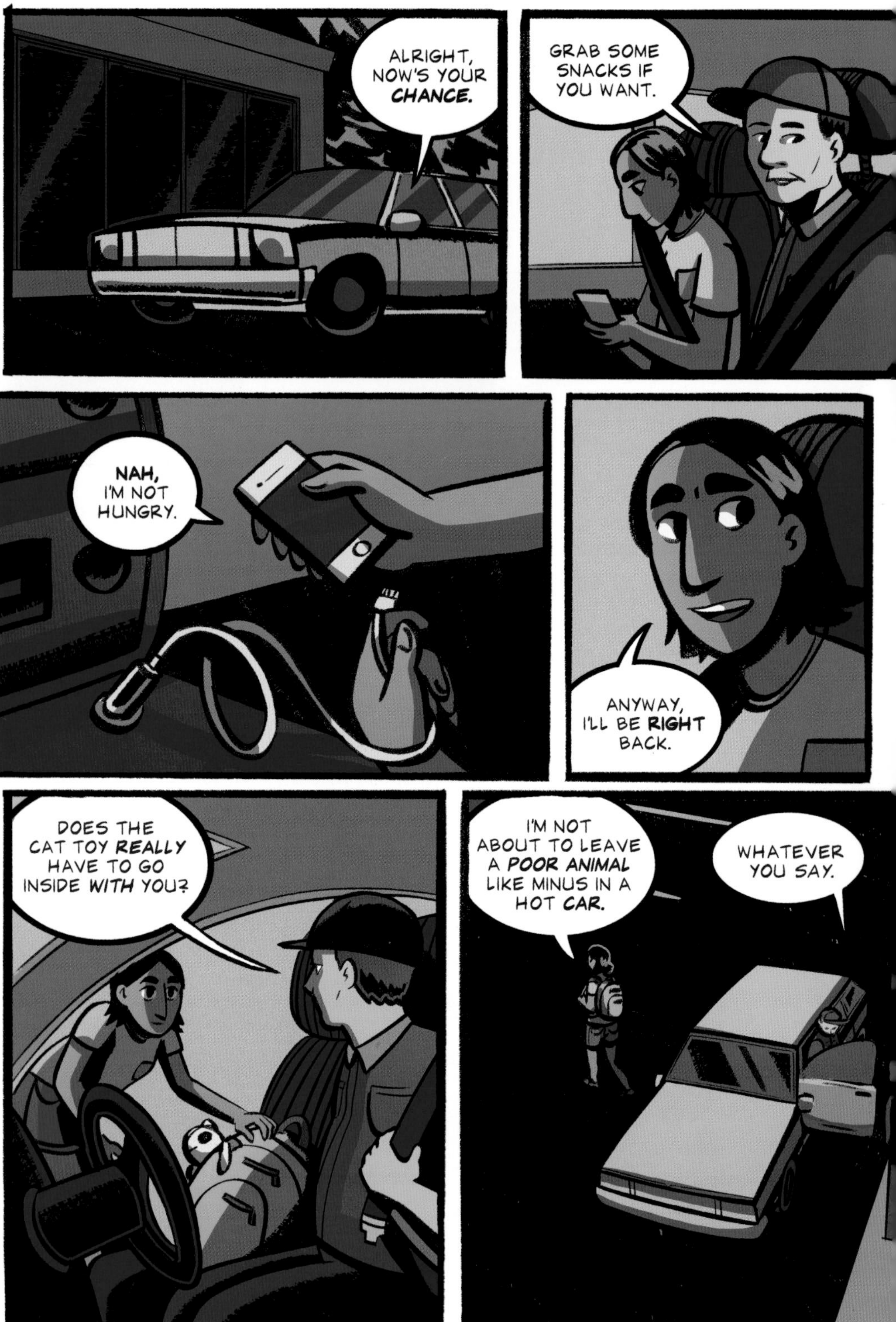
ALRIGHT, NOW'S YOUR **CHANCE.**
GRAB SOME SNACKS IF YOU WANT.
NAH, I'M NOT HUNGRY.
ANYWAY, I'LL BE **RIGHT** BACK.
DOES THE CAT TOY **REALLY** HAVE TO GO INSIDE **WITH** YOU?
I'M NOT ABOUT TO LEAVE A **POOR ANIMAL** LIKE MINUS IN A HOT **CAR.**
WHATEVER YOU SAY.

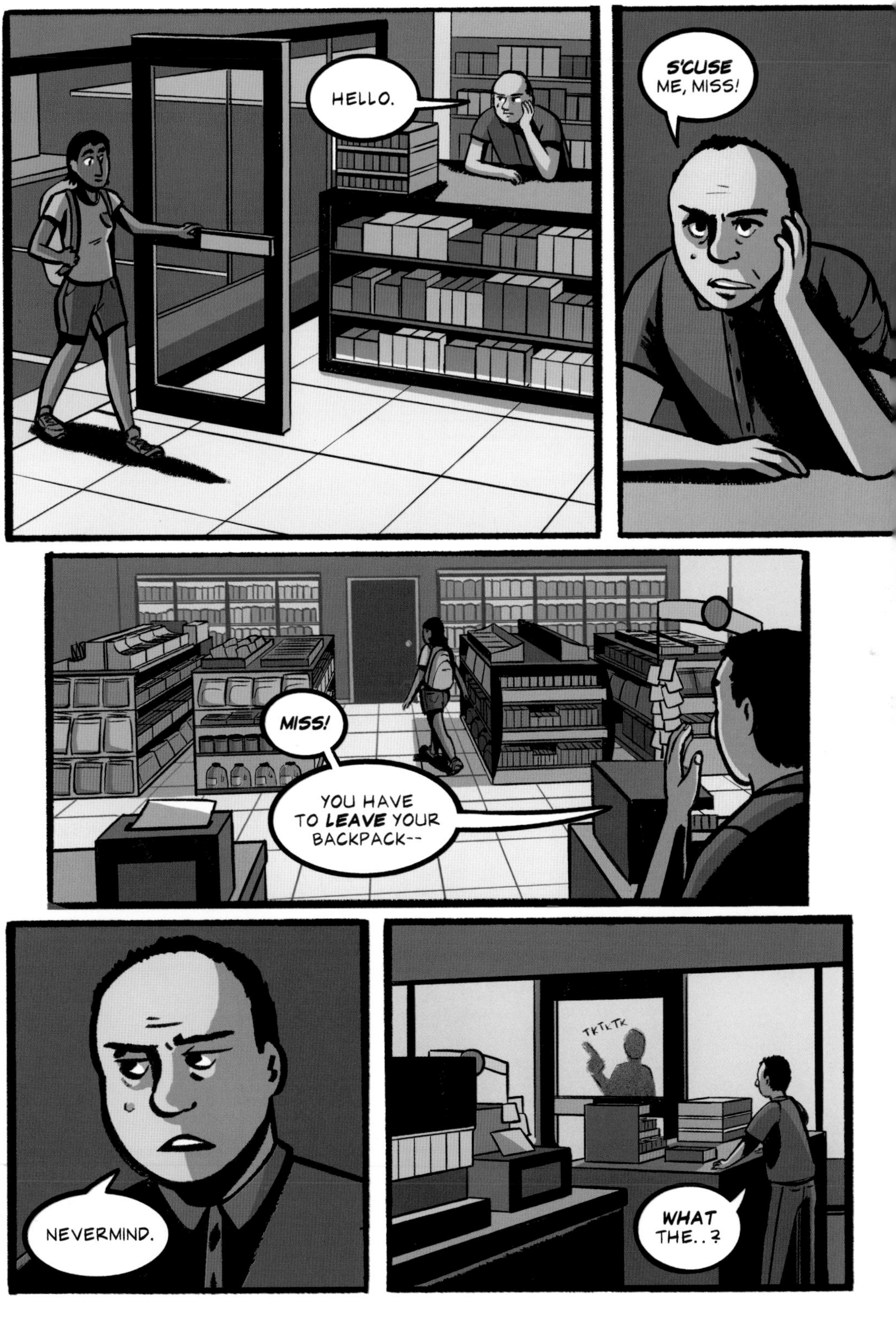
HELLO.
S'CUSE ME, MISS!
MISS!
YOU HAVE TO LEAVE YOUR BACKPACK--
NEVERMIND.
TKTKTK
WHAT THE..?

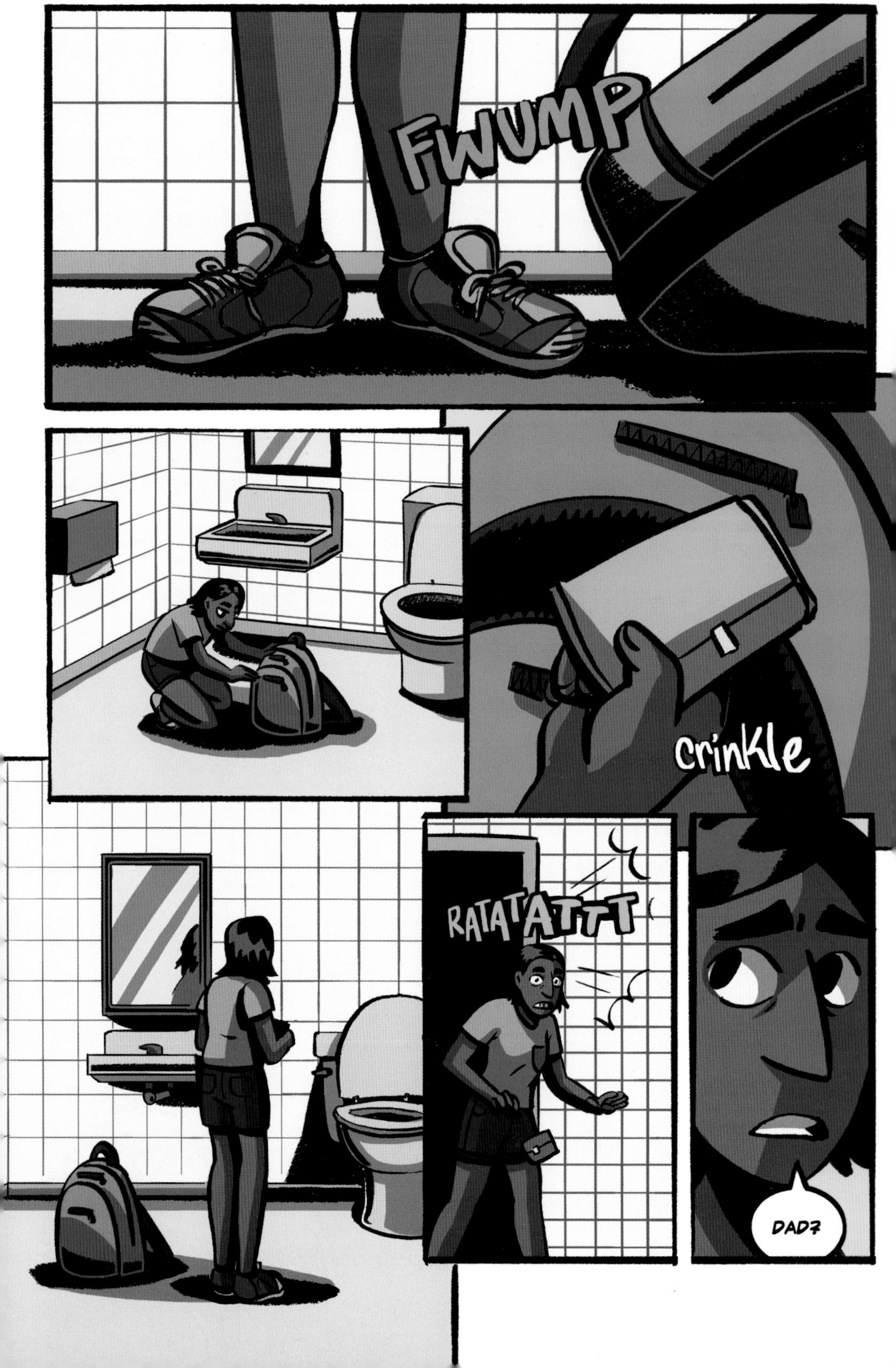
FWUMP
crinkle
RATATATTTT
DAD?

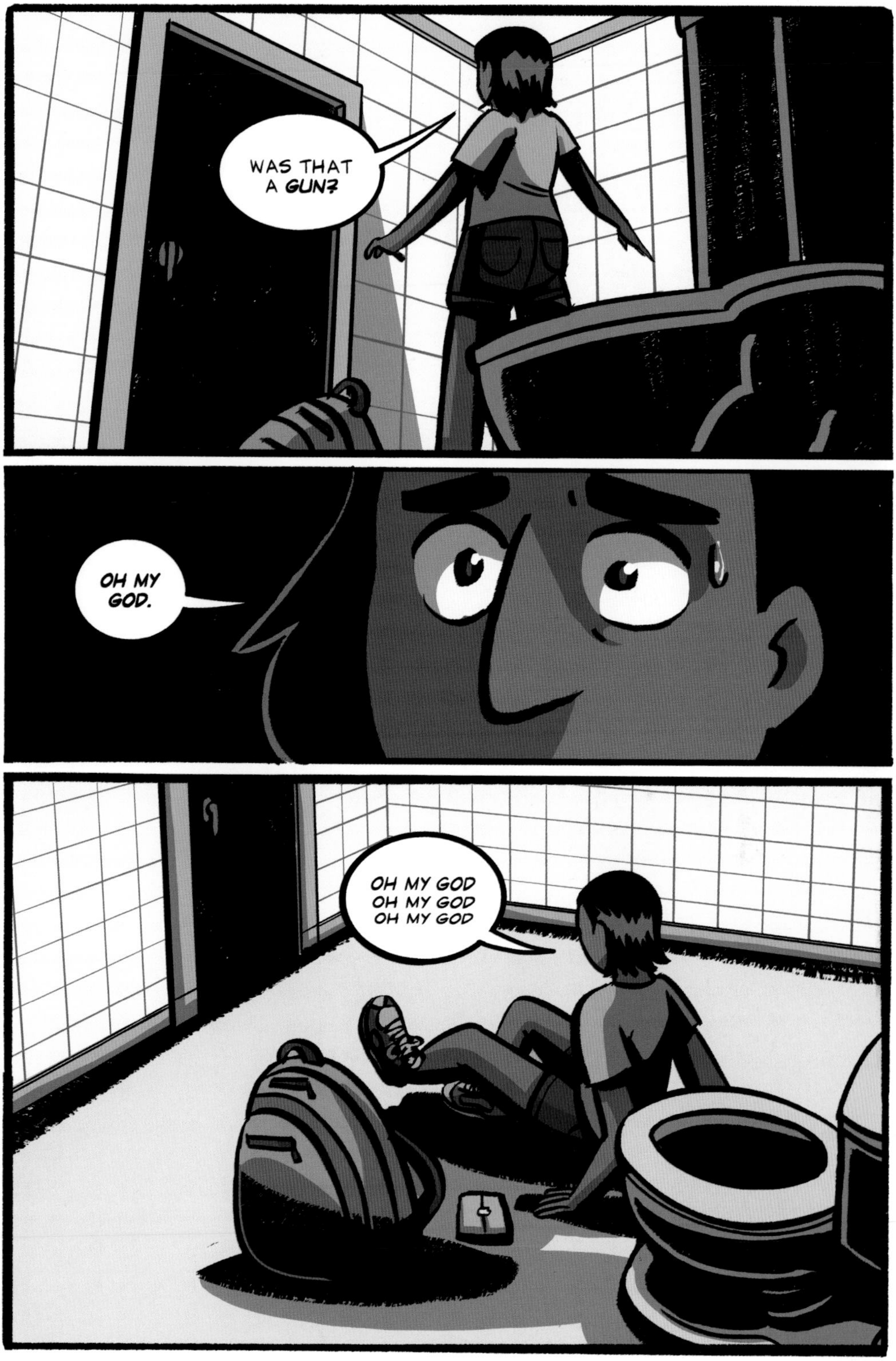
WAS THAT A GUN?
OH MY GOD.
OH MY GOD OH MY GOD OH MY GOD

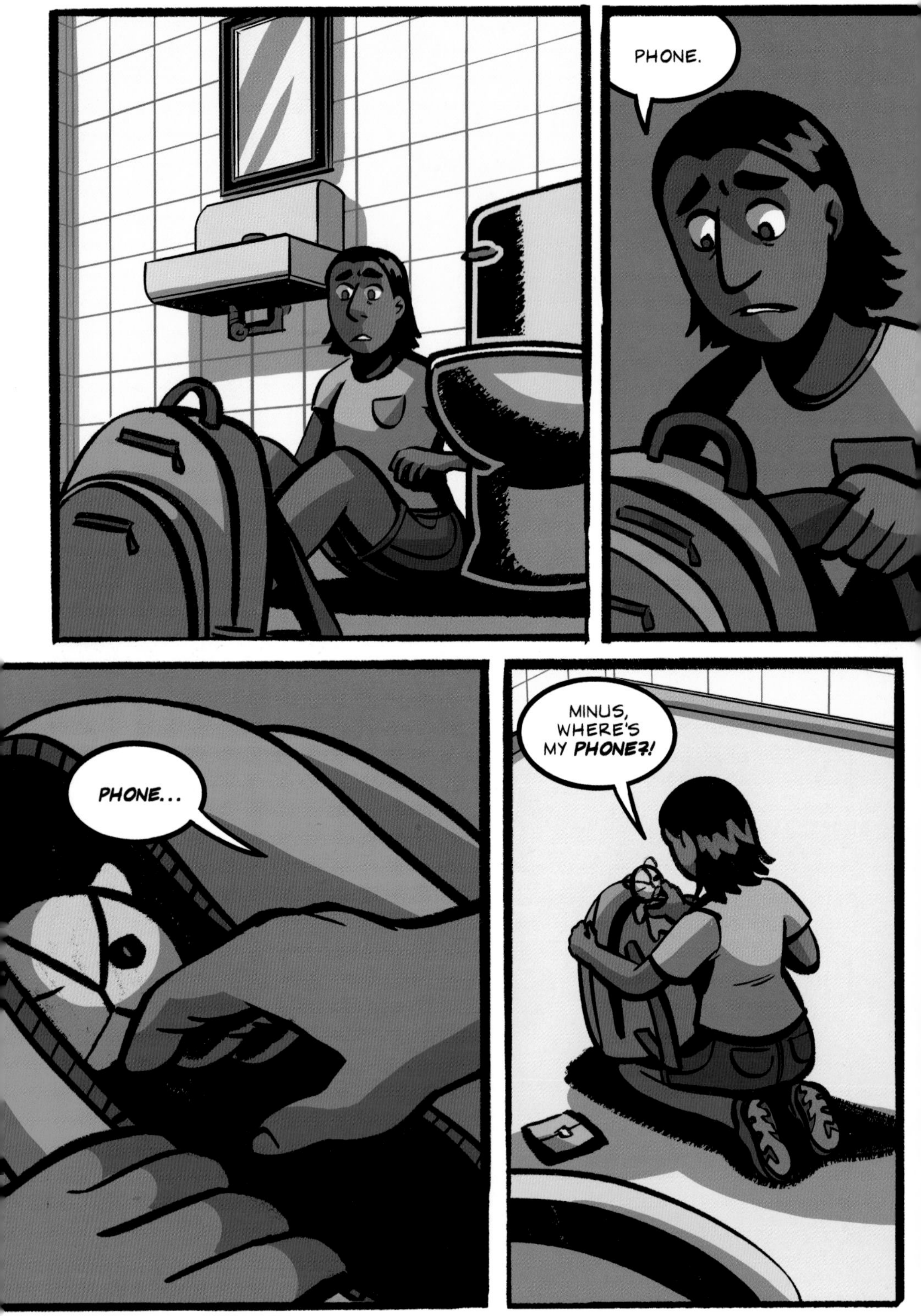
PHONE.
PHONE...
MINUS, WHERE'S MY **PHONE?!**

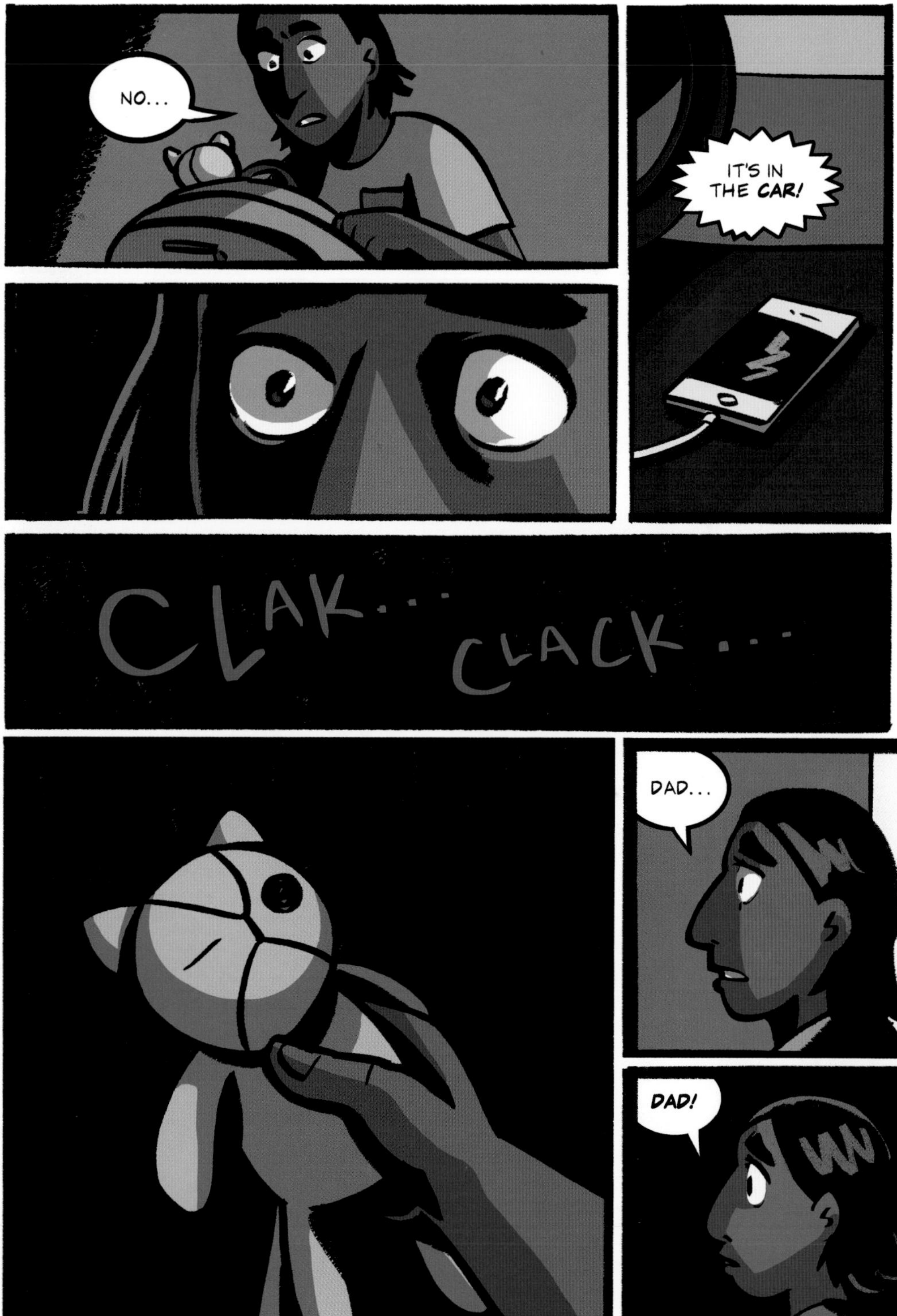
NO...
IT'S IN THE CAR!
CLAK... CLACK...
DAD...
DAD!

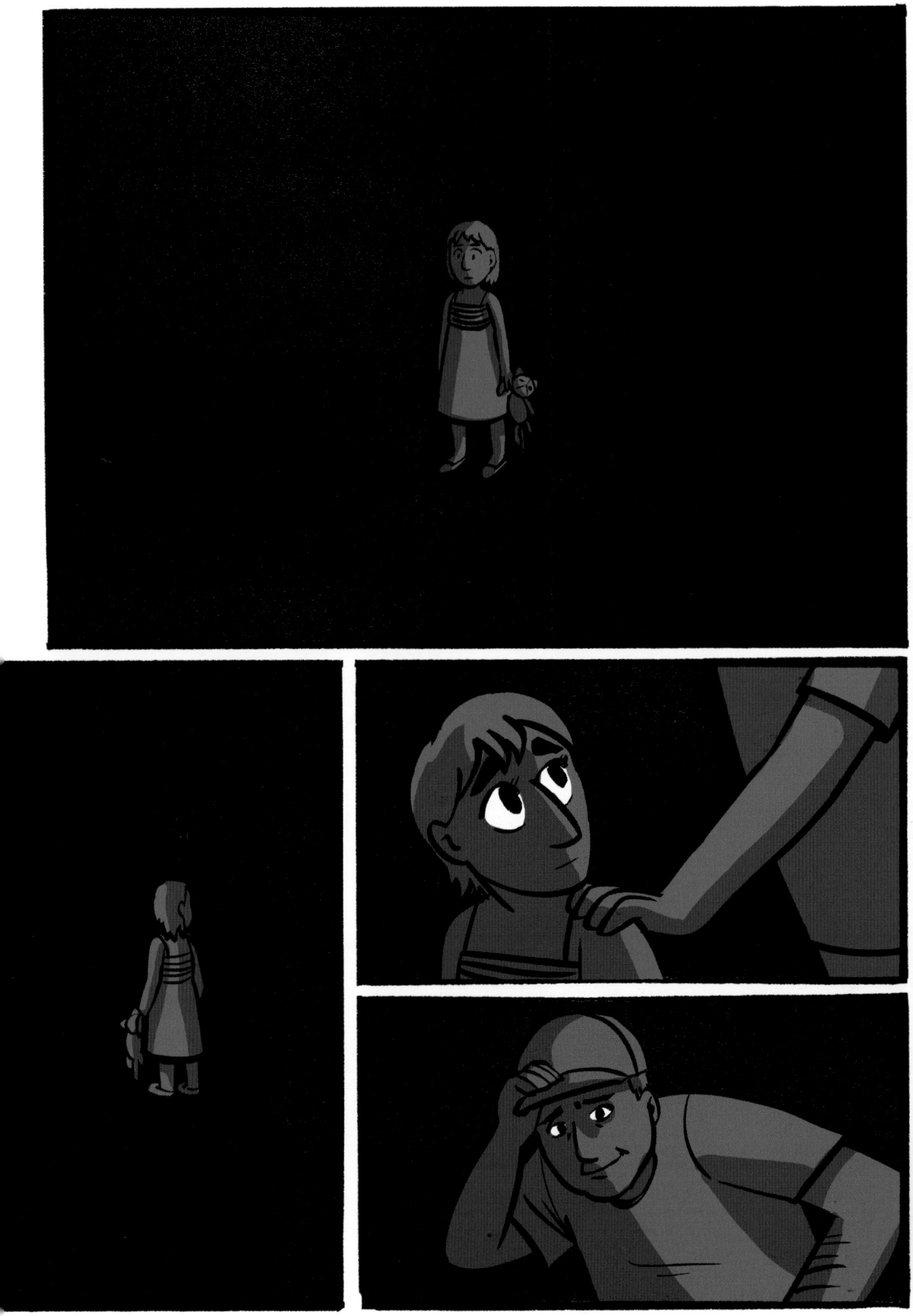

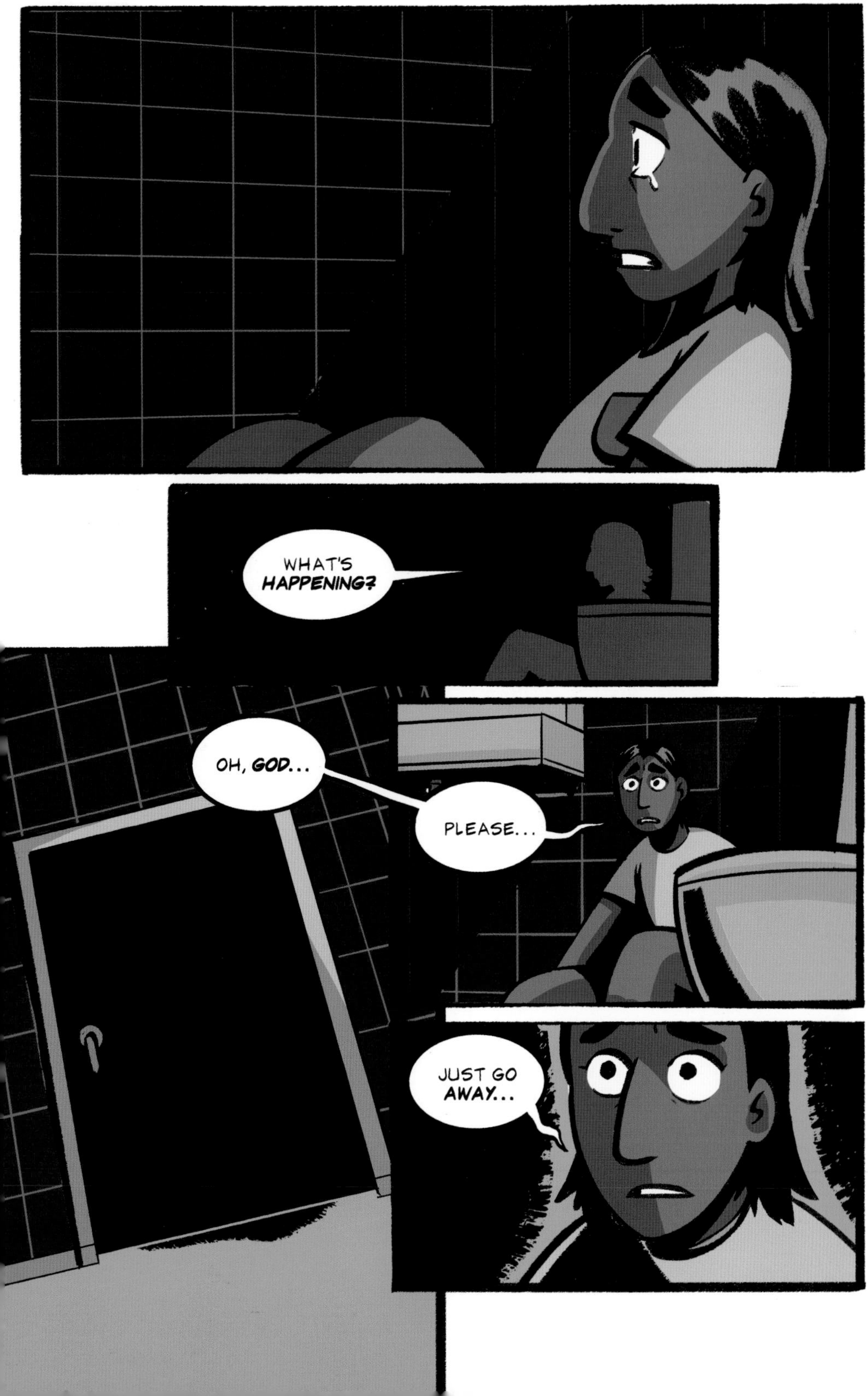
WHAT'S HAPPENING?
OH, GOD...
PLEASE...
JUST GO AWAY...

CHAPTER 2

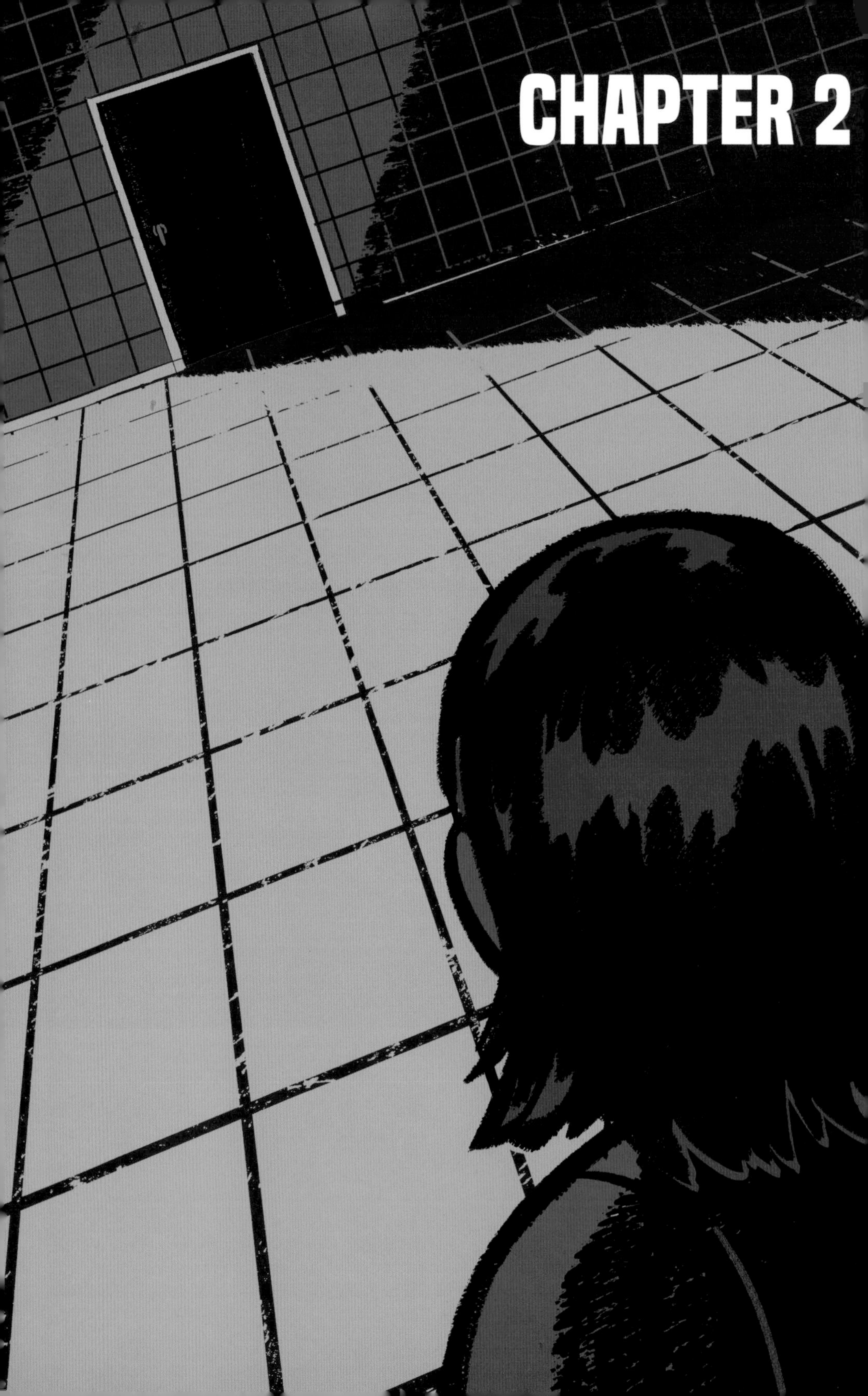

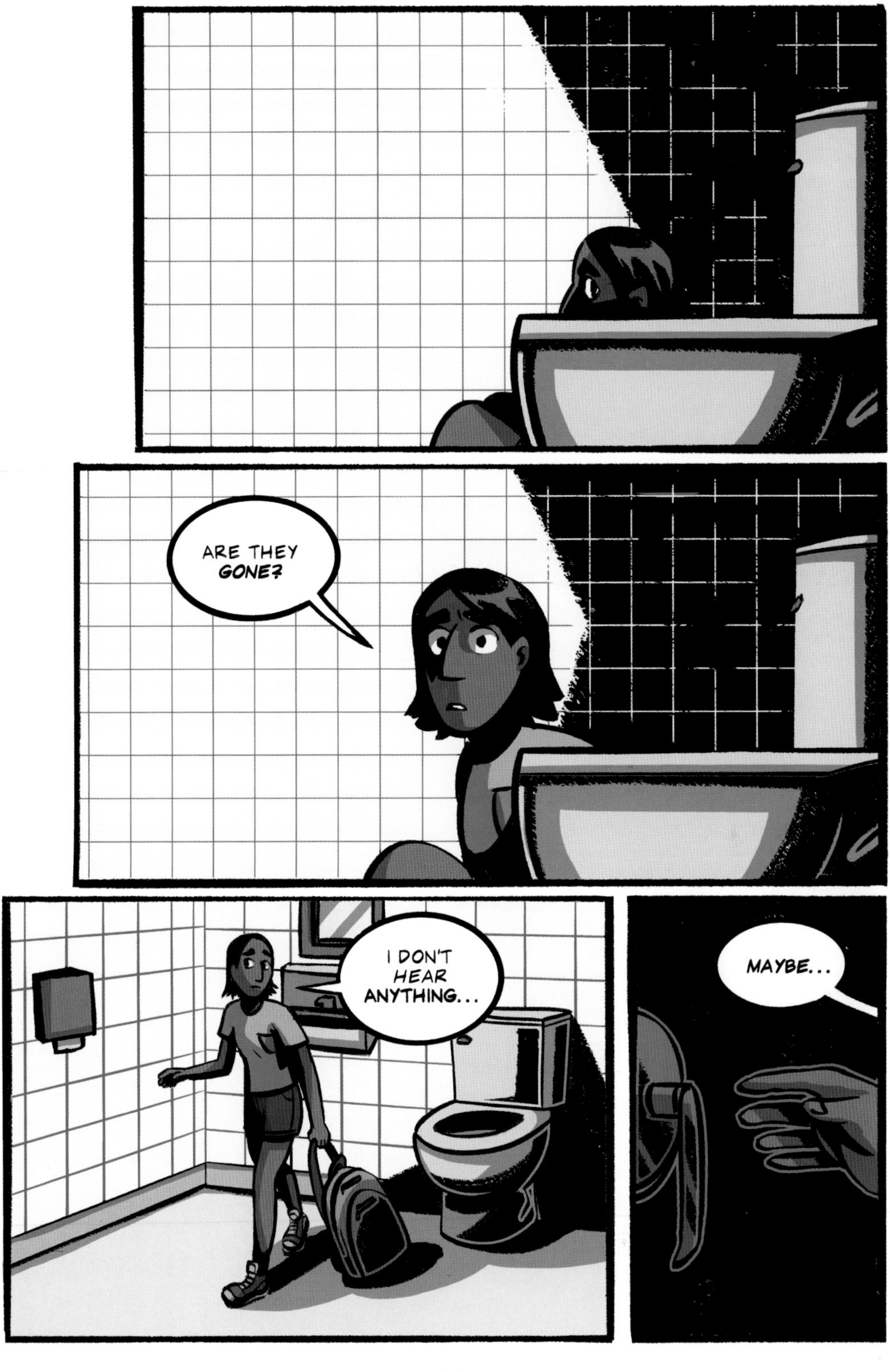
ARE THEY GONE?
I DON'T HEAR ANYTHING...
MAYBE...

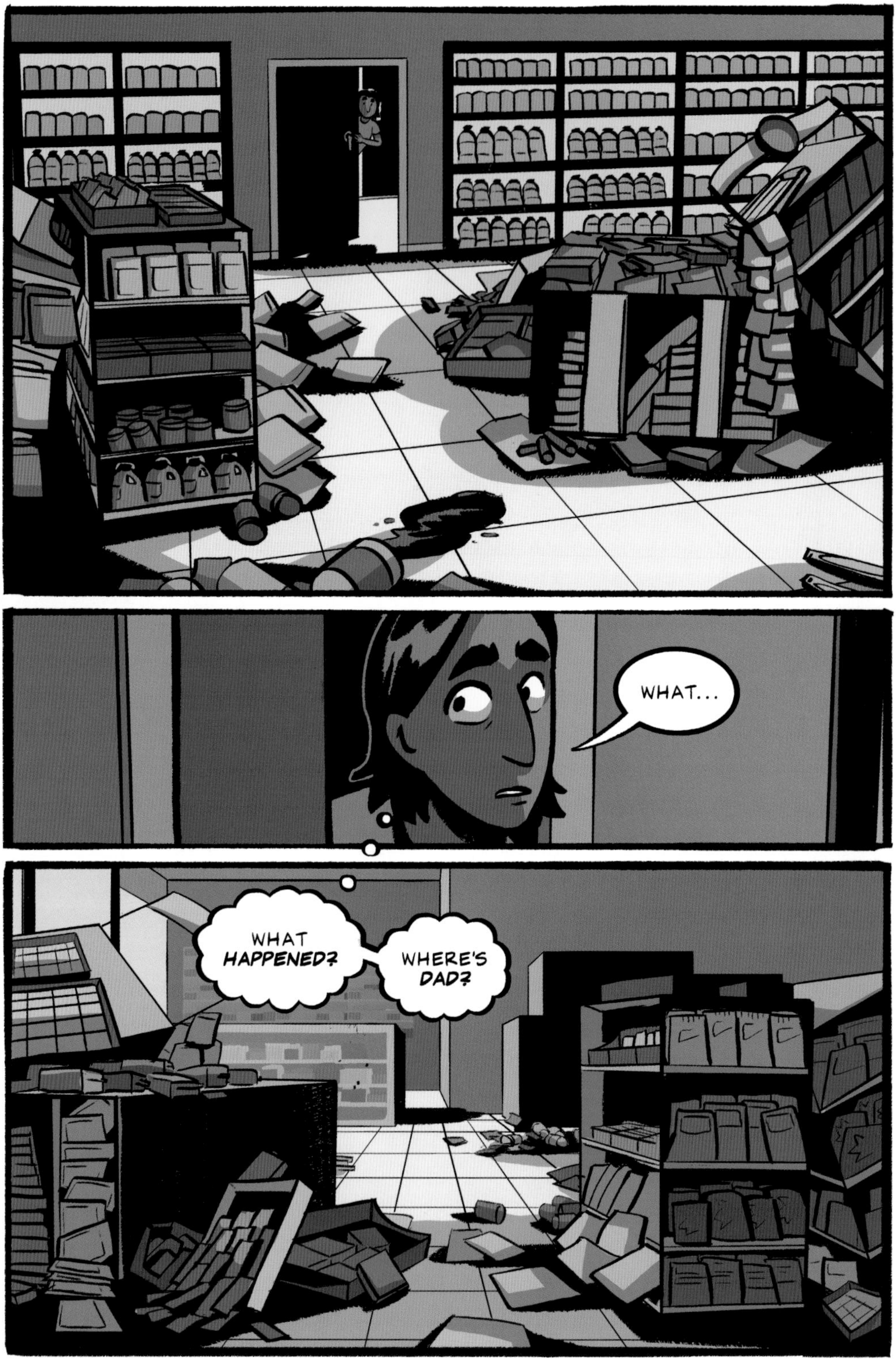
WHAT...
WHAT HAPPENED?
WHERE'S DAD?

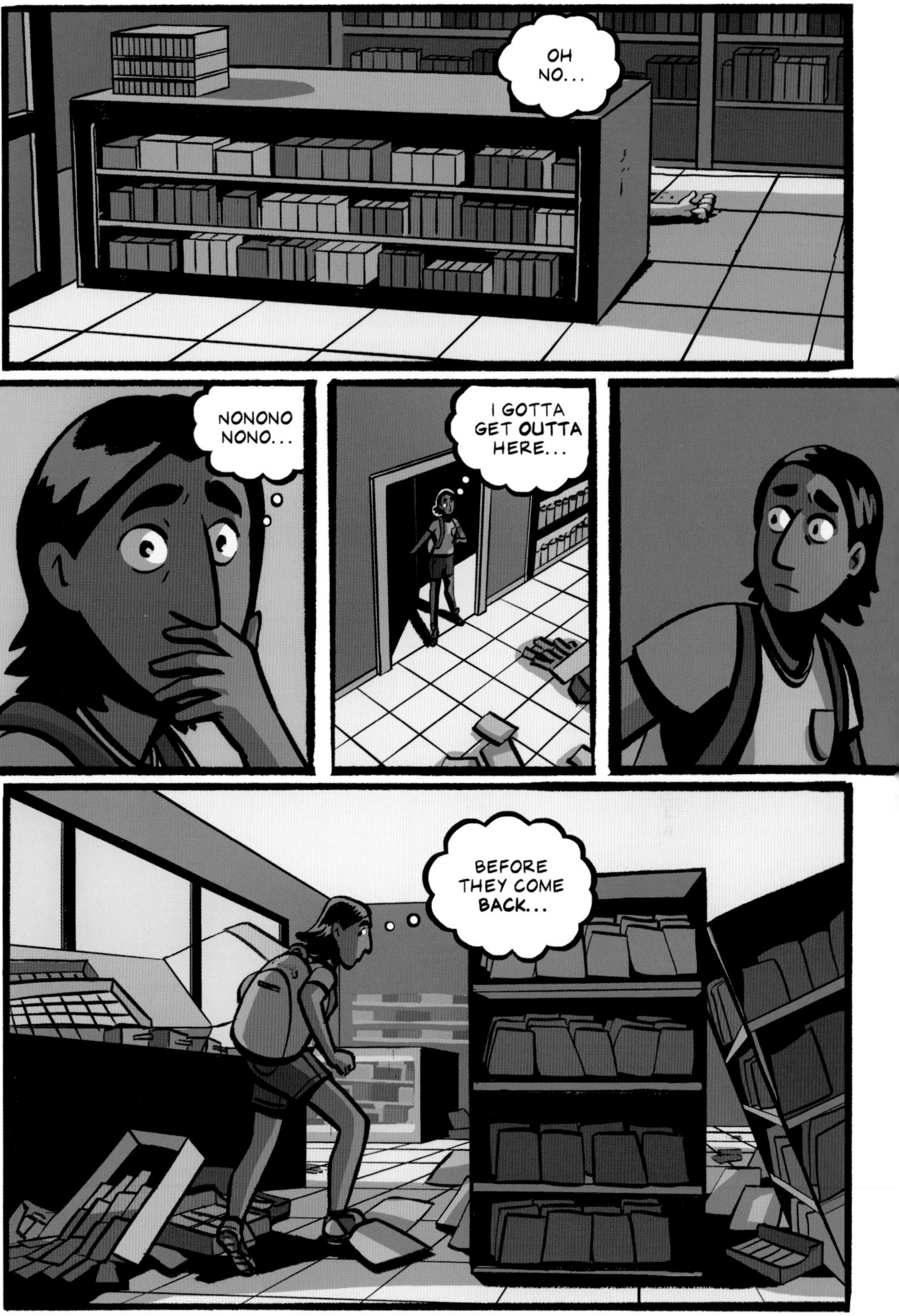
OH NO...
NONONO NONO...
I GOTTA GET OUTTA HERE...
BEFORE THEY COME BACK...

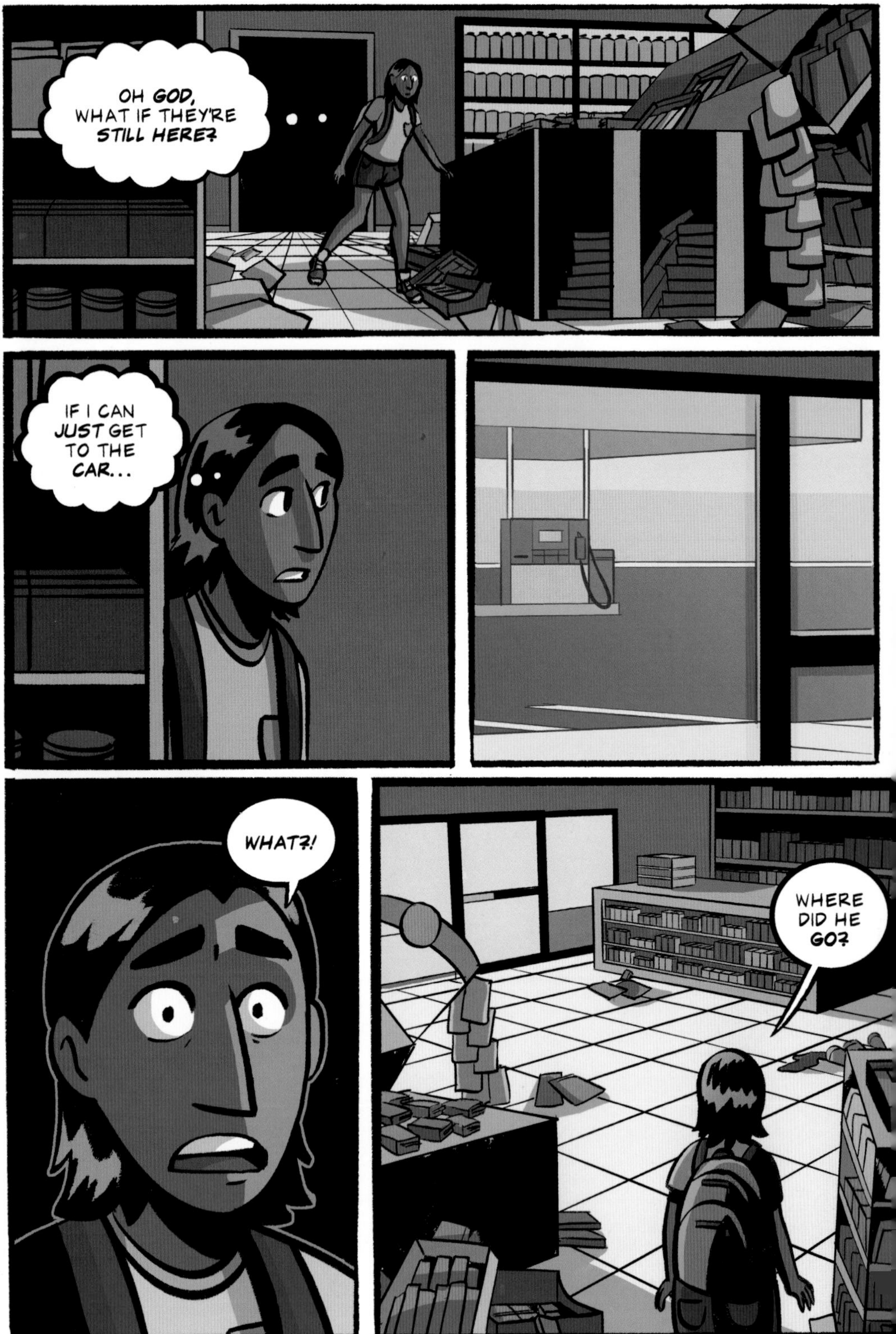
OH GOD, WHAT IF THEY'RE STILL HERE?
IF I CAN JUST GET TO THE CAR...
WHAT?!
WHERE DID HE GO?

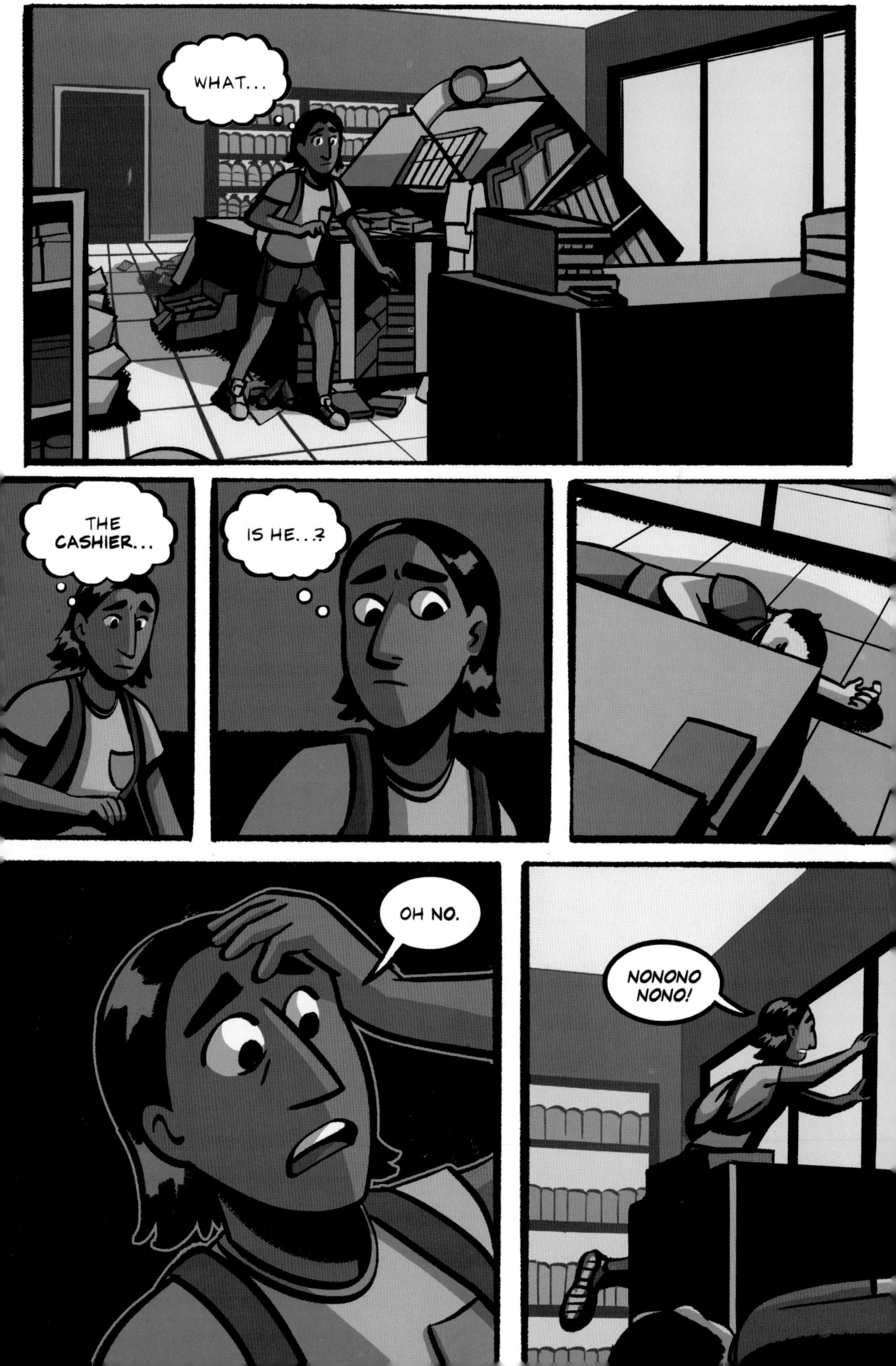
WHAT...
THE CASHIER...
IS HE...?
OH NO.
NONONO NONO!

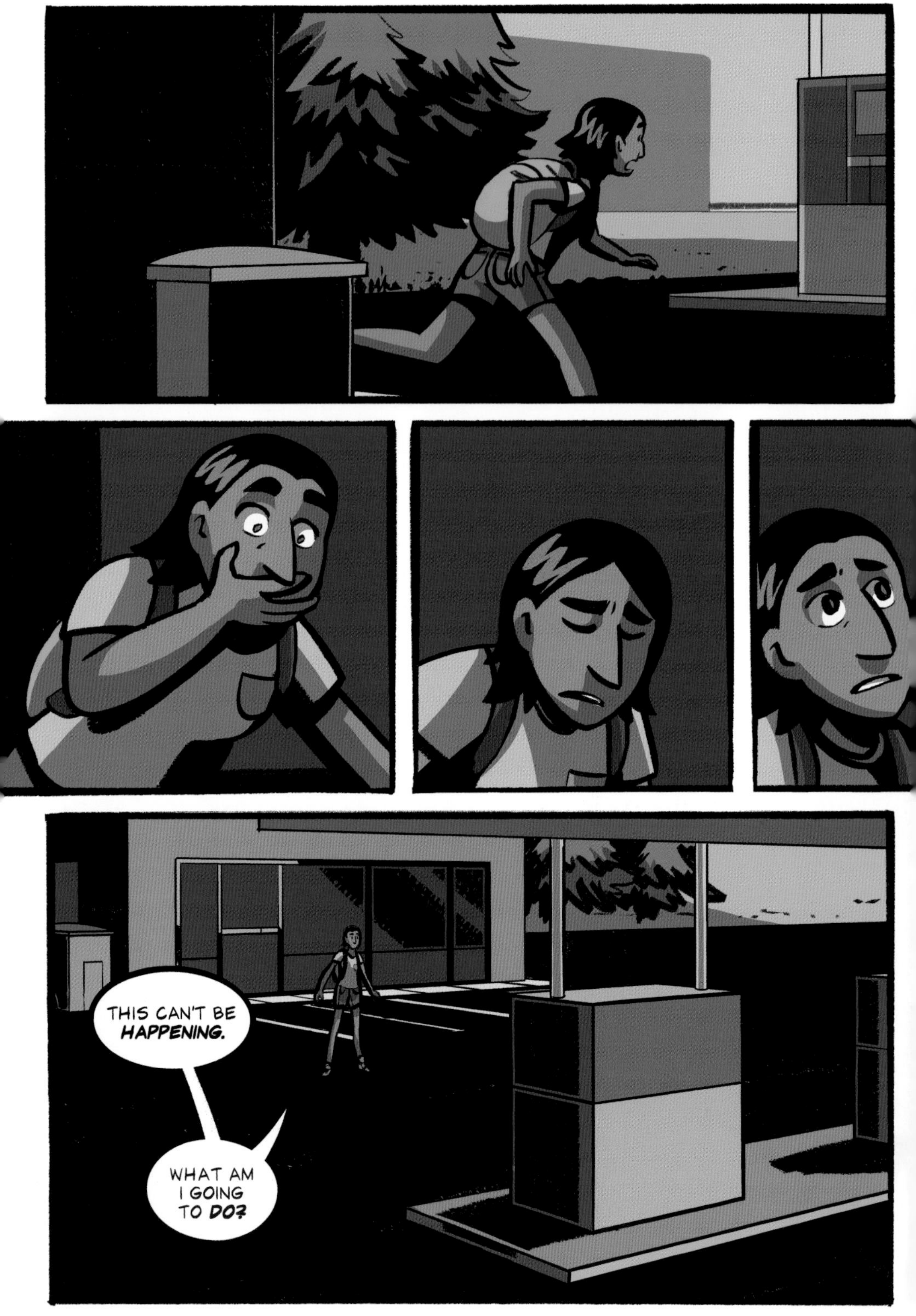
THIS CAN'T BE *HAPPENING.*
WHAT AM I GOING TO *DO?*

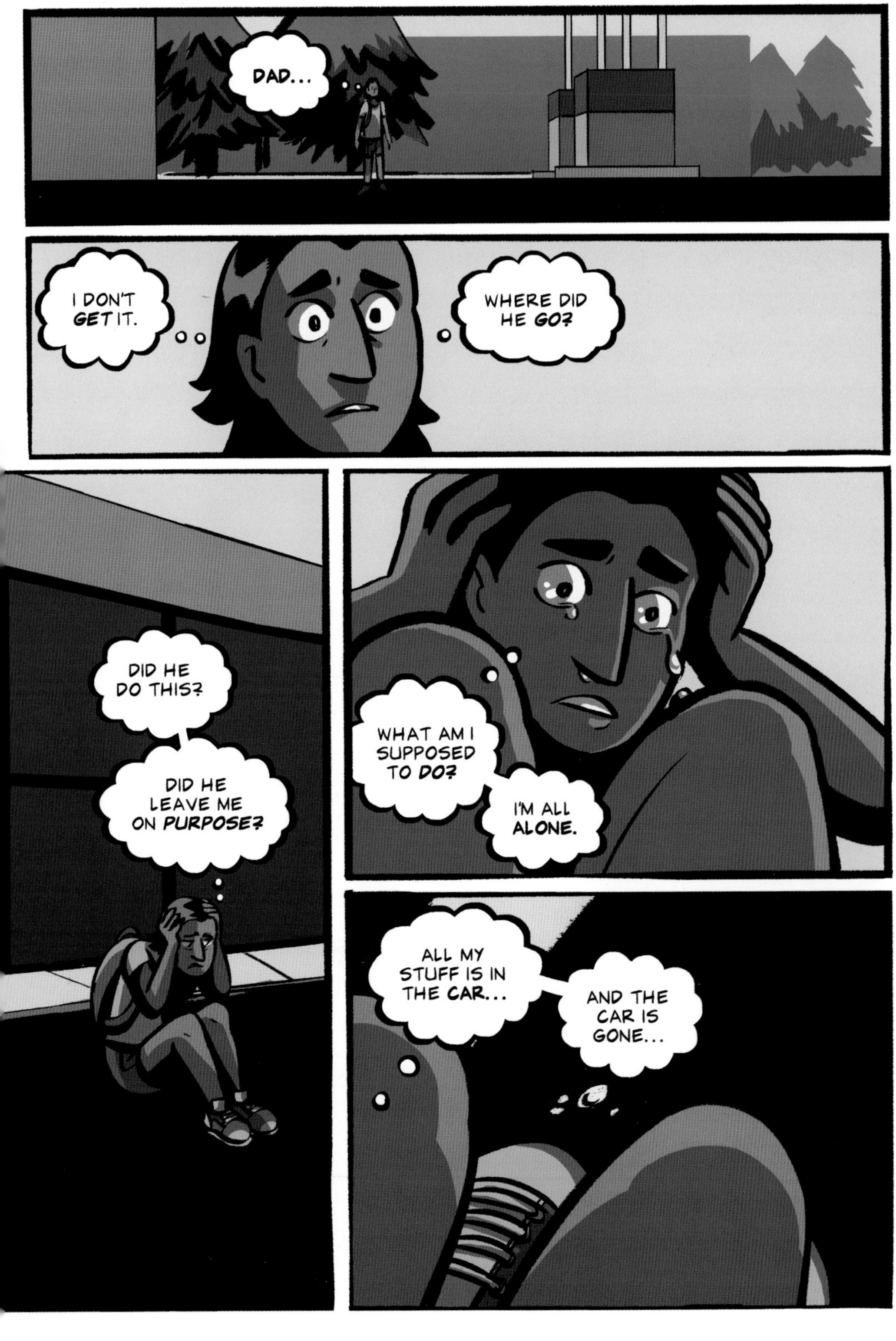
DAD...
I DON'T GET IT.
WHERE DID HE GO?
DID HE DO THIS?
DID HE LEAVE ME ON PURPOSE?
WHAT AM I SUPPOSED TO DO?
I'M ALL ALONE.
ALL MY STUFF IS IN THE CAR...
AND THE CAR IS GONE...

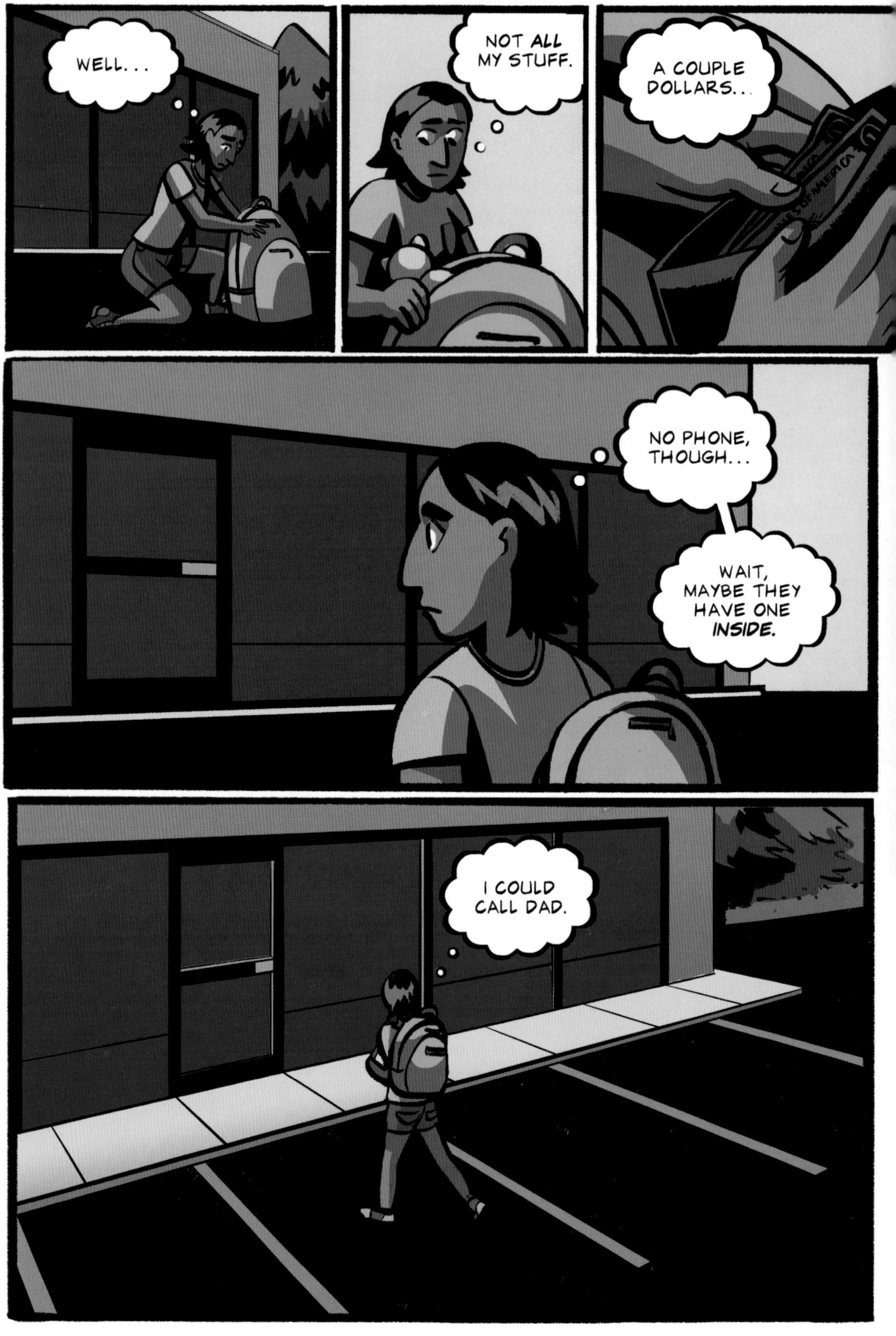
WELL...
NOT ALL MY STUFF.
A COUPLE DOLLARS...
NO PHONE, THOUGH...
WAIT, MAYBE THEY HAVE ONE INSIDE.
I COULD CALL DAD.

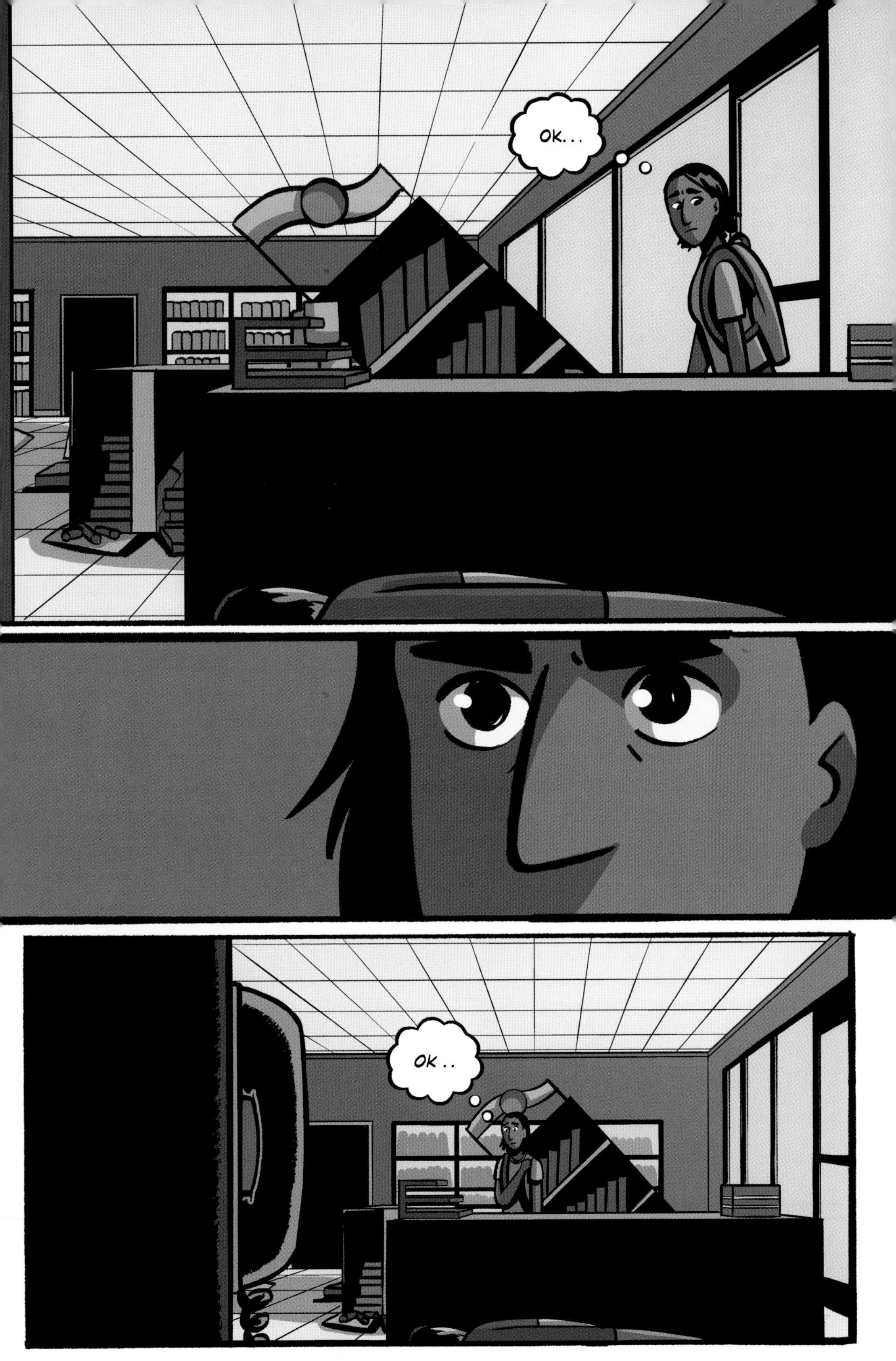
OK...
OK..

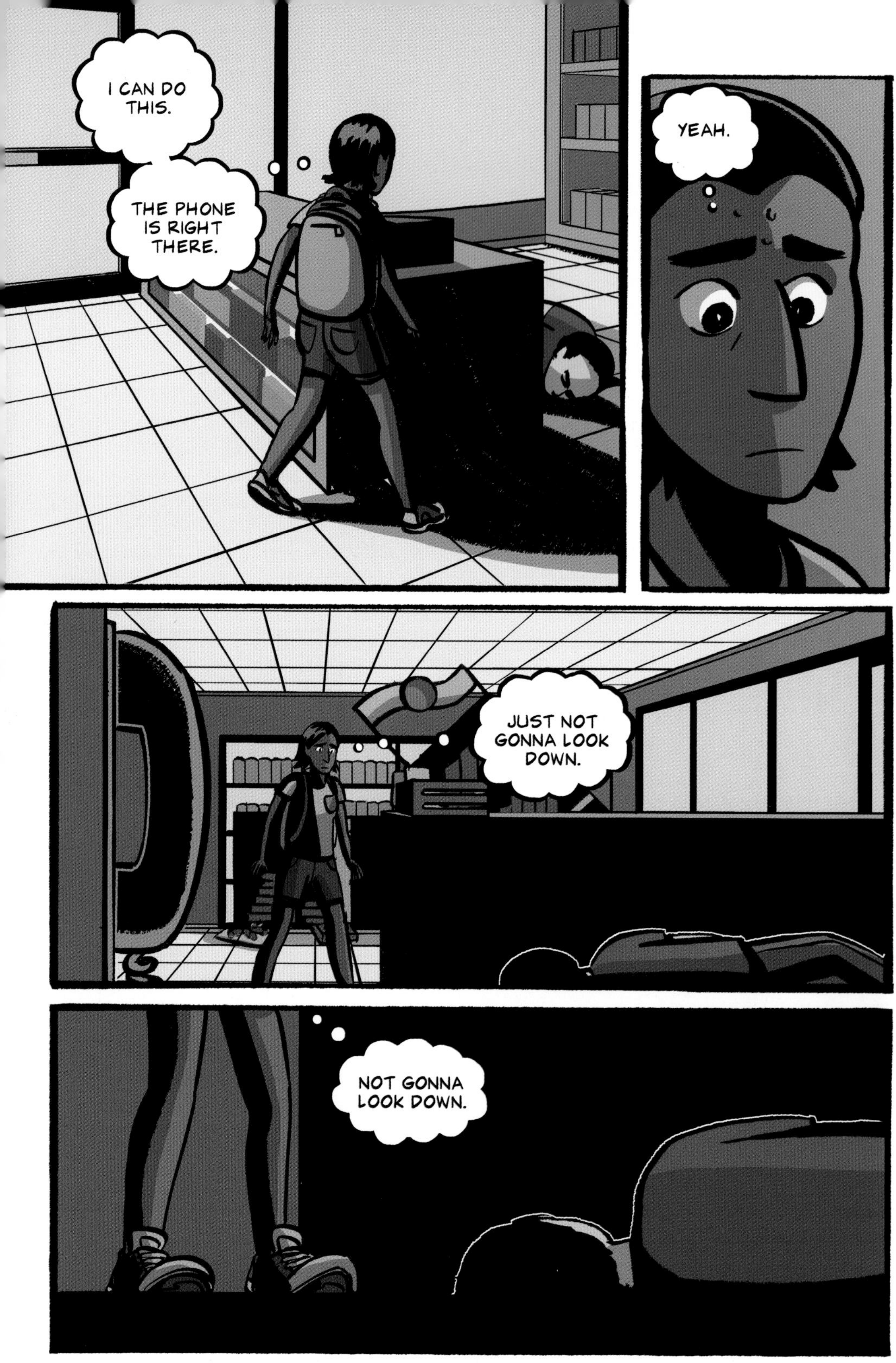
I CAN DO THIS.
THE PHONE IS RIGHT THERE.
YEAH.
JUST NOT GONNA LOOK DOWN.
NOT GONNA LOOK DOWN.

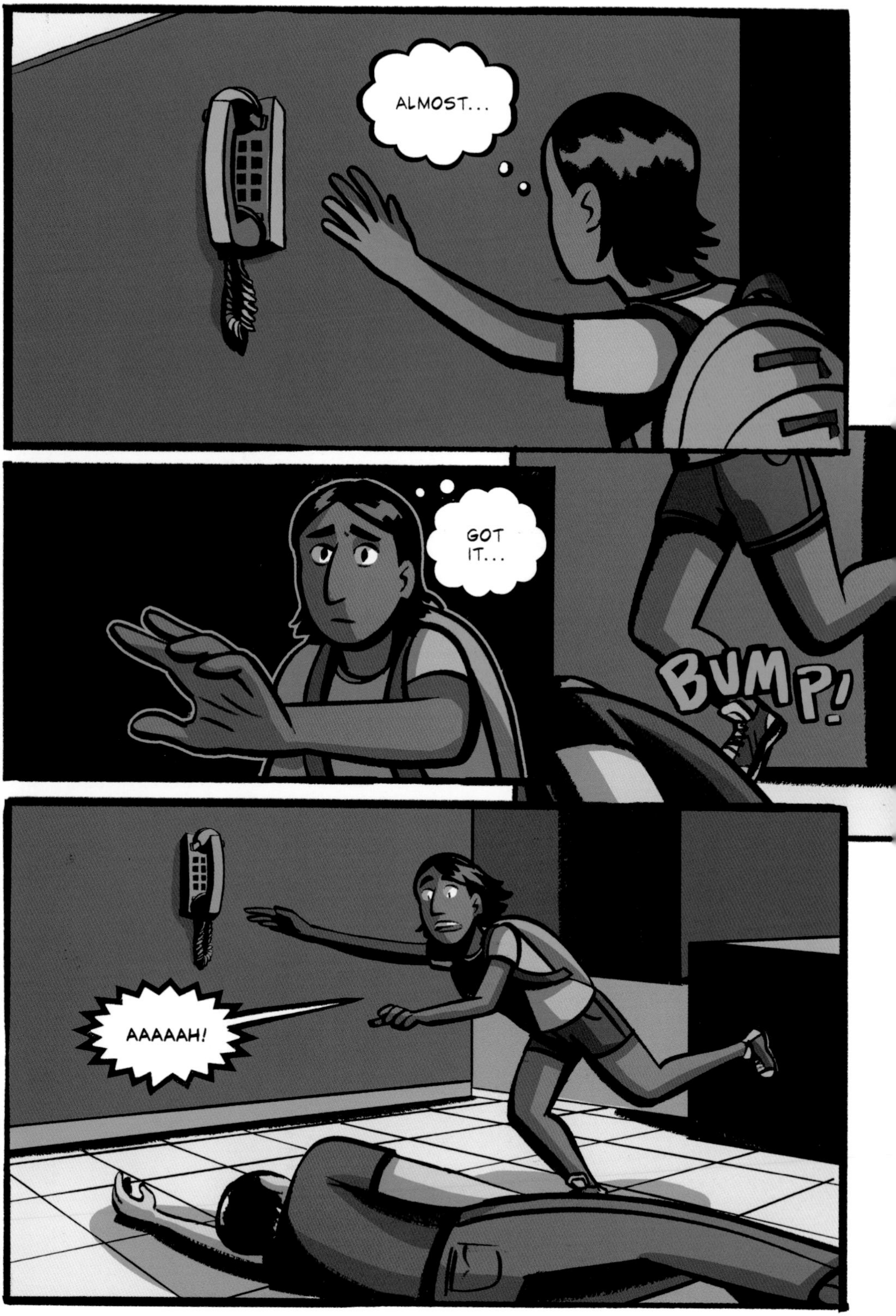
ALMOST...
GOT IT...
BUMP!
AAAAAH!

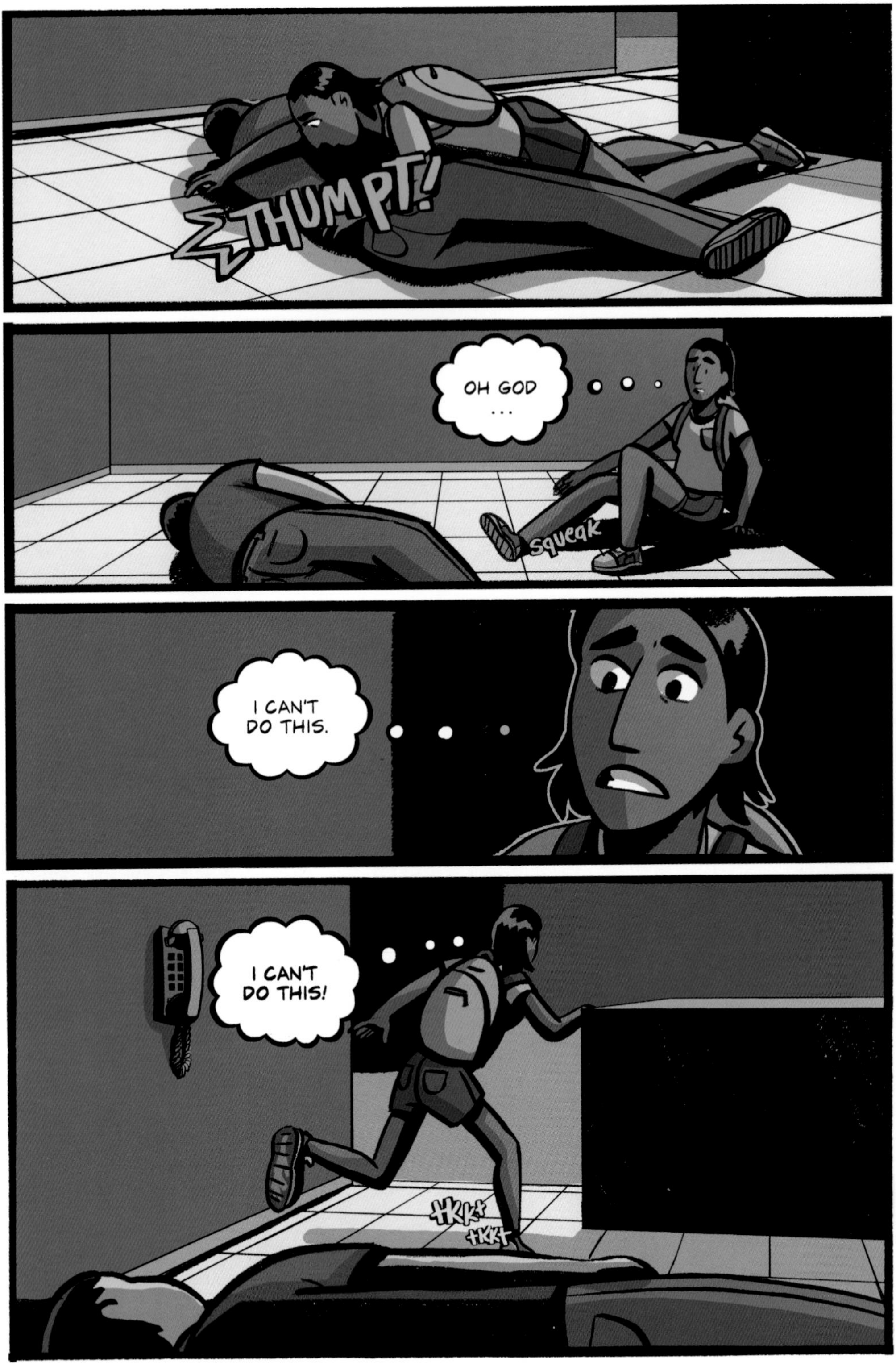
THUMPT!
OH GOD . . .
squeak
I CAN'T DO THIS.
I CAN'T DO THIS!
tkkt tkkt

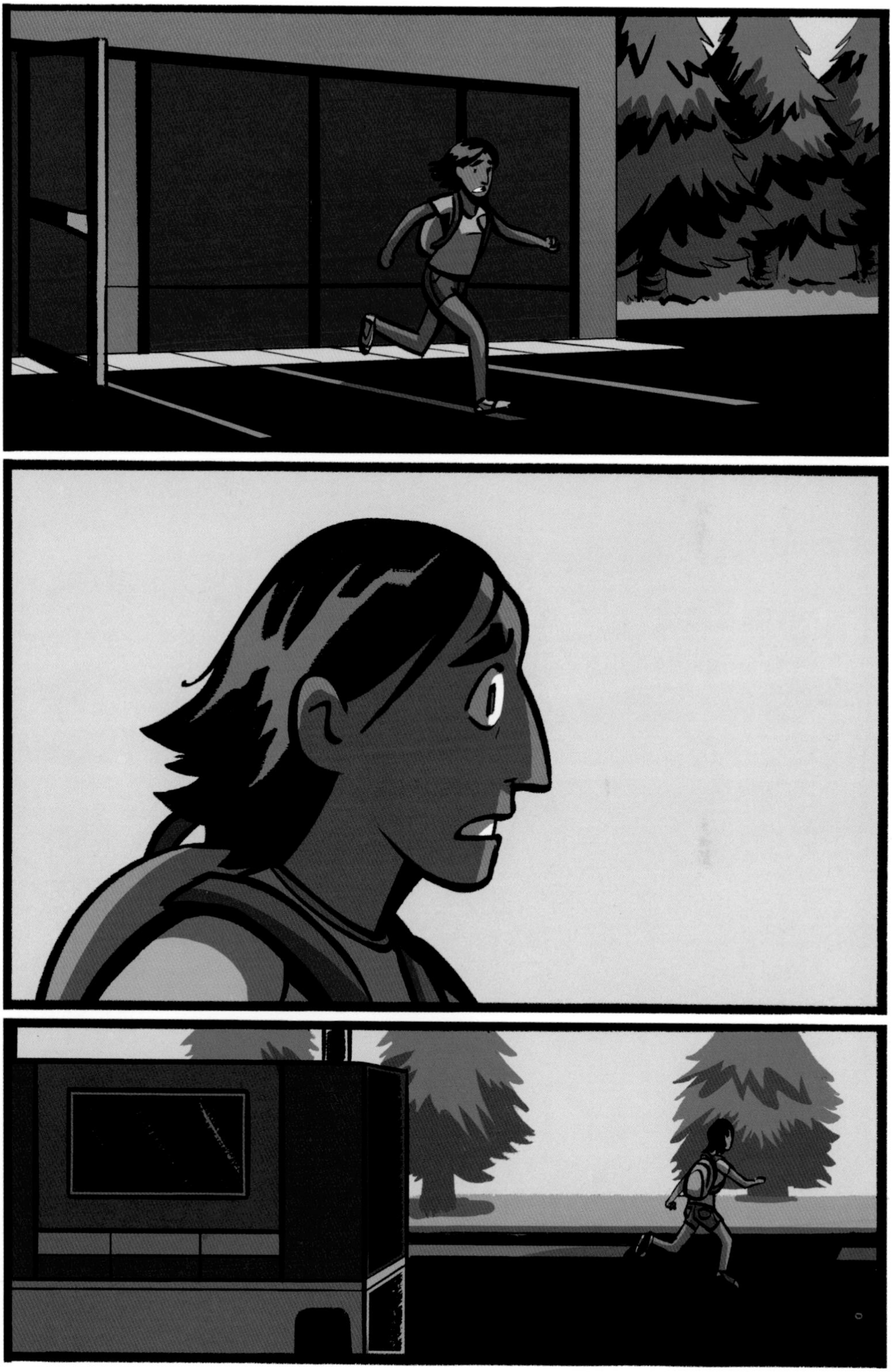

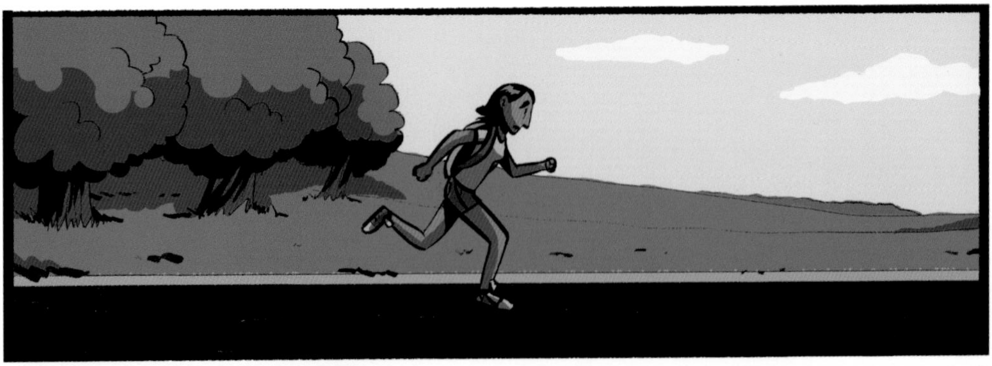

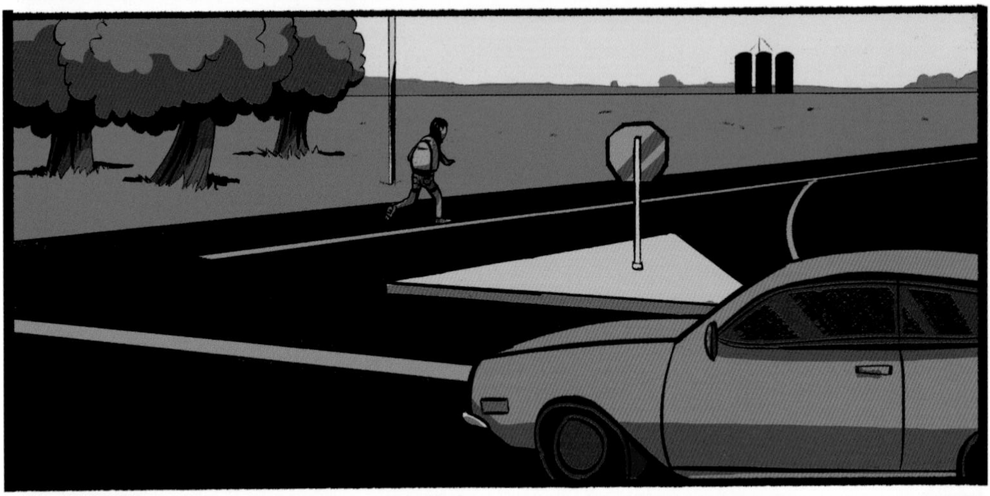

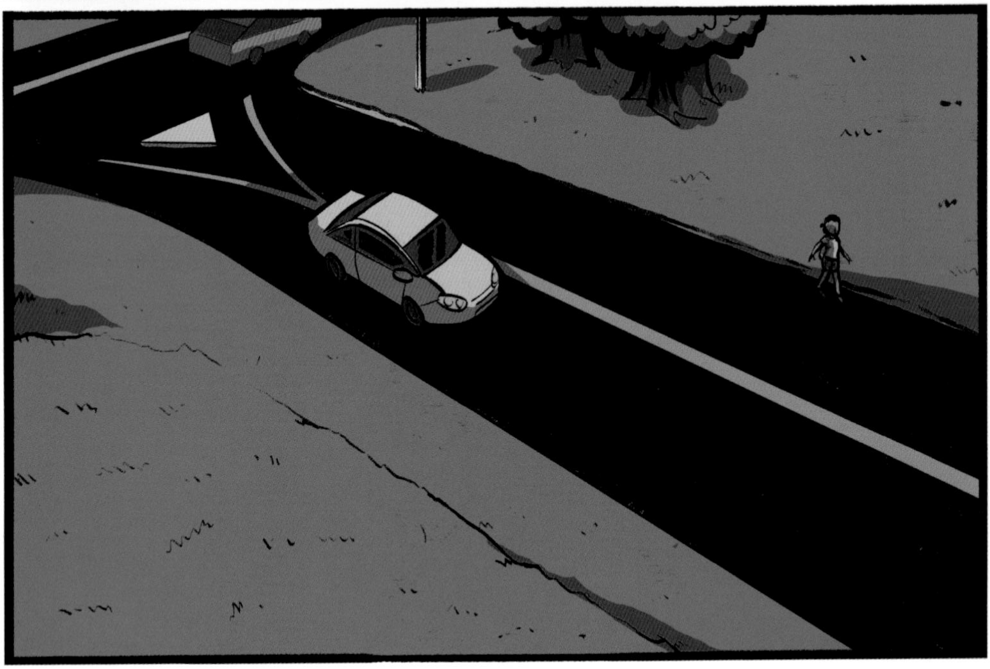

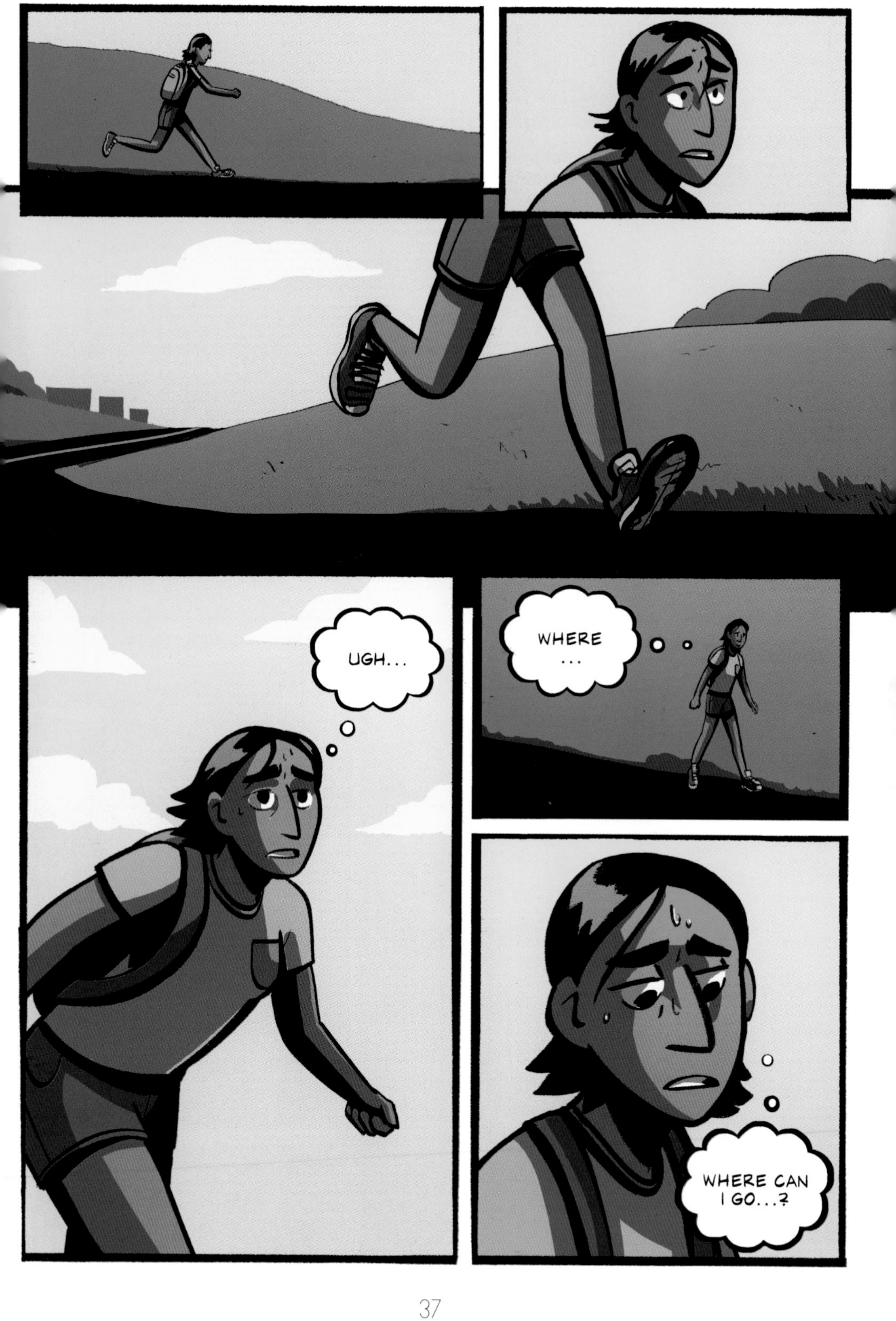
UGH...
WHERE ...
WHERE CAN I GO...?

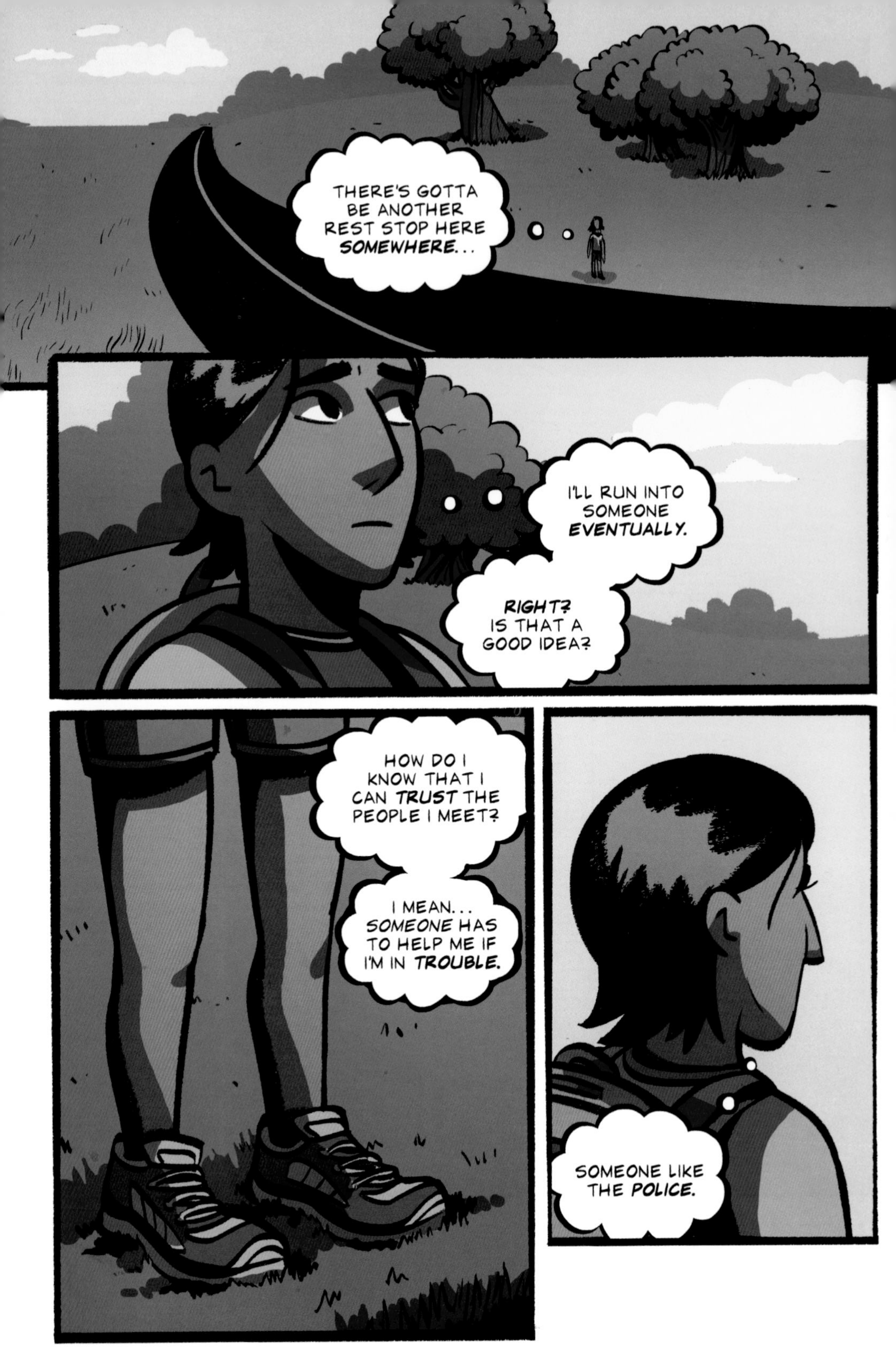
THERE'S GOTTA BE ANOTHER REST STOP HERE SOMEWHERE...
I'LL RUN INTO SOMEONE EVENTUALLY.
RIGHT? IS THAT A GOOD IDEA?
HOW DO I KNOW THAT I CAN TRUST THE PEOPLE I MEET?
I MEAN... SOMEONE HAS TO HELP ME IF I'M IN TROUBLE.
SOMEONE LIKE THE POLICE.

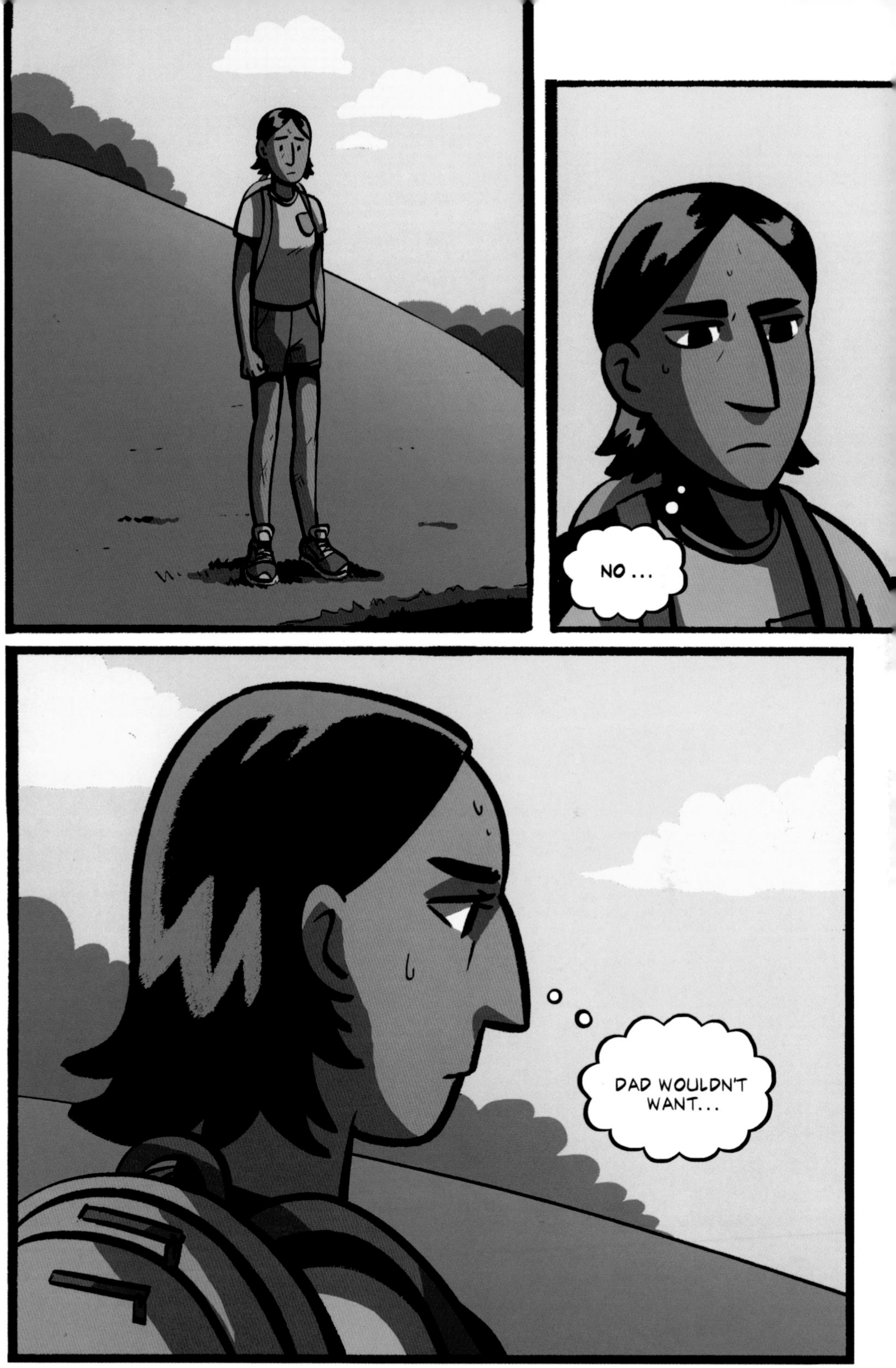
NO...
DAD WOULDN'T WANT...

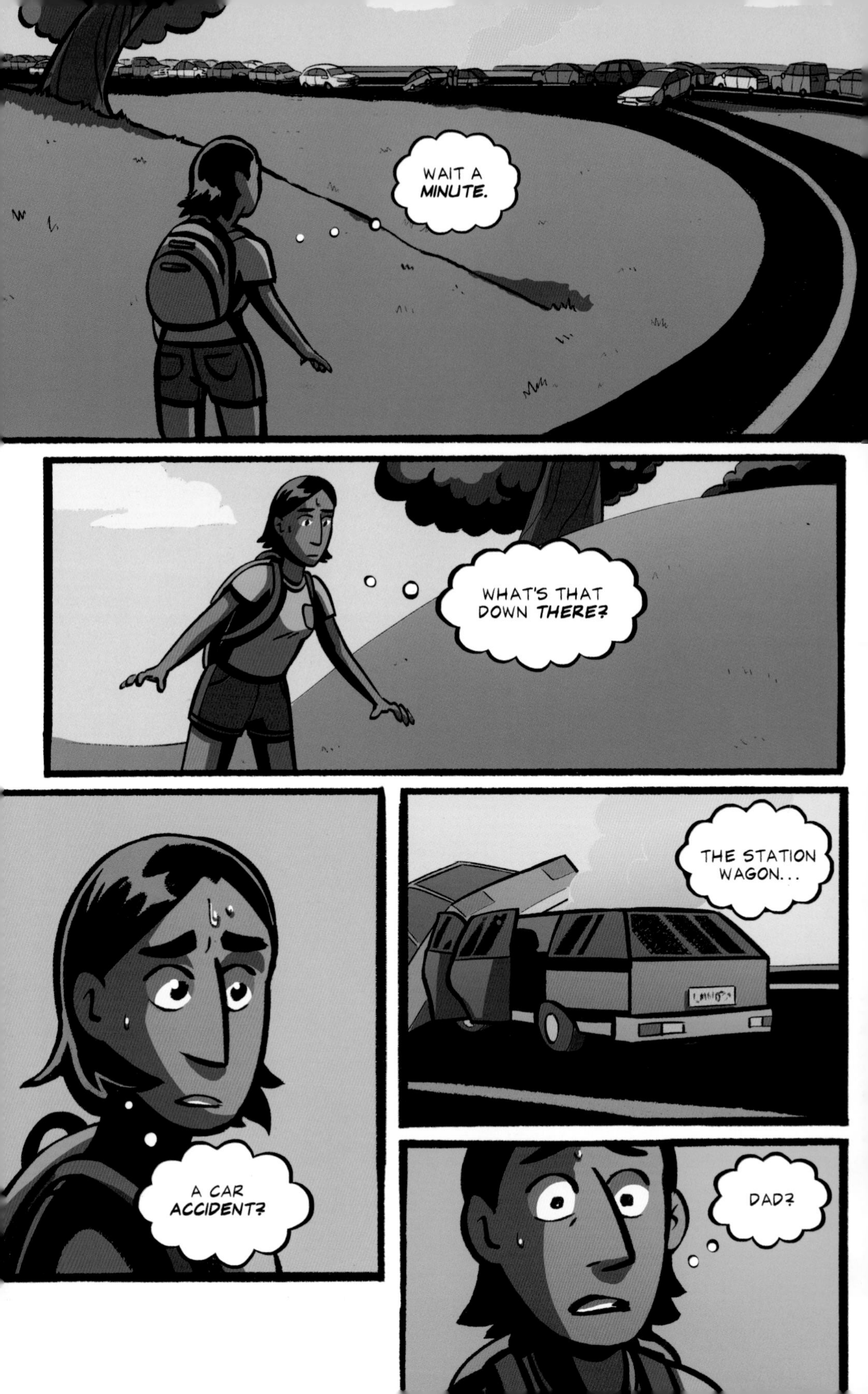
WAIT A MINUTE.
WHAT'S THAT DOWN THERE?
A CAR ACCIDENT?
THE STATION WAGON...
DAD?

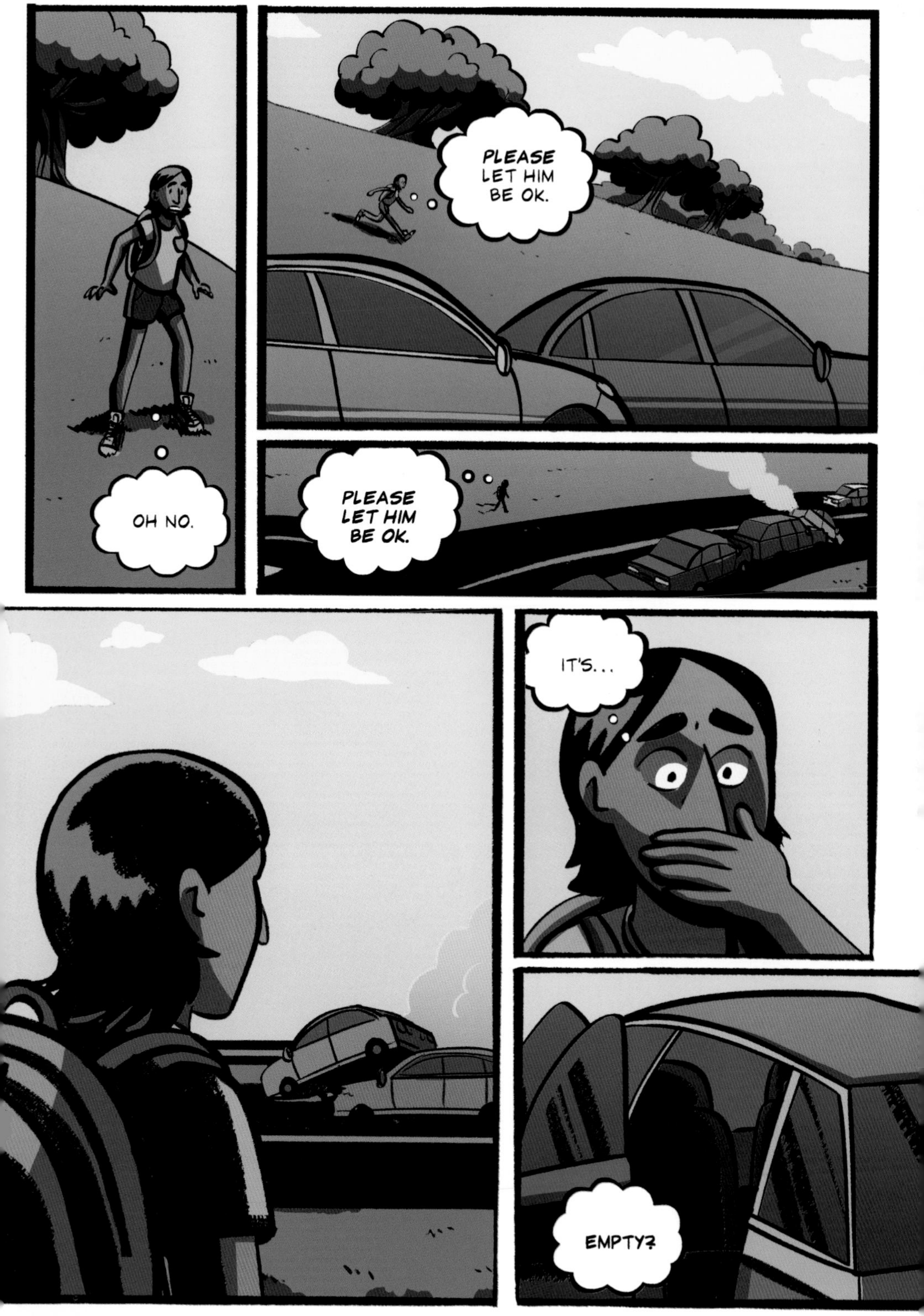
OH NO.
PLEASE LET HIM BE OK.
PLEASE LET HIM BE OK.
IT'S...
EMPTY?

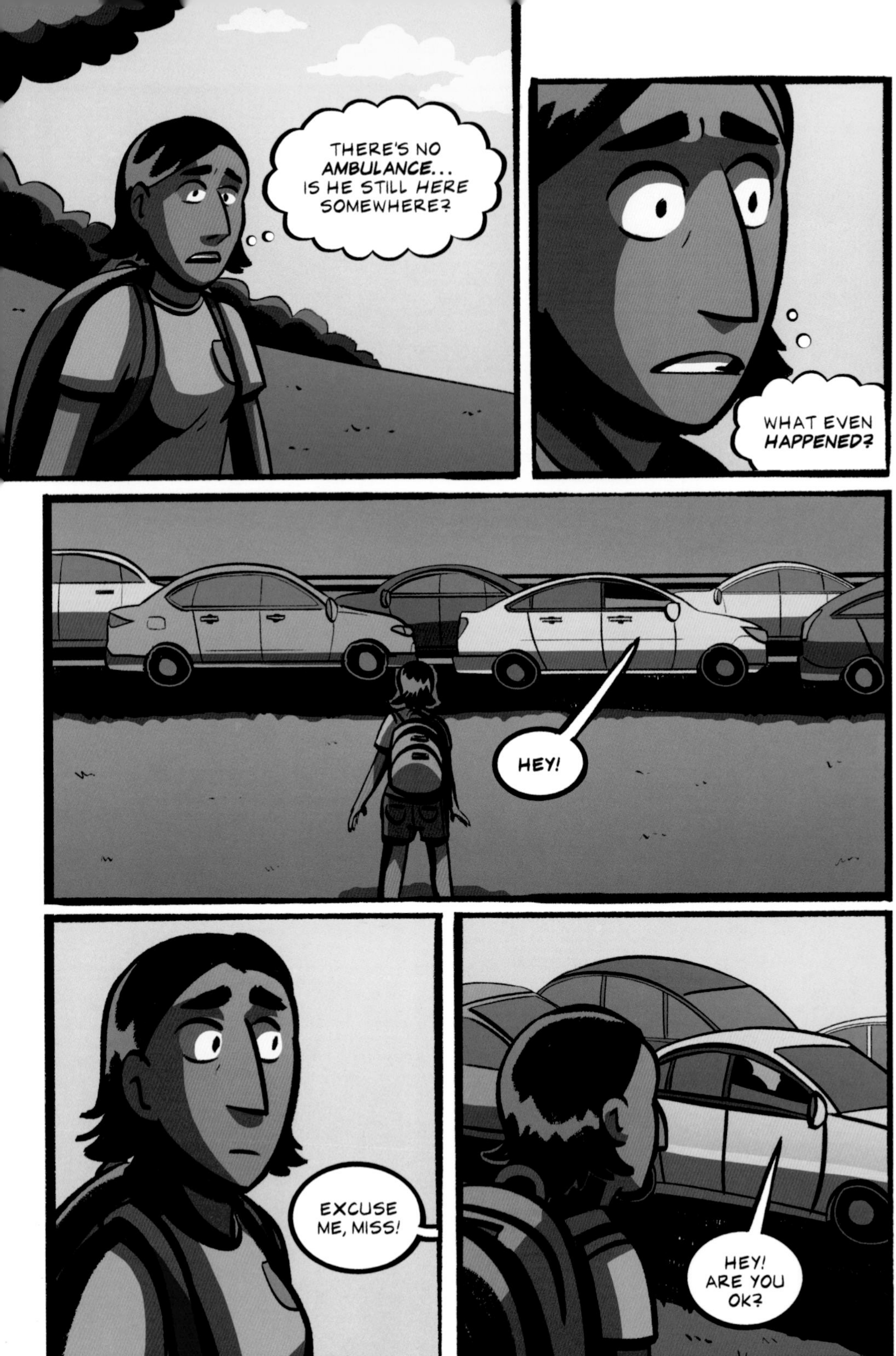
THERE'S NO AMBULANCE... IS HE STILL HERE SOMEWHERE?
WHAT EVEN HAPPENED?
HEY!
EXCUSE ME, MISS!
HEY! ARE YOU OK?

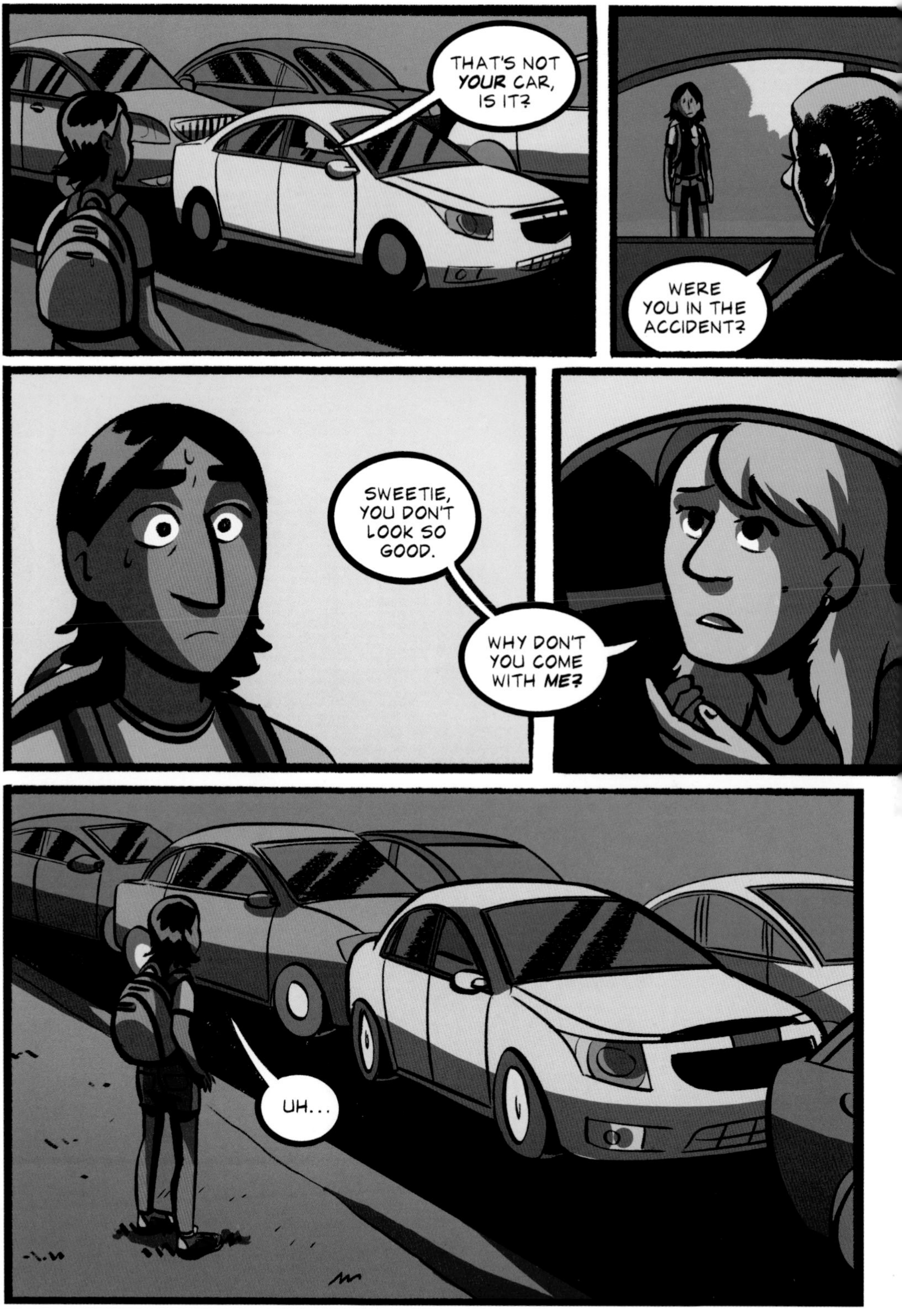
THAT'S NOT *YOUR* CAR, IS IT?
WERE YOU IN THE ACCIDENT?
SWEETIE, YOU DON'T LOOK SO GOOD.
WHY DON'T YOU COME WITH *ME*?
UH...

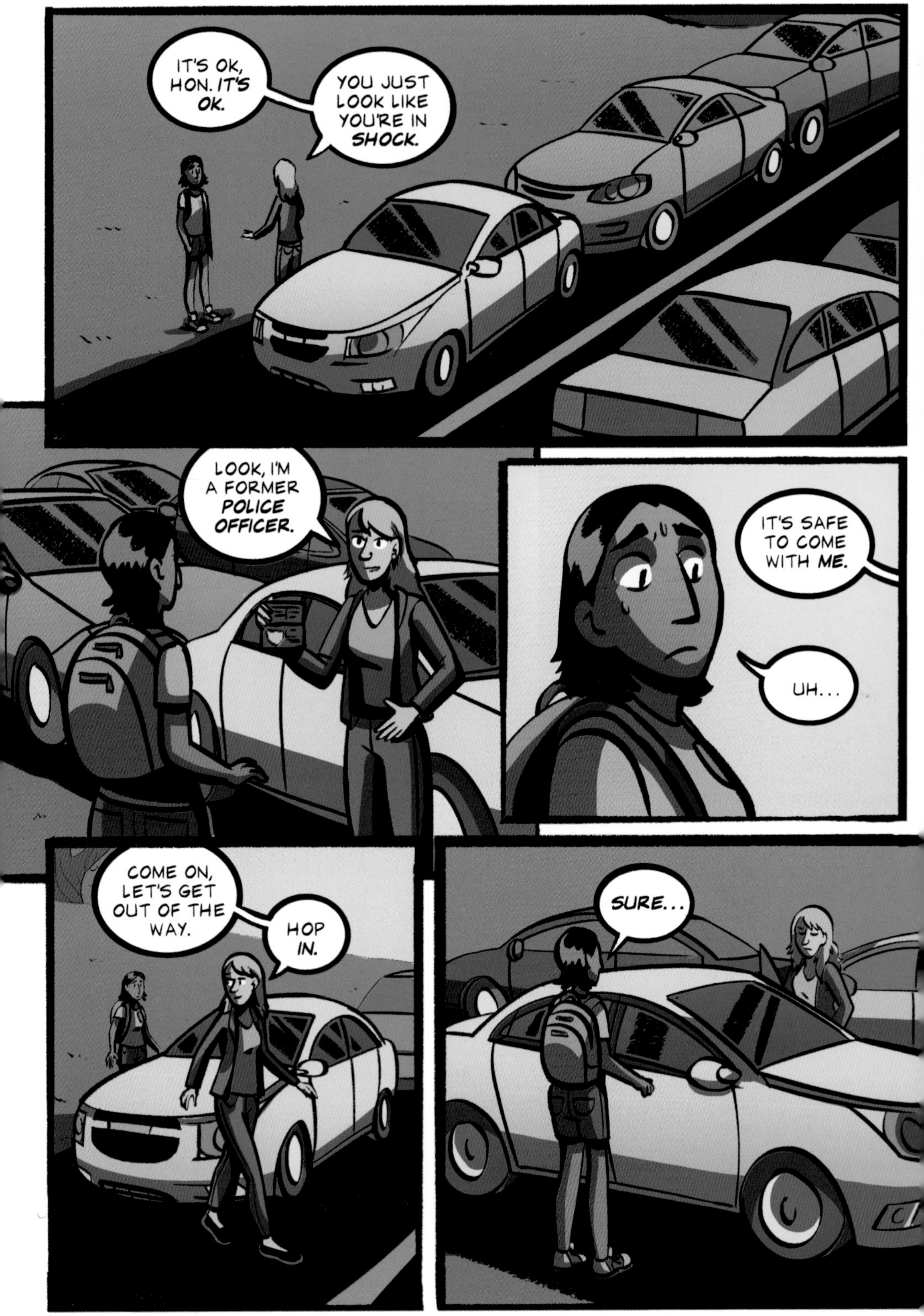
IT'S OK, HON. IT'S OK.
YOU JUST LOOK LIKE YOU'RE IN SHOCK.
LOOK, I'M A FORMER POLICE OFFICER.
IT'S SAFE TO COME WITH ME.
UH...
COME ON, LET'S GET OUT OF THE WAY.
HOP IN.
SURE...

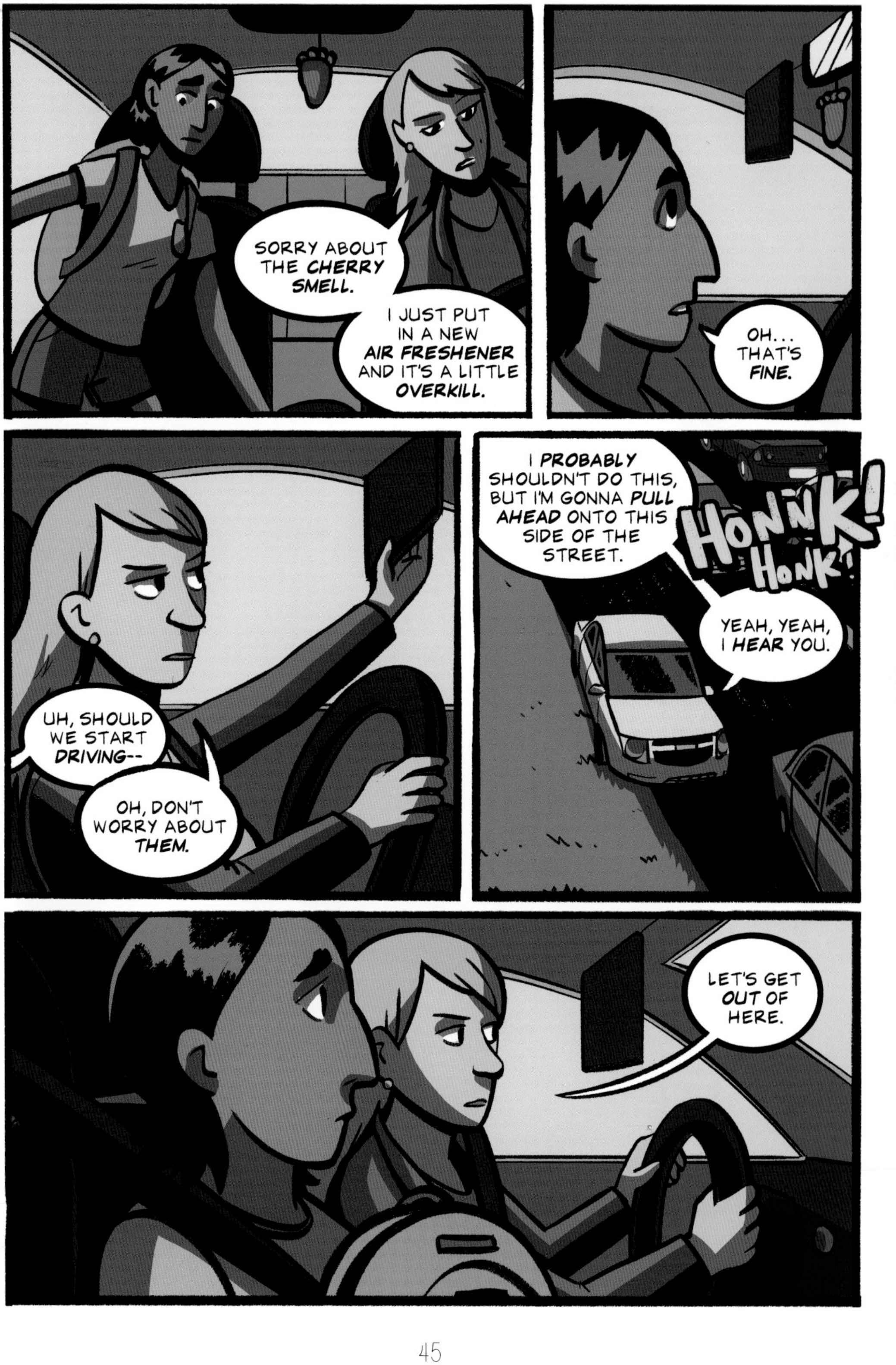
SORRY ABOUT THE CHERRY SMELL.
I JUST PUT IN A NEW AIR FRESHENER AND IT'S A LITTLE OVERKILL.
OH... THAT'S FINE.
UH, SHOULD WE START DRIVING--
OH, DON'T WORRY ABOUT THEM.
I PROBABLY SHOULDN'T DO THIS, BUT I'M GONNA PULL AHEAD ONTO THIS SIDE OF THE STREET.
HONNK! HONK!
YEAH, YEAH, I HEAR YOU.
LET'S GET OUT OF HERE.

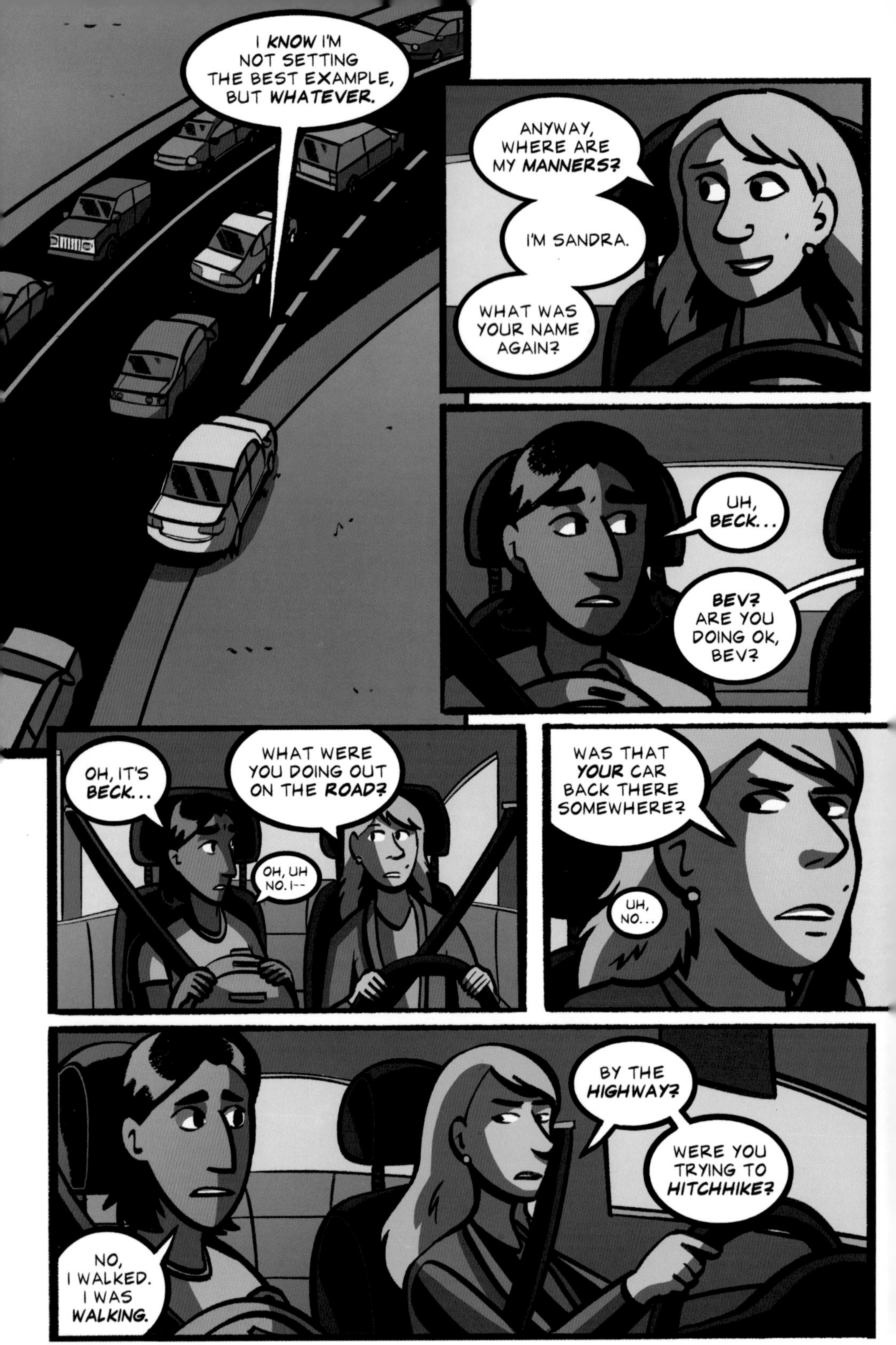
I KNOW I'M NOT SETTING THE BEST EXAMPLE, BUT WHATEVER.
ANYWAY, WHERE ARE MY MANNERS?
I'M SANDRA.
WHAT WAS YOUR NAME AGAIN?
UH, BECK...
BEV? ARE YOU DOING OK, BEV?
OH, IT'S BECK...
WHAT WERE YOU DOING OUT ON THE ROAD?
OH, UH NO. I--
WAS THAT YOUR CAR BACK THERE SOMEWHERE?
UH, NO...
BY THE HIGHWAY?
WERE YOU TRYING TO HITCHHIKE?
NO, I WALKED. I WAS WALKING.

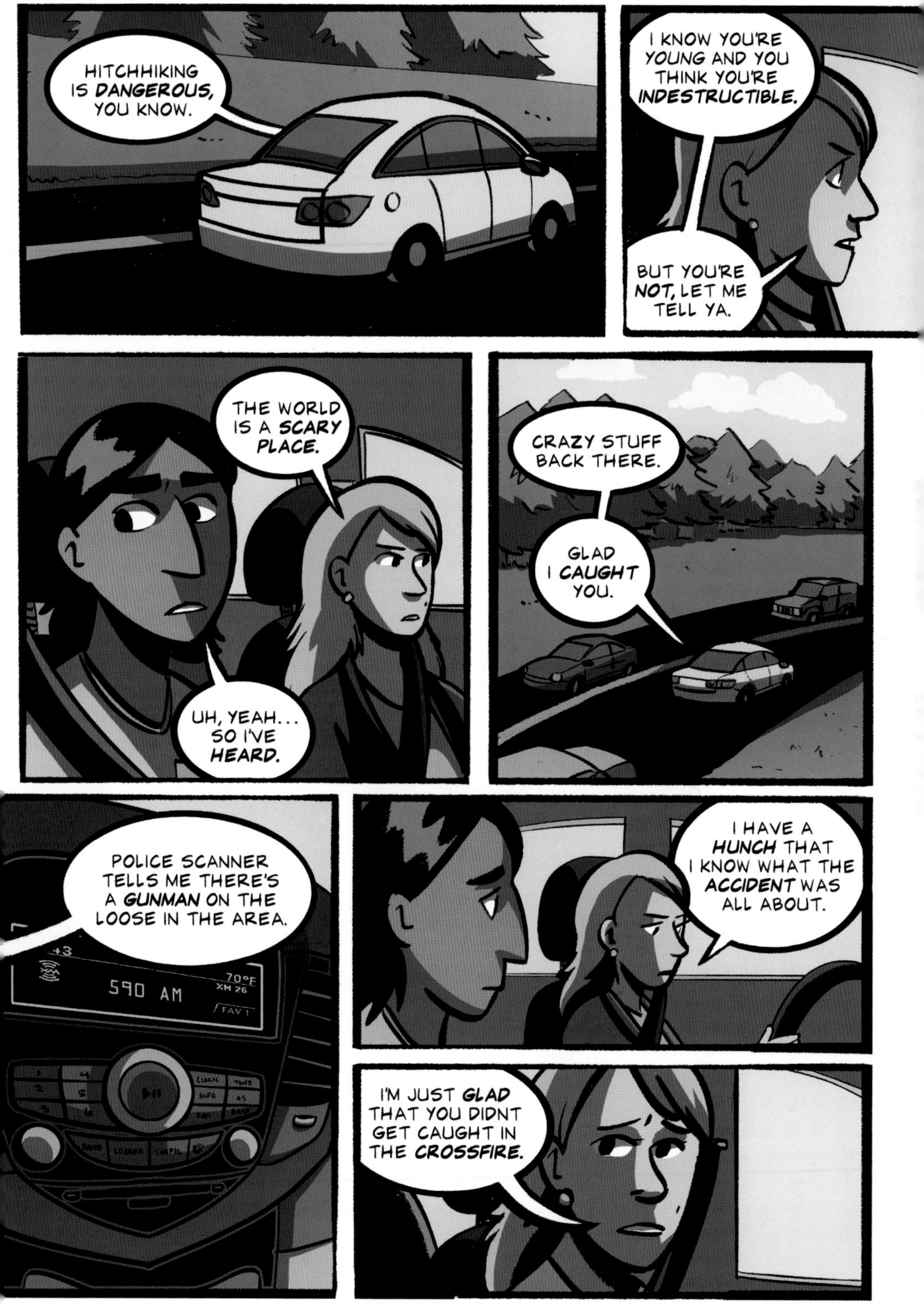
HITCHHIKING IS **DANGEROUS,** YOU KNOW.
I KNOW YOU'RE YOUNG AND YOU THINK YOU'RE **INDESTRUCTIBLE.**
BUT YOU'RE **NOT,** LET ME TELL YA.
THE WORLD IS A **SCARY PLACE.**
UH, YEAH... SO I'VE **HEARD.**
CRAZY STUFF BACK THERE.
GLAD I **CAUGHT** YOU.
POLICE SCANNER TELLS ME THERE'S A **GUNMAN** ON THE LOOSE IN THE AREA.
590 AM
70°F
XM 26
I HAVE A **HUNCH** THAT I KNOW WHAT THE **ACCIDENT** WAS ALL ABOUT.
I'M JUST **GLAD** THAT YOU DIDNT GET CAUGHT IN THE **CROSSFIRE.**

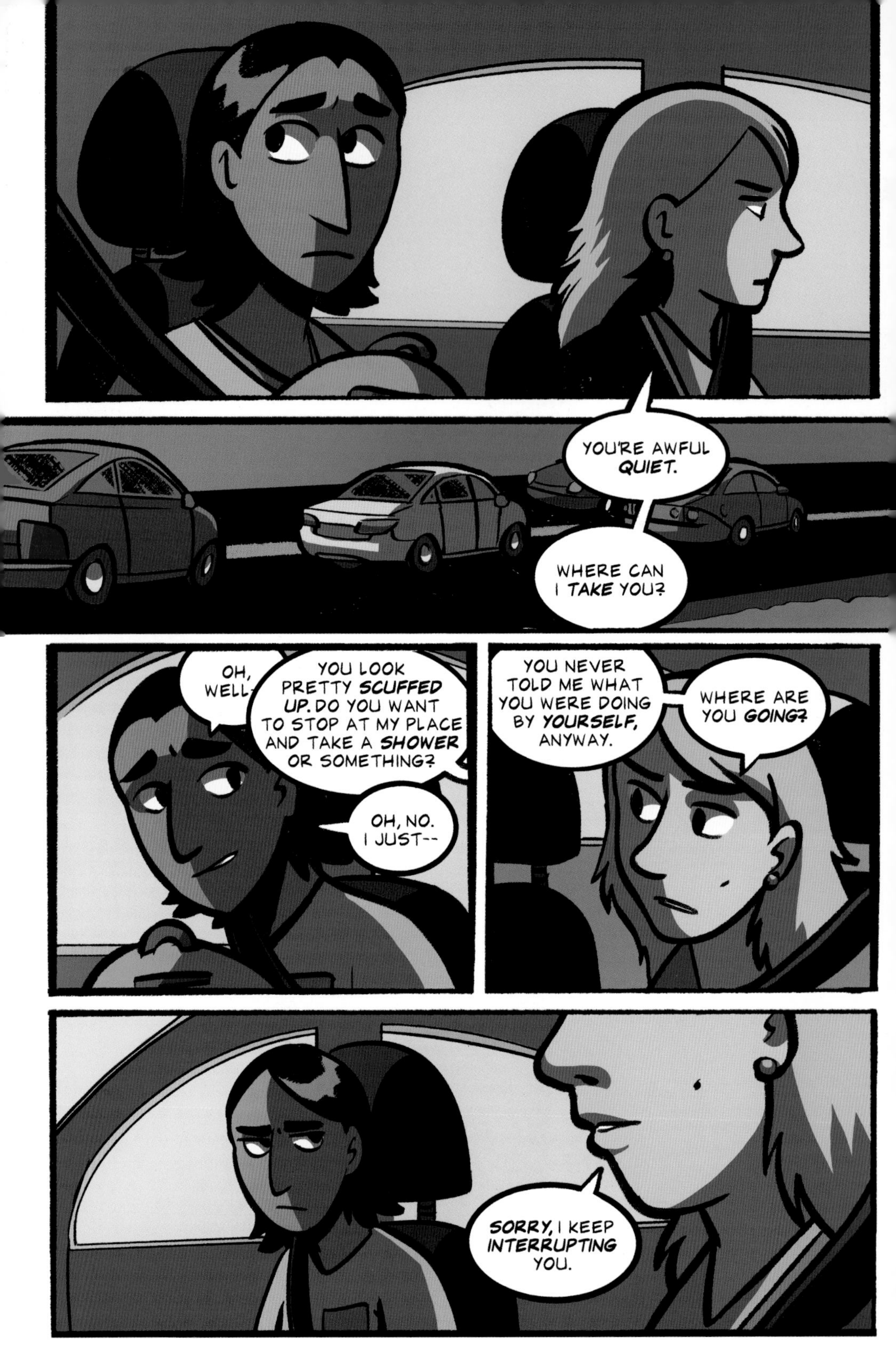
YOU'RE AWFUL QUIET.
WHERE CAN I TAKE YOU?
OH, WELL-
YOU LOOK PRETTY SCUFFED UP. DO YOU WANT TO STOP AT MY PLACE AND TAKE A SHOWER OR SOMETHING?
OH, NO. I JUST--
YOU NEVER TOLD ME WHAT YOU WERE DOING BY YOURSELF, ANYWAY.
WHERE ARE YOU GOING?
SORRY, I KEEP INTERRUPTING YOU.

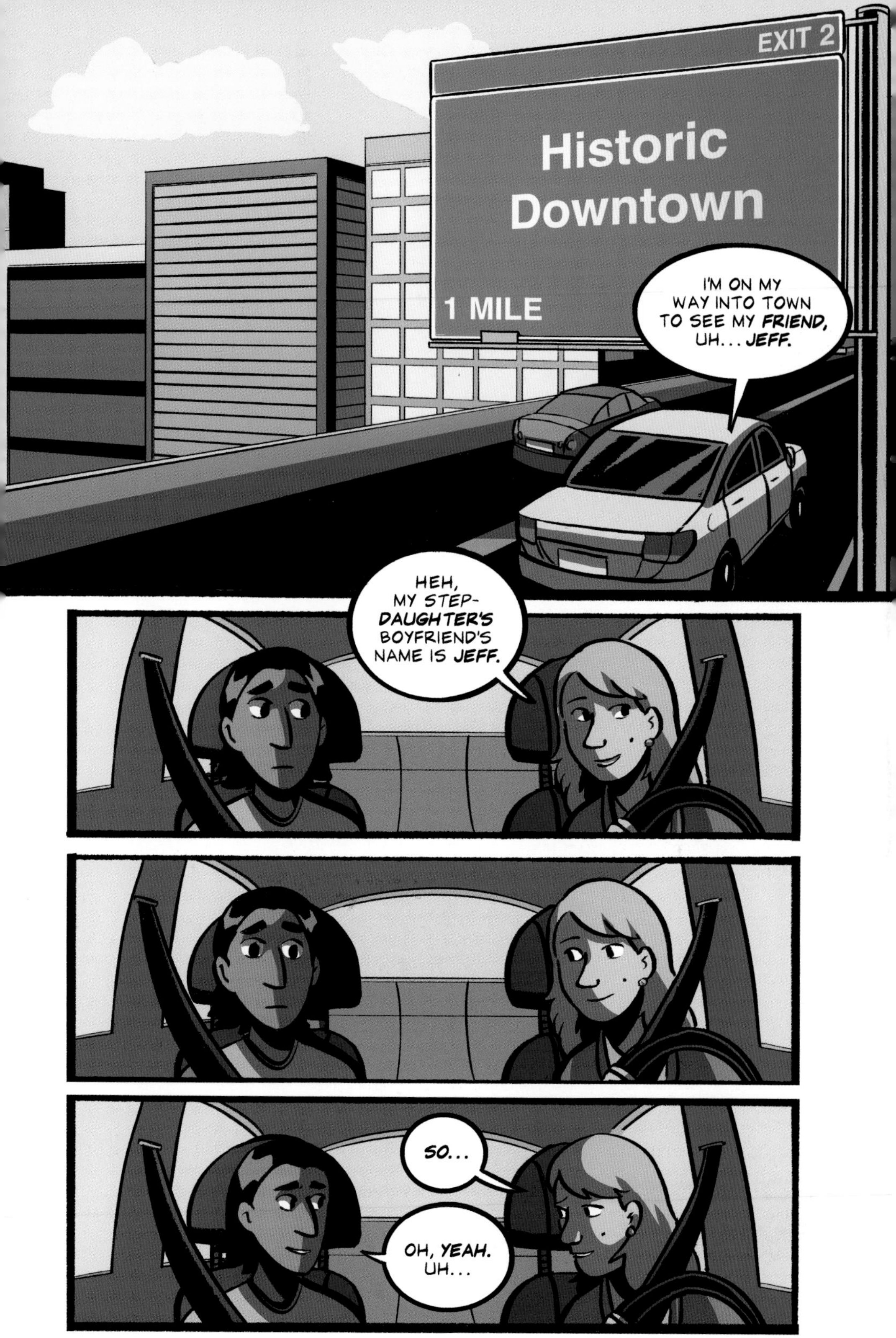
EXIT 2
Historic Downtown
1 MILE
I'M ON MY WAY INTO TOWN TO SEE MY FRIEND, UH... JEFF.
HEH, MY STEP-DAUGHTER'S BOYFRIEND'S NAME IS JEFF.
SO...
OH, YEAH. UH...

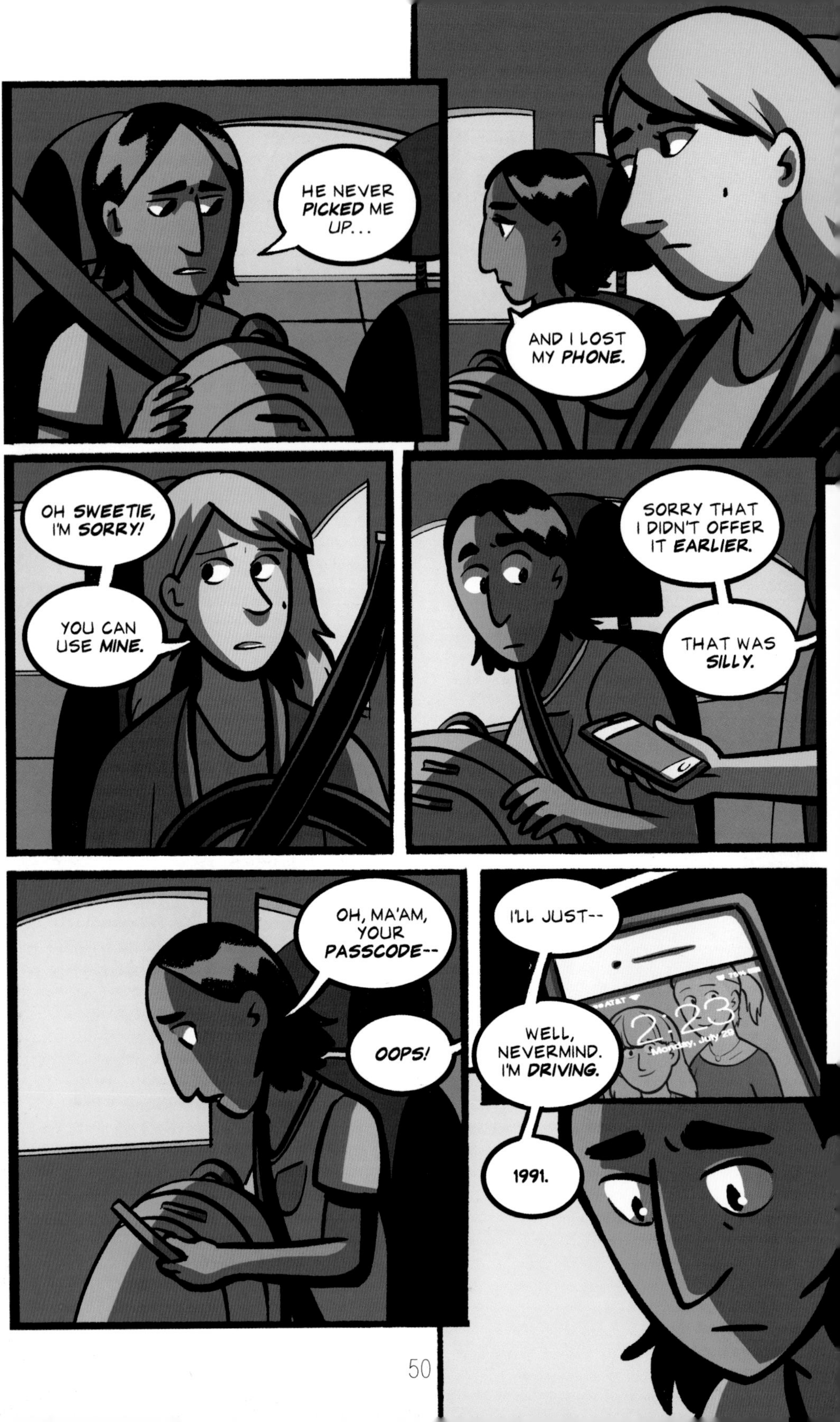
HE NEVER PICKED ME UP...
AND I LOST MY PHONE.
OH SWEETIE, I'M SORRY!
YOU CAN USE MINE.
SORRY THAT I DIDN'T OFFER IT EARLIER.
THAT WAS SILLY.
OH, MA'AM, YOUR PASSCODE--
OOPS!
I'LL JUST--
2:23
WELL, NEVERMIND. I'M DRIVING.
1991.

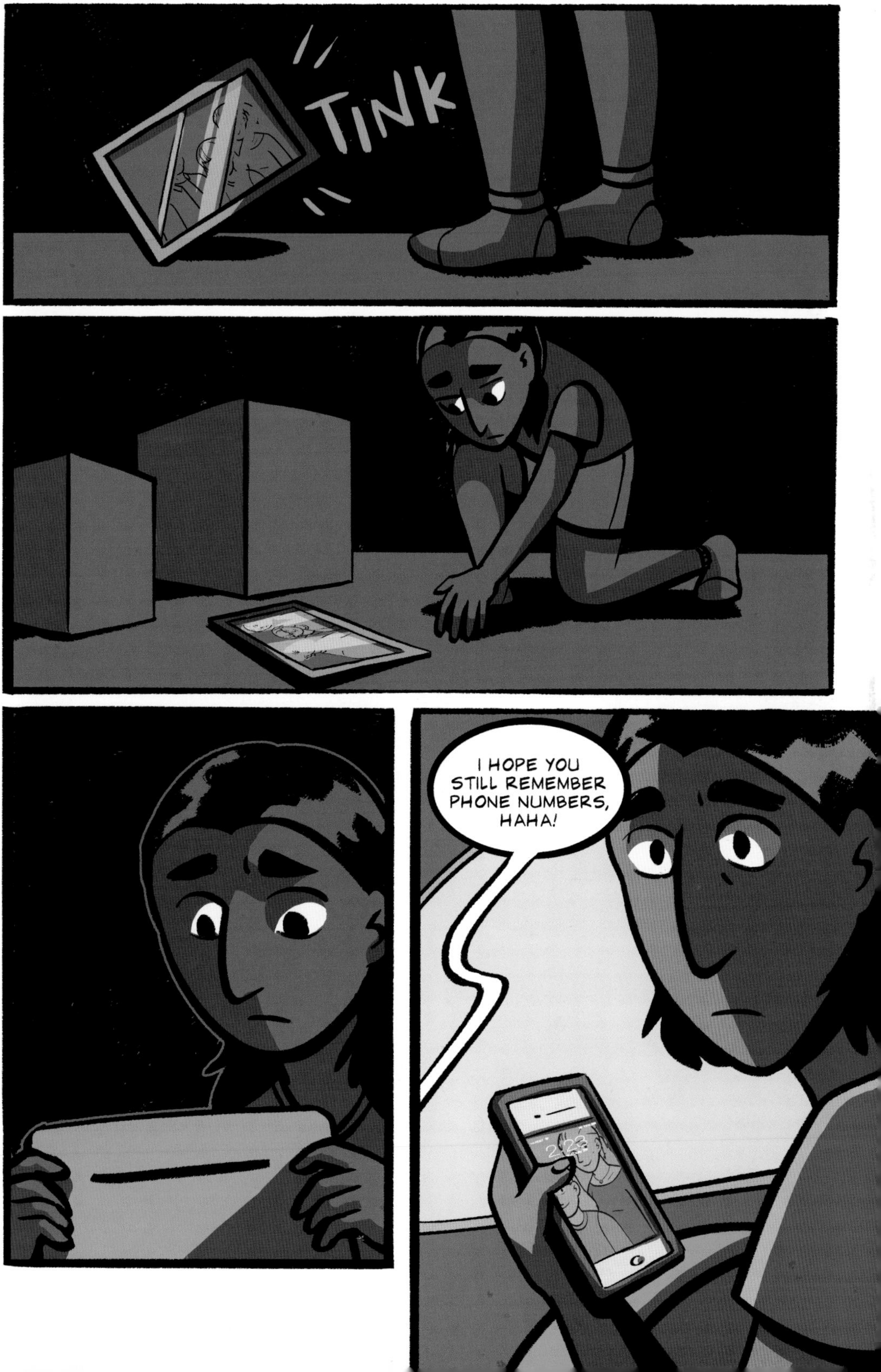
TINK
I HOPE YOU STILL REMEMBER PHONE NUMBERS, HAHA!

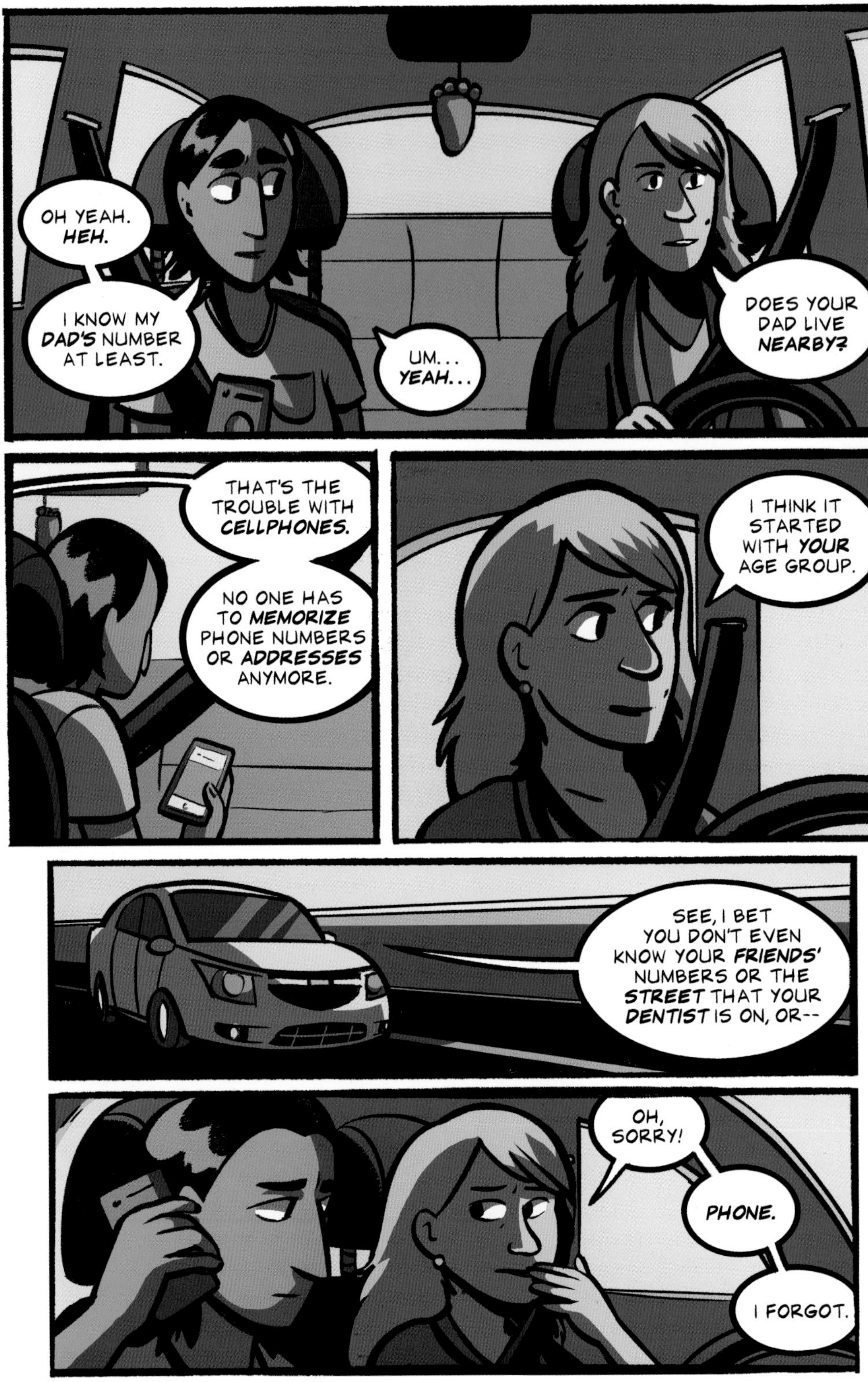
OH YEAH. HEH.
I KNOW MY DAD'S NUMBER AT LEAST.
UM... YEAH...
DOES YOUR DAD LIVE NEARBY?
THAT'S THE TROUBLE WITH CELLPHONES.
NO ONE HAS TO MEMORIZE PHONE NUMBERS OR ADDRESSES ANYMORE.
I THINK IT STARTED WITH YOUR AGE GROUP.
SEE, I BET YOU DON'T EVEN KNOW YOUR FRIENDS' NUMBERS OR THE STREET THAT YOUR DENTIST IS ON, OR--
OH, SORRY!
PHONE.
I FORGOT.

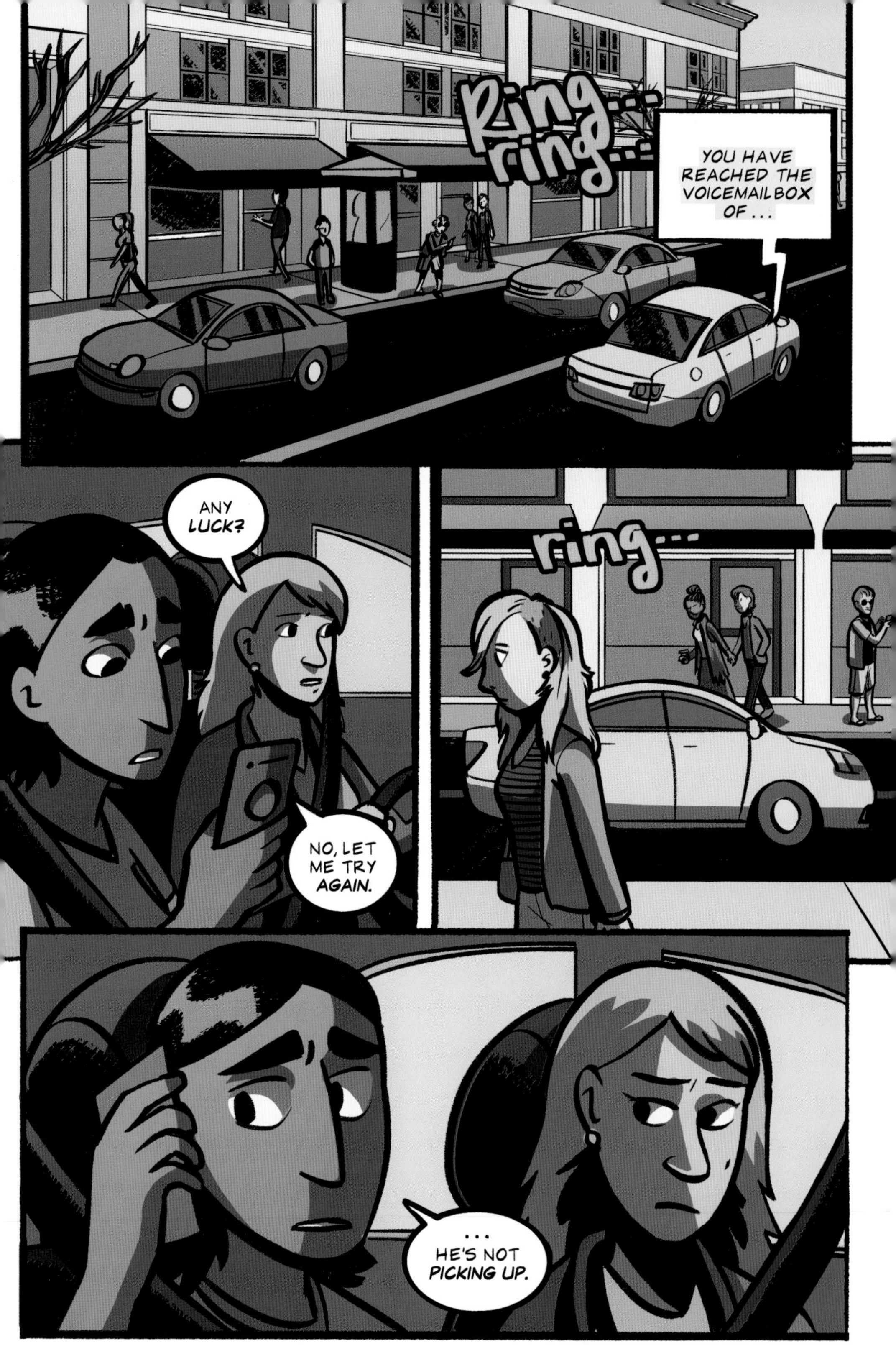
Ring... ring...
YOU HAVE REACHED THE VOICEMAILBOX OF...
ANY LUCK?
NO, LET ME TRY AGAIN.
ring...
... HE'S NOT PICKING UP.

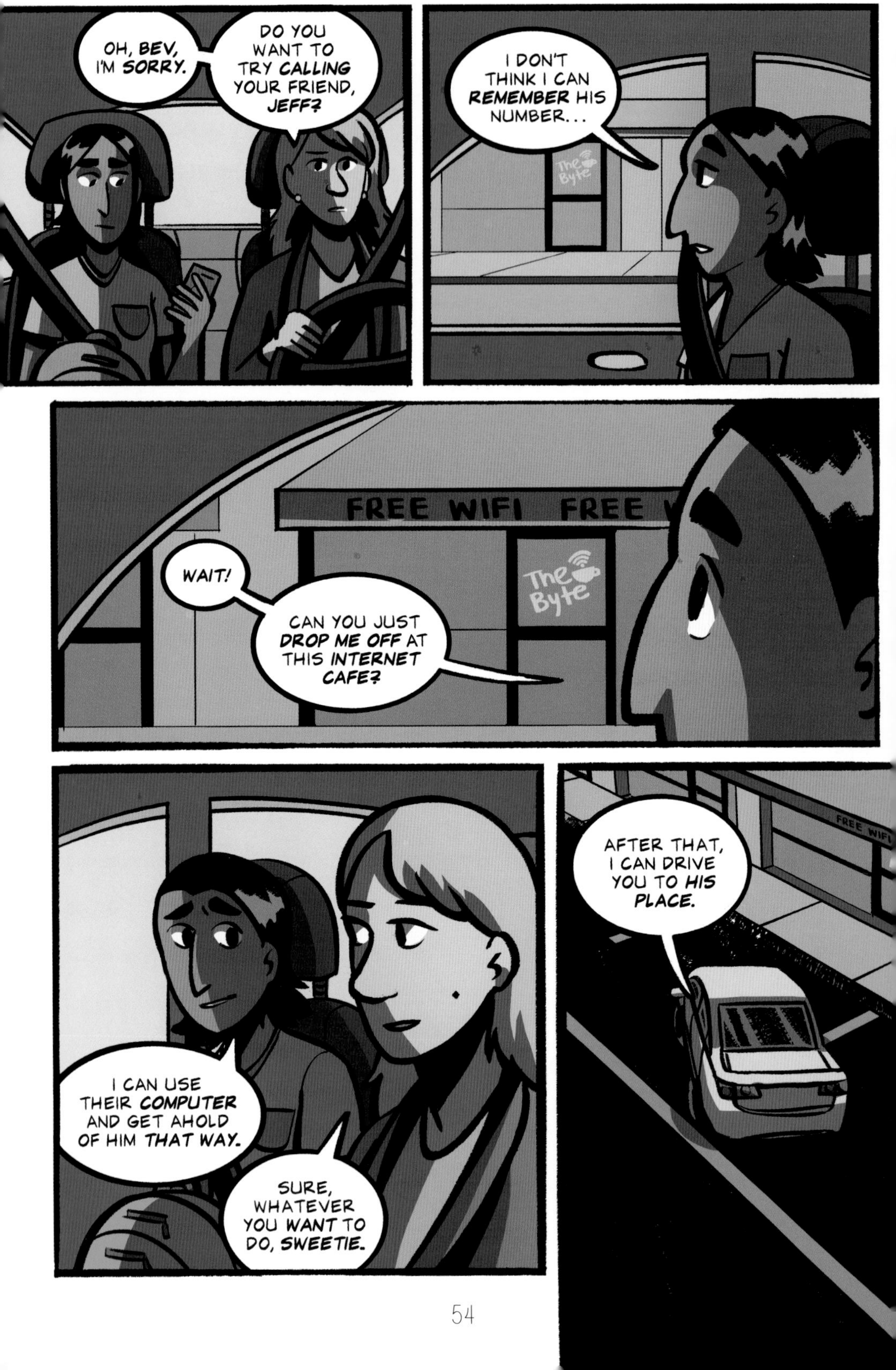
OH, BEV, I'M SORRY.
DO YOU WANT TO TRY CALLING YOUR FRIEND, JEFF?
I DON'T THINK I CAN REMEMBER HIS NUMBER...
The Byte
FREE WIFI FREE W
The Byte
WAIT!
CAN YOU JUST DROP ME OFF AT THIS INTERNET CAFE?
I CAN USE THEIR COMPUTER AND GET AHOLD OF HIM THAT WAY.
SURE, WHATEVER YOU WANT TO DO, SWEETIE.
FREE WIFI
AFTER THAT, I CAN DRIVE YOU TO HIS PLACE.

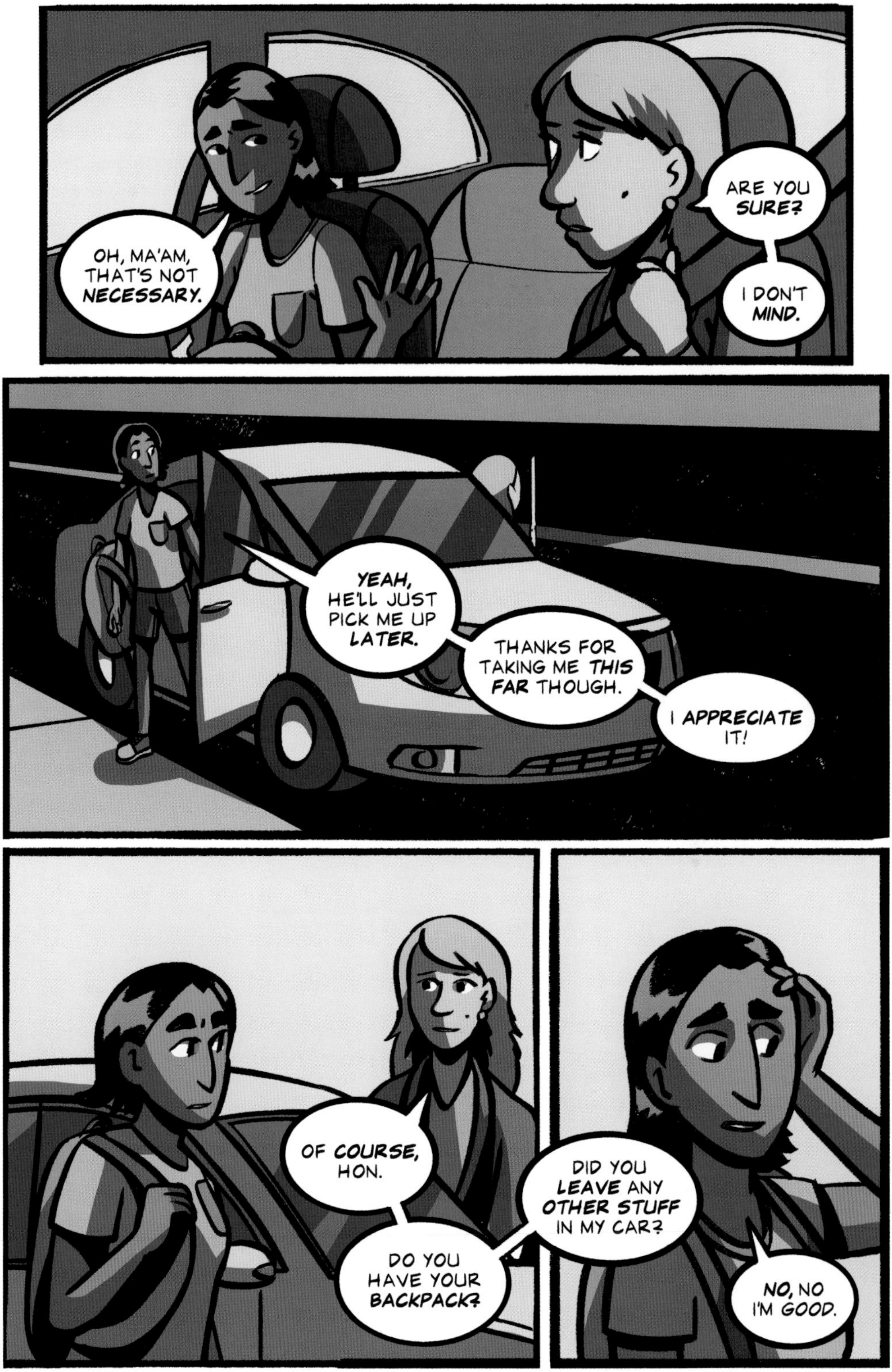
ARE YOU SURE?
I DON'T MIND.
OH, MA'AM, THAT'S NOT NECESSARY.
YEAH, HE'LL JUST PICK ME UP LATER.
THANKS FOR TAKING ME THIS FAR THOUGH.
I APPRECIATE IT!
OF COURSE, HON.
DO YOU HAVE YOUR BACKPACK?
DID YOU LEAVE ANY OTHER STUFF IN MY CAR?
NO, NO I'M GOOD.

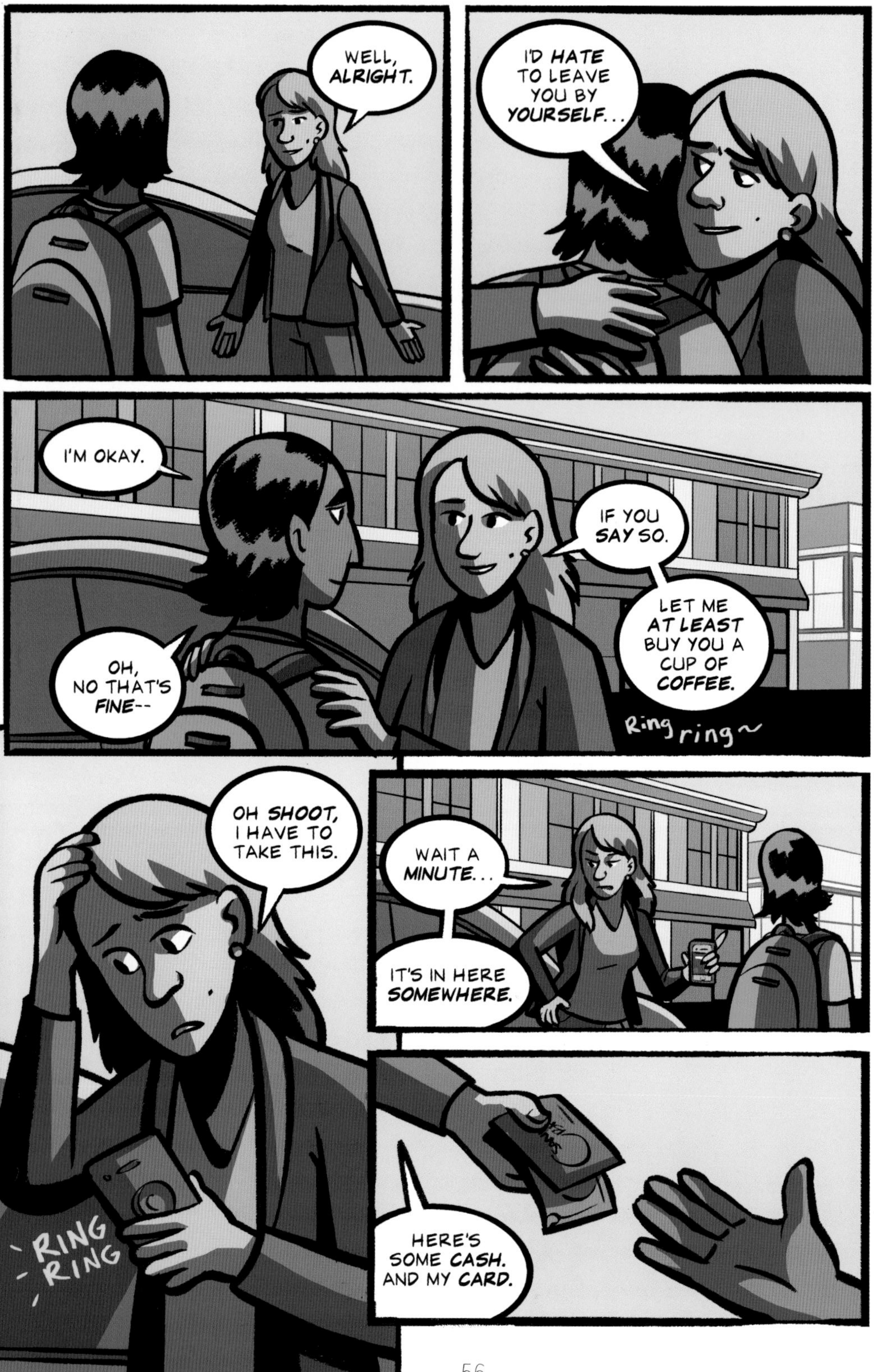
WELL, ALRIGHT.
I'D HATE TO LEAVE YOU BY YOURSELF...
I'M OKAY.
IF YOU SAY SO.
LET ME AT LEAST BUY YOU A CUP OF COFFEE.
OH, NO THAT'S FINE--
Ring ring~
OH SHOOT, I HAVE TO TAKE THIS.
RING RING
WAIT A MINUTE...
IT'S IN HERE SOMEWHERE.
HERE'S SOME CASH. AND MY CARD.

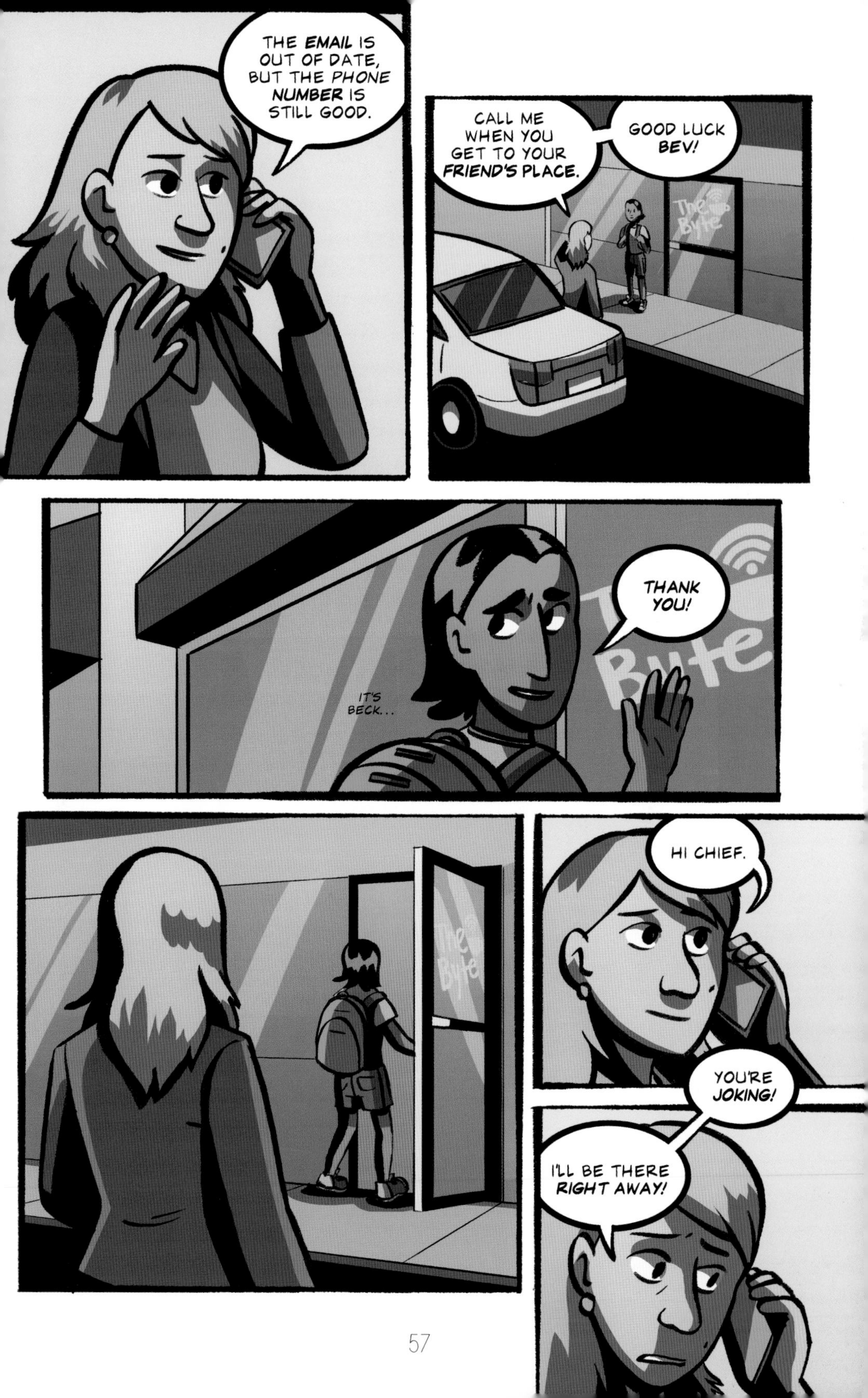
THE EMAIL IS OUT OF DATE, BUT THE PHONE NUMBER IS STILL GOOD.
CALL ME WHEN YOU GET TO YOUR FRIEND'S PLACE.
GOOD LUCK BEV!
The Byte
THANK YOU!
IT'S BECK...
HI CHIEF.
YOU'RE JOKING!
I'LL BE THERE RIGHT AWAY!

CHAPTER 3

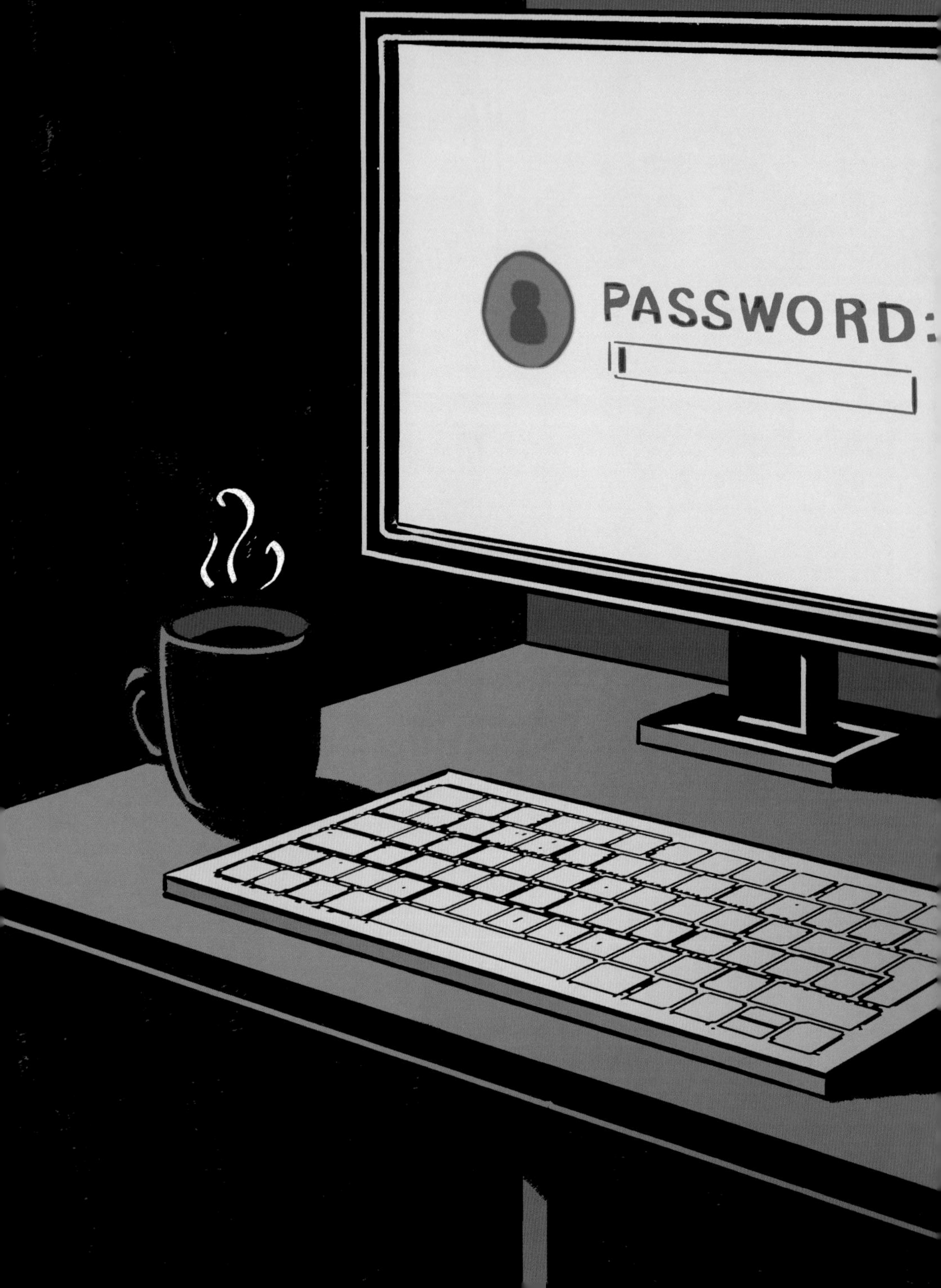
PASSWORD:

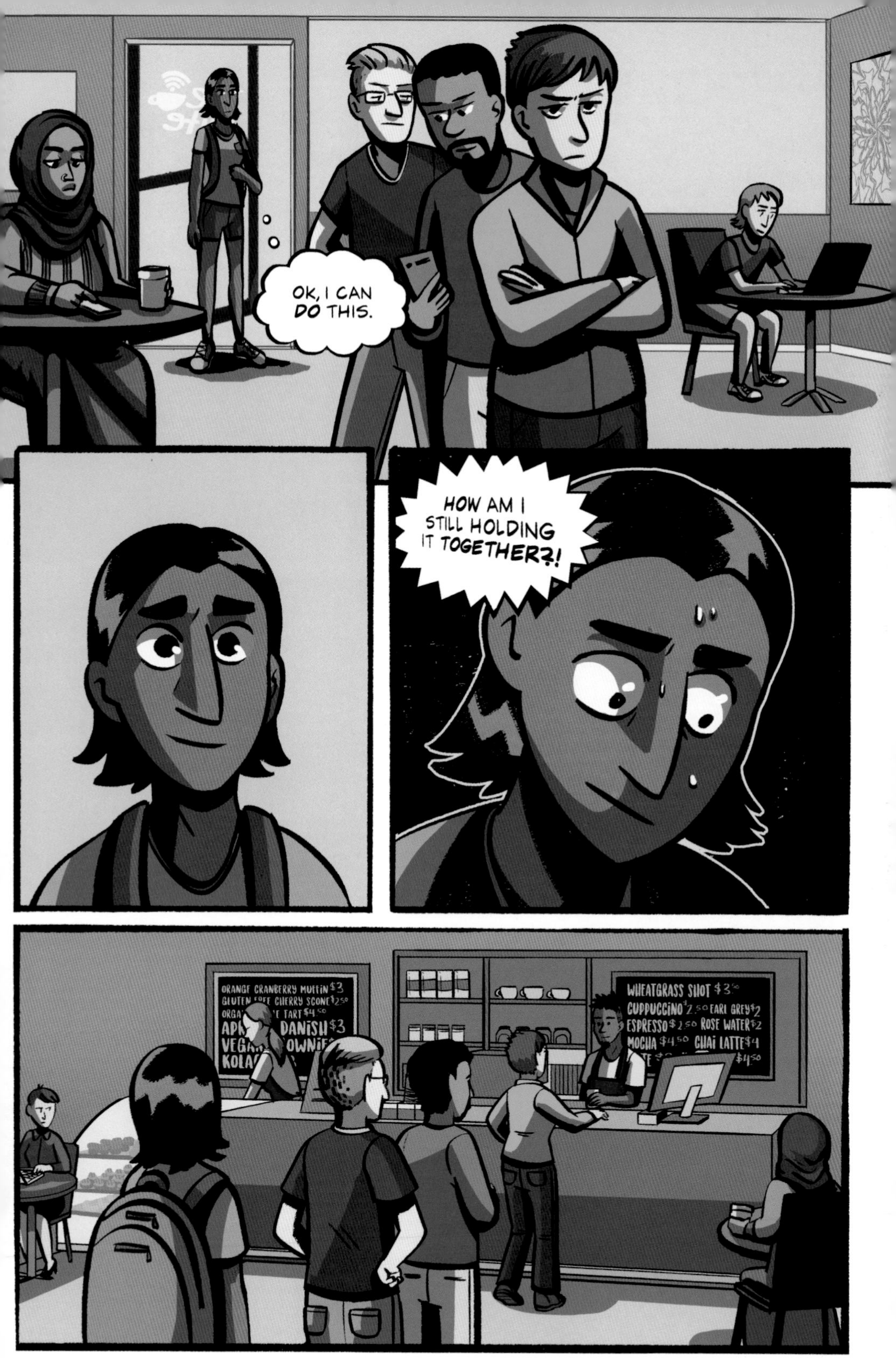

OK, I CAN *DO* THIS.
HOW AM I STILL HOLDING IT TOGETHER?!
ORANGE CRANBERRY MUFFIN $3
WHEATGRASS SHOT $3.50
CUPPUCCINO $2.50 EARL GREY $2
ESPRESSO $2.50 ROSE WATER $2
MOCHA $4.50 CHAI LATTE $4

I SHOULD PROBABLY *EAT* SOMETHING.

HOW AM I NOT *HUNGRY?*

WHAT'S ON THE *MENU,* ANYWAY?

BERRY MUFFIN $3
CHERRY SCONE $2.50
PLE TART $4.50
RICOT DANISH $3
VEGAN BROWNIE $2
KOLACHE $3

WHY IS EVERYTHING SO *EXPENSIVE?*

NBERRY MUFFIN $3
FREE CHERRY SCONE $2.50
ORGANIC APPLE TART $4.50
APRICOT DANISH $3
VEGAN BROWNIE $2
KOLACHE $3

I DON'T KNOW WHAT *HALF* OF THESE THINGS ARE...

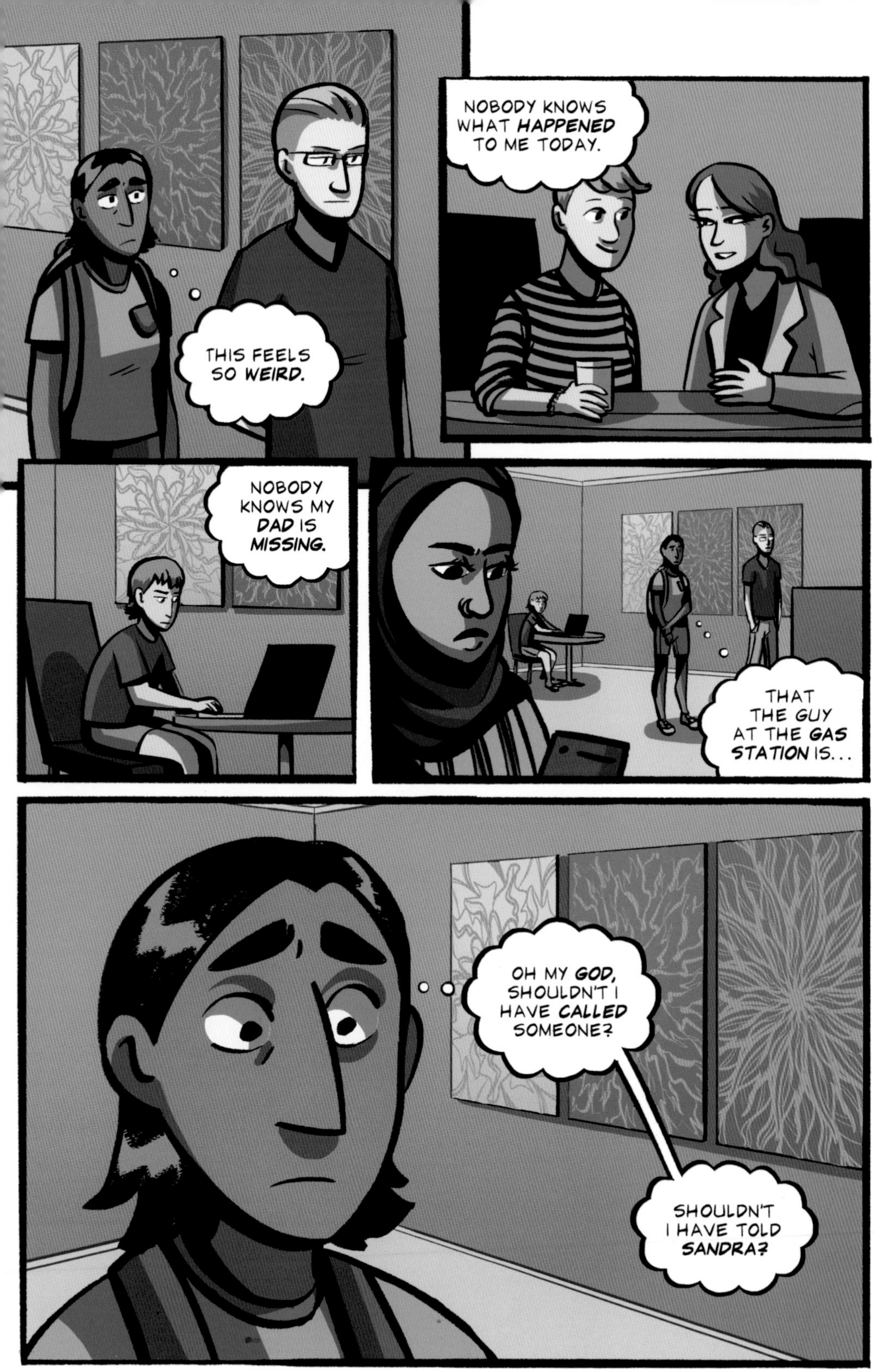
THIS FEELS SO WEIRD.
NOBODY KNOWS WHAT HAPPENED TO ME TODAY.
NOBODY KNOWS MY DAD IS MISSING.
THAT THE GUY AT THE GAS STATION IS...
OH MY GOD, SHOULDN'T I HAVE CALLED SOMEONE?
SHOULDN'T I HAVE TOLD SANDRA?

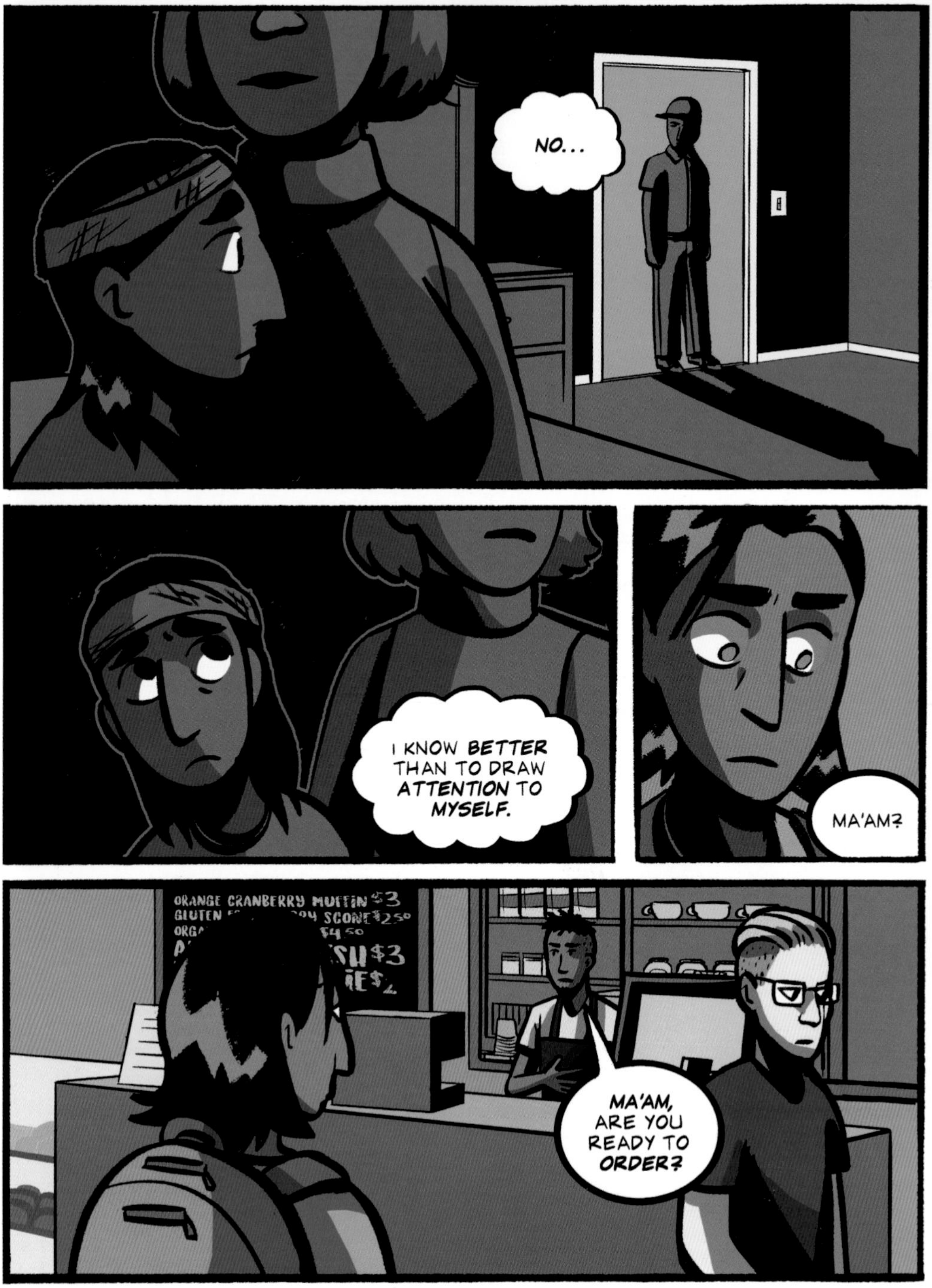
NO...
I KNOW BETTER THAN TO DRAW ATTENTION TO MYSELF.
MA'AM?
ORANGE CRANBERRY MUFFIN $3
MA'AM, ARE YOU READY TO ORDER?

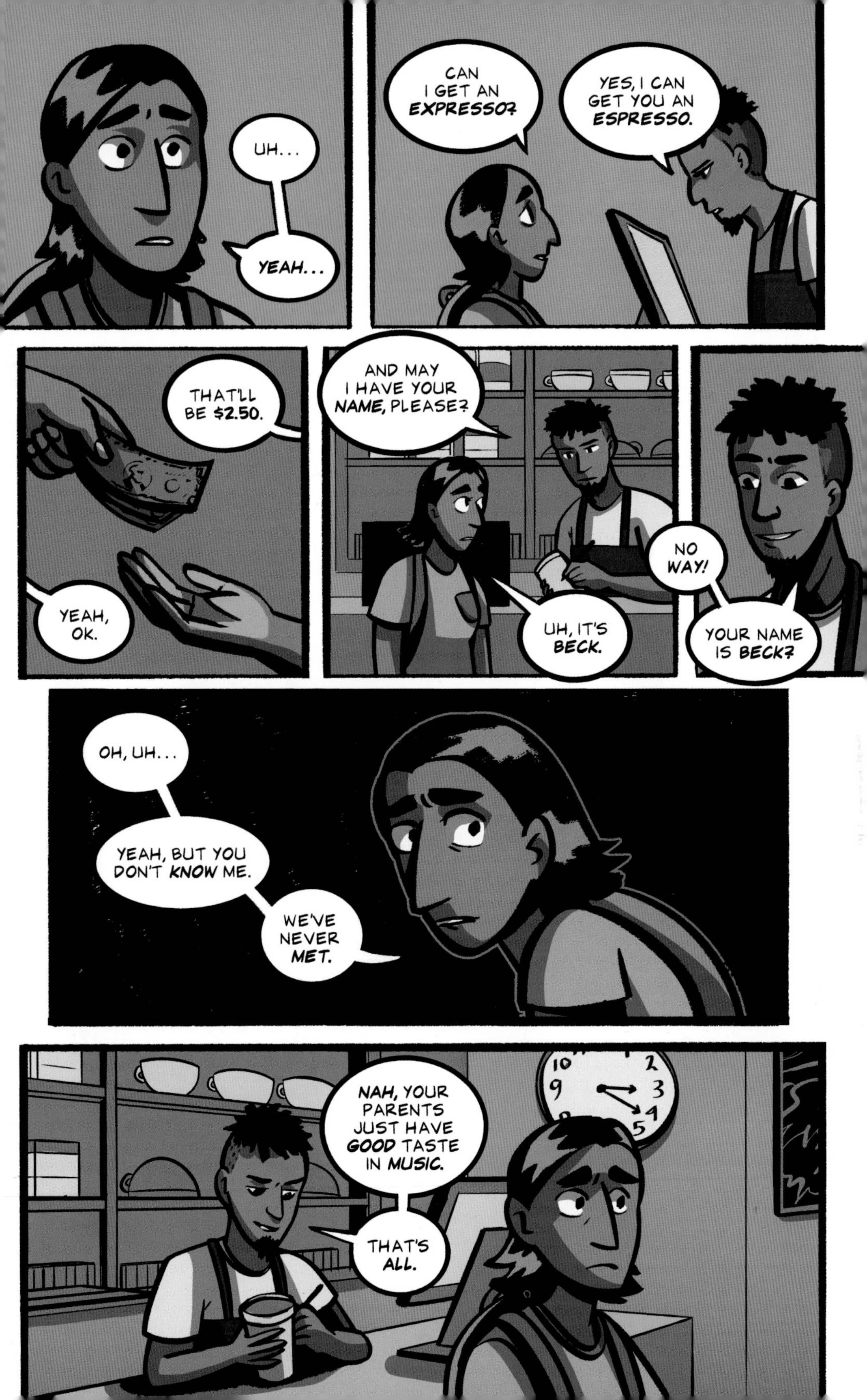
UH...
YEAH...
CAN I GET AN EXPRESSO?
YES, I CAN GET YOU AN ESPRESSO.
THAT'LL BE $2.50.
YEAH, OK.
AND MAY I HAVE YOUR NAME, PLEASE?
UH, IT'S BECK.
NO WAY!
YOUR NAME IS BECK?
OH, UH...
YEAH, BUT YOU DON'T KNOW ME.
WE'VE NEVER MET.
NAH, YOUR PARENTS JUST HAVE GOOD TASTE IN MUSIC.
THAT'S ALL.

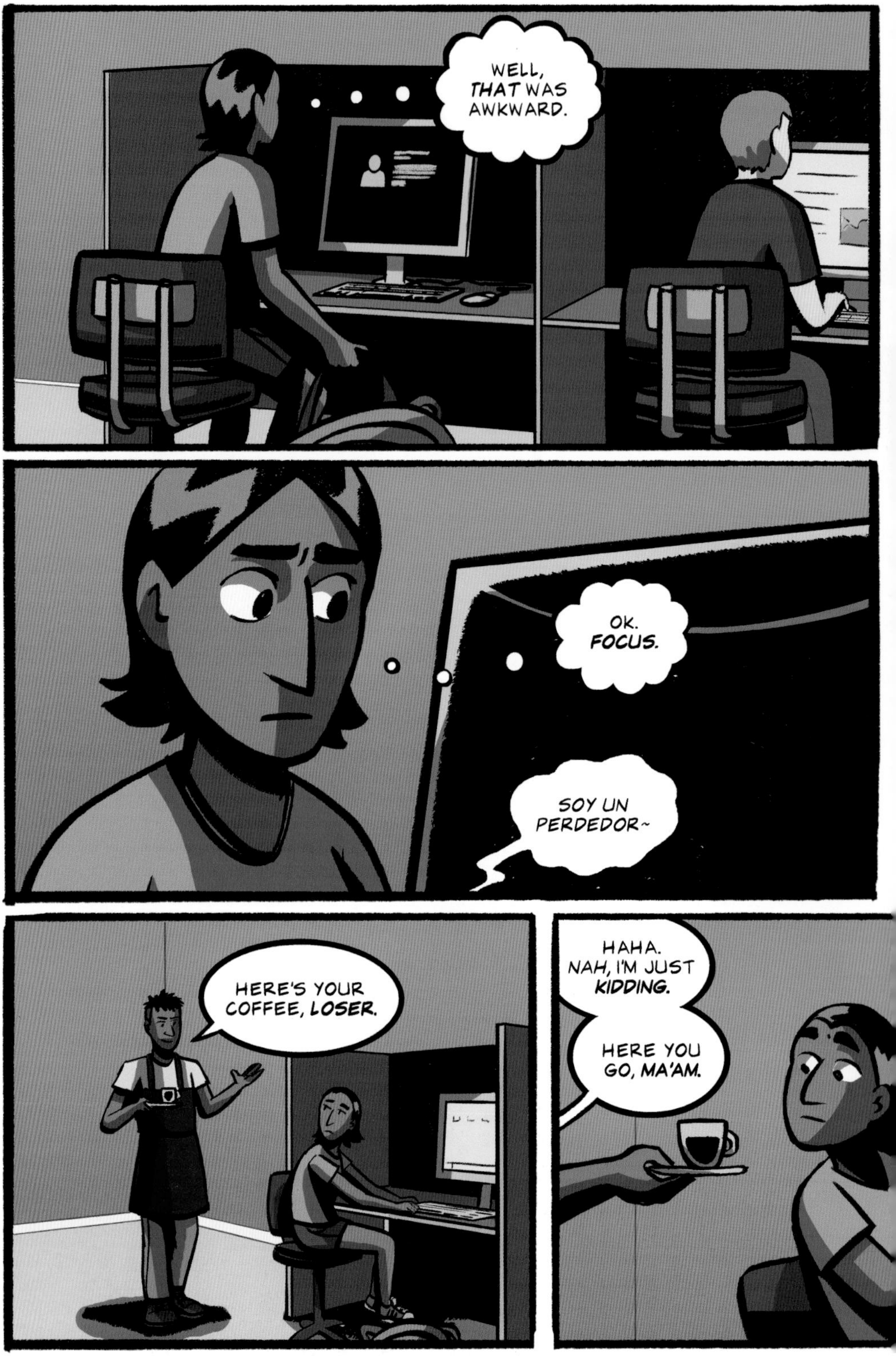
WELL, *THAT* WAS AWKWARD.
OK. *FOCUS.*
SOY UN PERDEDOR~
HERE'S YOUR COFFEE, *LOSER.*
HAHA. NAH, I'M JUST *KIDDING.*
HERE YOU GO, *MA'AM.*

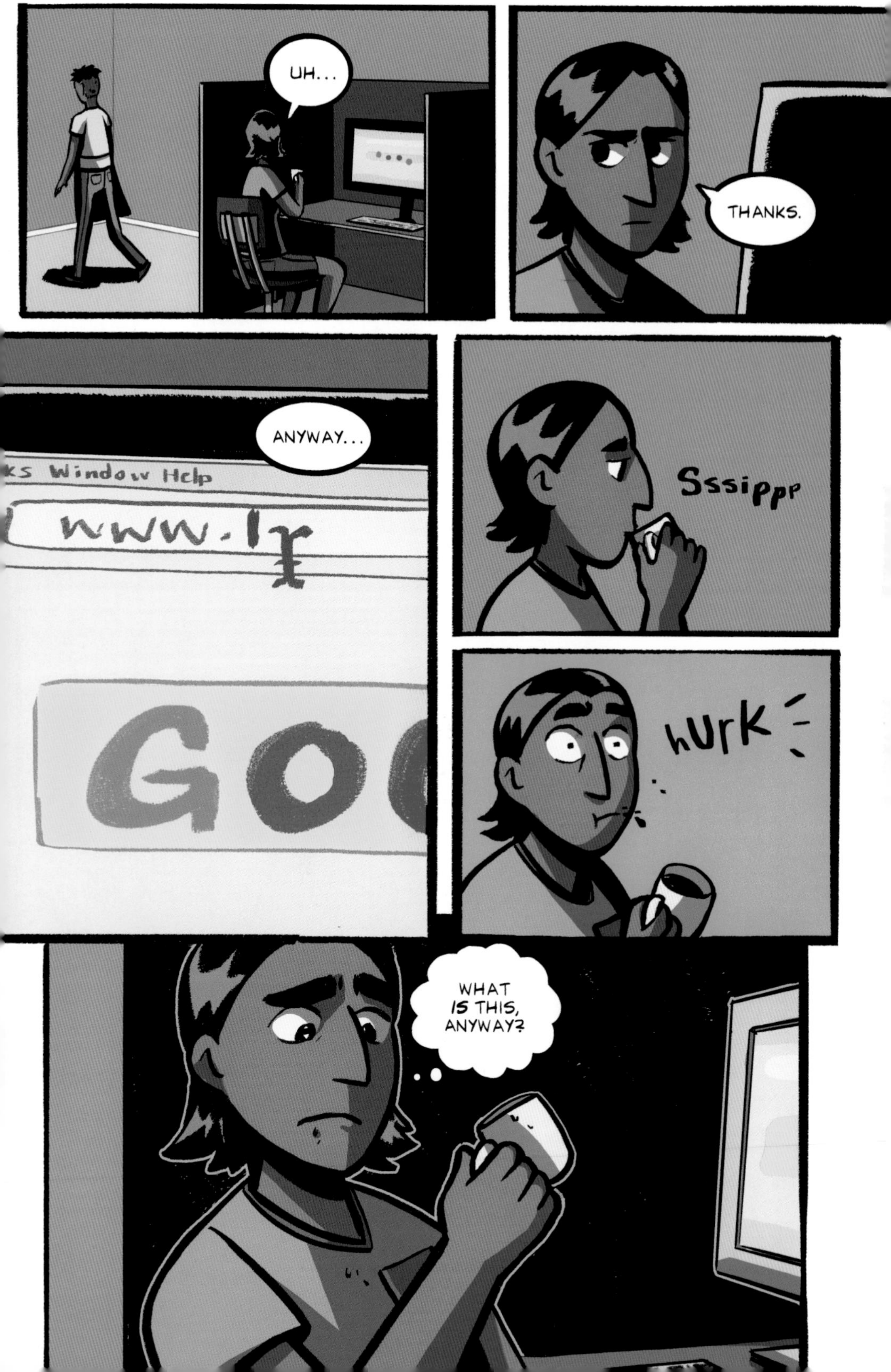
UH...
THANKS.
ANYWAY...
ks Window Help
www.l
GOO
Sssippp
hUrk
WHAT IS THIS, ANYWAY?

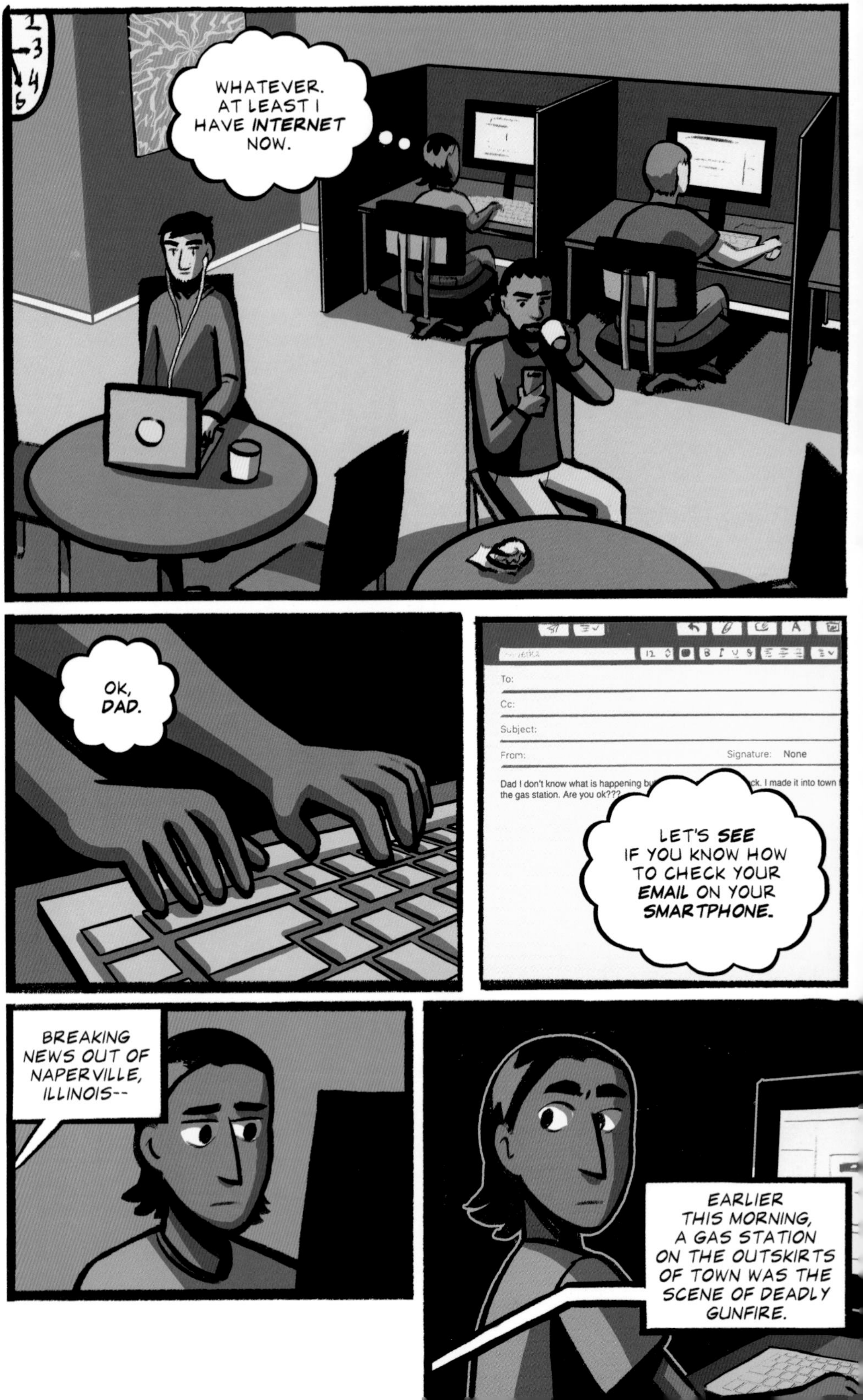
WHATEVER. AT LEAST I HAVE INTERNET NOW.
OK, DAD.
To:
Cc:
Subject:
From:
Signature: None
Dad I don't know what is happening
I made it into town
the gas station. Are you ok???
LET'S SEE IF YOU KNOW HOW TO CHECK YOUR EMAIL ON YOUR SMARTPHONE.
BREAKING NEWS OUT OF NAPERVILLE, ILLINOIS--
EARLIER THIS MORNING, A GAS STATION ON THE OUTSKIRTS OF TOWN WAS THE SCENE OF DEADLY GUNFIRE.

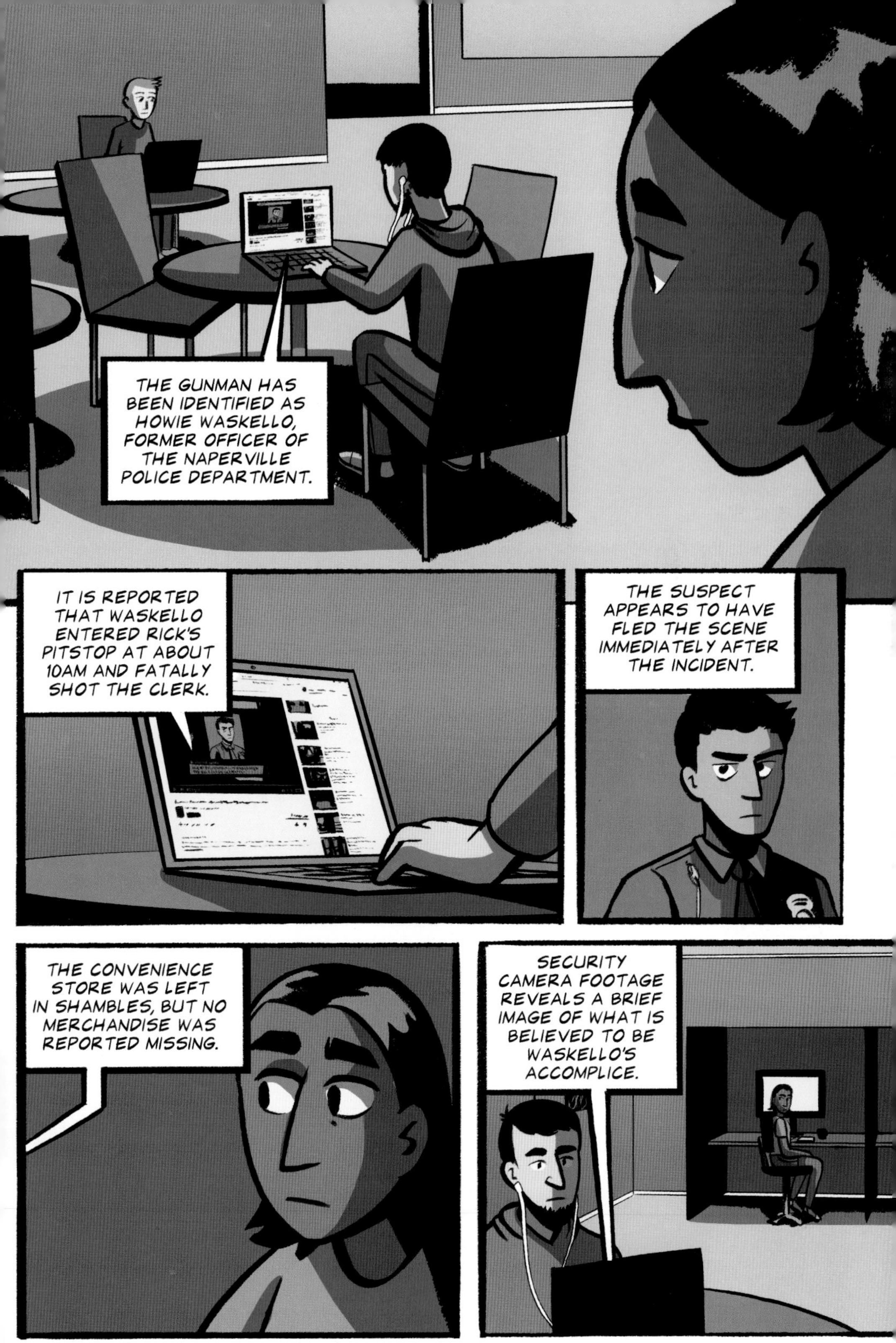
THE GUNMAN HAS BEEN IDENTIFIED AS HOWIE WASKELLO, FORMER OFFICER OF THE NAPERVILLE POLICE DEPARTMENT.
IT IS REPORTED THAT WASKELLO ENTERED RICK'S PITSTOP AT ABOUT 10AM AND FATALLY SHOT THE CLERK.
THE SUSPECT APPEARS TO HAVE FLED THE SCENE IMMEDIATELY AFTER THE INCIDENT.
THE CONVENIENCE STORE WAS LEFT IN SHAMBLES, BUT NO MERCHANDISE WAS REPORTED MISSING.
SECURITY CAMERA FOOTAGE REVEALS A BRIEF IMAGE OF WHAT IS BELIEVED TO BE WASKELLO'S ACCOMPLICE.

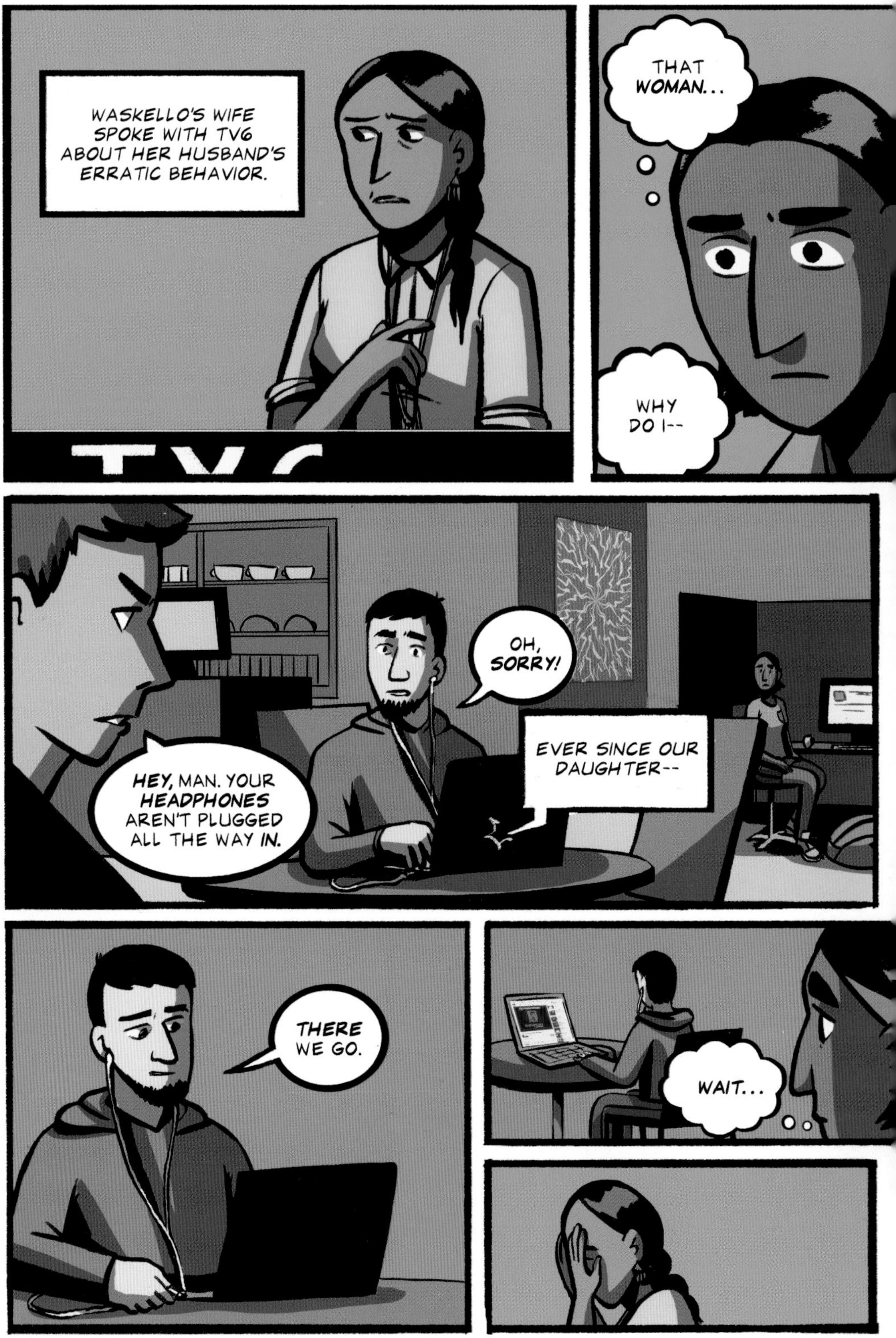
WASKELLO'S WIFE SPOKE WITH TV6 ABOUT HER HUSBAND'S ERRATIC BEHAVIOR.
TV6
THAT WOMAN...
WHY DO I--
HEY, MAN. YOUR HEADPHONES AREN'T PLUGGED ALL THE WAY IN.
OH, SORRY!
EVER SINCE OUR DAUGHTER--
THERE WE GO.
WAIT...

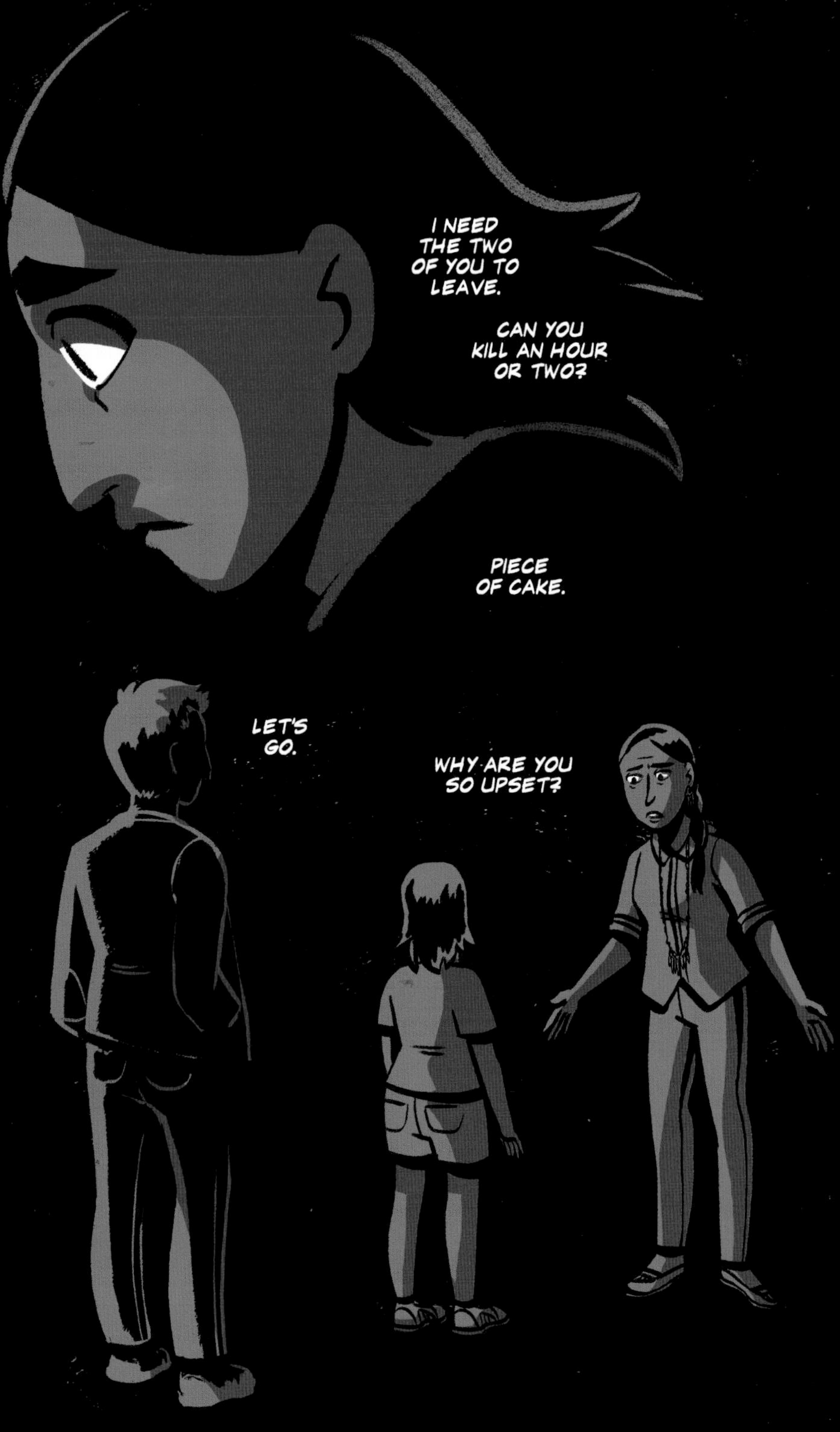
I NEED THE TWO OF YOU TO LEAVE.
CAN YOU KILL AN HOUR OR TWO?
PIECE OF CAKE.
LET'S GO.
WHY ARE YOU SO UPSET?

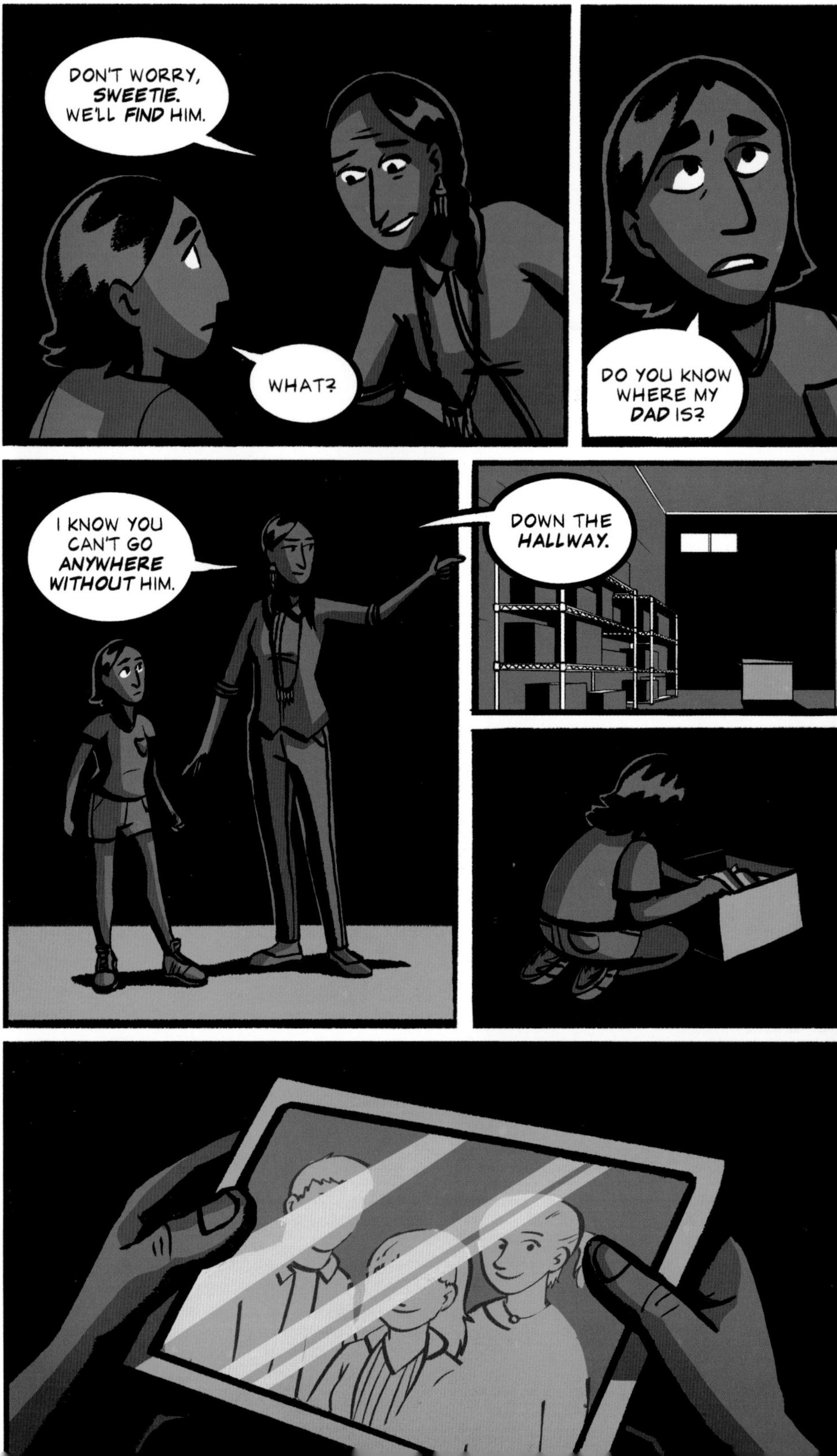
DON'T WORRY, SWEETIE. WE'LL FIND HIM.
WHAT?
DO YOU KNOW WHERE MY DAD IS?
I KNOW YOU CAN'T GO ANYWHERE WITHOUT HIM.
DOWN THE HALLWAY.

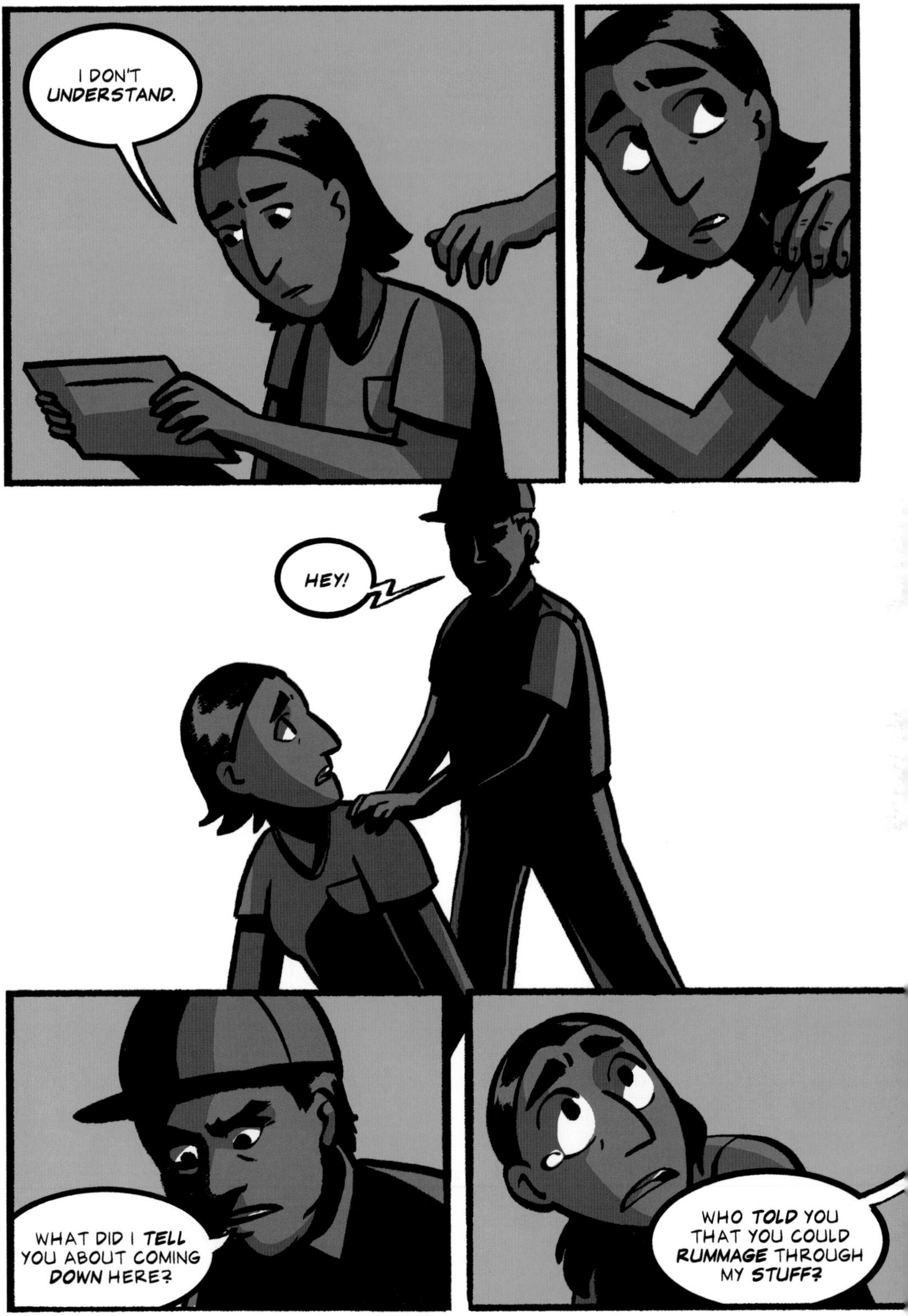
I DON'T UNDERSTAND.
HEY!
WHAT DID I TELL YOU ABOUT COMING DOWN HERE?
WHO TOLD YOU THAT YOU COULD RUMMAGE THROUGH MY STUFF?

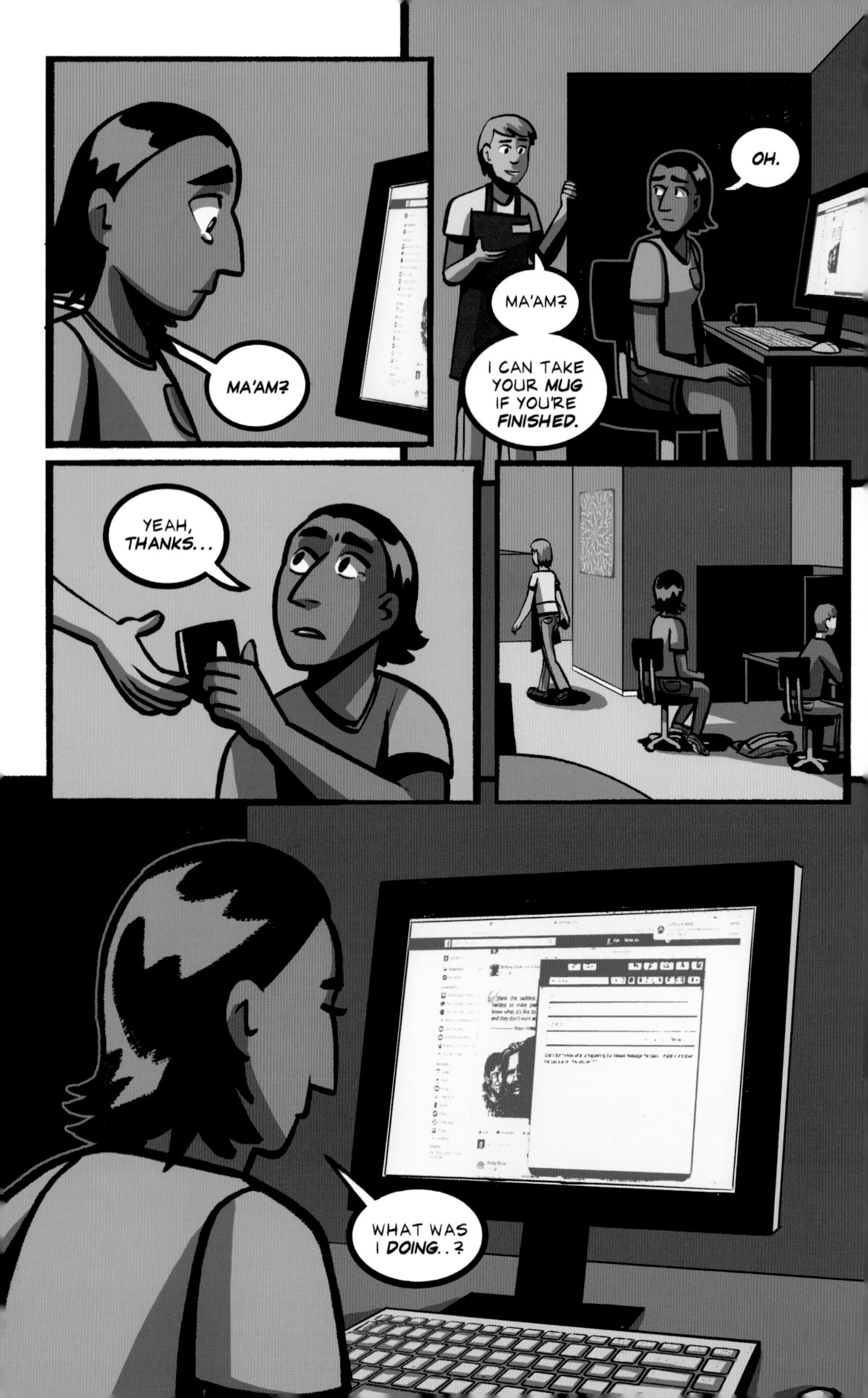
MA'AM?
MA'AM?
I CAN TAKE YOUR MUG IF YOU'RE FINISHED.
OH.
YEAH, THANKS...
WHAT WAS I DOING..?

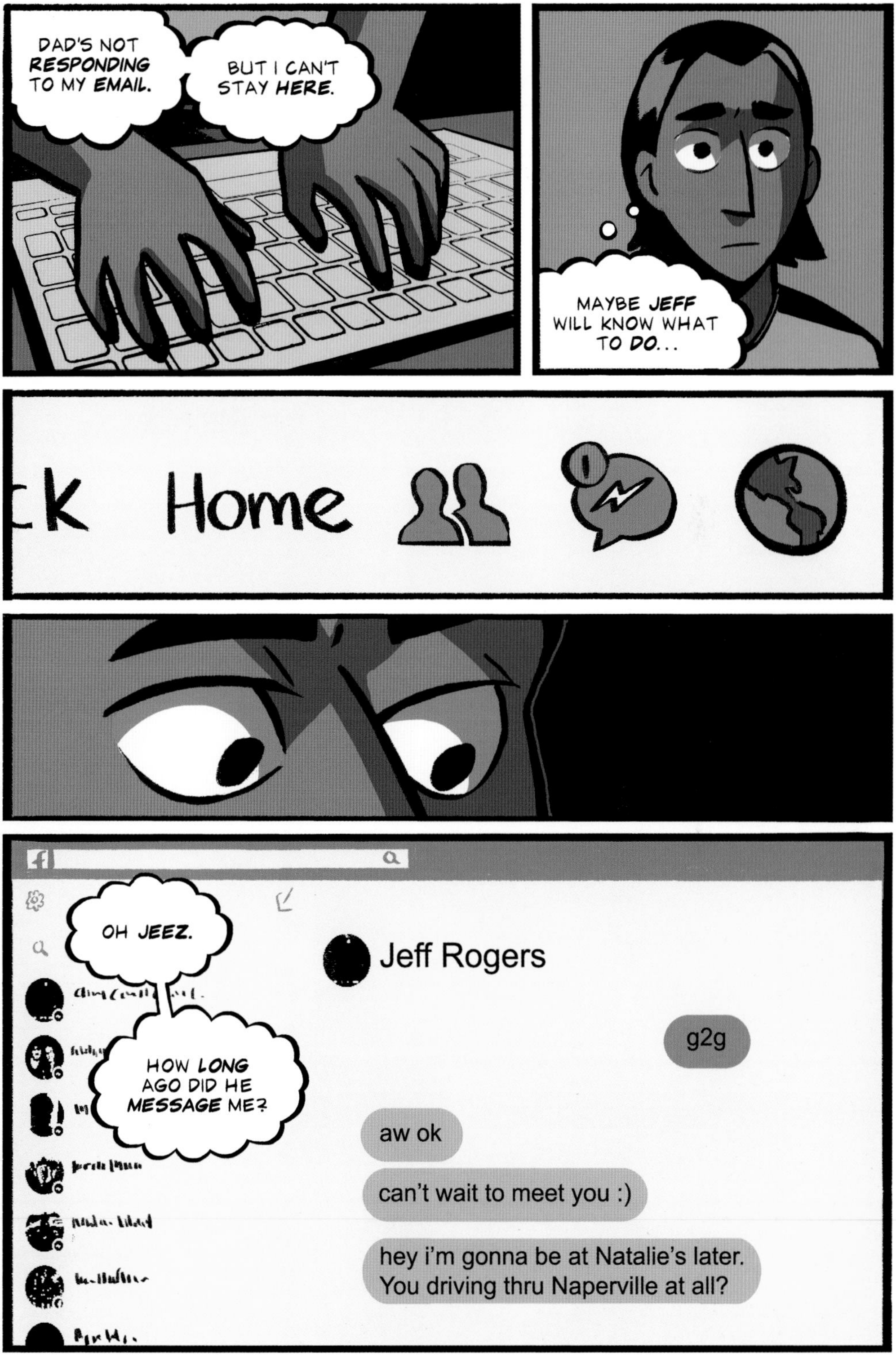
DAD'S NOT RESPONDING TO MY EMAIL.
BUT I CAN'T STAY HERE.
MAYBE JEFF WILL KNOW WHAT TO DO...
Home
OH JEEZ.
HOW LONG AGO DID HE MESSAGE ME?
Jeff Rogers
g2g
aw ok
can't wait to meet you :)
hey i'm gonna be at Natalie's later. You driving thru Naperville at all?

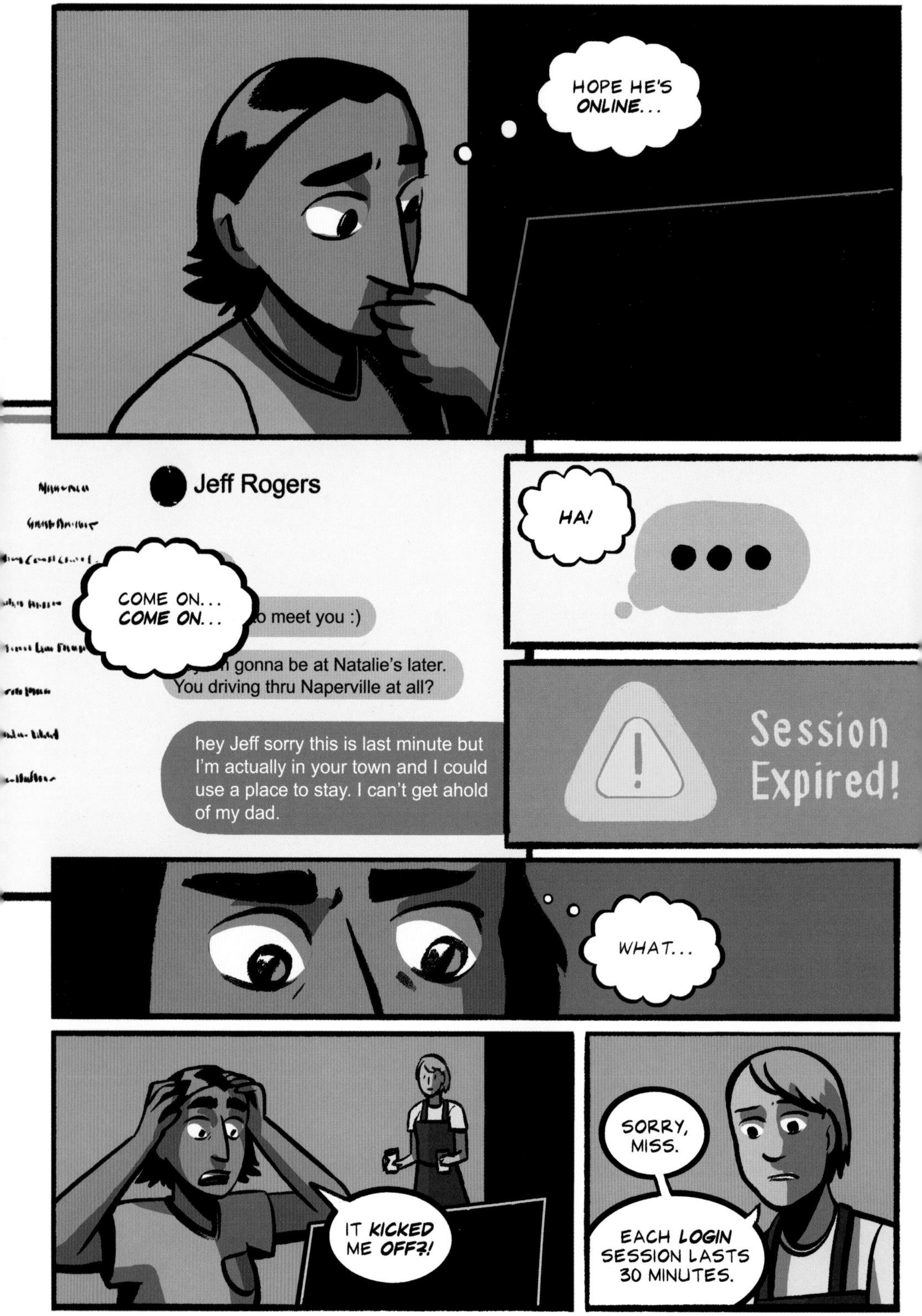
HOPE HE'S ONLINE...
Jeff Rogers
COME ON... COME ON...
o meet you :)
gonna be at Natalie's later. You driving thru Naperville at all?
hey Jeff sorry this is last minute but I'm actually in your town and I could use a place to stay. I can't get ahold of my dad.
HA!
Session Expired!
WHAT...
IT KICKED ME OFF?!
SORRY, MISS.
EACH LOGIN SESSION LASTS 30 MINUTES.

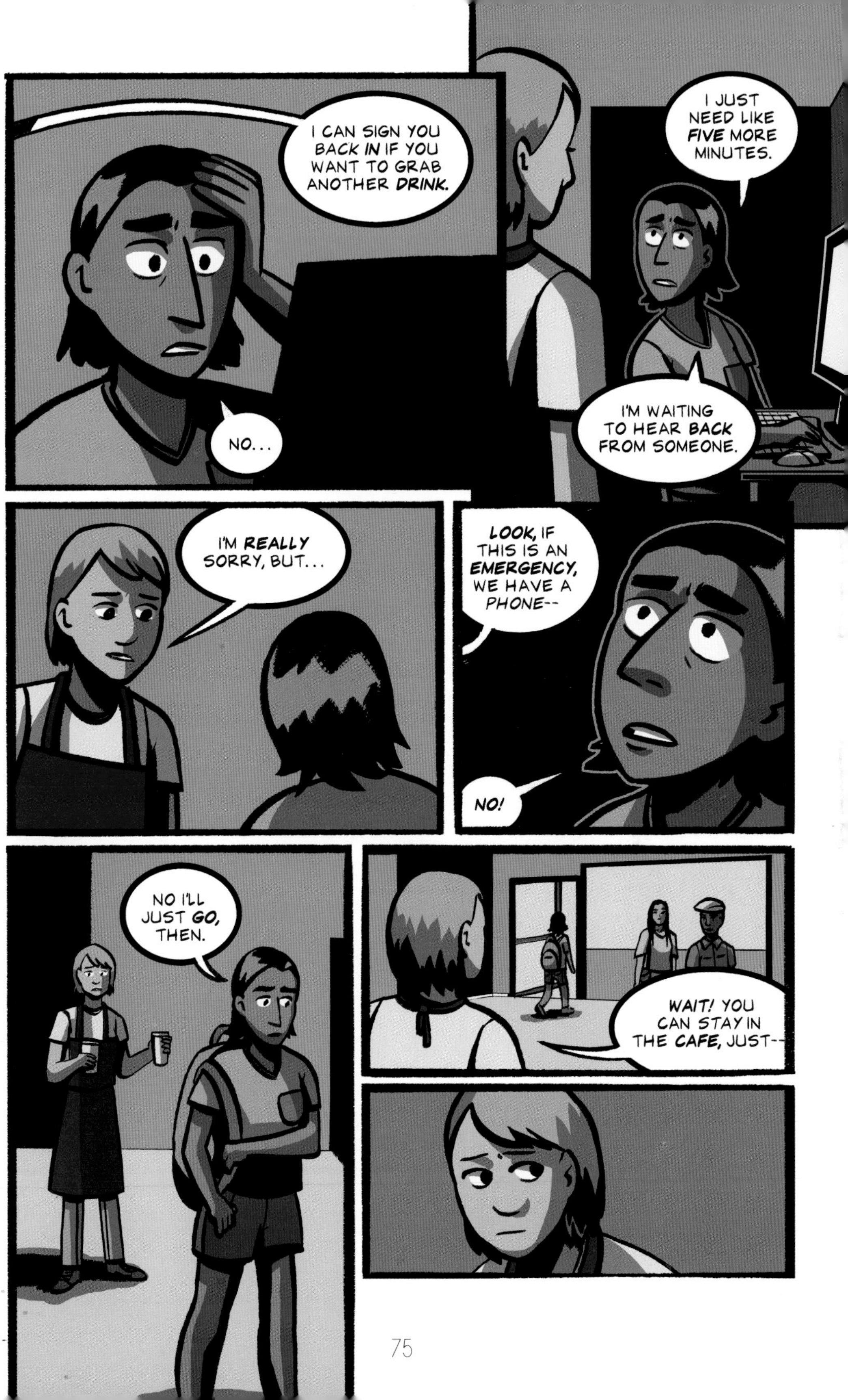
I CAN SIGN YOU BACK **IN** IF YOU WANT TO GRAB ANOTHER **DRINK.**
NO...
I JUST NEED LIKE **FIVE** MORE MINUTES.
I'M WAITING TO HEAR **BACK** FROM SOMEONE.
I'M **REALLY** SORRY, BUT...
LOOK, IF THIS IS AN **EMERGENCY,** WE HAVE A PHONE--
NO!
NO I'LL JUST **GO,** THEN.
WAIT! YOU CAN STAY IN THE **CAFE,** JUST--

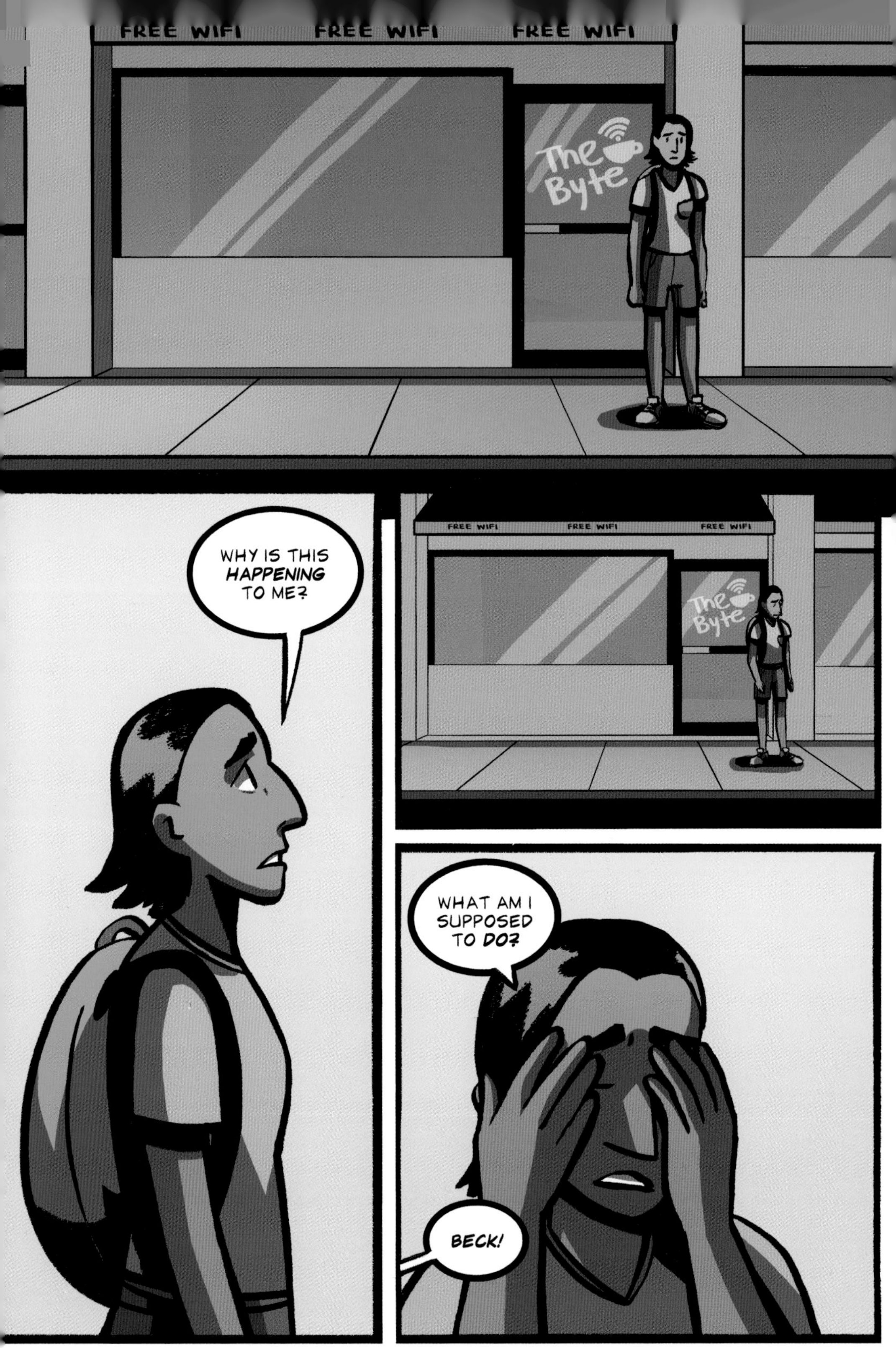
FREE WIFI FREE WIFI FREE WIFI
The Byte
WHY IS THIS HAPPENING TO ME?
WHAT AM I SUPPOSED TO DO?
BECK!

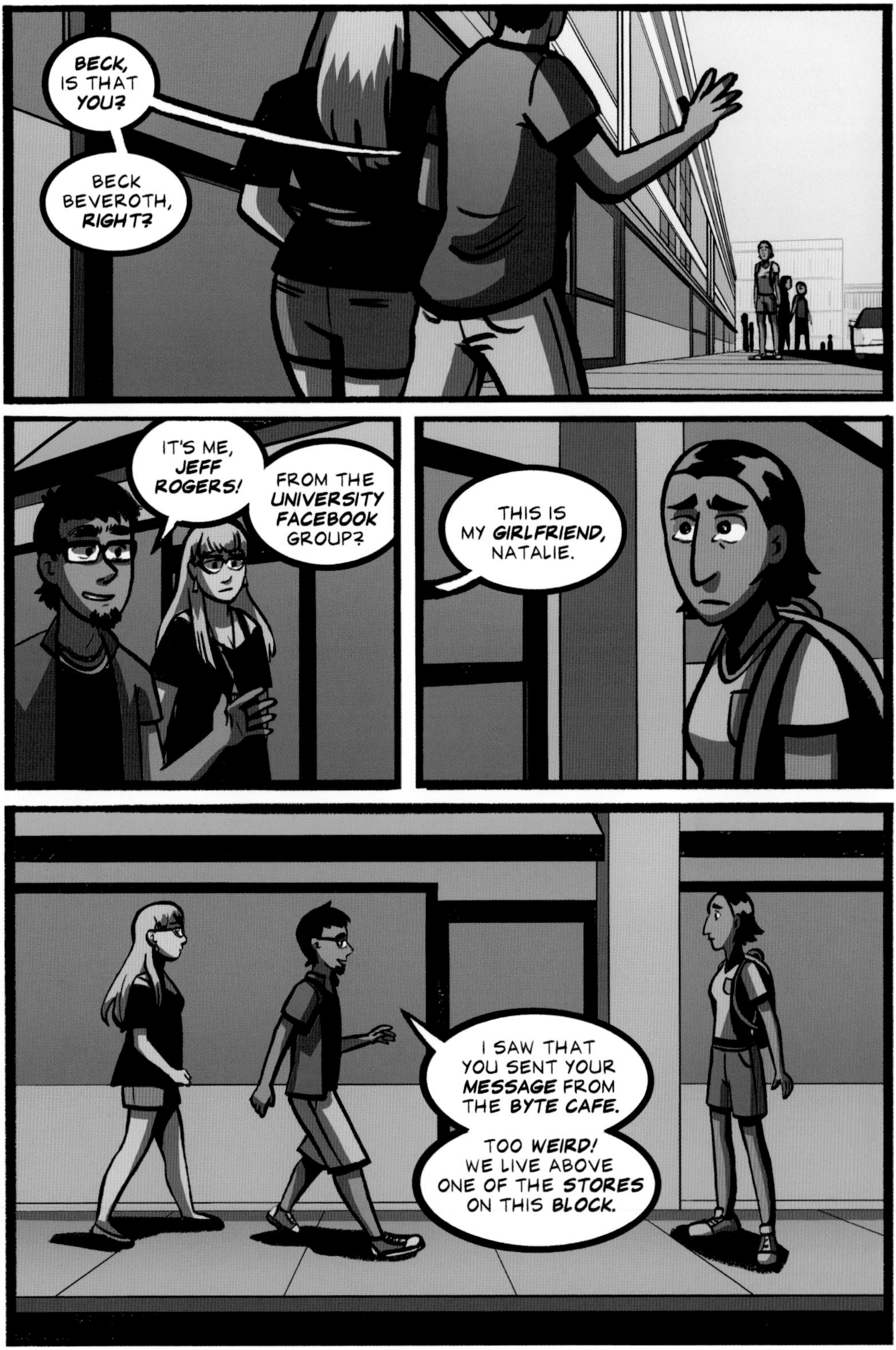
BECK, IS THAT YOU?
BECK BEVEROTH, RIGHT?
IT'S ME, JEFF ROGERS!
FROM THE UNIVERSITY FACEBOOK GROUP?
THIS IS MY GIRLFRIEND, NATALIE.
I SAW THAT YOU SENT YOUR MESSAGE FROM THE BYTE CAFE.
TOO WEIRD! WE LIVE ABOVE ONE OF THE STORES ON THIS BLOCK.

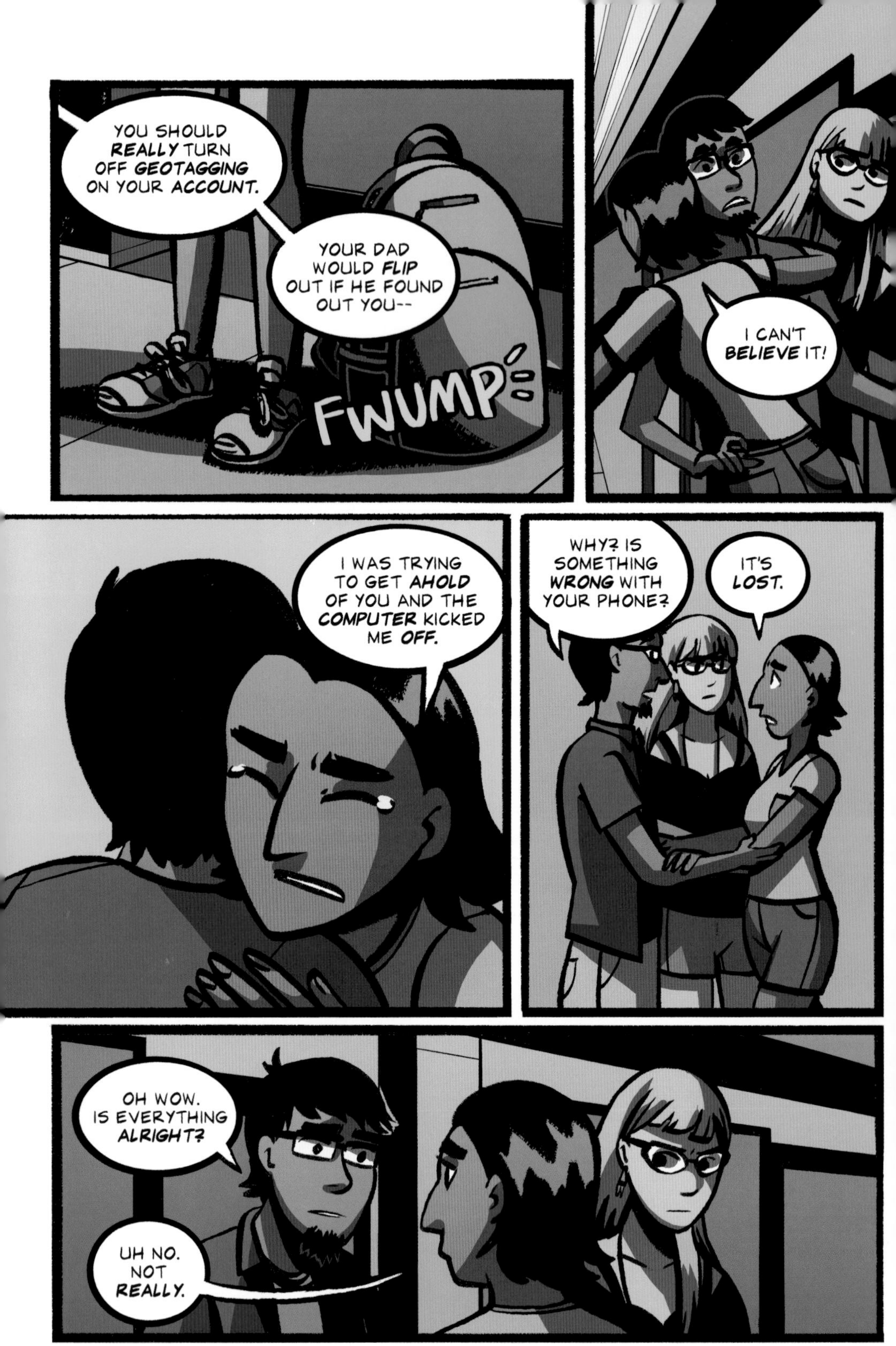
YOU SHOULD REALLY TURN OFF GEOTAGGING ON YOUR ACCOUNT.
YOUR DAD WOULD FLIP OUT IF HE FOUND OUT YOU--
FWUMP
I CAN'T BELIEVE IT!
I WAS TRYING TO GET AHOLD OF YOU AND THE COMPUTER KICKED ME OFF.
WHY? IS SOMETHING WRONG WITH YOUR PHONE?
IT'S LOST.
OH WOW. IS EVERYTHING ALRIGHT?
UH NO. NOT REALLY.

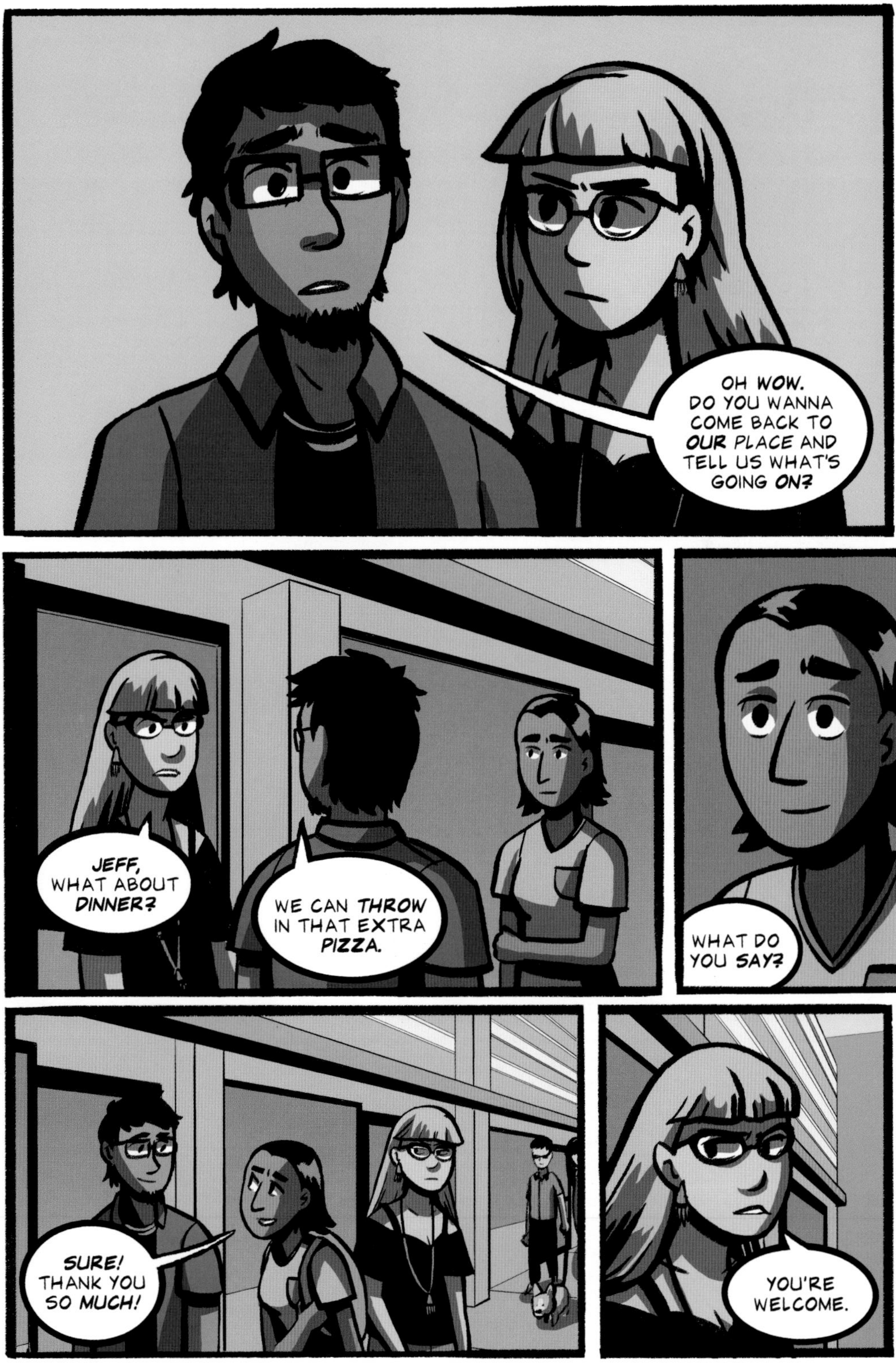
OH WOW. DO YOU WANNA COME BACK TO OUR PLACE AND TELL US WHAT'S GOING ON?
JEFF, WHAT ABOUT DINNER?
WE CAN THROW IN THAT EXTRA PIZZA.
WHAT DO YOU SAY?
SURE! THANK YOU SO MUCH!
YOU'RE WELCOME.

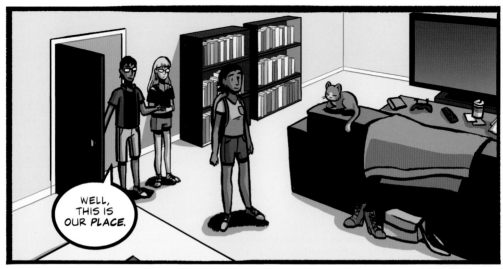

WELL, THIS IS OUR PLACE.

OH! YOU CAN HAVE PETS IN YOUR APARTMENT?

NOPE.

SO DON'T MENTION THE CAT TO ANYONE.

IT'S GOING TO BE SO WEIRD NOT HAVING ANIMALS FOR A YEAR.

I GREW UP ON A FARM, SO THIS IS GOING TO BE TOTALLY NEW.

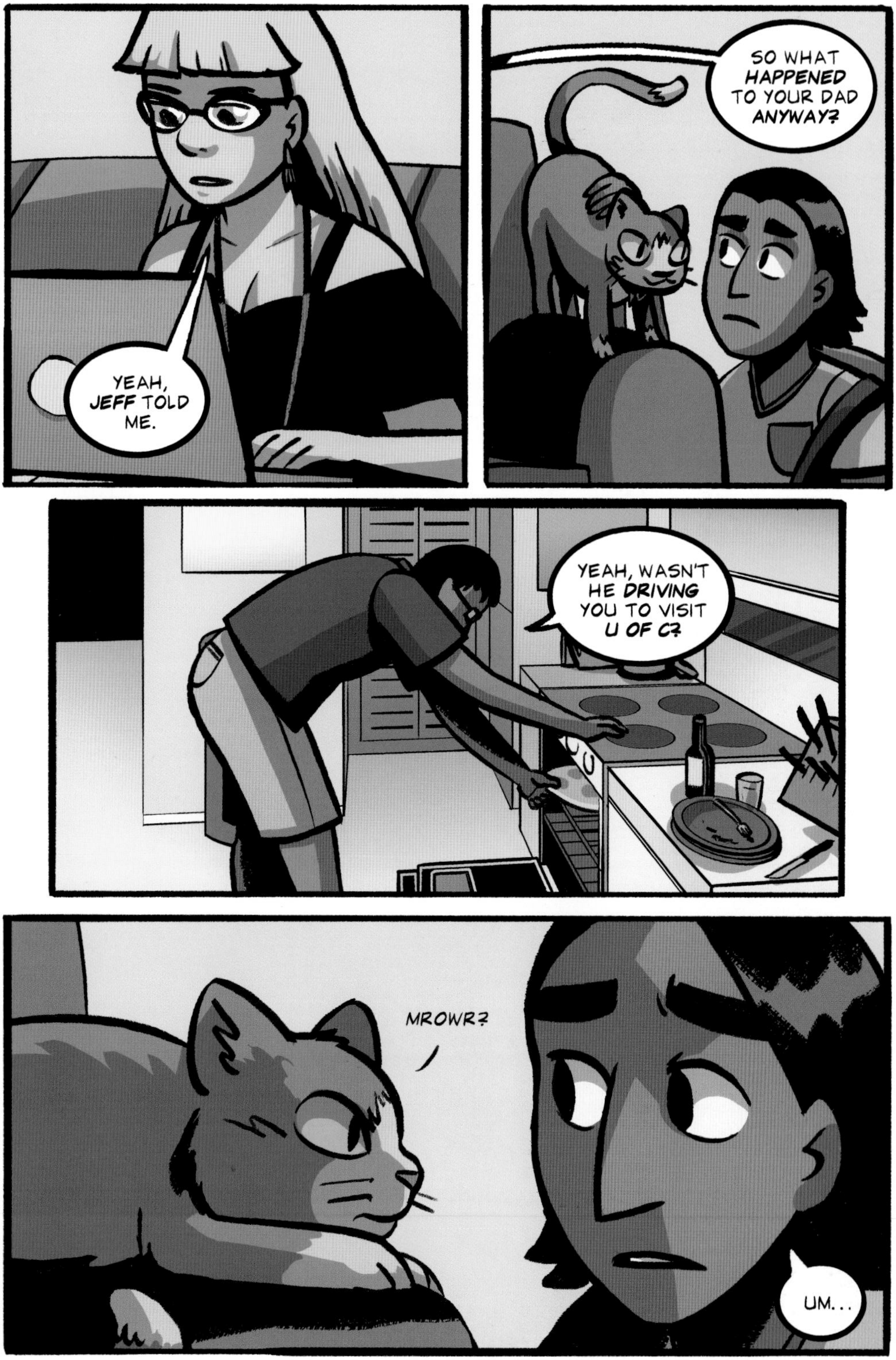
YEAH, JEFF TOLD ME.
SO WHAT HAPPENED TO YOUR DAD ANYWAY?
YEAH, WASN'T HE DRIVING YOU TO VISIT U OF C?
MROWR?
UM...

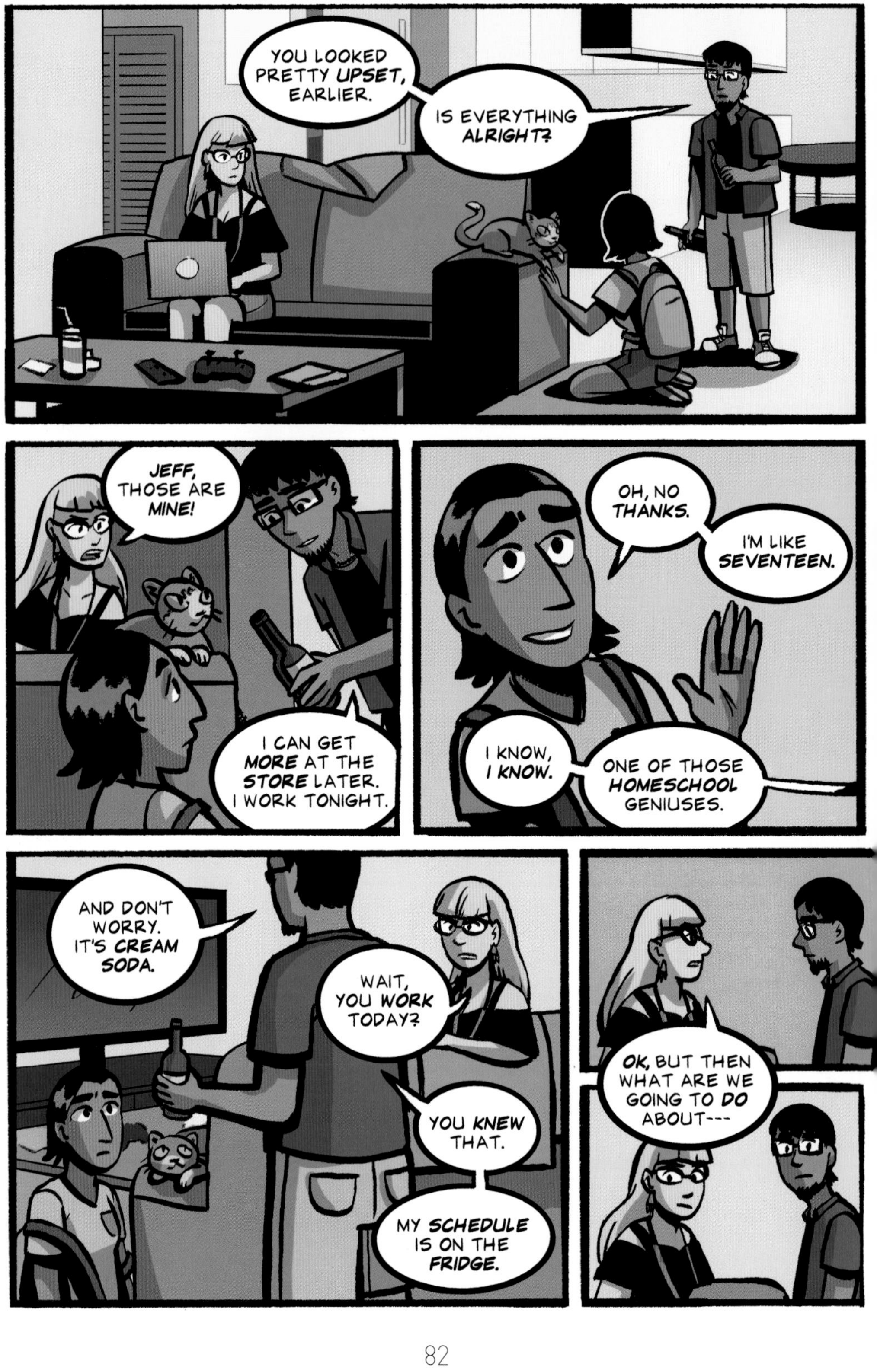
YOU LOOKED PRETTY UPSET, EARLIER.
IS EVERYTHING ALRIGHT?
JEFF, THOSE ARE MINE!
I CAN GET MORE AT THE STORE LATER. I WORK TONIGHT.
OH, NO THANKS.
I'M LIKE SEVENTEEN.
ONE OF THOSE HOMESCHOOL GENIUSES.
I KNOW, I KNOW.
AND DON'T WORRY. IT'S CREAM SODA.
WAIT, YOU WORK TODAY?
YOU KNEW THAT.
MY SCHEDULE IS ON THE FRIDGE.
OK, BUT THEN WHAT ARE WE GOING TO DO ABOUT---

JEFF, CAN I TALK TO YOU FOR A MINUTE?

HEYYYY ACTUALLY, I WAS GONNA GO USE THE BATHROOM.

WHERE IS IT?

FIRST DOOR DOWN THE HALLWAY.

THANKS!

JEFF, SHE'S YOUR FRIEND.

IT'S A SHORT SHIFT TONIGHT.

YOU CAN'T JUST LEAVE.

I'LL BE BACK IN FOUR HOURS.

I DON'T NEED ANY MORE STRESS TONIGHT.

MOM HAS BEEN WORKED UP BECAUSE HER EX HUSBAND--

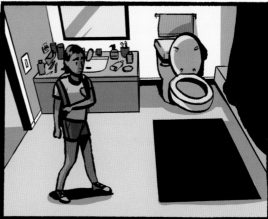

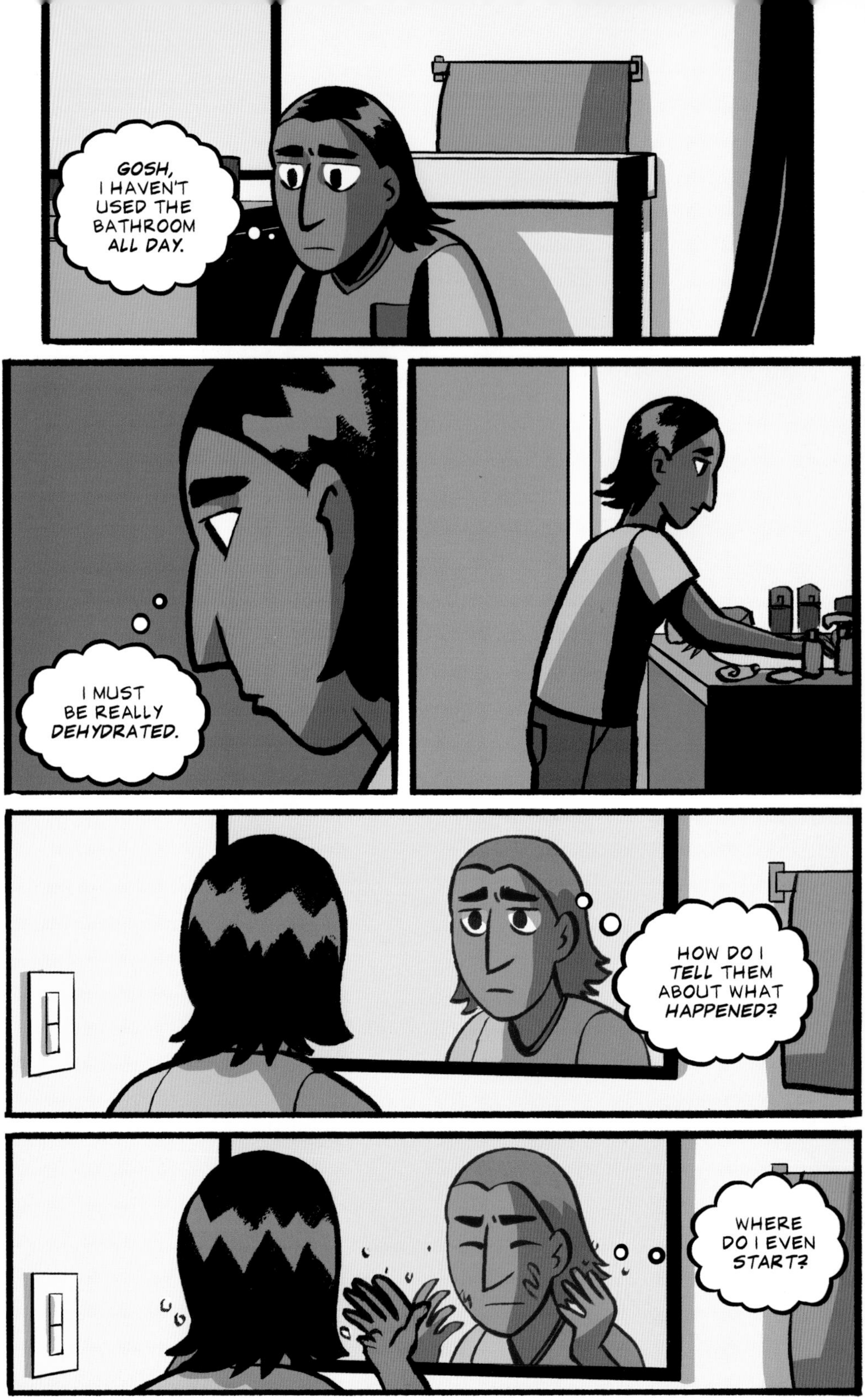
GOSH, I HAVEN'T USED THE BATHROOM ALL DAY.
I MUST BE REALLY DEHYDRATED.
HOW DO I TELL THEM ABOUT WHAT HAPPENED?
WHERE DO I EVEN START?

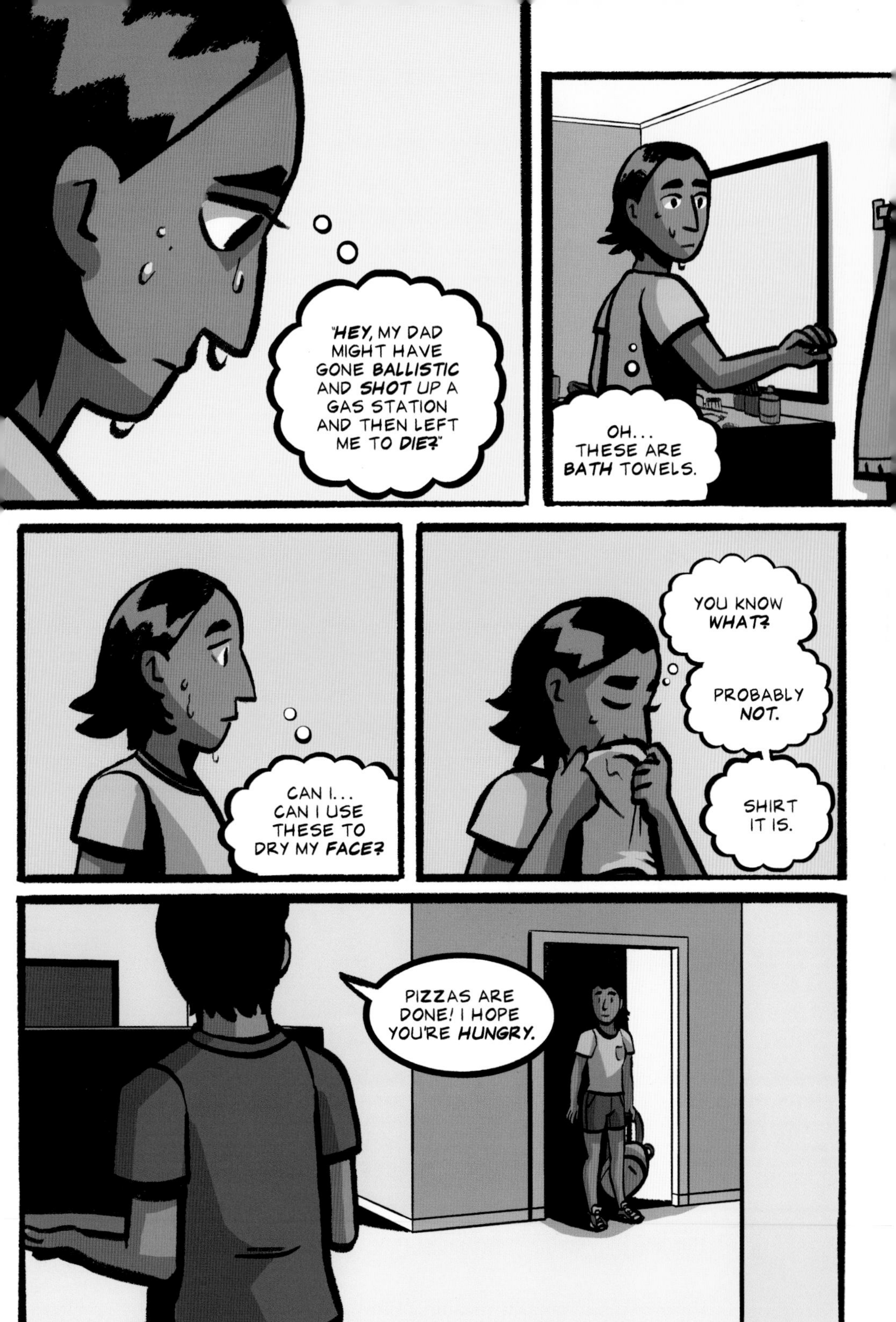
"HEY, MY DAD MIGHT HAVE GONE BALLISTIC AND SHOT UP A GAS STATION AND THEN LEFT ME TO DIE?"
OH... THESE ARE BATH TOWELS.
CAN I... CAN I USE THESE TO DRY MY FACE?
YOU KNOW WHAT?
PROBABLY NOT.
SHIRT IT IS.
PIZZAS ARE DONE! I HOPE YOU'RE HUNGRY.

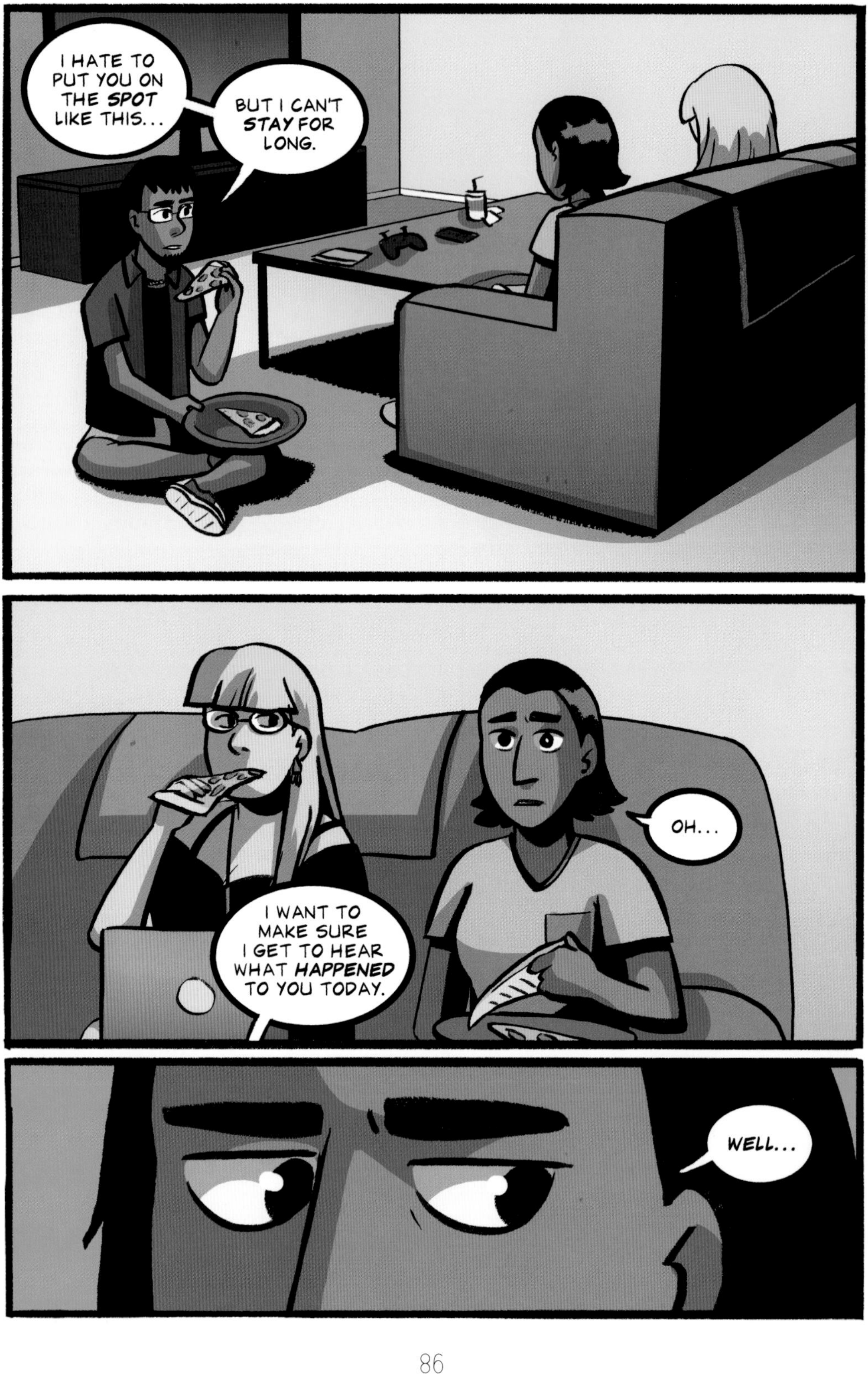
I HATE TO PUT YOU ON THE SPOT LIKE THIS...
BUT I CAN'T STAY FOR LONG.
OH...
I WANT TO MAKE SURE I GET TO HEAR WHAT HAPPENED TO YOU TODAY.
WELL...

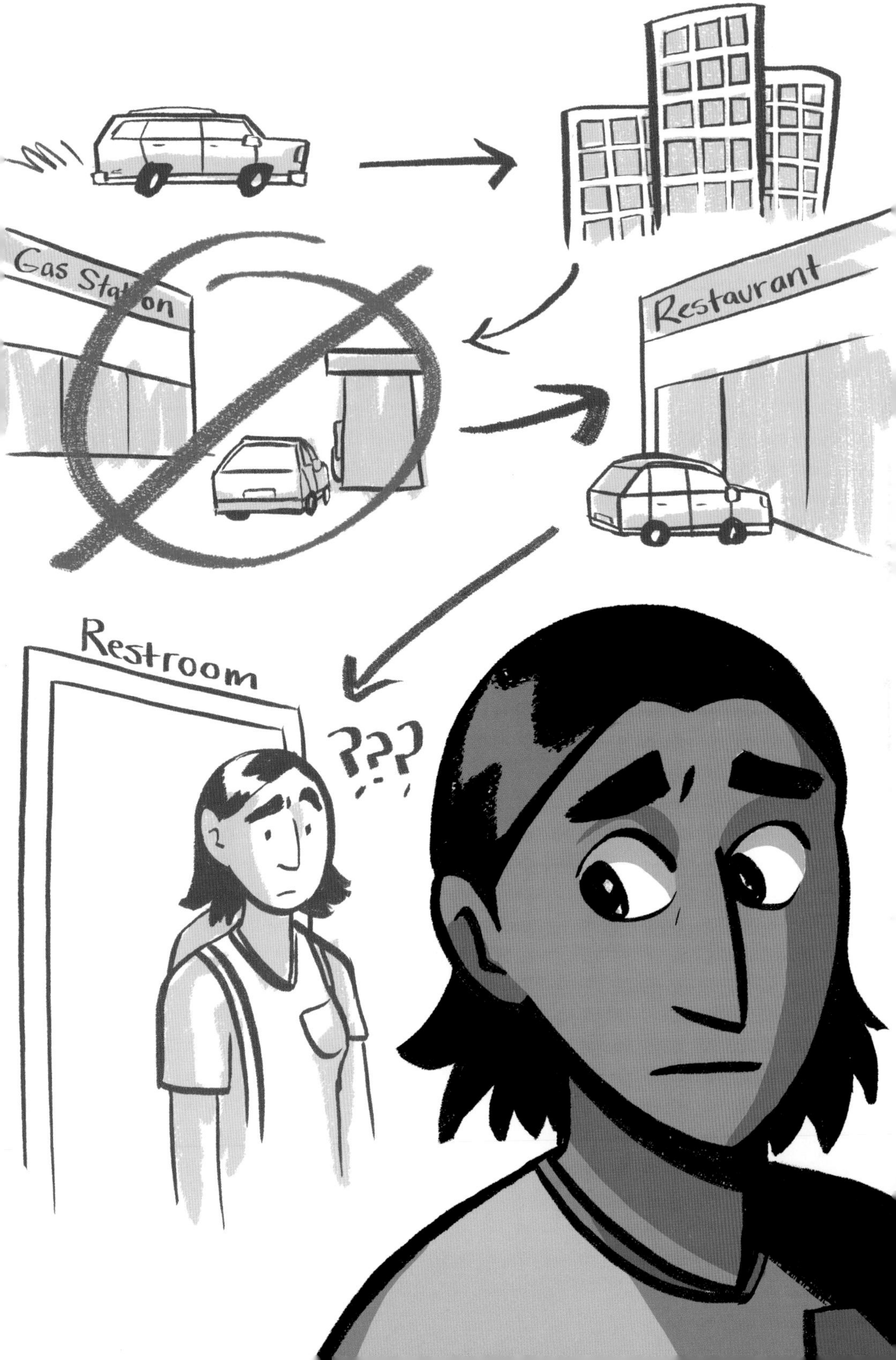
Gas Station
Restaurant
Restroom
???

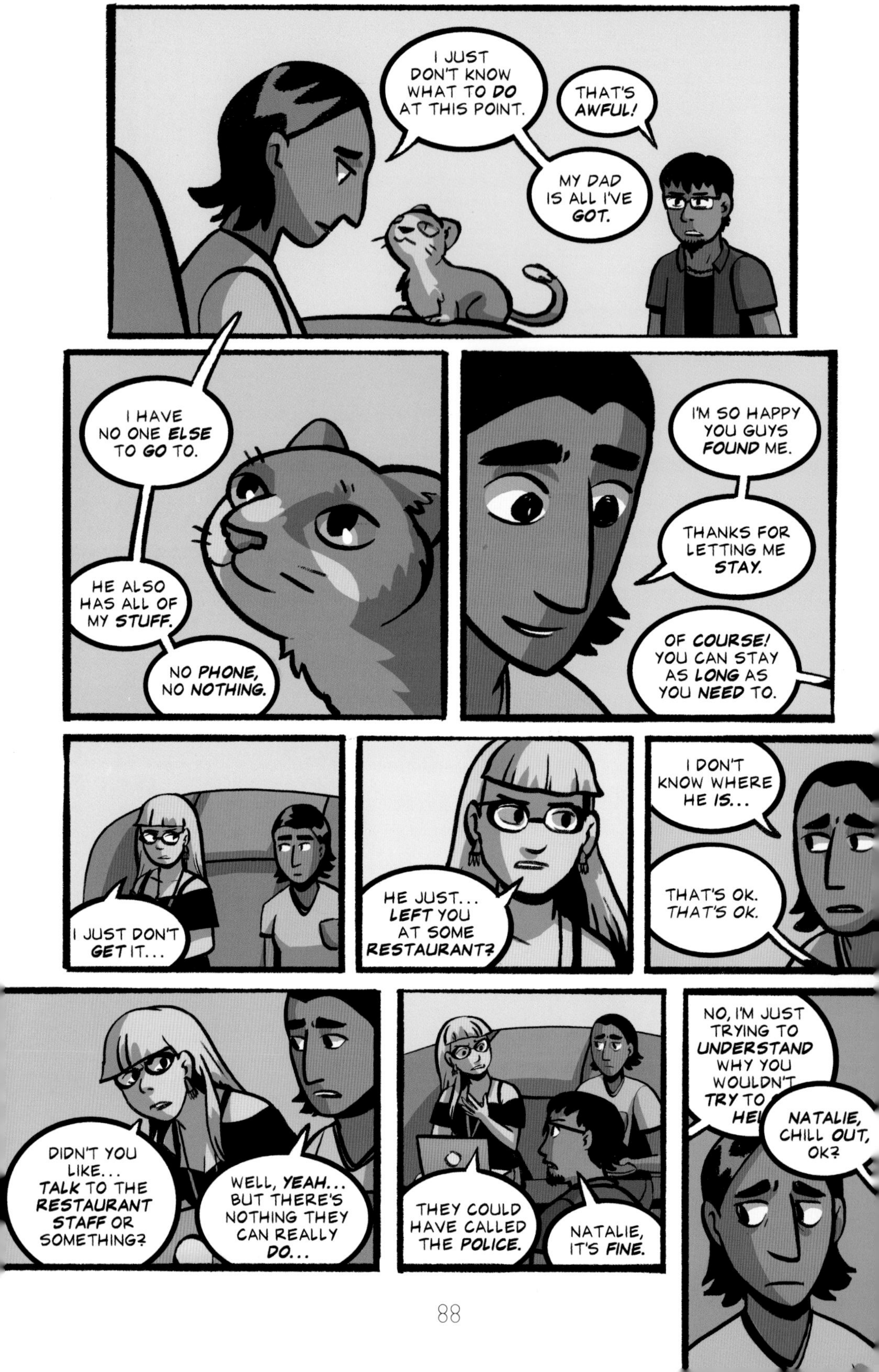
I JUST DON'T KNOW WHAT TO DO AT THIS POINT.
MY DAD IS ALL I'VE GOT.
THAT'S AWFUL!
I HAVE NO ONE ELSE TO GO TO.
HE ALSO HAS ALL OF MY STUFF.
NO PHONE, NO NOTHING.
I'M SO HAPPY YOU GUYS FOUND ME.
THANKS FOR LETTING ME STAY.
OF COURSE! YOU CAN STAY AS LONG AS YOU NEED TO.
I JUST DON'T GET IT...
HE JUST... LEFT YOU AT SOME RESTAURANT?
I DON'T KNOW WHERE HE IS...
THAT'S OK. THAT'S OK.
DIDN'T YOU LIKE... TALK TO THE RESTAURANT STAFF OR SOMETHING?
WELL, YEAH... BUT THERE'S NOTHING THEY CAN REALLY DO...
THEY COULD HAVE CALLED THE POLICE.
NATALIE, IT'S FINE.
NATALIE, CHILL OUT, OK?

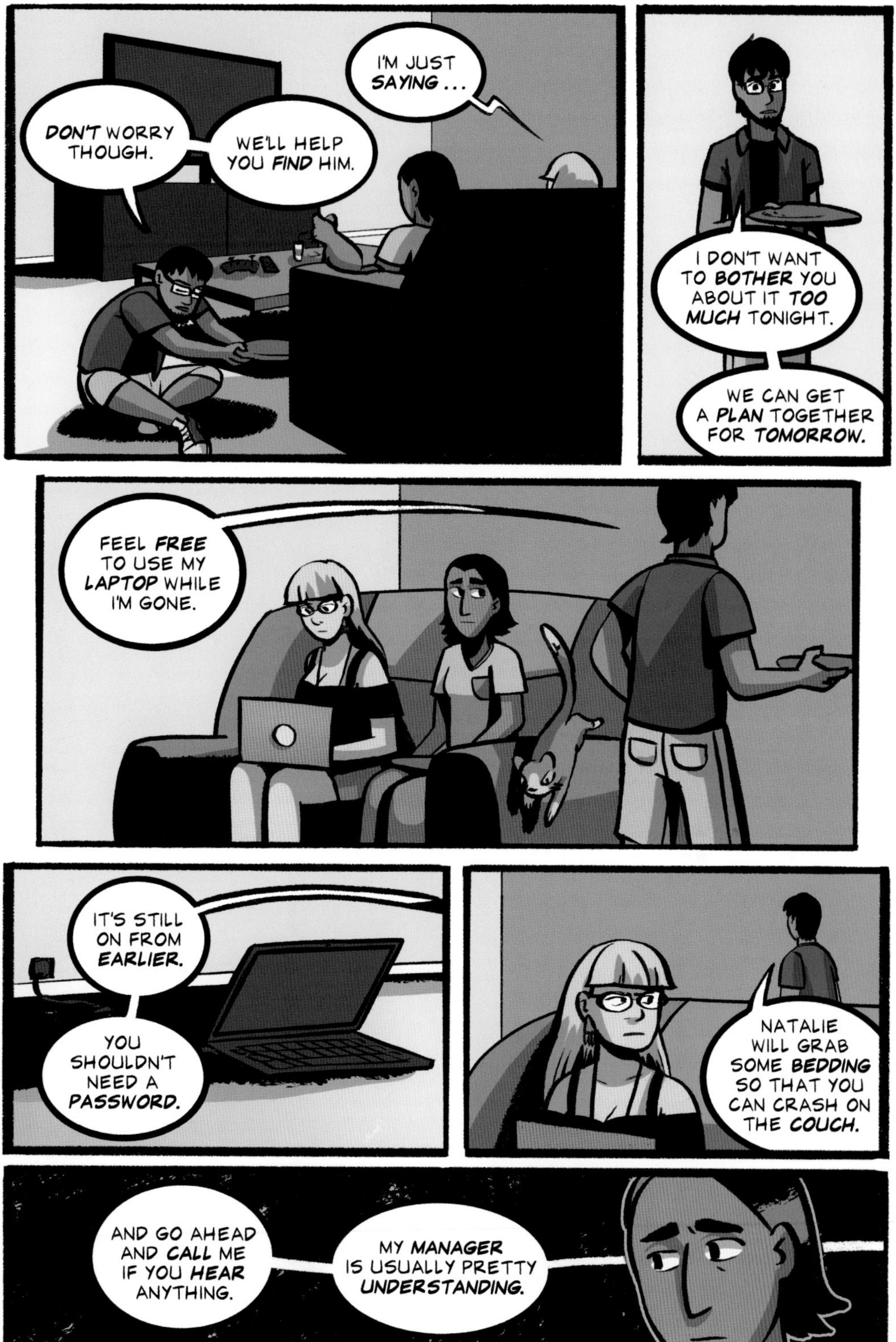
I'M JUST SAYING . . .
DON'T WORRY THOUGH.
WE'LL HELP YOU FIND HIM.
I DON'T WANT TO BOTHER YOU ABOUT IT TOO MUCH TONIGHT.
WE CAN GET A PLAN TOGETHER FOR TOMORROW.
FEEL FREE TO USE MY LAPTOP WHILE I'M GONE.
IT'S STILL ON FROM EARLIER.
YOU SHOULDN'T NEED A PASSWORD.
NATALIE WILL GRAB SOME BEDDING SO THAT YOU CAN CRASH ON THE COUCH.
AND GO AHEAD AND CALL ME IF YOU HEAR ANYTHING.
MY MANAGER IS USUALLY PRETTY UNDERSTANDING.

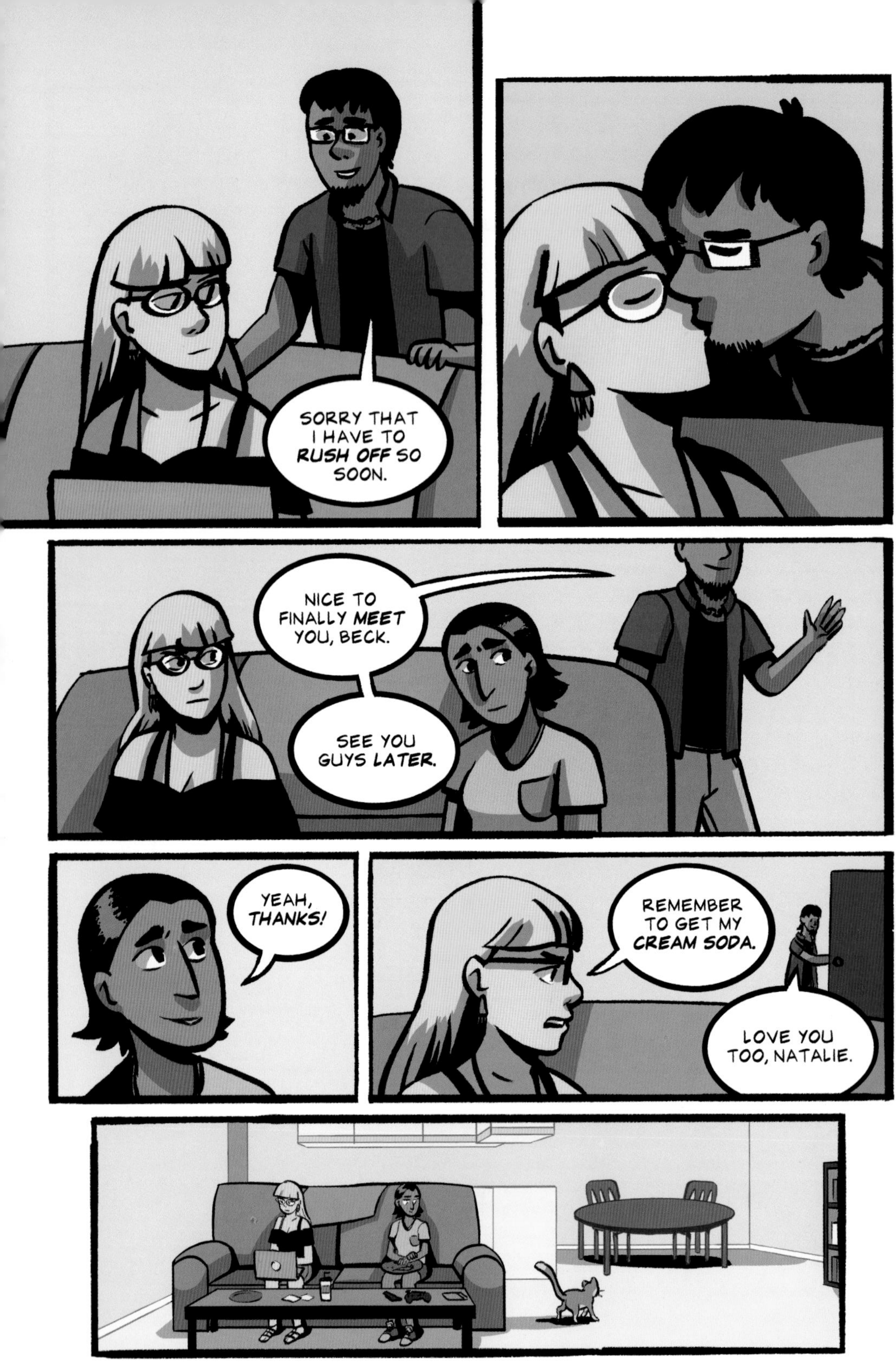
SORRY THAT I HAVE TO RUSH OFF SO SOON.
NICE TO FINALLY MEET YOU, BECK.
SEE YOU GUYS LATER.
YEAH, THANKS!
REMEMBER TO GET MY CREAM SODA.
LOVE YOU TOO, NATALIE.

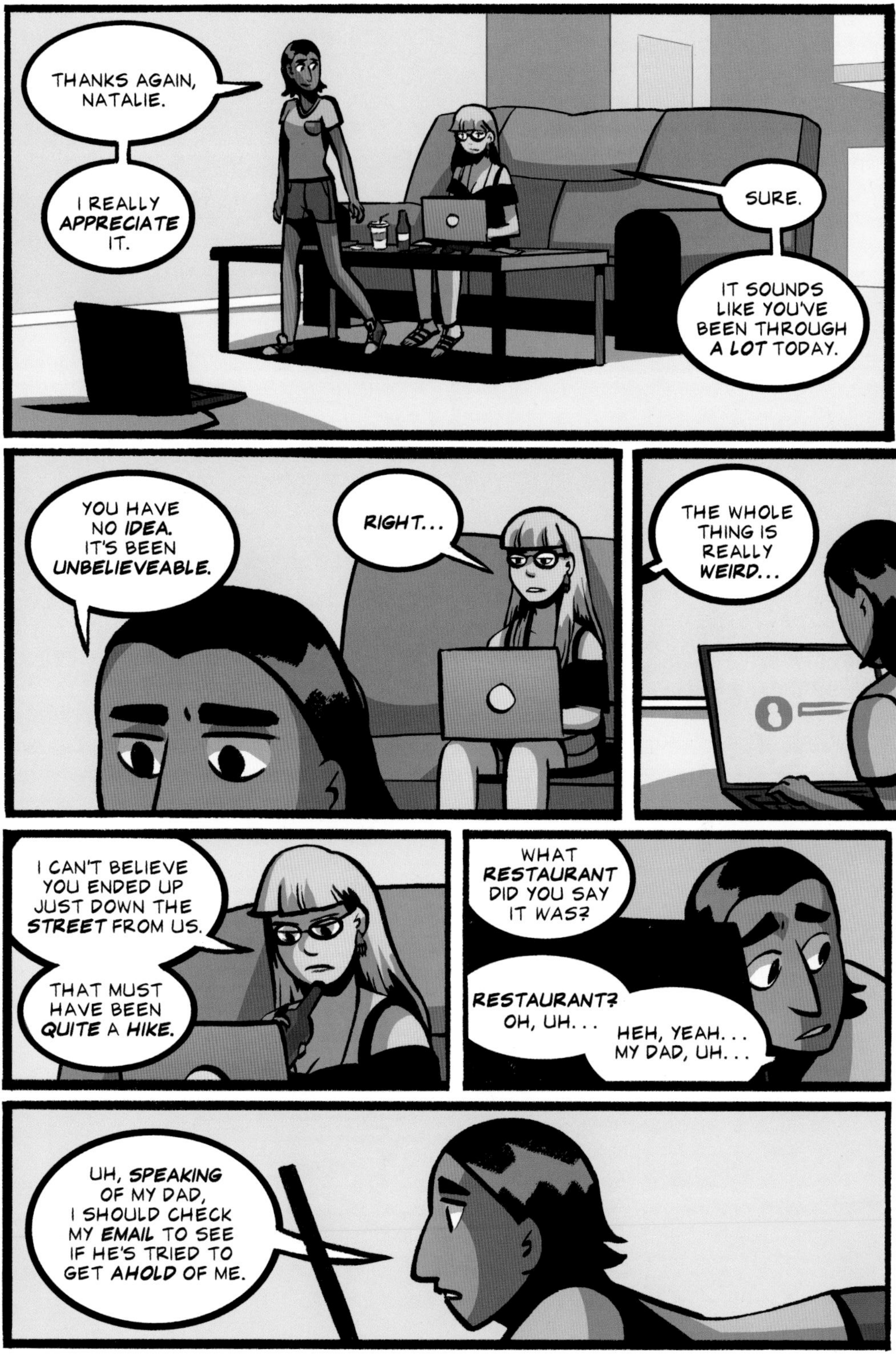
THANKS AGAIN, NATALIE.
I REALLY **APPRECIATE** IT.
SURE.
IT SOUNDS LIKE YOU'VE BEEN THROUGH **A LOT** TODAY.
YOU HAVE NO **IDEA.** IT'S BEEN **UNBELIEVEABLE.**
RIGHT...
THE WHOLE THING IS REALLY **WEIRD...**
I CAN'T BELIEVE YOU ENDED UP JUST DOWN THE **STREET** FROM US.
THAT MUST HAVE BEEN **QUITE** A **HIKE.**
WHAT **RESTAURANT** DID YOU SAY IT WAS?
RESTAURANT? OH, UH...
HEH, YEAH... MY DAD, UH...
UH, **SPEAKING** OF MY DAD, I SHOULD CHECK MY **EMAIL** TO SEE IF HE'S TRIED TO GET **AHOLD** OF ME.

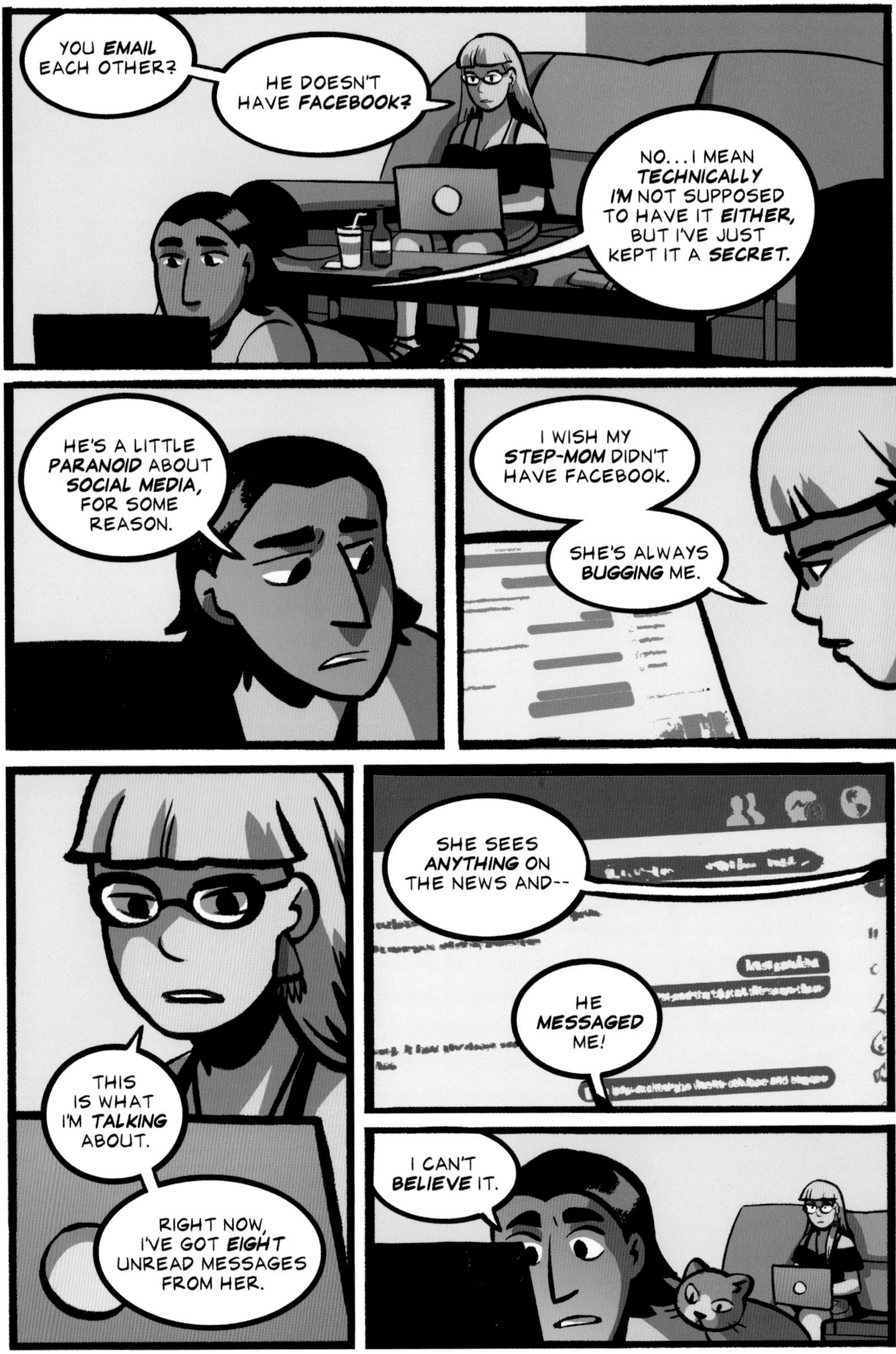
YOU EMAIL EACH OTHER?
HE DOESN'T HAVE FACEBOOK?
NO... I MEAN TECHNICALLY I'M NOT SUPPOSED TO HAVE IT EITHER, BUT I'VE JUST KEPT IT A SECRET.
HE'S A LITTLE PARANOID ABOUT SOCIAL MEDIA, FOR SOME REASON.
I WISH MY STEP-MOM DIDN'T HAVE FACEBOOK.
SHE'S ALWAYS BUGGING ME.
THIS IS WHAT I'M TALKING ABOUT.
RIGHT NOW, I'VE GOT EIGHT UNREAD MESSAGES FROM HER.
SHE SEES ANYTHING ON THE NEWS AND--
HE MESSAGED ME!
I CAN'T BELIEVE IT.

News

Dragnet for Suspected Rest Sto... Killer Widens
The search continues for Howie Waske...
413 shares

...e Hunt for Gas Station ...han Continues
...rties say that suspected killer...
...shares

NOT *MUCH.* BUT HE'S *ALIVE.*

OH, *GOOD...*

OH *YEAH?* WHAT DOES THE EMAIL *SAY?*

WOW, IT WAS ONLY SENT A FEW *MINUTES* AGO.

WHAT *ELSE* DOES IT SAY?

Gill Beveroth
Hey, it's me.
I've been looking for you. I'll tell you what happened later.
I'm downtown. Can you meet me at the Dillon Industrial Park?
I love you.

HOLD ON, I'M TRYING TO READ.

MOVE, KITTY!

HE WANTS ME TO MEET HIM AT THE OLD *INDUSTRIAL* PARK.

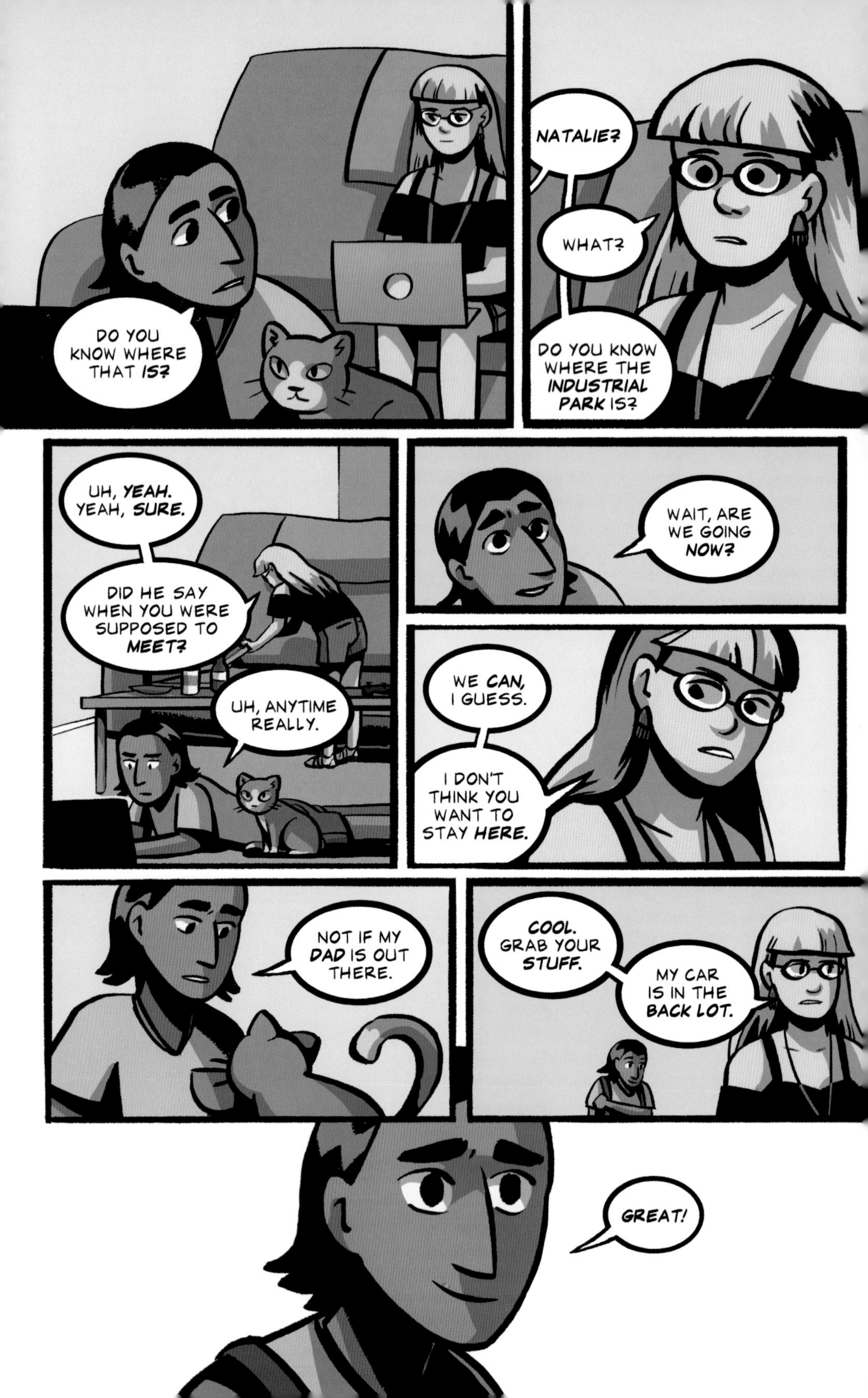

DO YOU KNOW WHERE THAT IS?
NATALIE?
WHAT?
DO YOU KNOW WHERE THE INDUSTRIAL PARK IS?
UH, YEAH. YEAH, SURE.
DID HE SAY WHEN YOU WERE SUPPOSED TO MEET?
UH, ANYTIME REALLY.
WAIT, ARE WE GOING NOW?
WE CAN, I GUESS.
I DON'T THINK YOU WANT TO STAY HERE.
NOT IF MY DAD IS OUT THERE.
COOL. GRAB YOUR STUFF.
MY CAR IS IN THE BACK LOT.
GREAT!

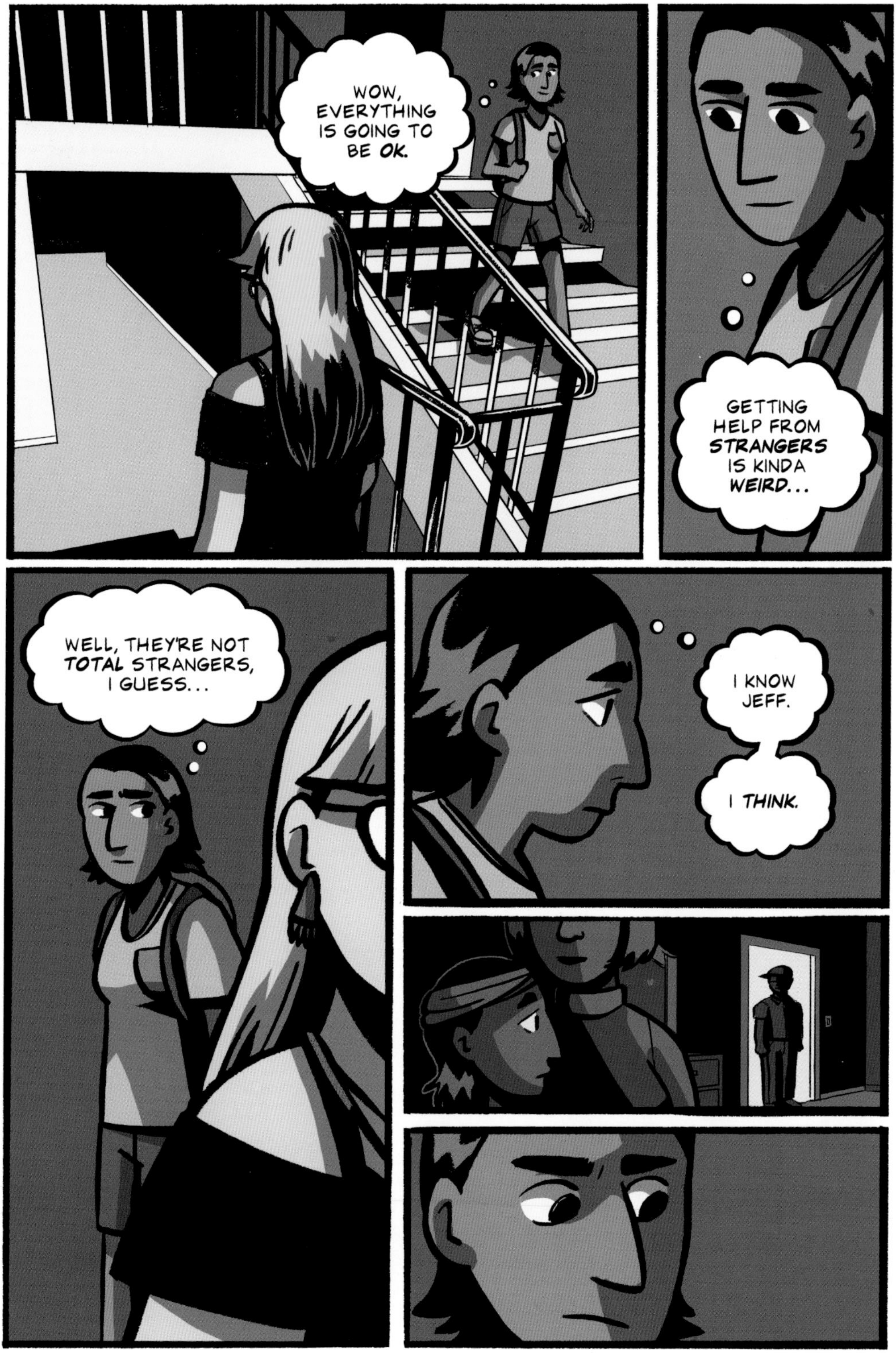
WOW, EVERYTHING IS GOING TO BE OK.
GETTING HELP FROM STRANGERS IS KINDA WEIRD...
WELL, THEY'RE NOT TOTAL STRANGERS, I GUESS...
I KNOW JEFF.
I THINK.

CHAPTER 4

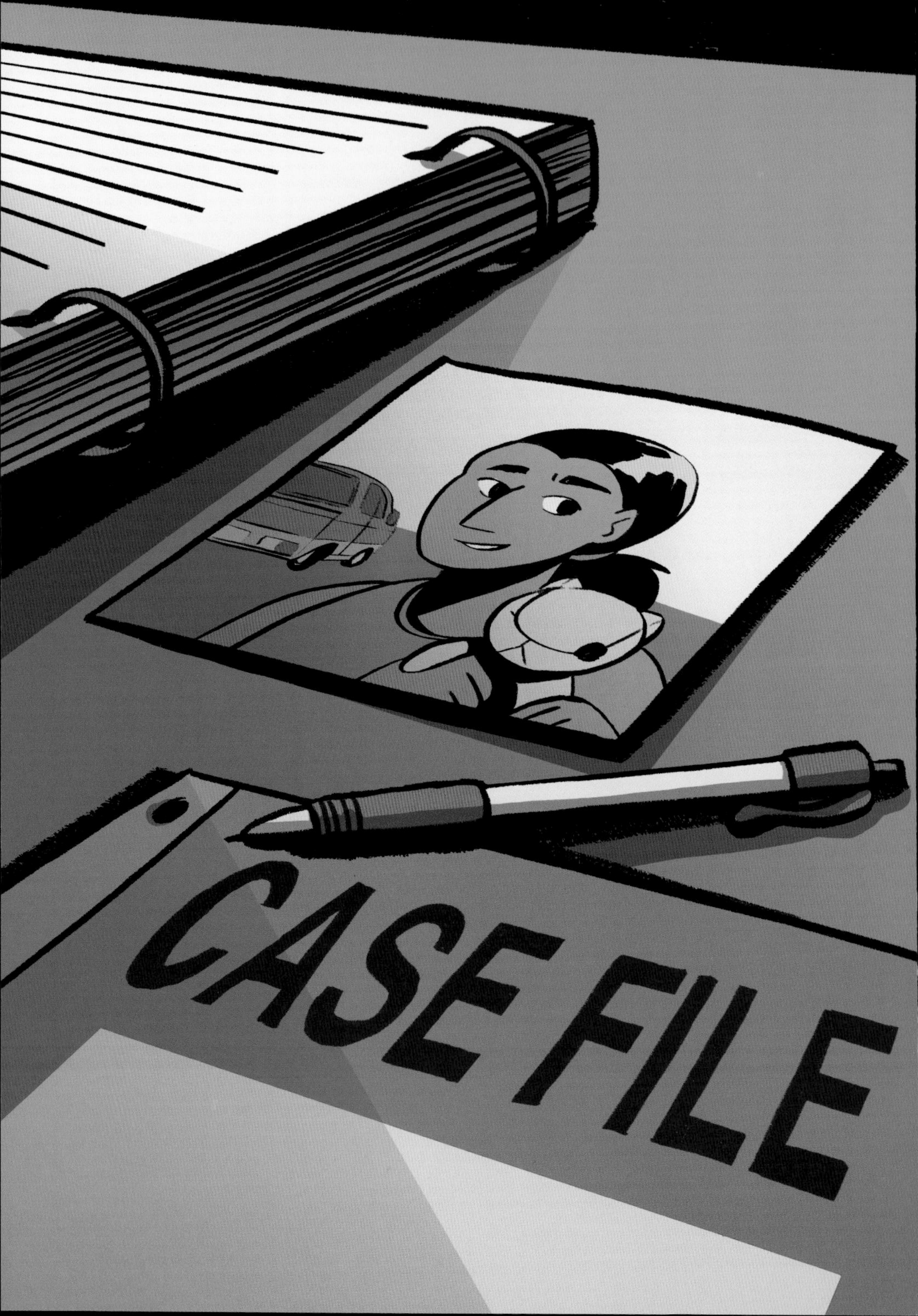
CASE FILE

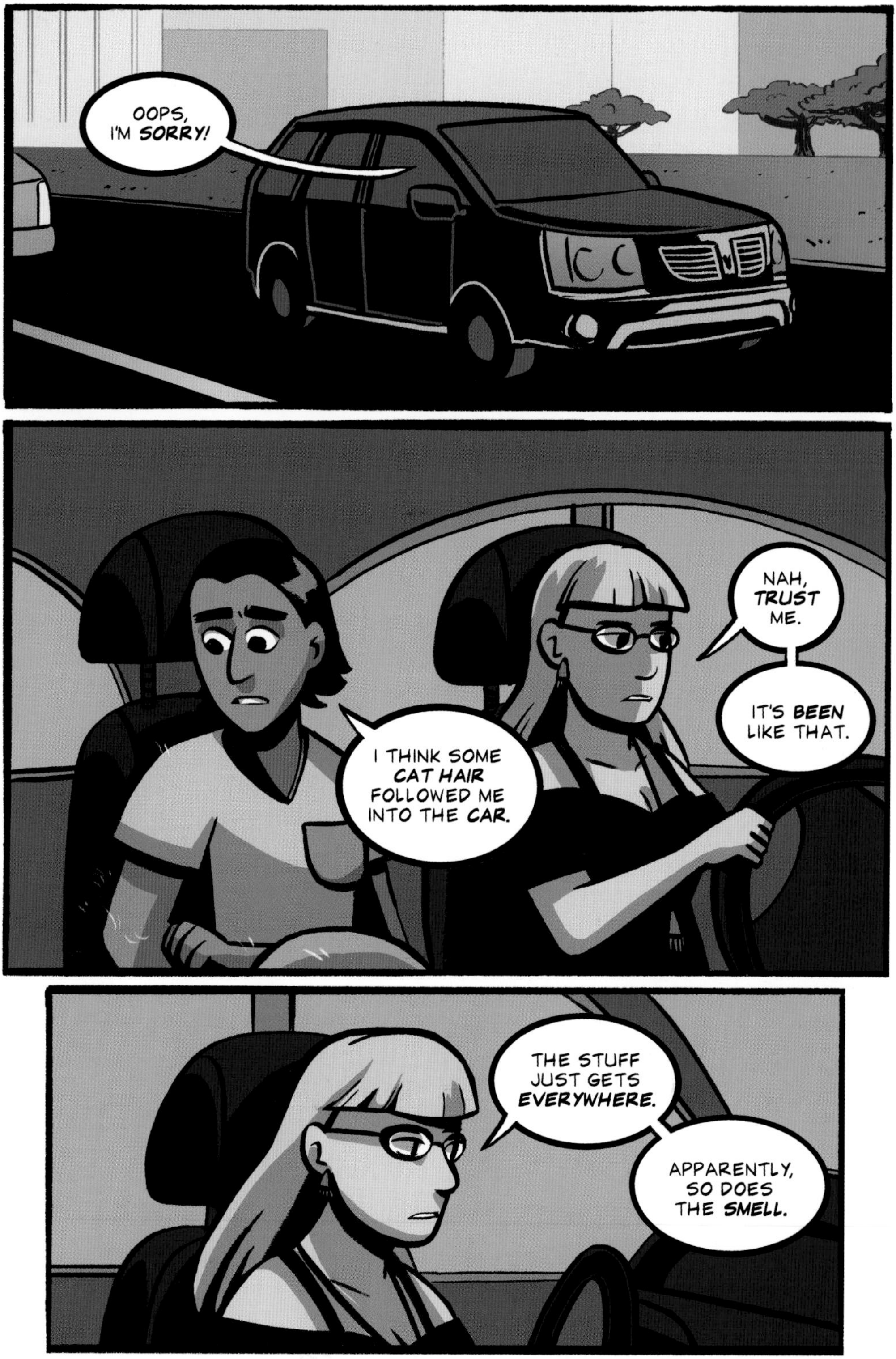
OOPS, I'M SORRY!
I THINK SOME CAT HAIR FOLLOWED ME INTO THE CAR.
NAH, TRUST ME.
IT'S BEEN LIKE THAT.
THE STUFF JUST GETS EVERYWHERE.
APPARENTLY, SO DOES THE SMELL.

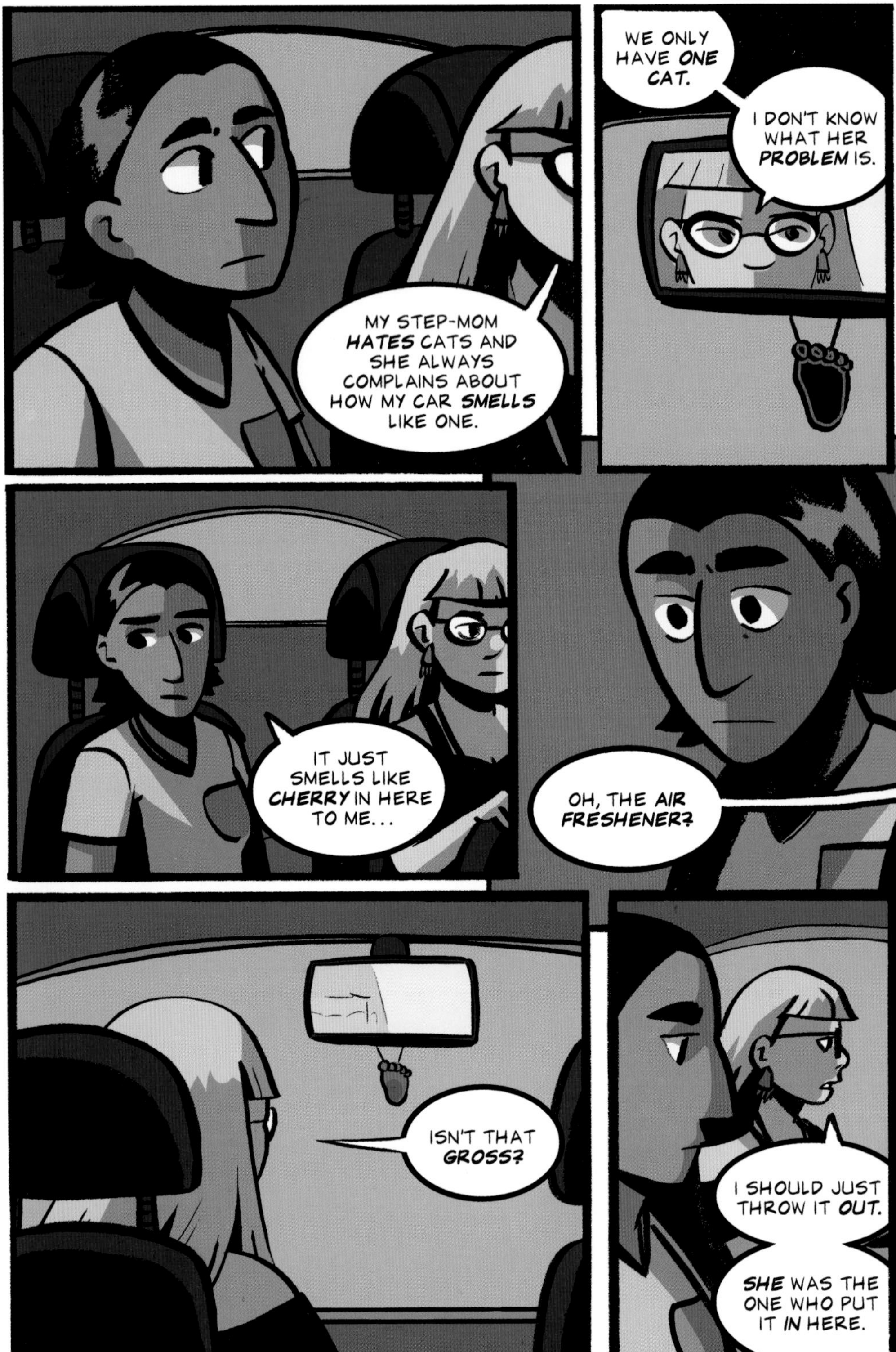
MY STEP-MOM HATES CATS AND SHE ALWAYS COMPLAINS ABOUT HOW MY CAR SMELLS LIKE ONE.
WE ONLY HAVE ONE CAT.
I DON'T KNOW WHAT HER PROBLEM IS.
IT JUST SMELLS LIKE CHERRY IN HERE TO ME...
OH, THE AIR FRESHENER?
ISN'T THAT GROSS?
I SHOULD JUST THROW IT OUT.
SHE WAS THE ONE WHO PUT IT IN HERE.

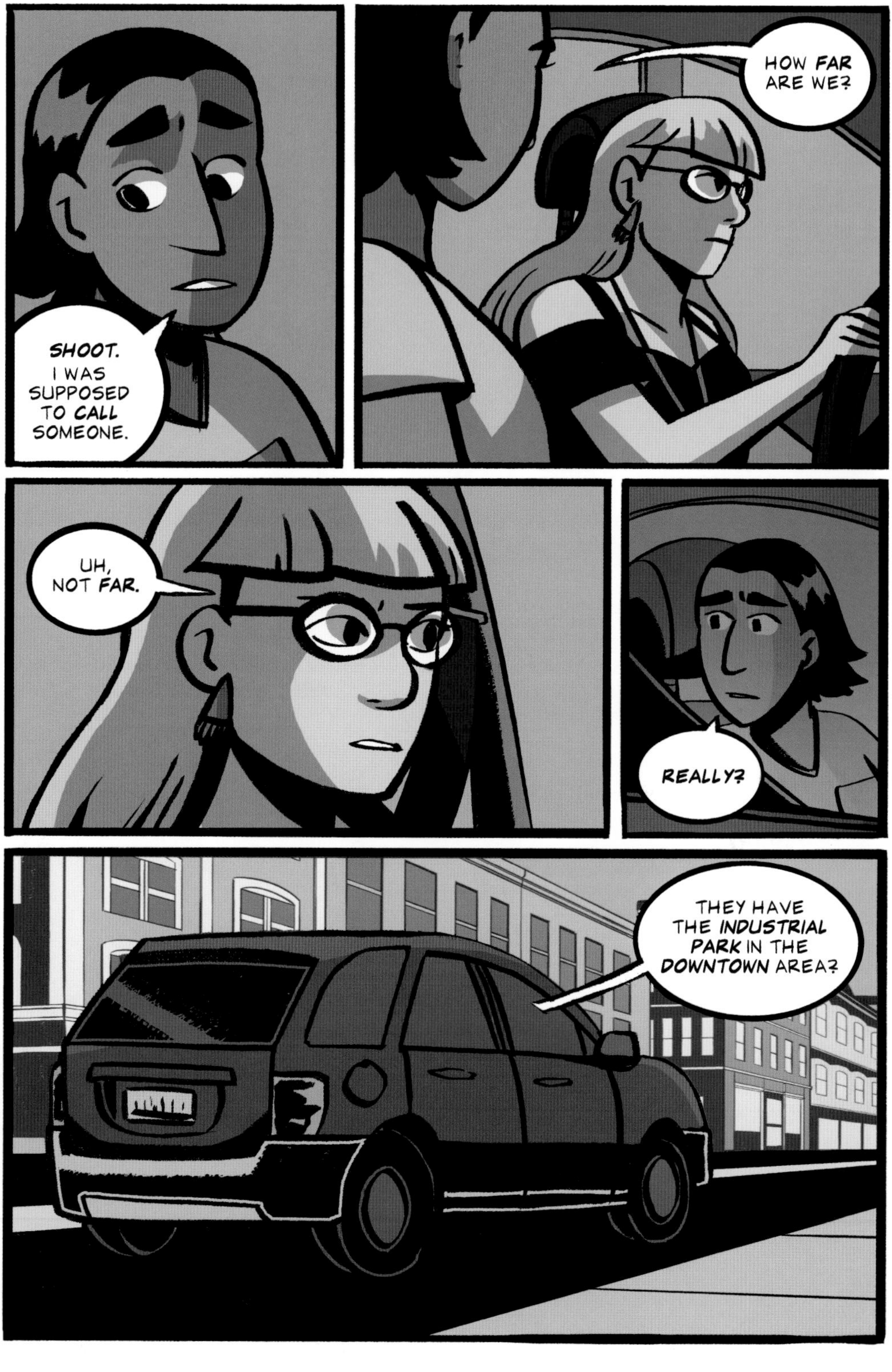
SHOOT. I WAS SUPPOSED TO CALL SOMEONE.
HOW FAR ARE WE?
UH, NOT FAR.
REALLY?
THEY HAVE THE INDUSTRIAL PARK IN THE DOWNTOWN AREA?

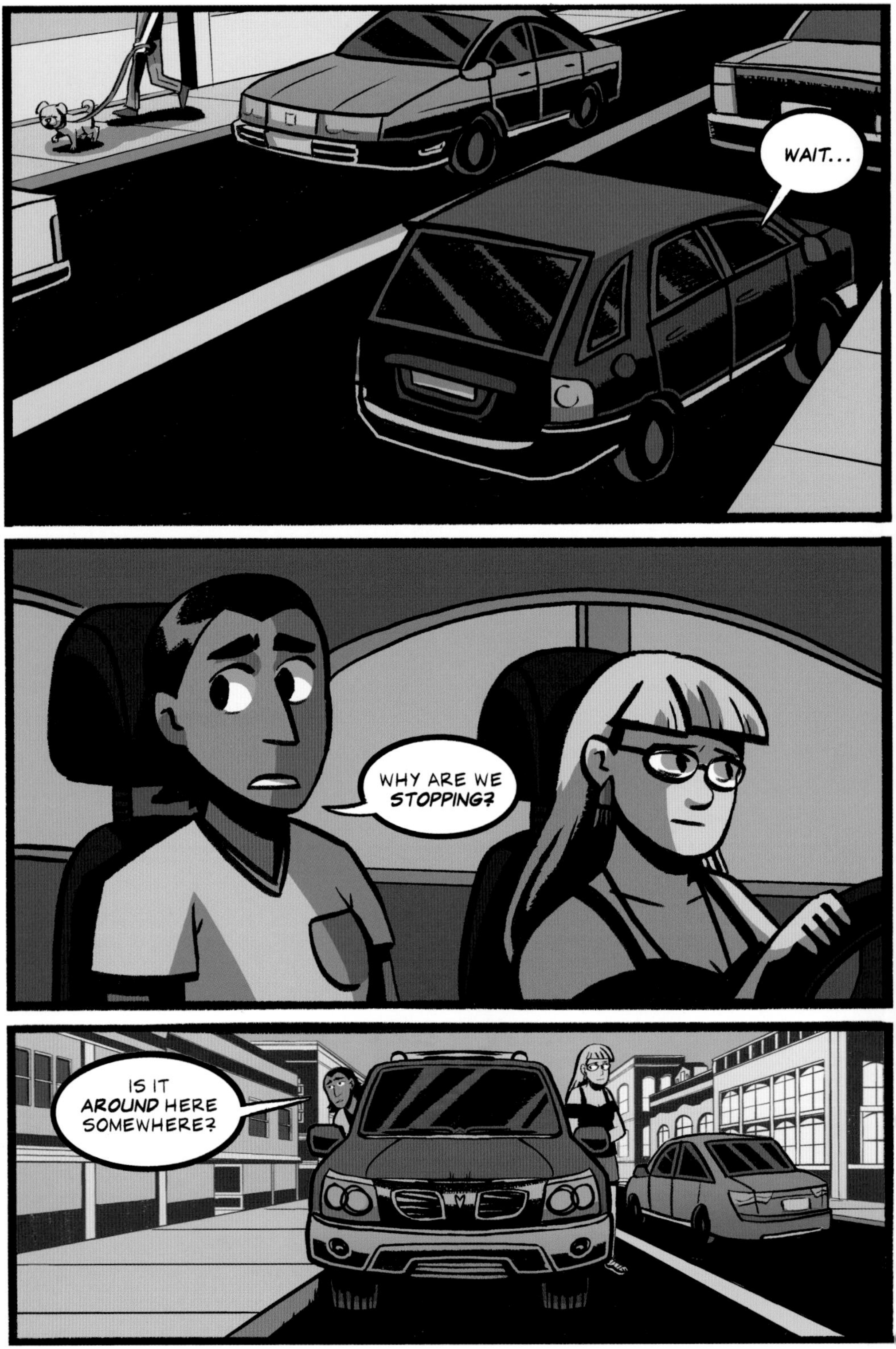
WAIT...
WHY ARE WE STOPPING?
IS IT AROUND HERE SOMEWHERE?

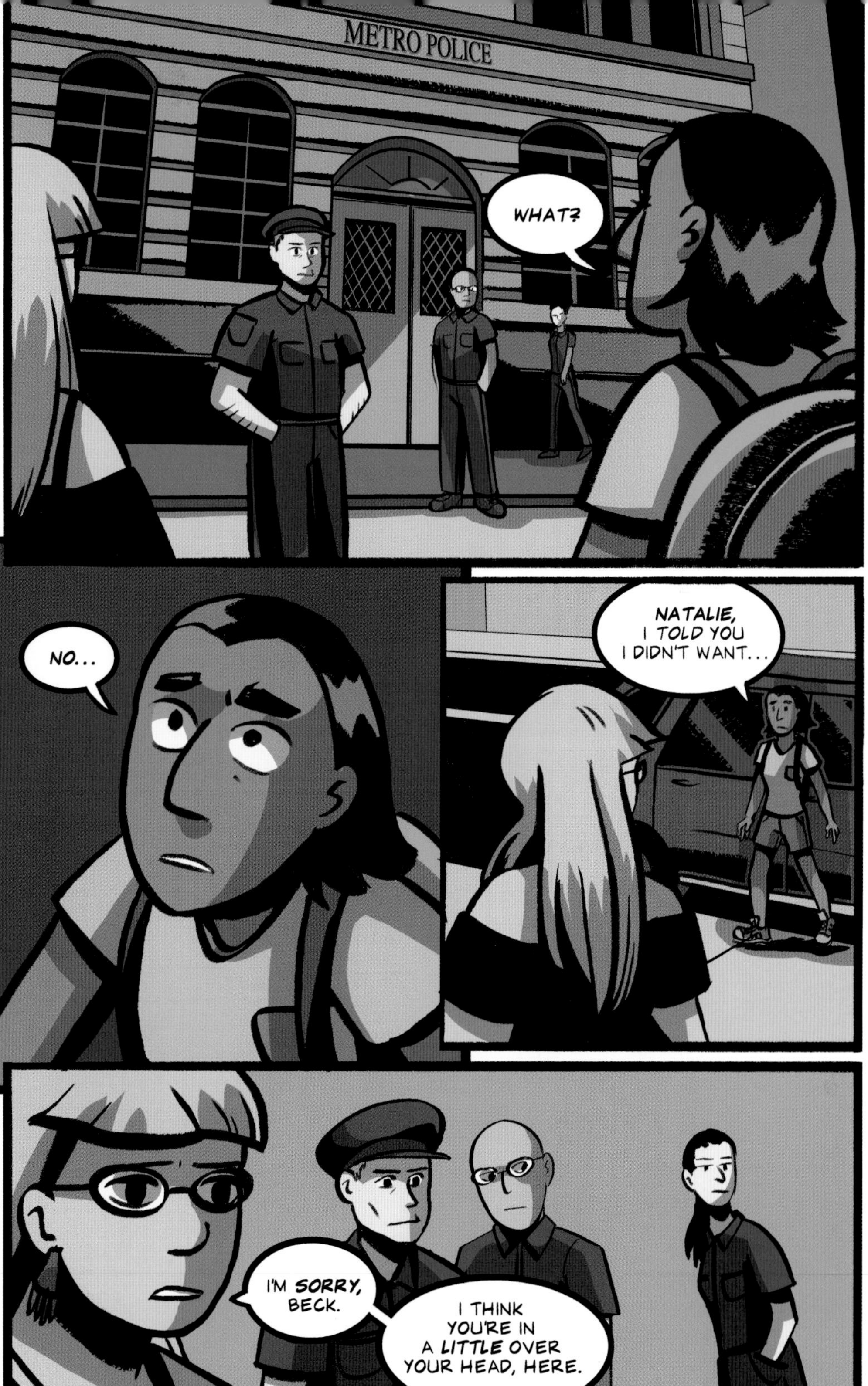
METRO POLICE
WHAT?
NO...
NATALIE, I TOLD YOU I DIDN'T WANT...
I'M SORRY, BECK.
I THINK YOU'RE IN A LITTLE OVER YOUR HEAD, HERE.

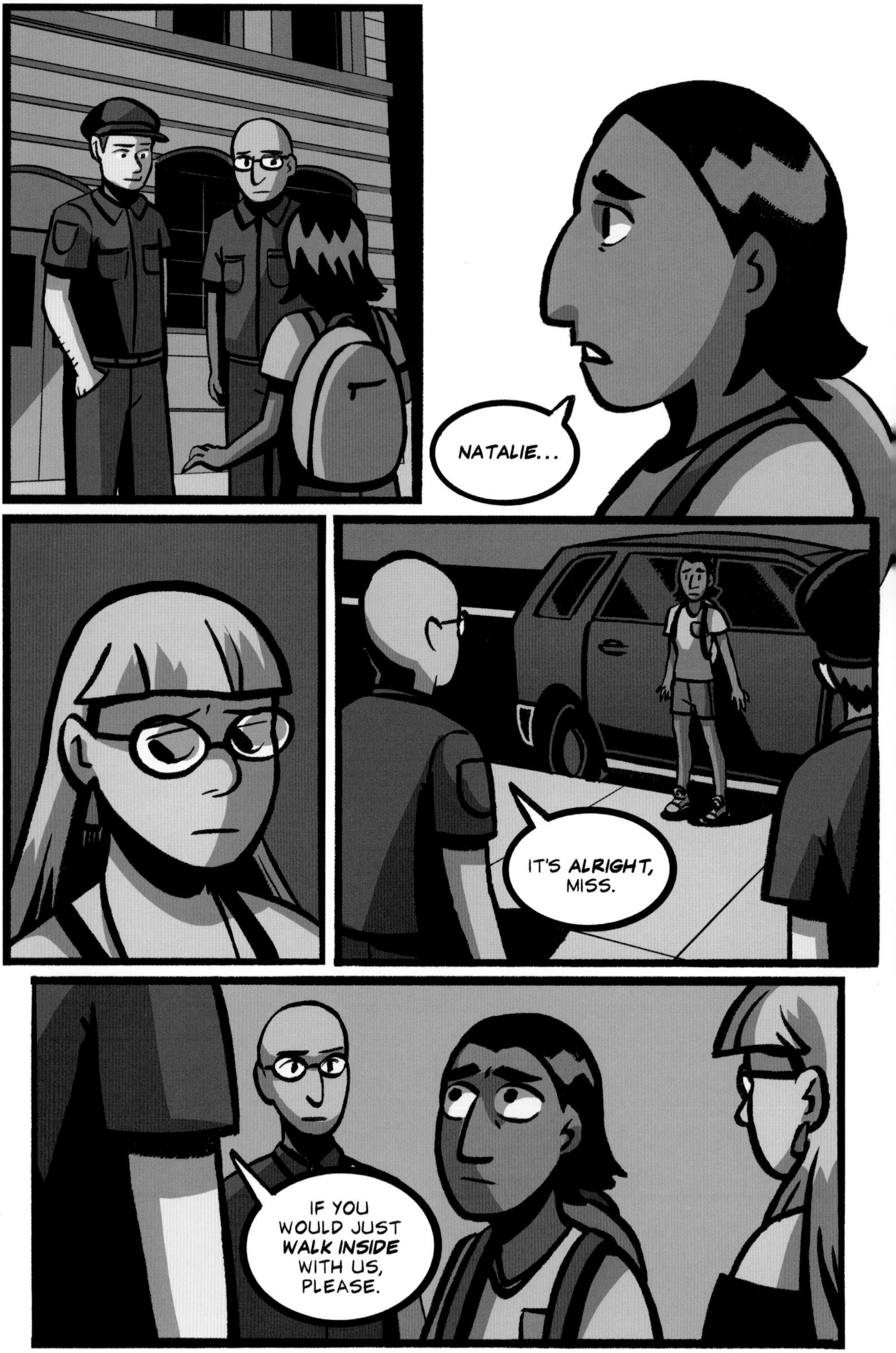
NATALIE...
IT'S ALRIGHT, MISS.
IF YOU WOULD JUST WALK INSIDE WITH US, PLEASE.

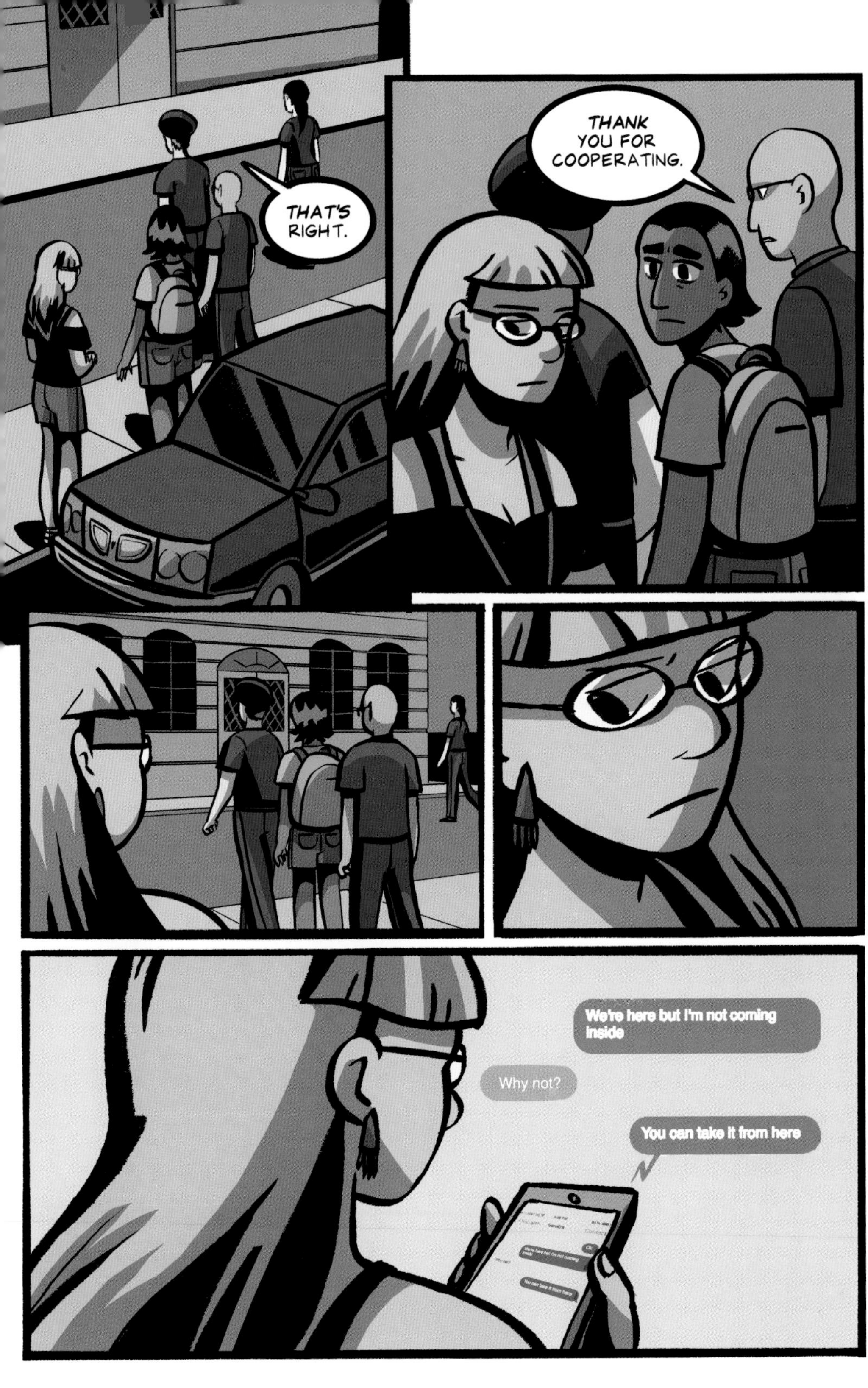
THAT'S RIGHT.
THANK YOU FOR COOPERATING.
We're here but I'm not coming inside
Why not?
You can take it from here

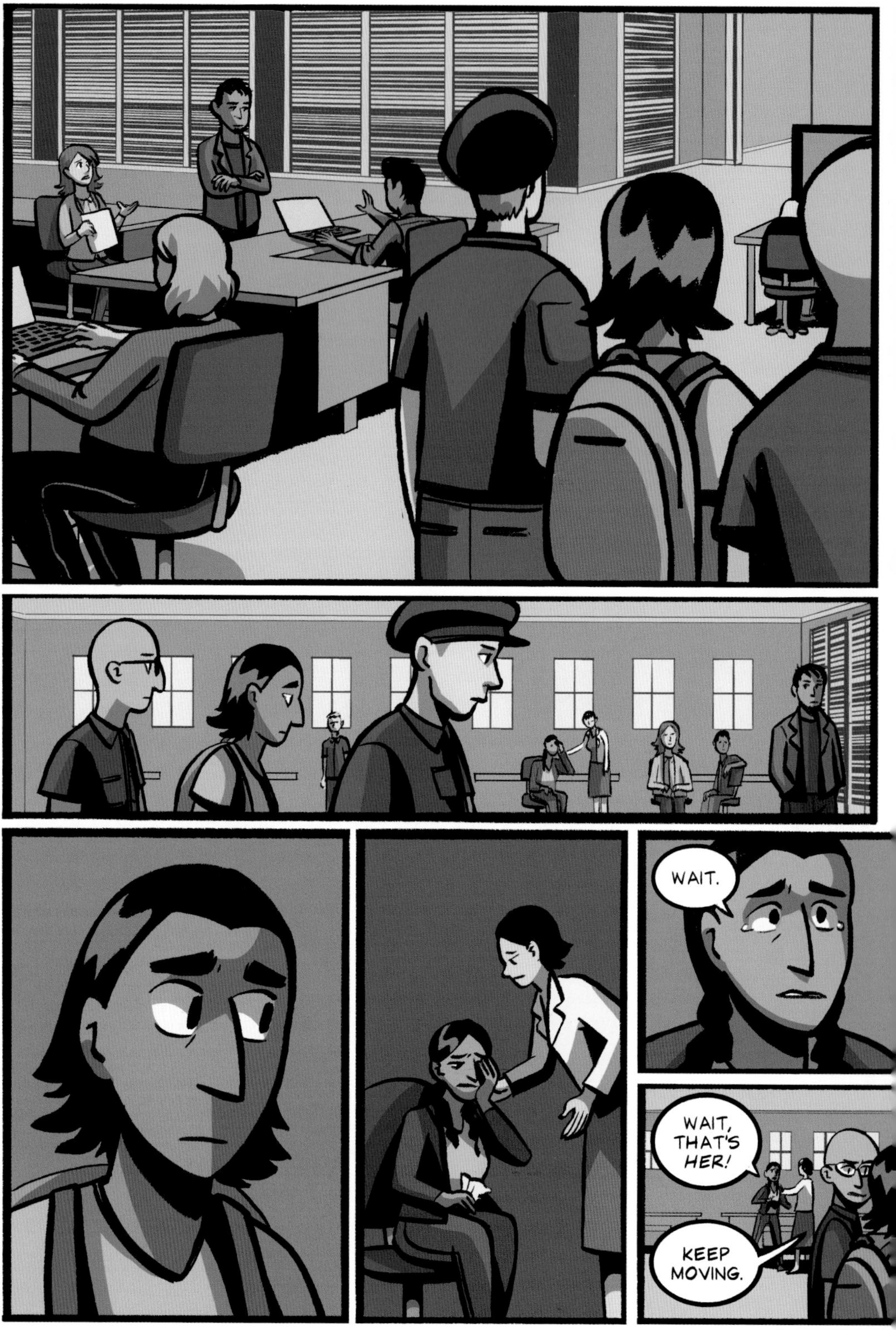
WAIT.
WAIT, THAT'S HER!
KEEP MOVING.

JUST A FEW MORE ROOMS DOWN THE *HALL*.

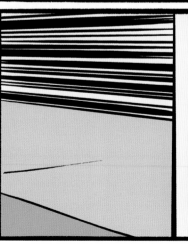

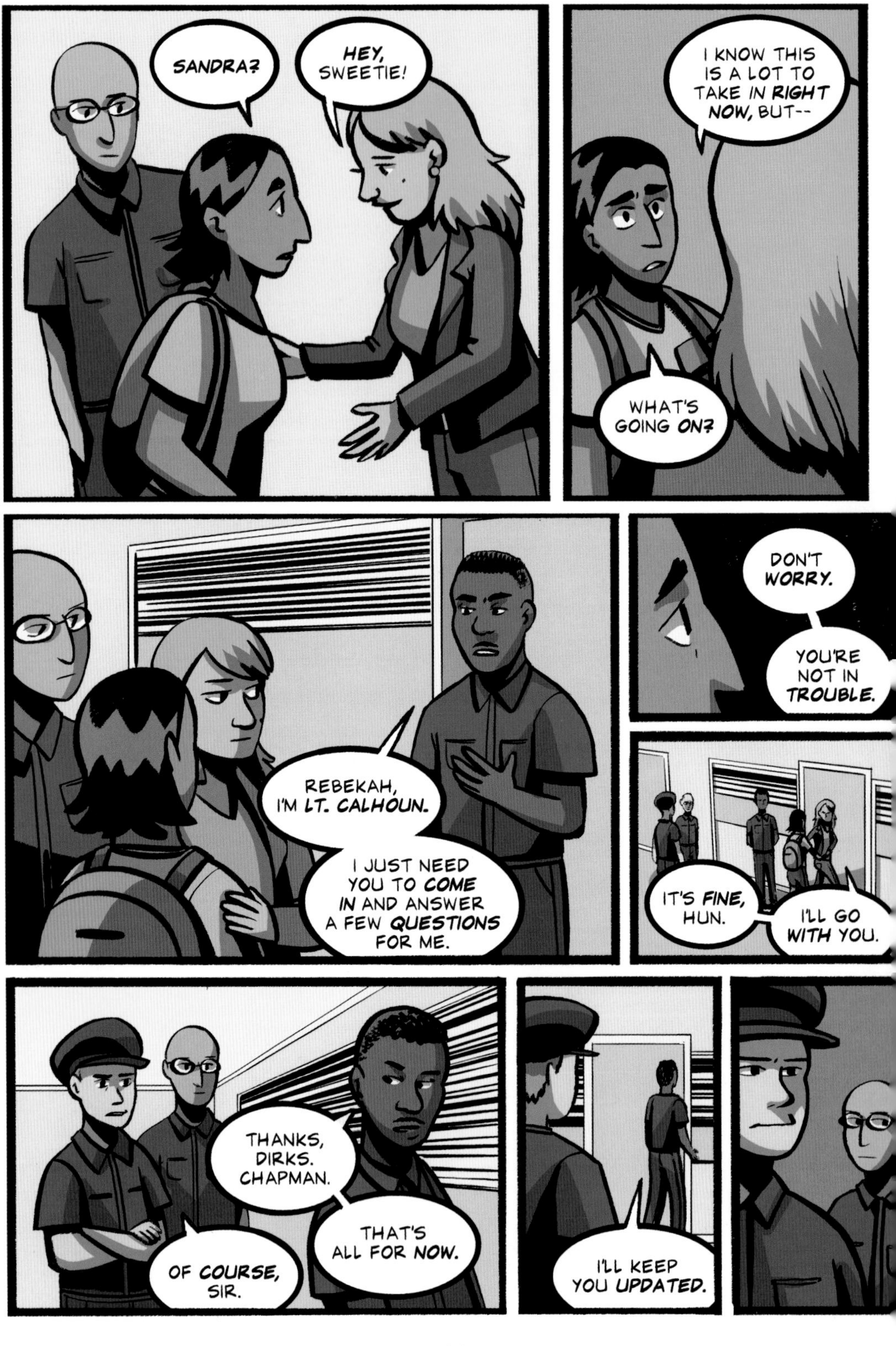
SANDRA?
HEY, SWEETIE!
I KNOW THIS IS A LOT TO TAKE IN RIGHT NOW, BUT--
WHAT'S GOING ON?
REBEKAH, I'M LT. CALHOUN.
I JUST NEED YOU TO COME IN AND ANSWER A FEW QUESTIONS FOR ME.
DON'T WORRY.
YOU'RE NOT IN TROUBLE.
IT'S FINE, HUN.
I'LL GO WITH YOU.
THANKS, DIRKS. CHAPMAN.
THAT'S ALL FOR NOW.
OF COURSE, SIR.
I'LL KEEP YOU UPDATED.

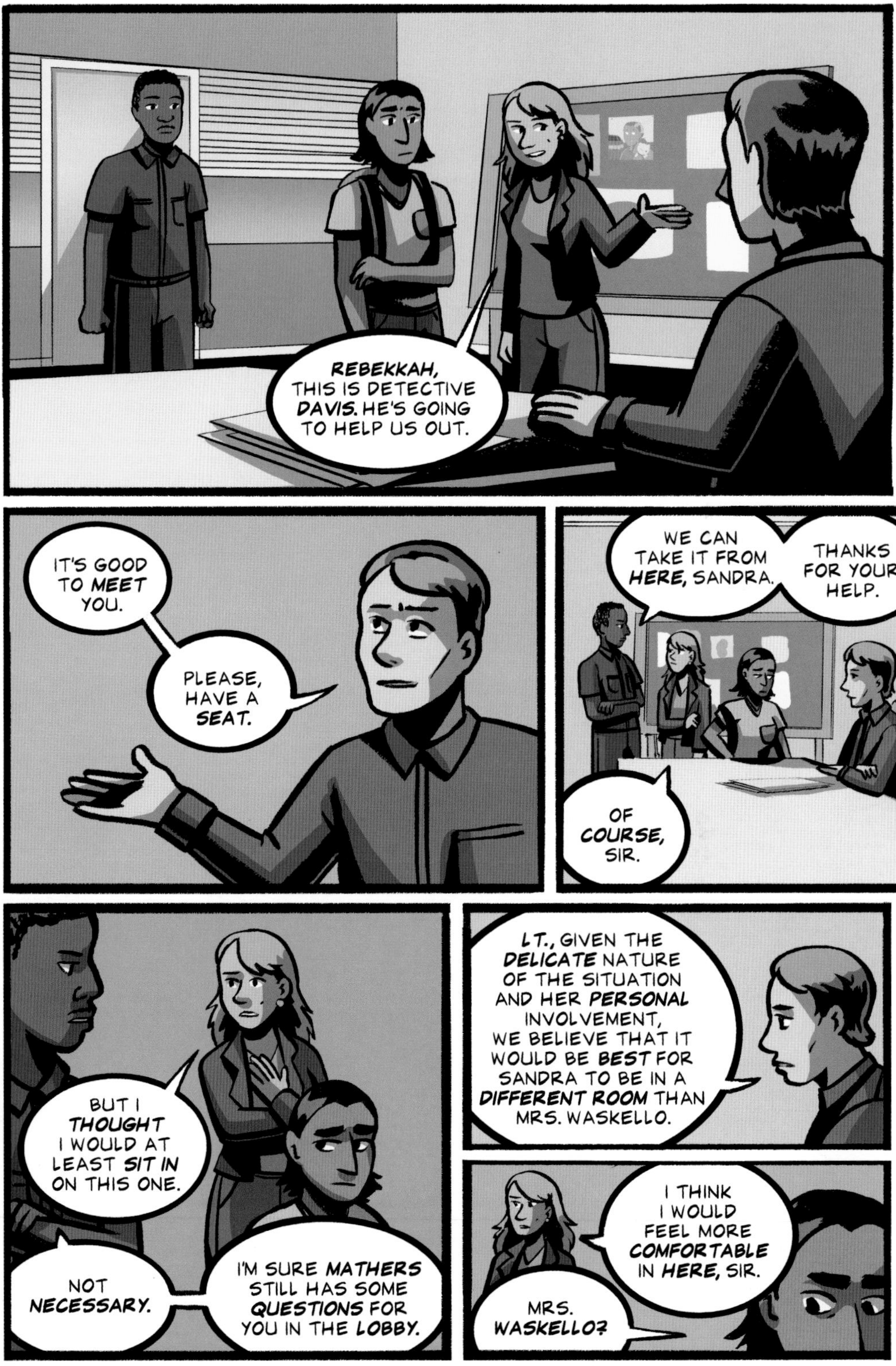
REBEKKAH, THIS IS DETECTIVE DAVIS. HE'S GOING TO HELP US OUT.
IT'S GOOD TO MEET YOU.
PLEASE, HAVE A SEAT.
WE CAN TAKE IT FROM HERE, SANDRA.
THANKS FOR YOUR HELP.
OF COURSE, SIR.
BUT I THOUGHT I WOULD AT LEAST SIT IN ON THIS ONE.
NOT NECESSARY.
I'M SURE MATHERS STILL HAS SOME QUESTIONS FOR YOU IN THE LOBBY.
LT., GIVEN THE DELICATE NATURE OF THE SITUATION AND HER PERSONAL INVOLVEMENT, WE BELIEVE THAT IT WOULD BE BEST FOR SANDRA TO BE IN A DIFFERENT ROOM THAN MRS. WASKELLO.
MRS. WASKELLO?
I THINK I WOULD FEEL MORE COMFORTABLE IN HERE, SIR.

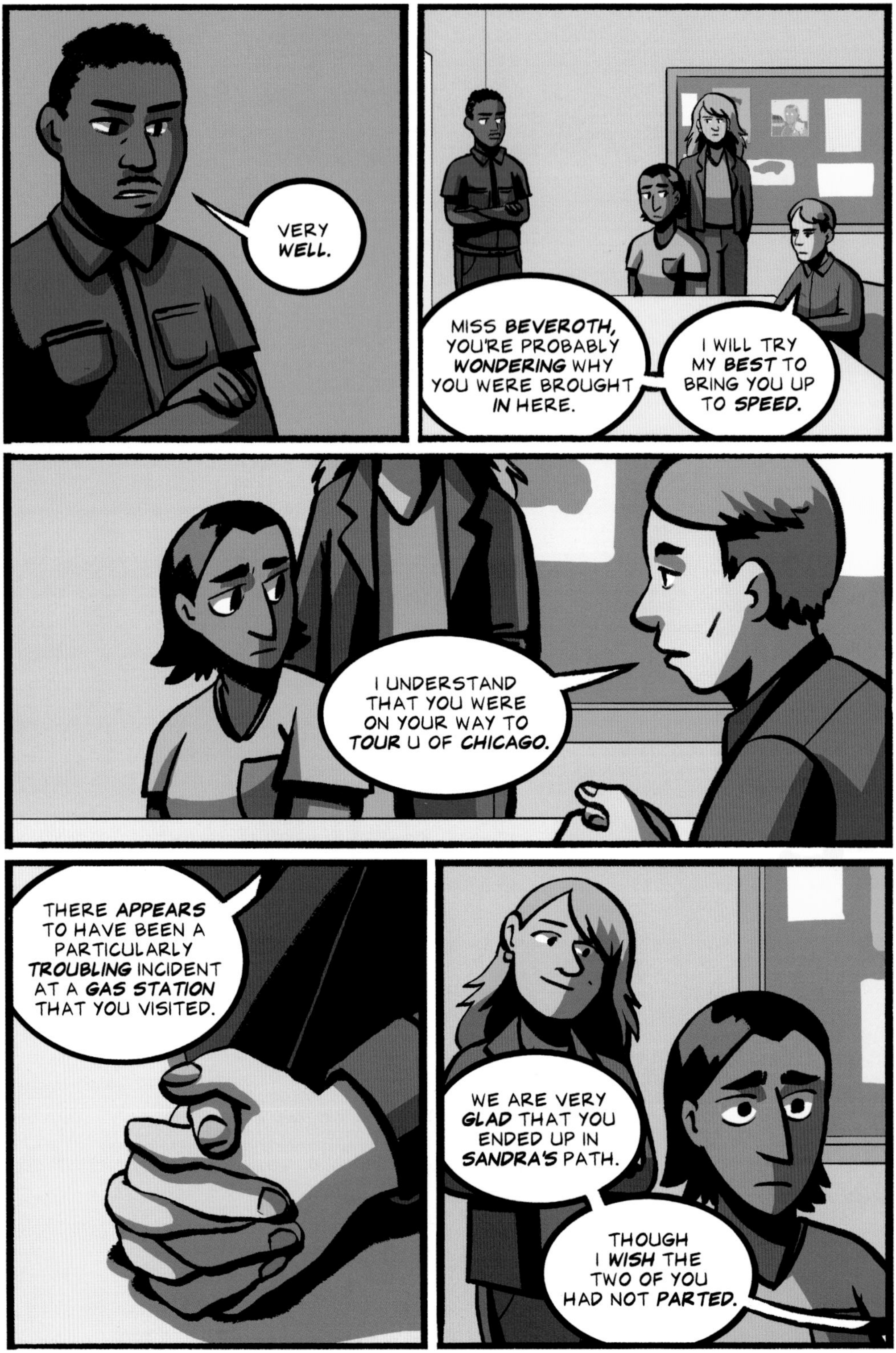
VERY WELL.
MISS BEVEROTH, YOU'RE PROBABLY WONDERING WHY YOU WERE BROUGHT IN HERE.
I WILL TRY MY BEST TO BRING YOU UP TO SPEED.
I UNDERSTAND THAT YOU WERE ON YOUR WAY TO TOUR U OF CHICAGO.
THERE APPEARS TO HAVE BEEN A PARTICULARLY TROUBLING INCIDENT AT A GAS STATION THAT YOU VISITED.
WE ARE VERY GLAD THAT YOU ENDED UP IN SANDRA'S PATH.
THOUGH I WISH THE TWO OF YOU HAD NOT PARTED.

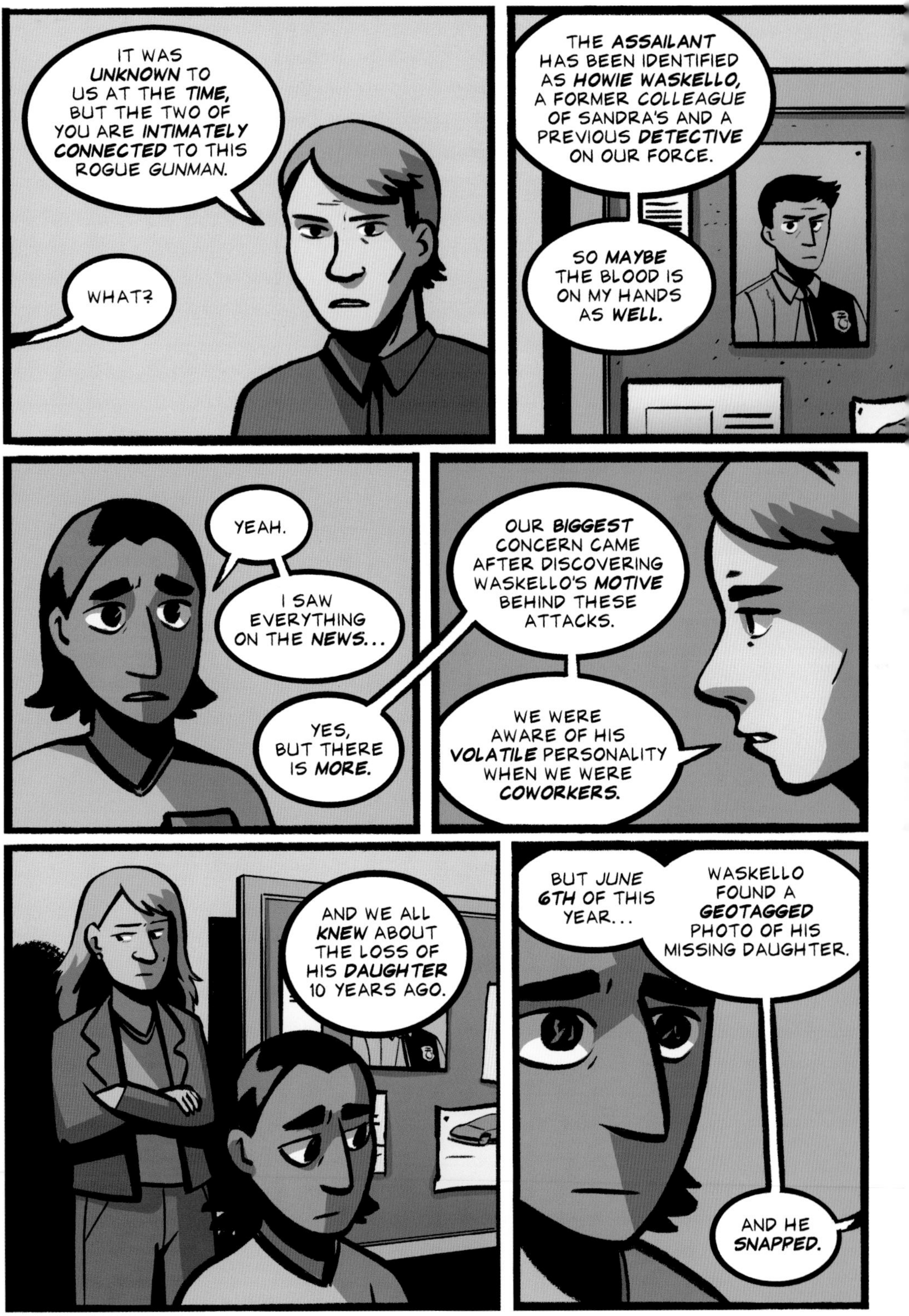
IT WAS UNKNOWN TO US AT THE TIME, BUT THE TWO OF YOU ARE INTIMATELY CONNECTED TO THIS ROGUE GUNMAN.
WHAT?
THE ASSAILANT HAS BEEN IDENTIFIED AS HOWIE WASKELLO, A FORMER COLLEAGUE OF SANDRA'S AND A PREVIOUS DETECTIVE ON OUR FORCE.
SO MAYBE THE BLOOD IS ON MY HANDS AS WELL.
YEAH.
I SAW EVERYTHING ON THE NEWS...
YES, BUT THERE IS MORE.
OUR BIGGEST CONCERN CAME AFTER DISCOVERING WASKELLO'S MOTIVE BEHIND THESE ATTACKS.
WE WERE AWARE OF HIS VOLATILE PERSONALITY WHEN WE WERE COWORKERS.
AND WE ALL KNEW ABOUT THE LOSS OF HIS DAUGHTER 10 YEARS AGO.
BUT JUNE 6TH OF THIS YEAR...
WASKELLO FOUND A GEOTAGGED PHOTO OF HIS MISSING DAUGHTER.
AND HE SNAPPED.

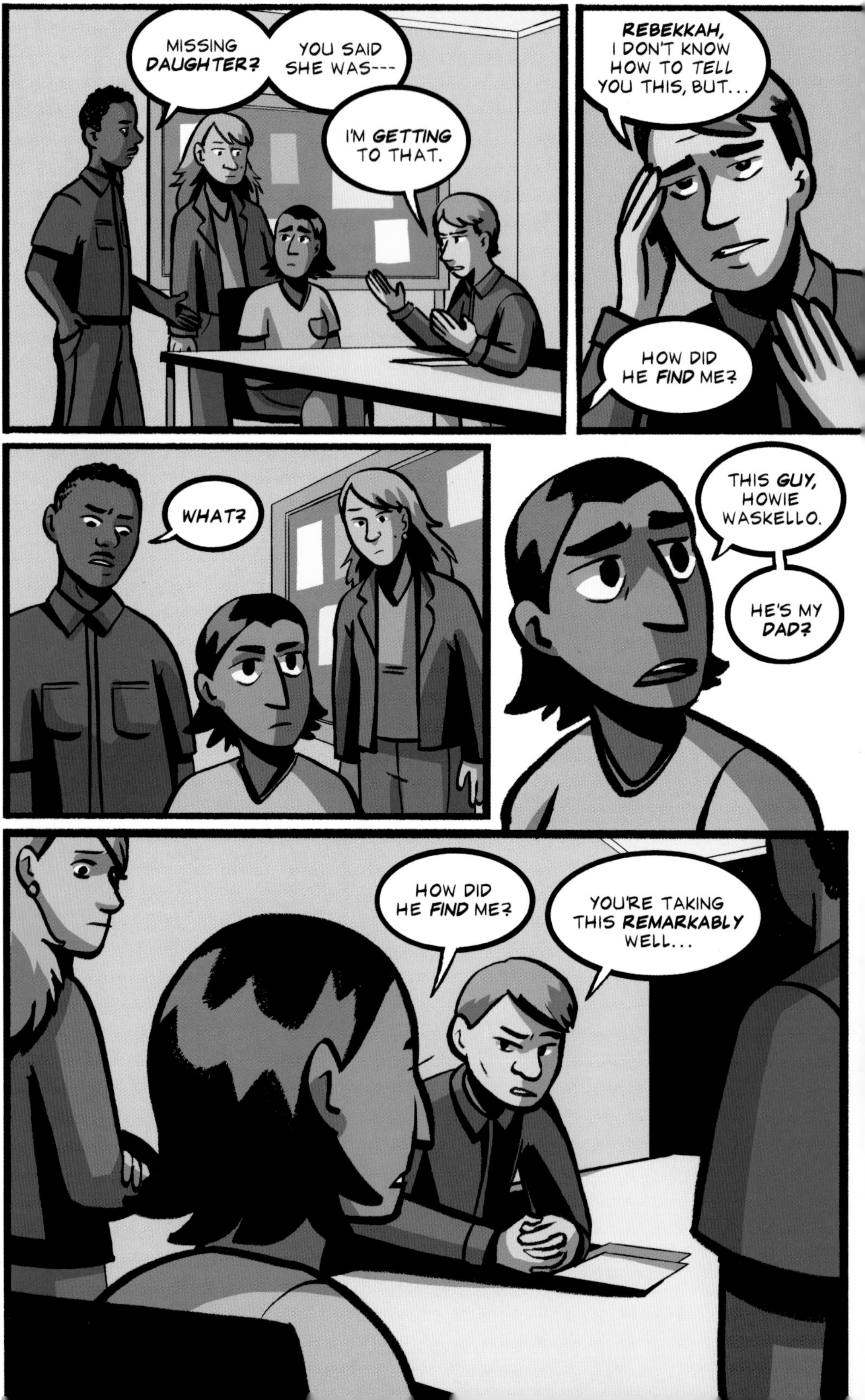
MISSING DAUGHTER?
YOU SAID SHE WAS---
I'M GETTING TO THAT.
REBEKKAH, I DON'T KNOW HOW TO TELL YOU THIS, BUT...
HOW DID HE FIND ME?
WHAT?
THIS GUY, HOWIE WASKELLO.
HE'S MY DAD?
HOW DID HE FIND ME?
YOU'RE TAKING THIS REMARKABLY WELL...

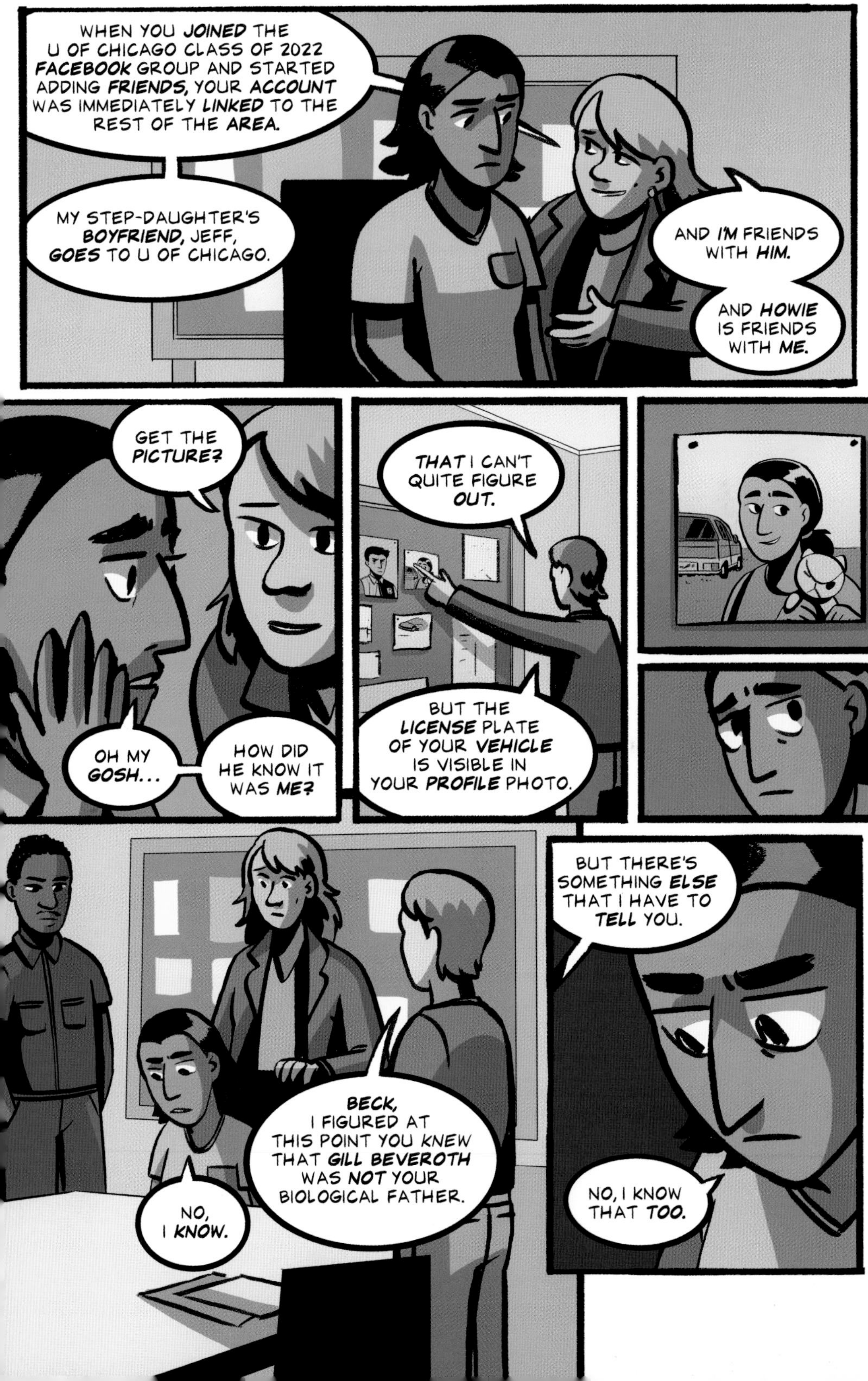
WHEN YOU JOINED THE U OF CHICAGO CLASS OF 2022 FACEBOOK GROUP AND STARTED ADDING FRIENDS, YOUR ACCOUNT WAS IMMEDIATELY LINKED TO THE REST OF THE AREA.
MY STEP-DAUGHTER'S BOYFRIEND, JEFF, GOES TO U OF CHICAGO.
AND I'M FRIENDS WITH HIM.
AND HOWIE IS FRIENDS WITH ME.
GET THE PICTURE?
OH MY GOSH...
HOW DID HE KNOW IT WAS ME?
THAT I CAN'T QUITE FIGURE OUT.
BUT THE LICENSE PLATE OF YOUR VEHICLE IS VISIBLE IN YOUR PROFILE PHOTO.
BUT THERE'S SOMETHING ELSE THAT I HAVE TO TELL YOU.
BECK, I FIGURED AT THIS POINT YOU KNEW THAT GILL BEVEROTH WAS NOT YOUR BIOLOGICAL FATHER.
NO, I KNOW.
NO, I KNOW THAT TOO.

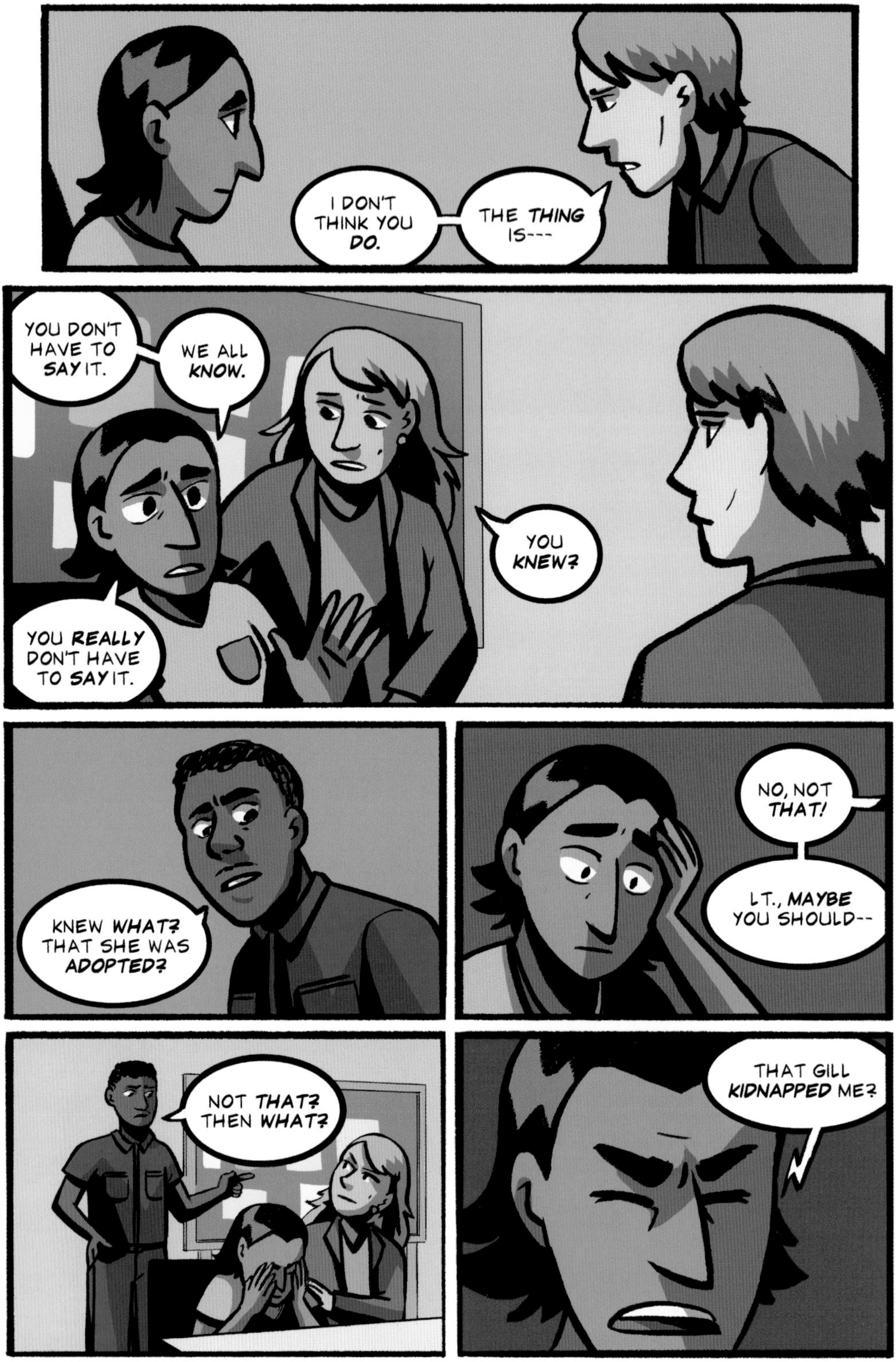

I DON'T THINK YOU DO.
THE THING IS---
YOU DON'T HAVE TO SAY IT.
WE ALL KNOW.
YOU KNEW?
YOU REALLY DON'T HAVE TO SAY IT.
KNEW WHAT? THAT SHE WAS ADOPTED?
NO, NOT THAT!
LT., MAYBE YOU SHOULD--
NOT THAT? THEN WHAT?
THAT GILL KIDNAPPED ME?

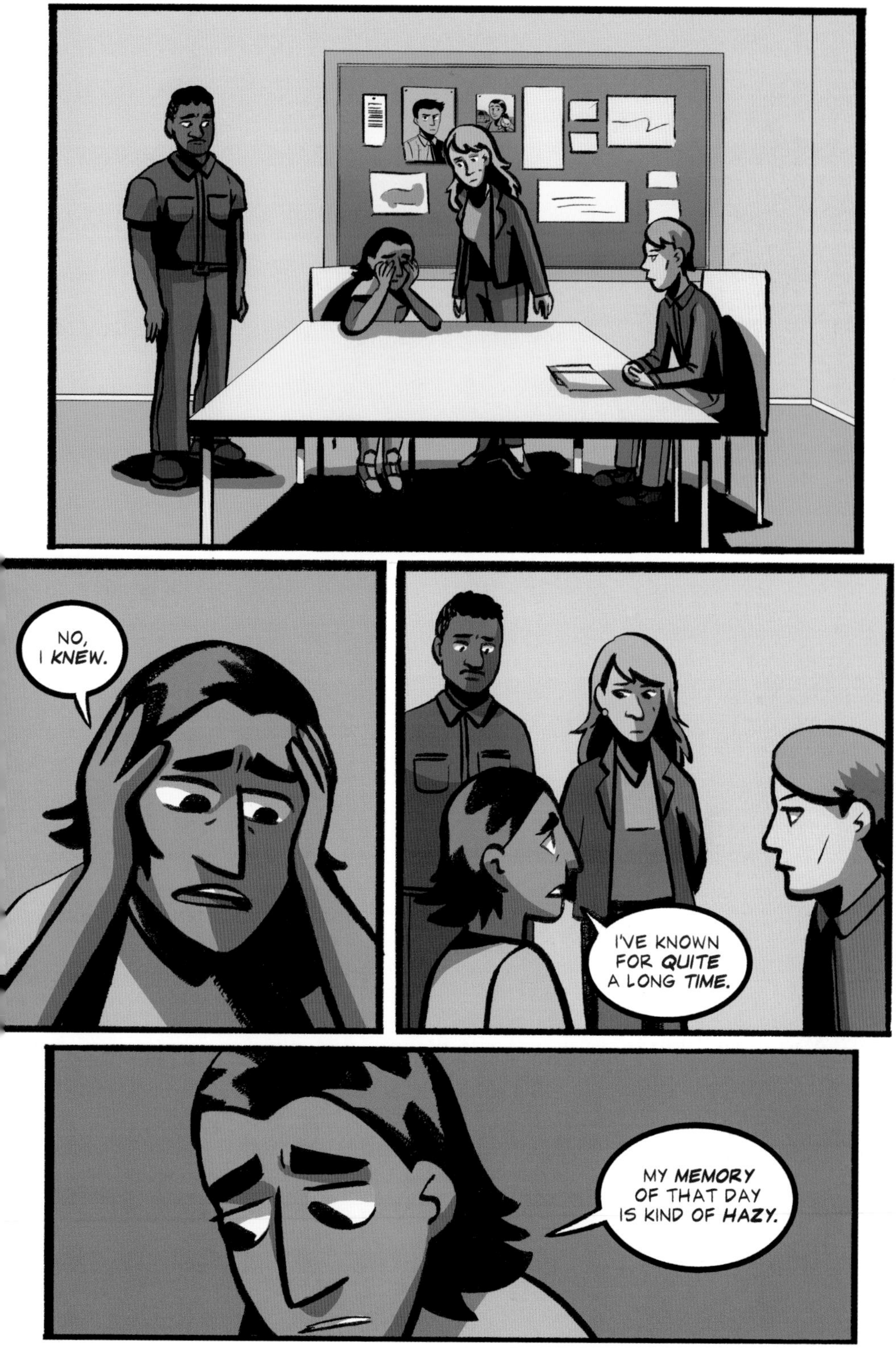
NO, I KNEW.
I'VE KNOWN FOR QUITE A LONG TIME.
MY MEMORY OF THAT DAY IS KIND OF HAZY.

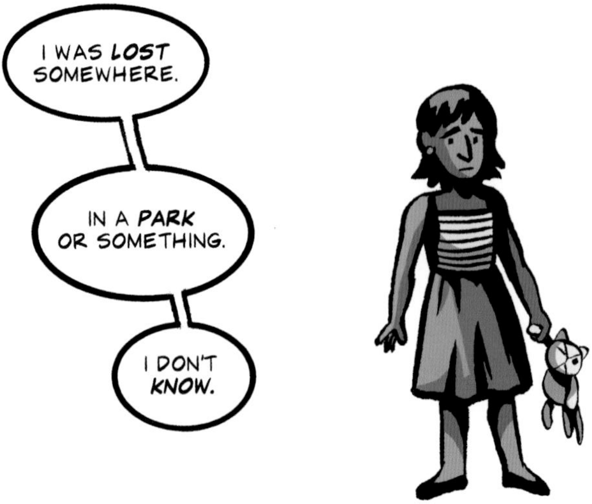
I WAS **LOST** SOMEWHERE.
IN A **PARK** OR SOMETHING.
I DON'T **KNOW.**

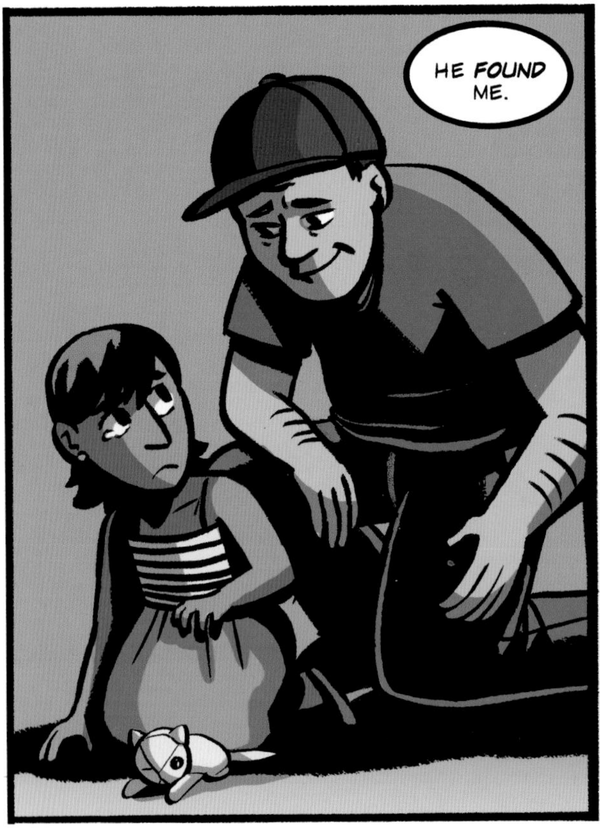
HE **FOUND** ME.

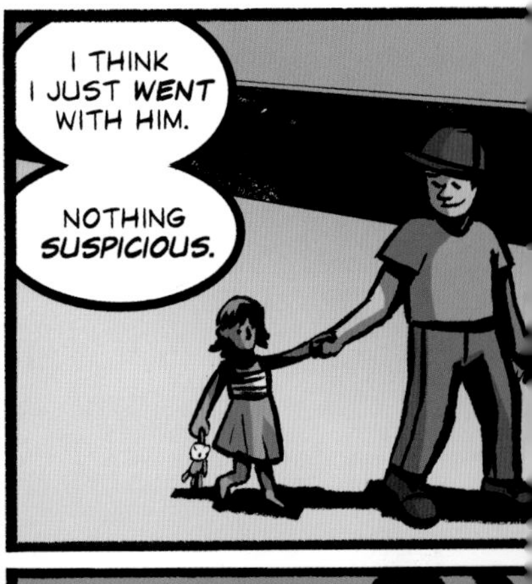
I THINK I JUST **WENT** WITH HIM.
NOTHING **SUSPICIOUS.**

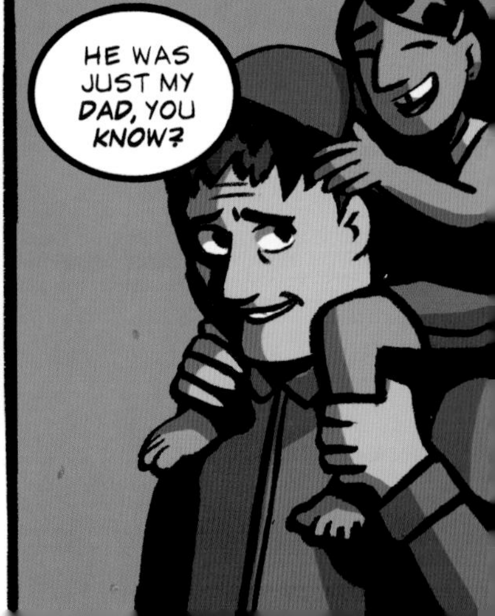
HE WAS JUST MY **DAD,** YOU **KNOW?**

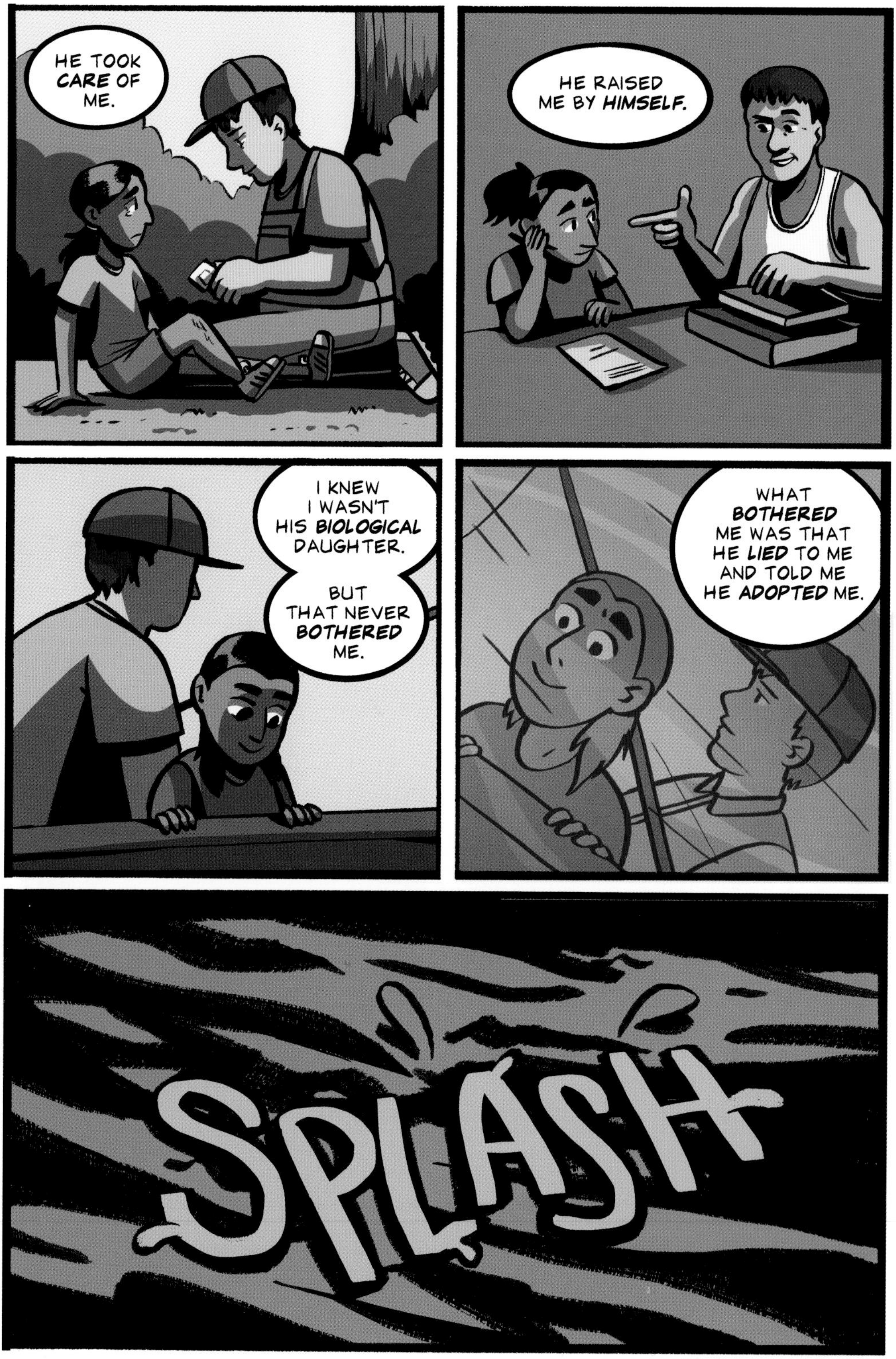
HE TOOK CARE OF ME.
HE RAISED ME BY HIMSELF.
I KNEW I WASN'T HIS BIOLOGICAL DAUGHTER.
BUT THAT NEVER BOTHERED ME.
WHAT BOTHERED ME WAS THAT HE LIED TO ME AND TOLD ME HE ADOPTED ME.
SPLASH

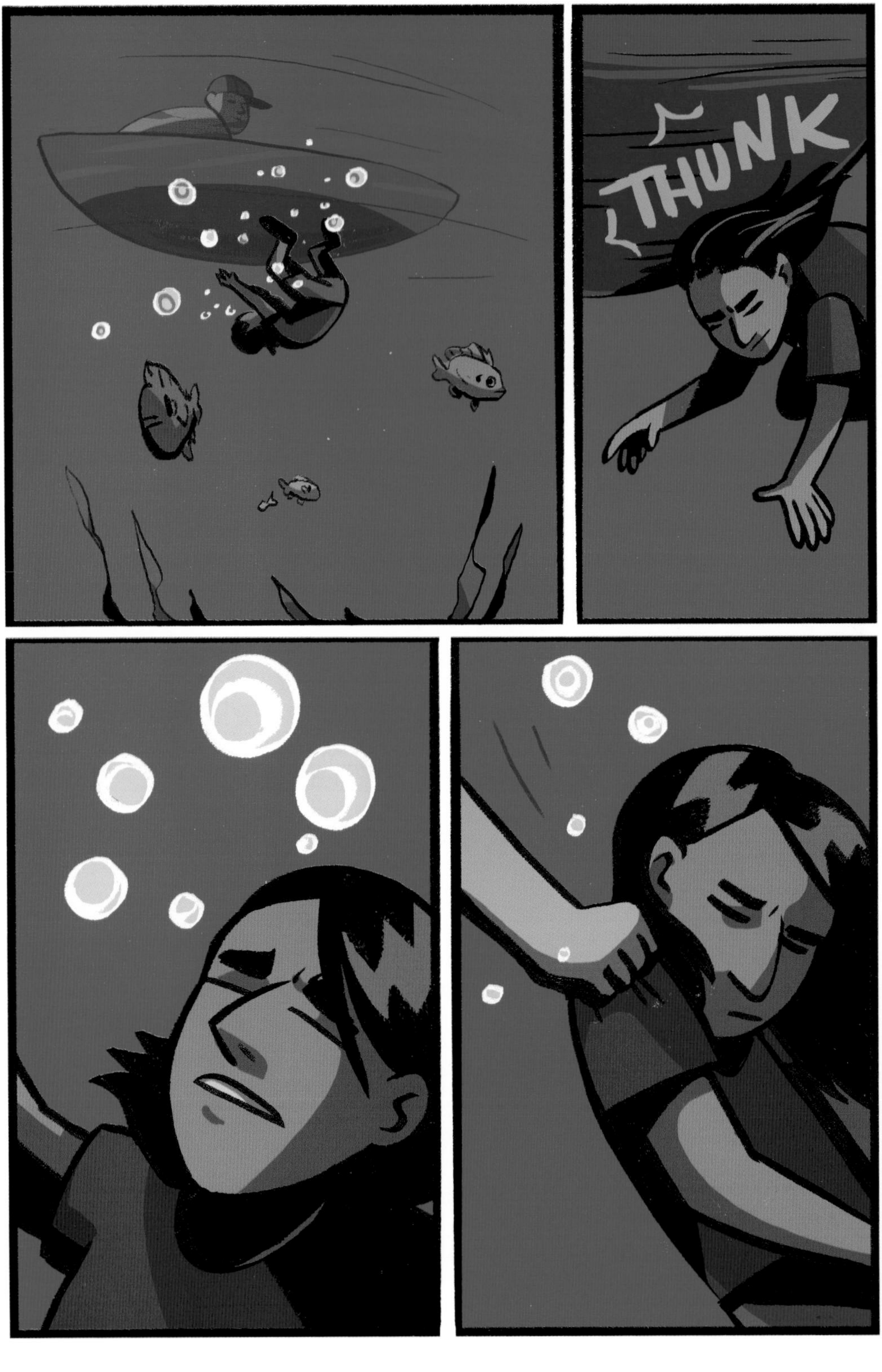
THUNK

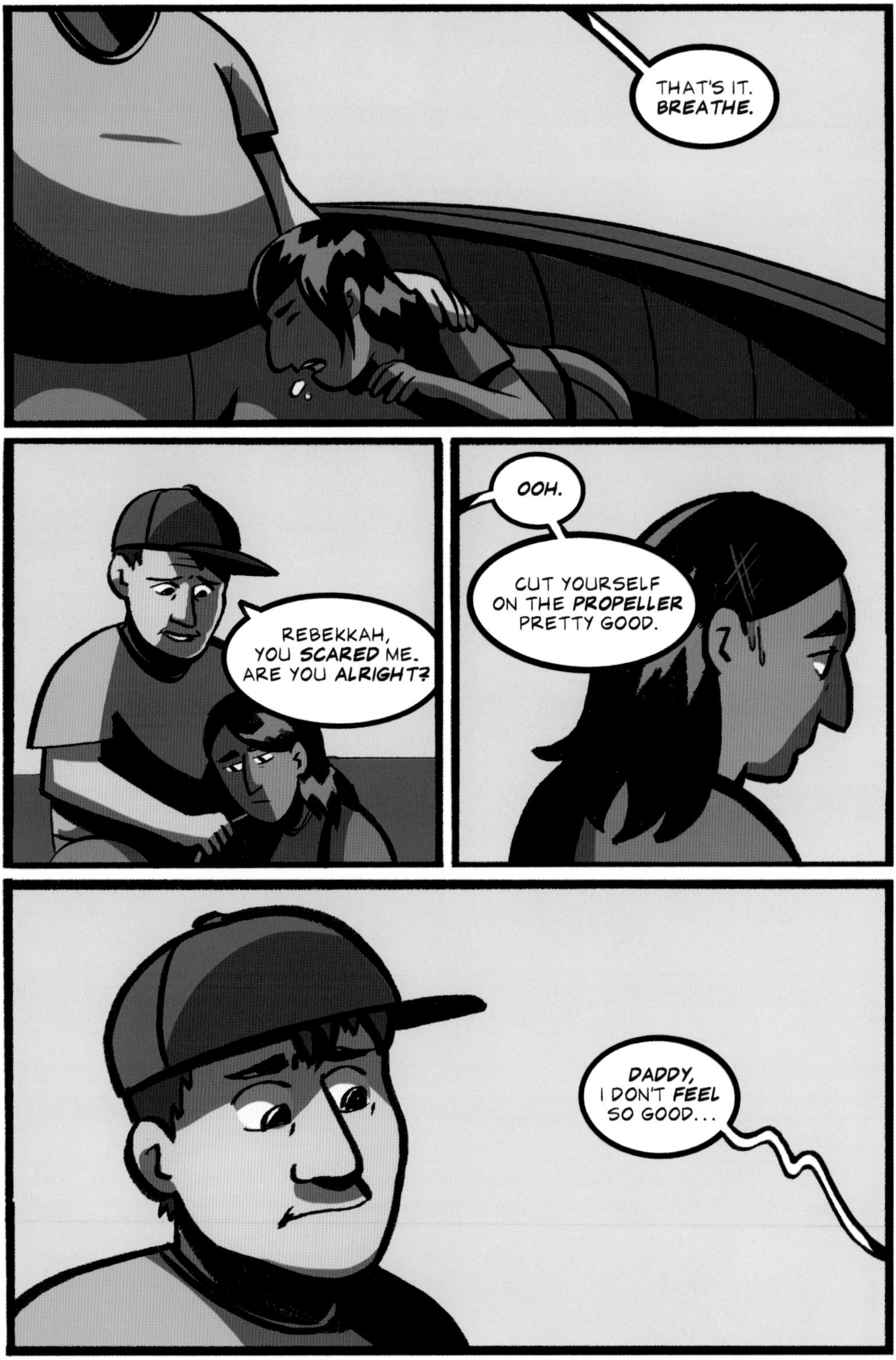
THAT'S IT. BREATHE.
REBEKKAH, YOU SCARED ME. ARE YOU ALRIGHT?
OOH.
CUT YOURSELF ON THE PROPELLER PRETTY GOOD.
DADDY, I DON'T FEEL SO GOOD...

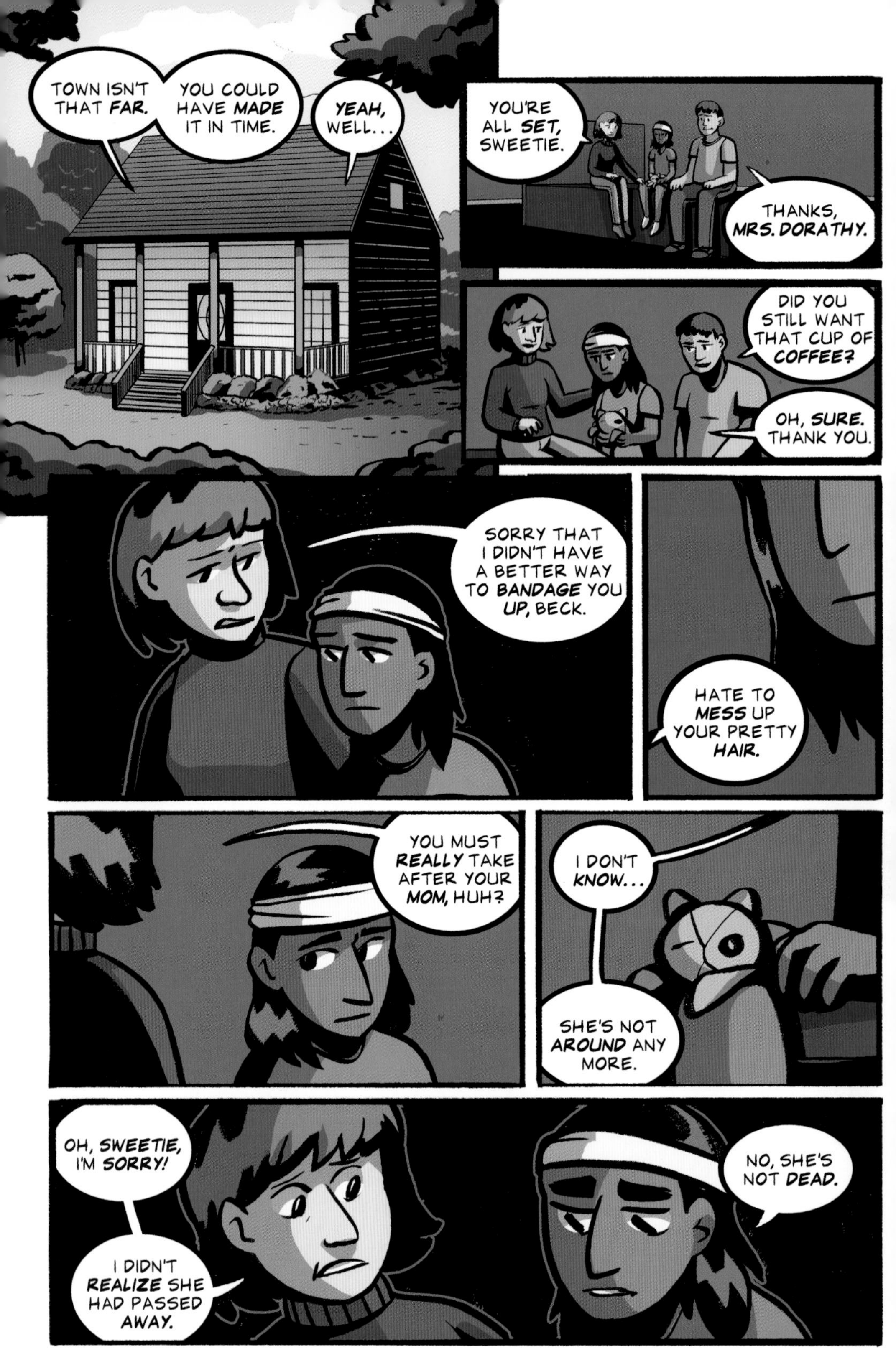
TOWN ISN'T THAT FAR.
YOU COULD HAVE MADE IT IN TIME.
YEAH, WELL...
YOU'RE ALL SET, SWEETIE.
THANKS, MRS. DORATHY.
DID YOU STILL WANT THAT CUP OF COFFEE?
OH, SURE. THANK YOU.
SORRY THAT I DIDN'T HAVE A BETTER WAY TO BANDAGE YOU UP, BECK.
HATE TO MESS UP YOUR PRETTY HAIR.
YOU MUST REALLY TAKE AFTER YOUR MOM, HUH?
I DON'T KNOW...
SHE'S NOT AROUND ANY MORE.
OH, SWEETIE, I'M SORRY!
I DIDN'T REALIZE SHE HAD PASSED AWAY.
NO, SHE'S NOT DEAD.

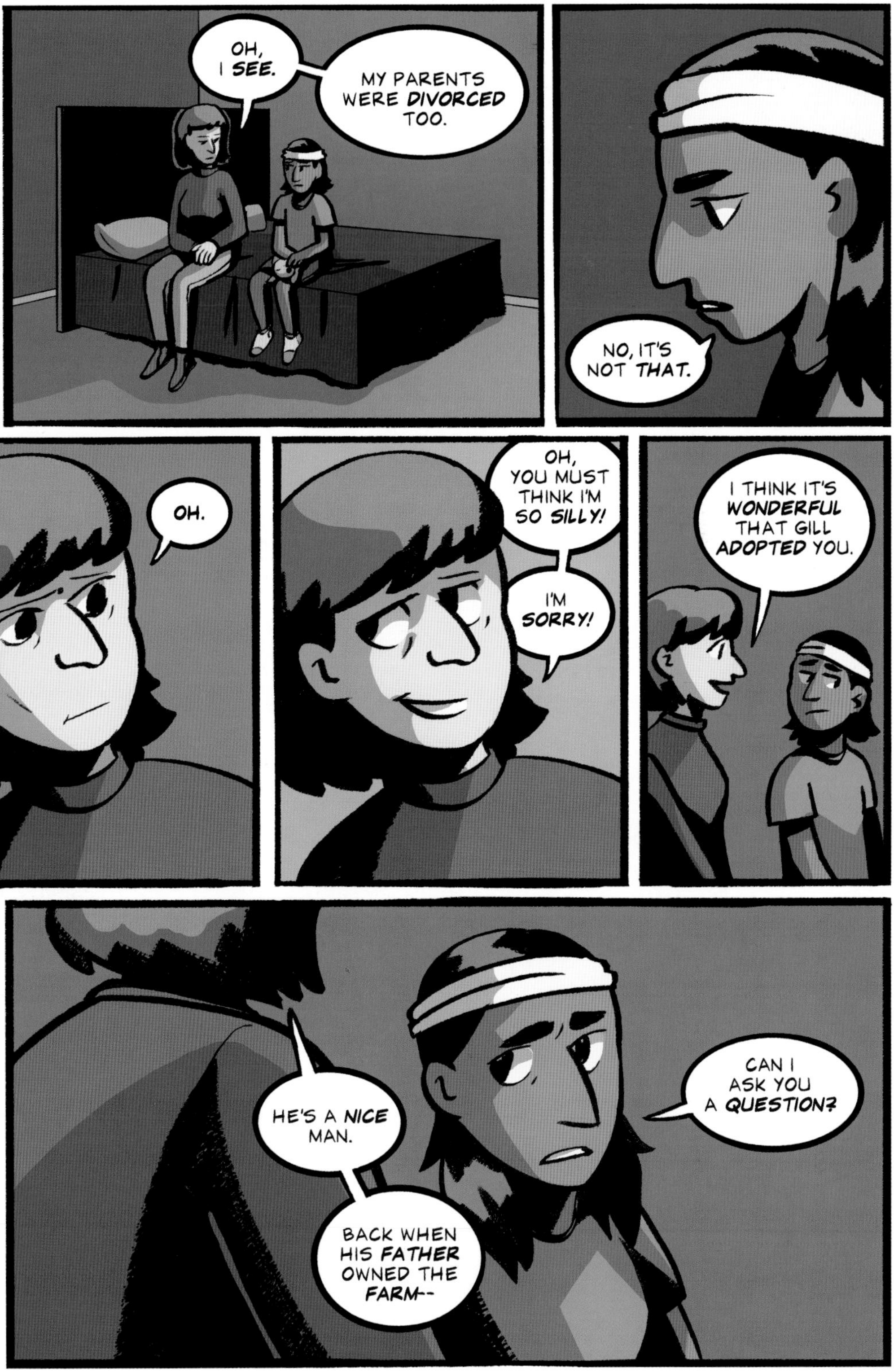
OH, I SEE.
MY PARENTS WERE DIVORCED TOO.
NO, IT'S NOT THAT.
OH.
OH, YOU MUST THINK I'M SO SILLY!
I'M SORRY!
I THINK IT'S WONDERFUL THAT GILL ADOPTED YOU.
CAN I ASK YOU A QUESTION?
HE'S A NICE MAN.
BACK WHEN HIS FATHER OWNED THE FARM--

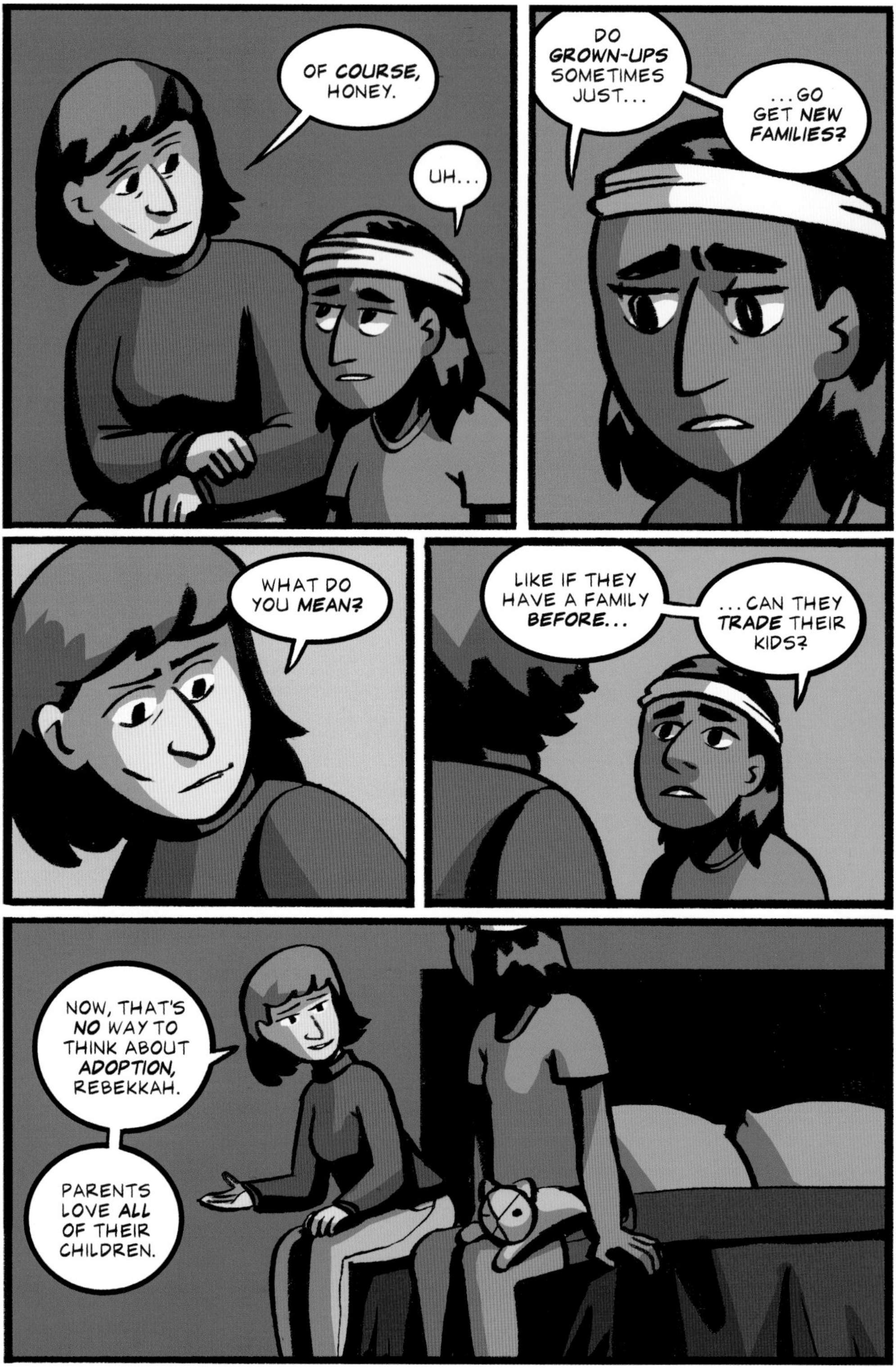
OF **COURSE,** HONEY.
UH...
DO **GROWN-UPS** SOMETIMES JUST...
...GO GET **NEW FAMILIES?**
WHAT DO YOU **MEAN?**
LIKE IF THEY HAVE A FAMILY **BEFORE...**
...CAN THEY **TRADE** THEIR KIDS?
NOW, THAT'S **NO** WAY TO THINK ABOUT **ADOPTION,** REBEKKAH.
PARENTS LOVE **ALL** OF THEIR CHILDREN.

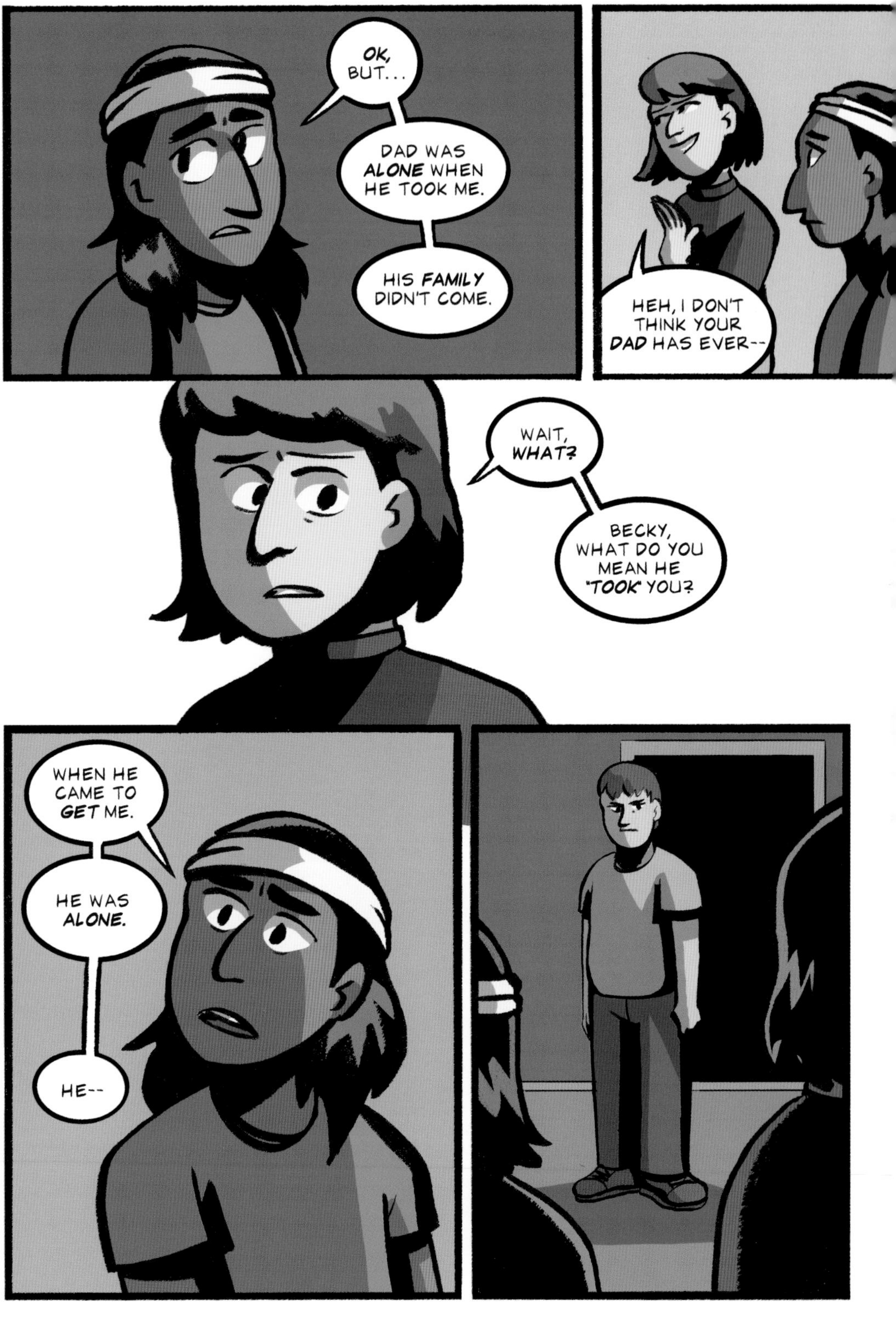
OK, BUT...
DAD WAS ALONE WHEN HE TOOK ME.
HIS FAMILY DIDN'T COME.
HEH, I DON'T THINK YOUR DAD HAS EVER--
WAIT, WHAT?
BECKY, WHAT DO YOU MEAN HE "TOOK" YOU?
WHEN HE CAME TO GET ME.
HE WAS ALONE.
HE--

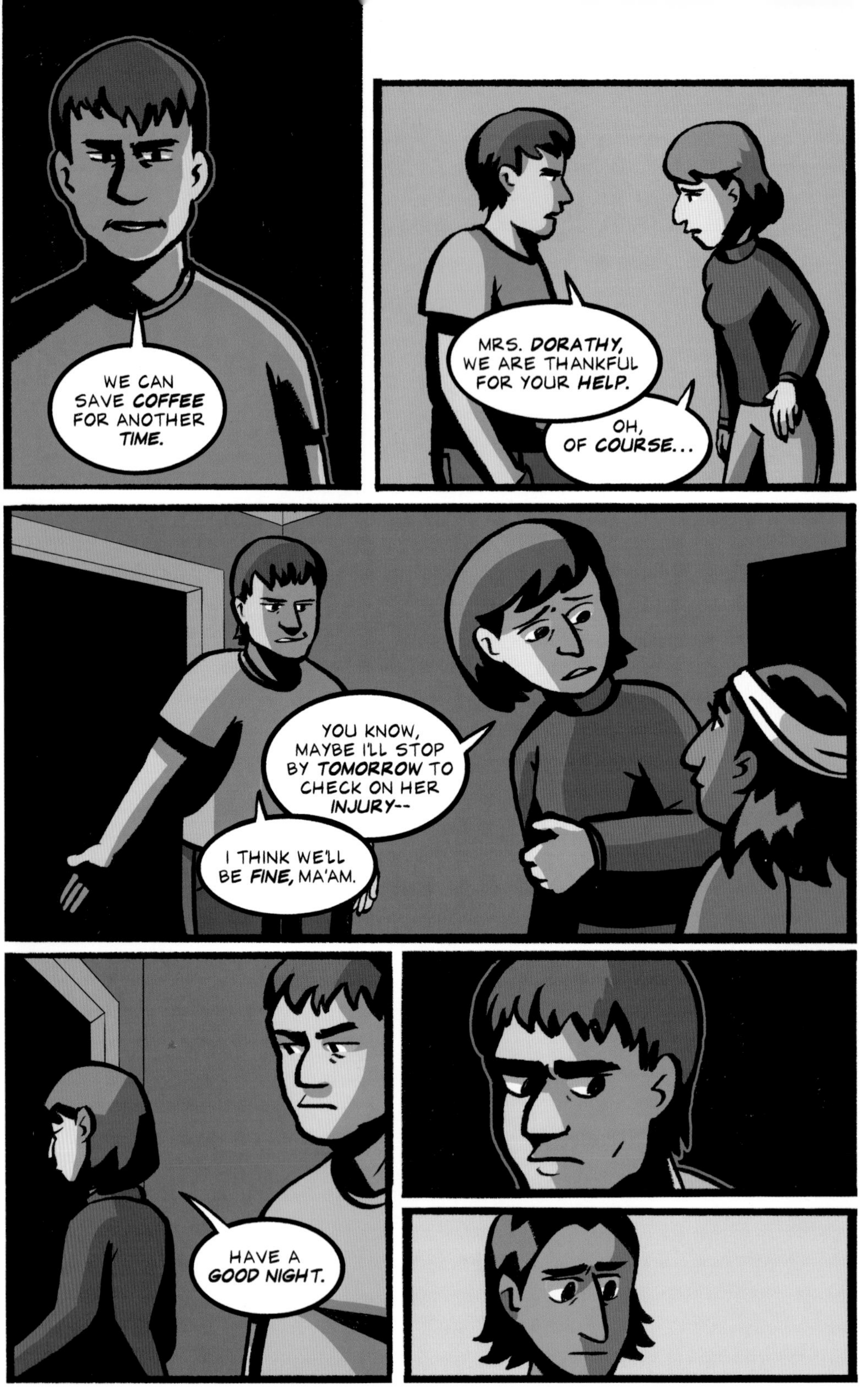
WE CAN SAVE COFFEE FOR ANOTHER TIME.
MRS. DORATHY, WE ARE THANKFUL FOR YOUR HELP.
OH, OF COURSE...
YOU KNOW, MAYBE I'LL STOP BY TOMORROW TO CHECK ON HER INJURY--
I THINK WE'LL BE FINE, MA'AM.
HAVE A GOOD NIGHT.

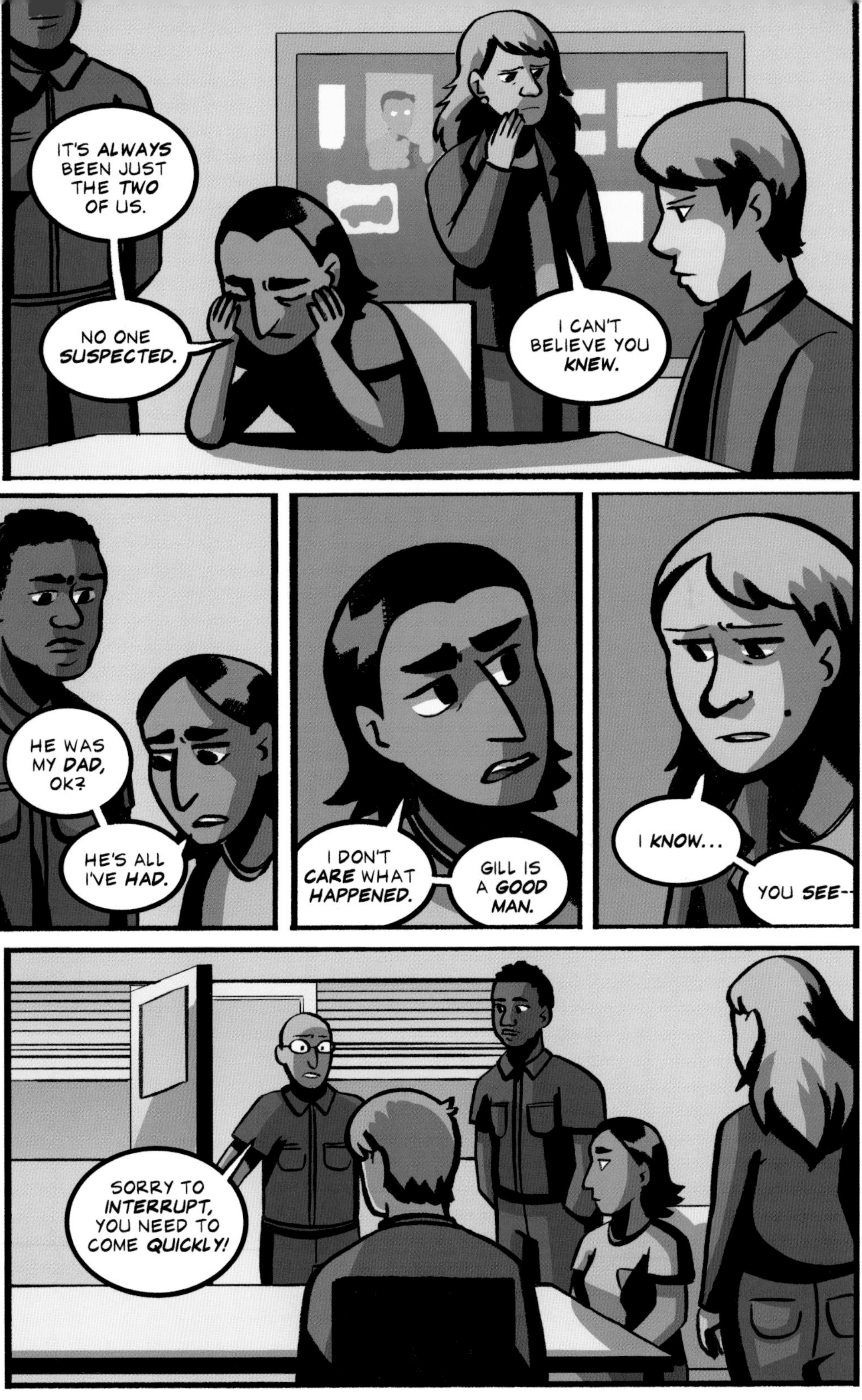
IT'S ALWAYS BEEN JUST THE TWO OF US.
NO ONE SUSPECTED.
I CAN'T BELIEVE YOU KNEW.
HE WAS MY DAD, OK?
HE'S ALL I'VE HAD.
I DON'T CARE WHAT HAPPENED.
GILL IS A GOOD MAN.
I KNOW...
YOU SEE--
SORRY TO INTERRUPT, YOU NEED TO COME QUICKLY!

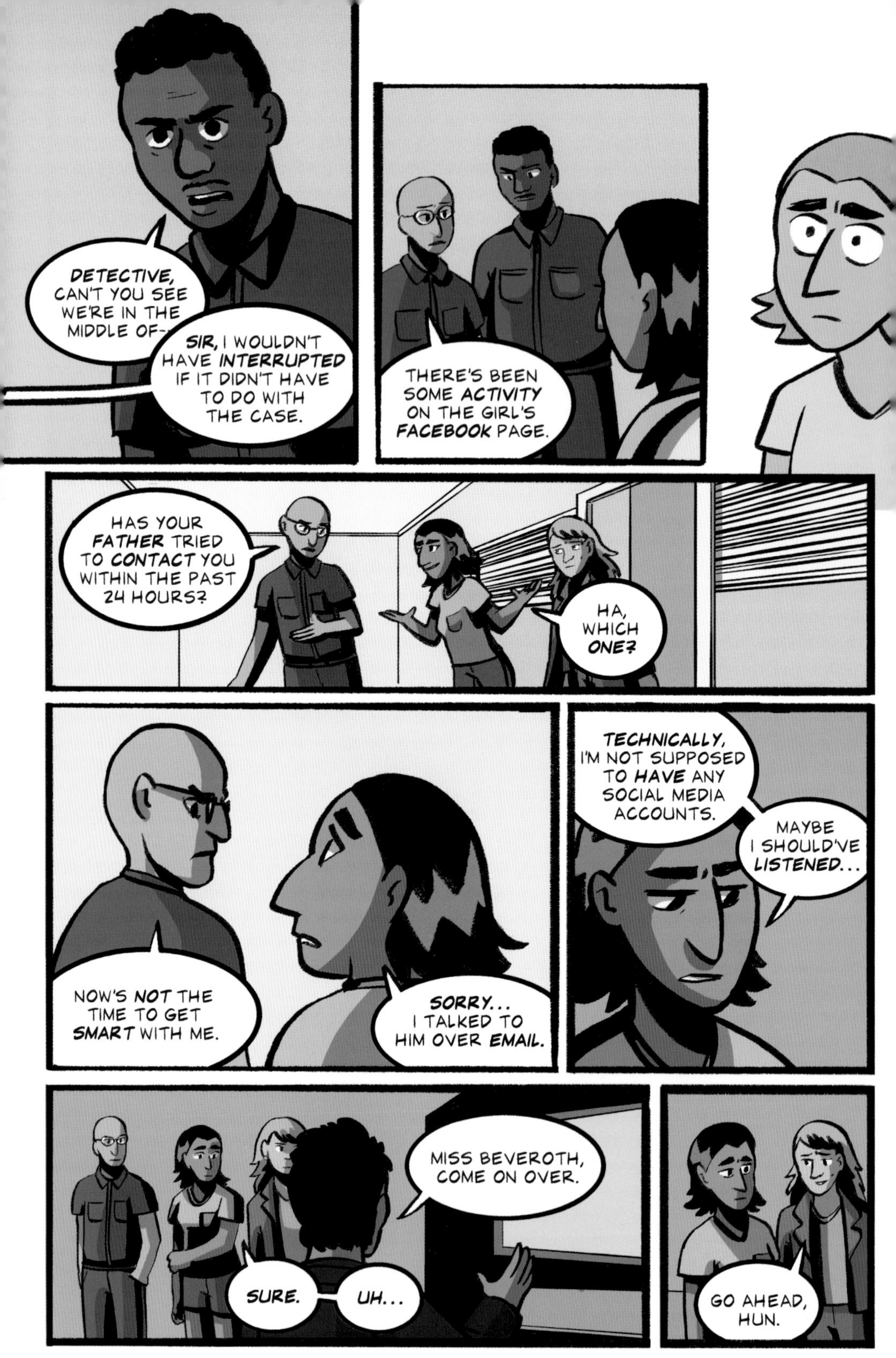
DETECTIVE, CAN'T YOU SEE WE'RE IN THE MIDDLE OF--
SIR, I WOULDN'T HAVE INTERRUPTED IF IT DIDN'T HAVE TO DO WITH THE CASE.
THERE'S BEEN SOME ACTIVITY ON THE GIRL'S FACEBOOK PAGE.
HAS YOUR FATHER TRIED TO CONTACT YOU WITHIN THE PAST 24 HOURS?
HA, WHICH ONE?
NOW'S NOT THE TIME TO GET SMART WITH ME.
SORRY... I TALKED TO HIM OVER EMAIL.
TECHNICALLY, I'M NOT SUPPOSED TO HAVE ANY SOCIAL MEDIA ACCOUNTS.
MAYBE I SHOULD'VE LISTENED...
MISS BEVEROTH, COME ON OVER.
SURE.
UH...
GO AHEAD, HUN.

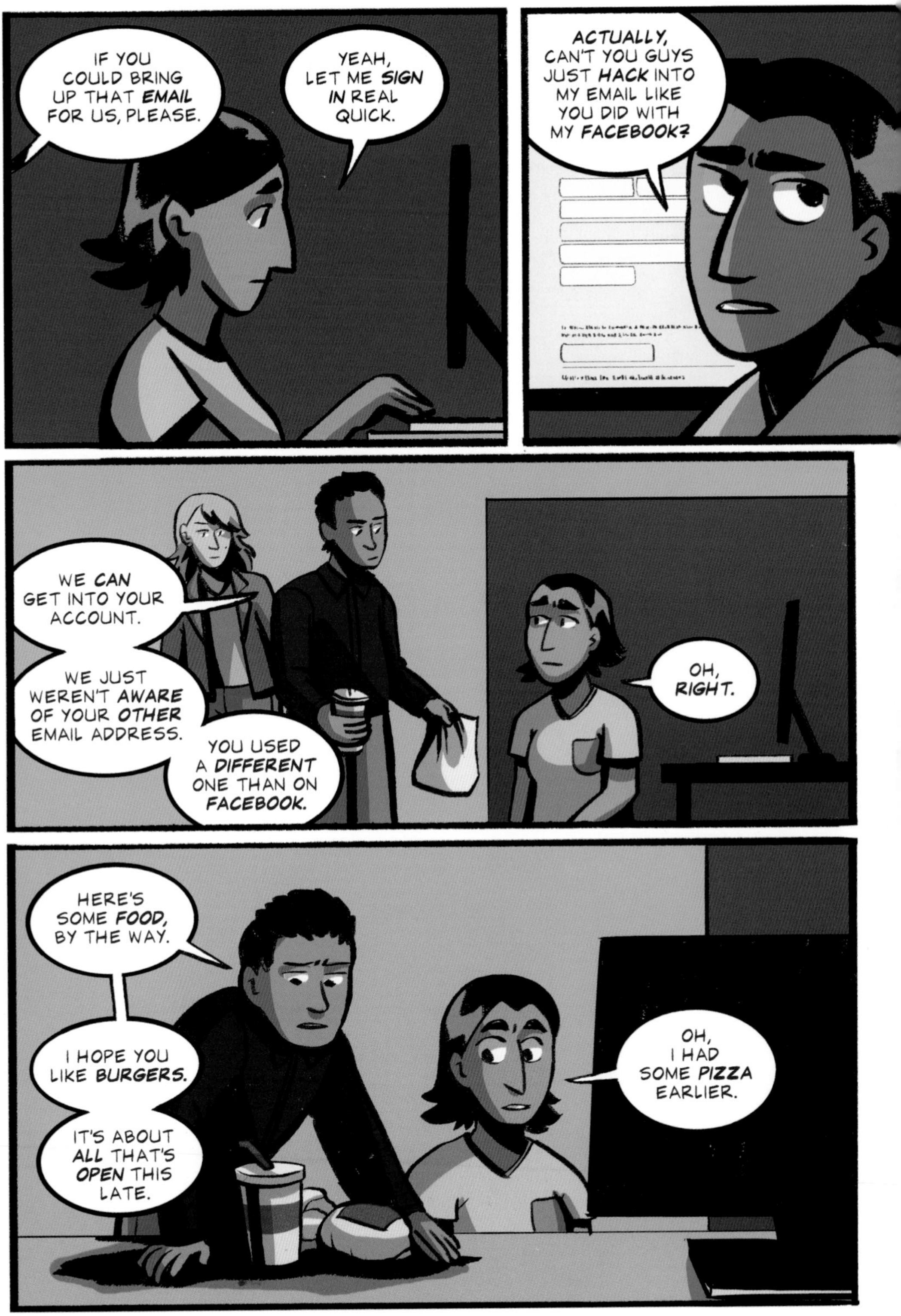
IF YOU COULD BRING UP THAT EMAIL FOR US, PLEASE.
YEAH, LET ME SIGN IN REAL QUICK.
ACTUALLY, CAN'T YOU GUYS JUST HACK INTO MY EMAIL LIKE YOU DID WITH MY FACEBOOK?
WE CAN GET INTO YOUR ACCOUNT.
WE JUST WEREN'T AWARE OF YOUR OTHER EMAIL ADDRESS.
YOU USED A DIFFERENT ONE THAN ON FACEBOOK.
OH, RIGHT.
HERE'S SOME FOOD, BY THE WAY.
I HOPE YOU LIKE BURGERS.
IT'S ABOUT ALL THAT'S OPEN THIS LATE.
OH, I HAD SOME PIZZA EARLIER.

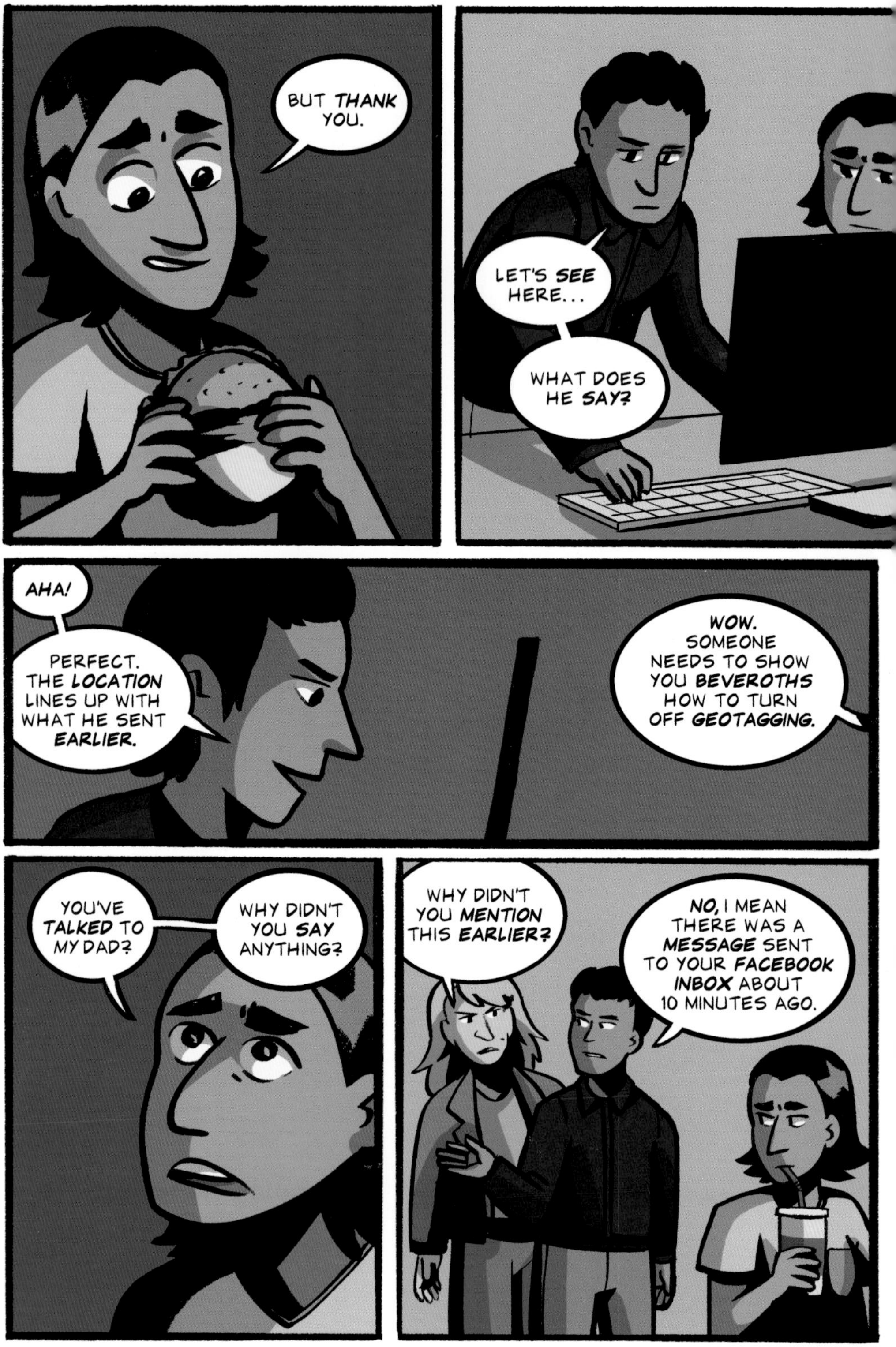
BUT THANK YOU.
LET'S SEE HERE...
WHAT DOES HE SAY?
AHA!
PERFECT. THE LOCATION LINES UP WITH WHAT HE SENT EARLIER.
WOW. SOMEONE NEEDS TO SHOW YOU BEVEROTHS HOW TO TURN OFF GEOTAGGING.
YOU'VE TALKED TO MY DAD?
WHY DIDN'T YOU SAY ANYTHING?
WHY DIDN'T YOU MENTION THIS EARLIER?
NO, I MEAN THERE WAS A MESSAGE SENT TO YOUR FACEBOOK INBOX ABOUT 10 MINUTES AGO.

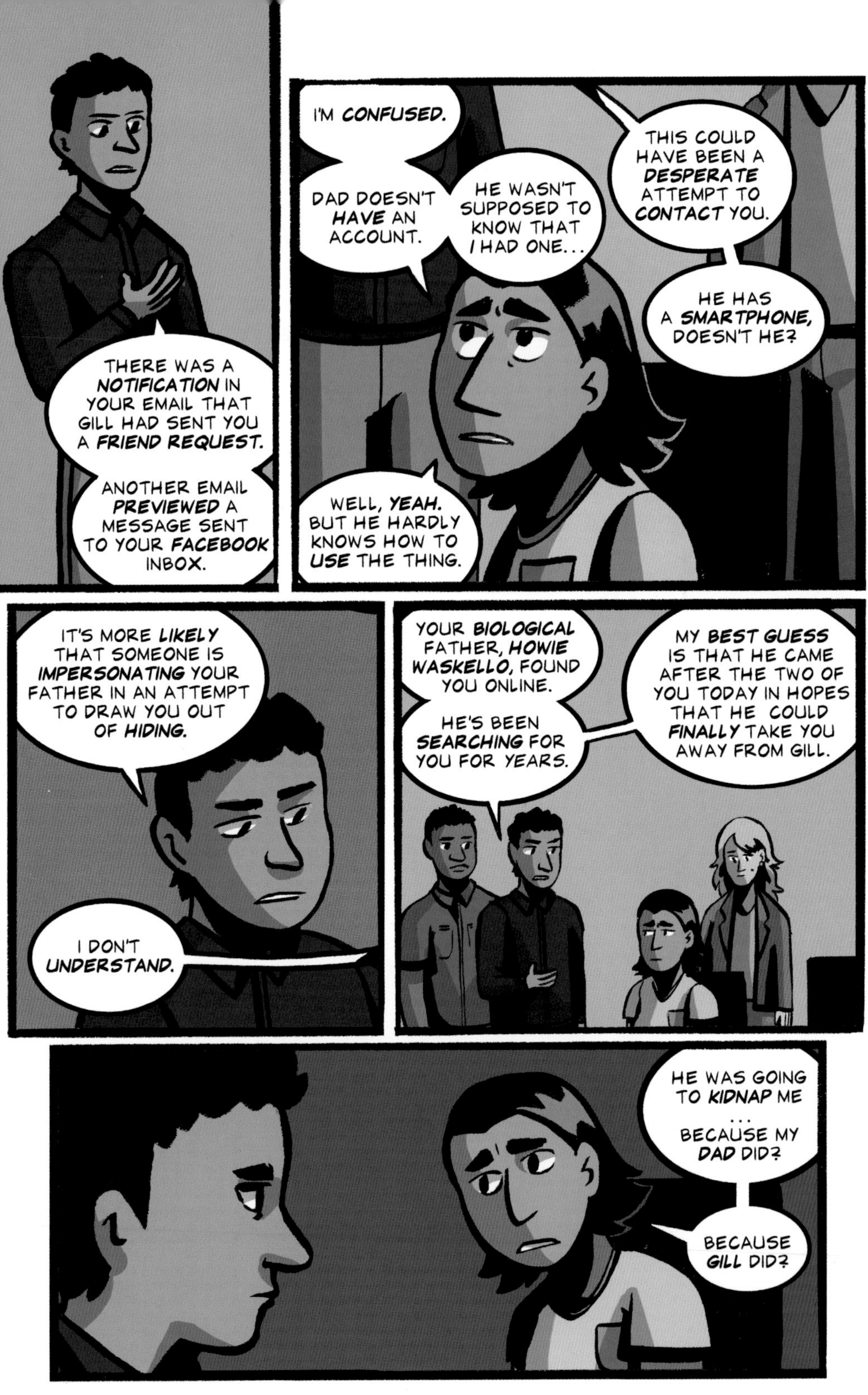
THERE WAS A NOTIFICATION IN YOUR EMAIL THAT GILL HAD SENT YOU A FRIEND REQUEST.
ANOTHER EMAIL PREVIEWED A MESSAGE SENT TO YOUR FACEBOOK INBOX.
I'M CONFUSED.
DAD DOESN'T HAVE AN ACCOUNT.
HE WASN'T SUPPOSED TO KNOW THAT I HAD ONE...
THIS COULD HAVE BEEN A DESPERATE ATTEMPT TO CONTACT YOU.
HE HAS A SMARTPHONE, DOESN'T HE?
WELL, YEAH. BUT HE HARDLY KNOWS HOW TO USE THE THING.
IT'S MORE LIKELY THAT SOMEONE IS IMPERSONATING YOUR FATHER IN AN ATTEMPT TO DRAW YOU OUT OF HIDING.
I DON'T UNDERSTAND.
YOUR BIOLOGICAL FATHER, HOWIE WASKELLO, FOUND YOU ONLINE.
HE'S BEEN SEARCHING FOR YOU FOR YEARS.
MY BEST GUESS IS THAT HE CAME AFTER THE TWO OF YOU TODAY IN HOPES THAT HE COULD FINALLY TAKE YOU AWAY FROM GILL.
HE WAS GOING TO KIDNAP ME ... BECAUSE MY DAD DID?
BECAUSE GILL DID?

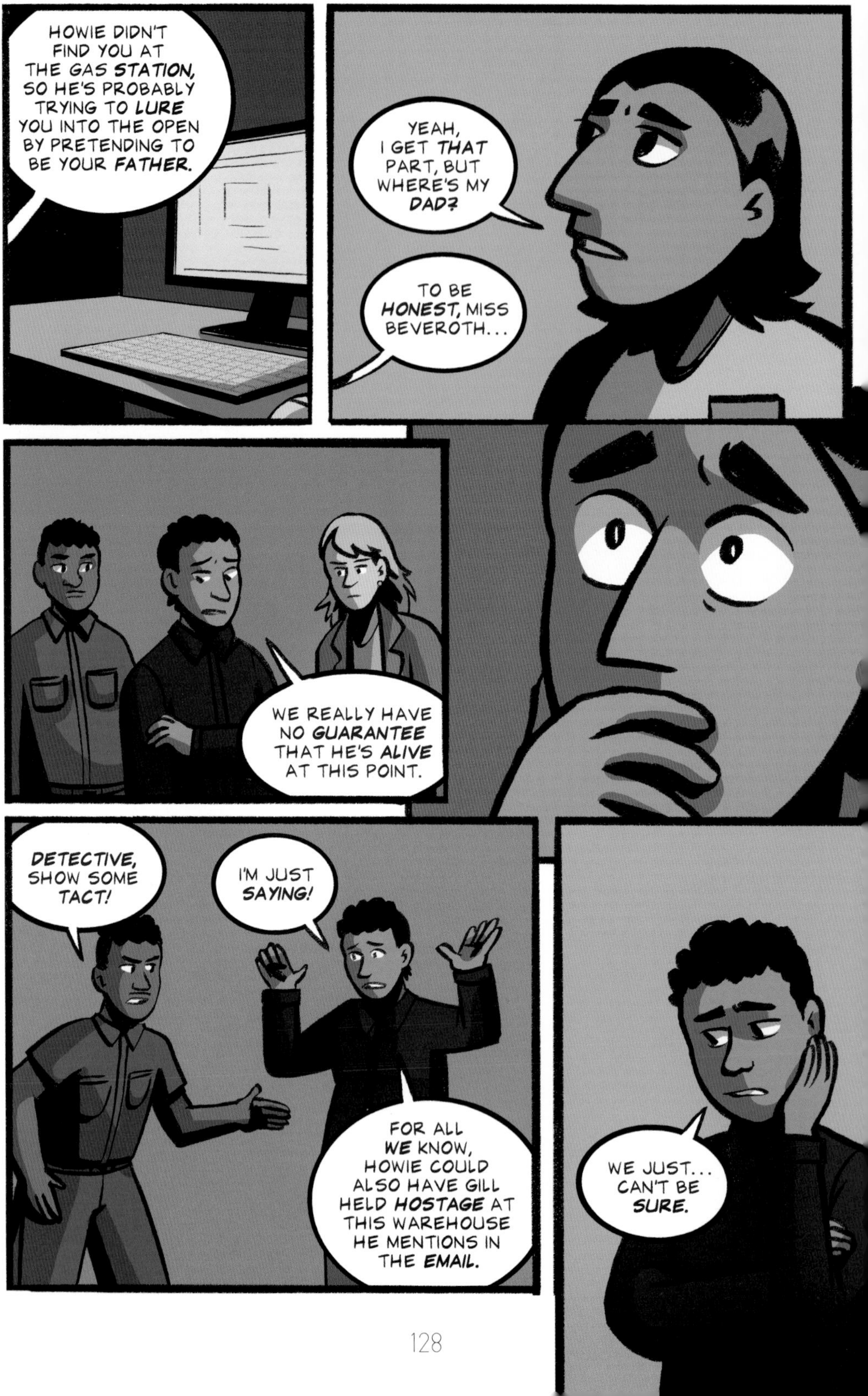
HOWIE DIDN'T FIND YOU AT THE GAS STATION, SO HE'S PROBABLY TRYING TO LURE YOU INTO THE OPEN BY PRETENDING TO BE YOUR FATHER.
YEAH, I GET THAT PART, BUT WHERE'S MY DAD?
TO BE HONEST, MISS BEVEROTH...
WE REALLY HAVE NO GUARANTEE THAT HE'S ALIVE AT THIS POINT.
DETECTIVE, SHOW SOME TACT!
I'M JUST SAYING!
FOR ALL WE KNOW, HOWIE COULD ALSO HAVE GILL HELD HOSTAGE AT THIS WAREHOUSE HE MENTIONS IN THE EMAIL.
WE JUST... CAN'T BE SURE.

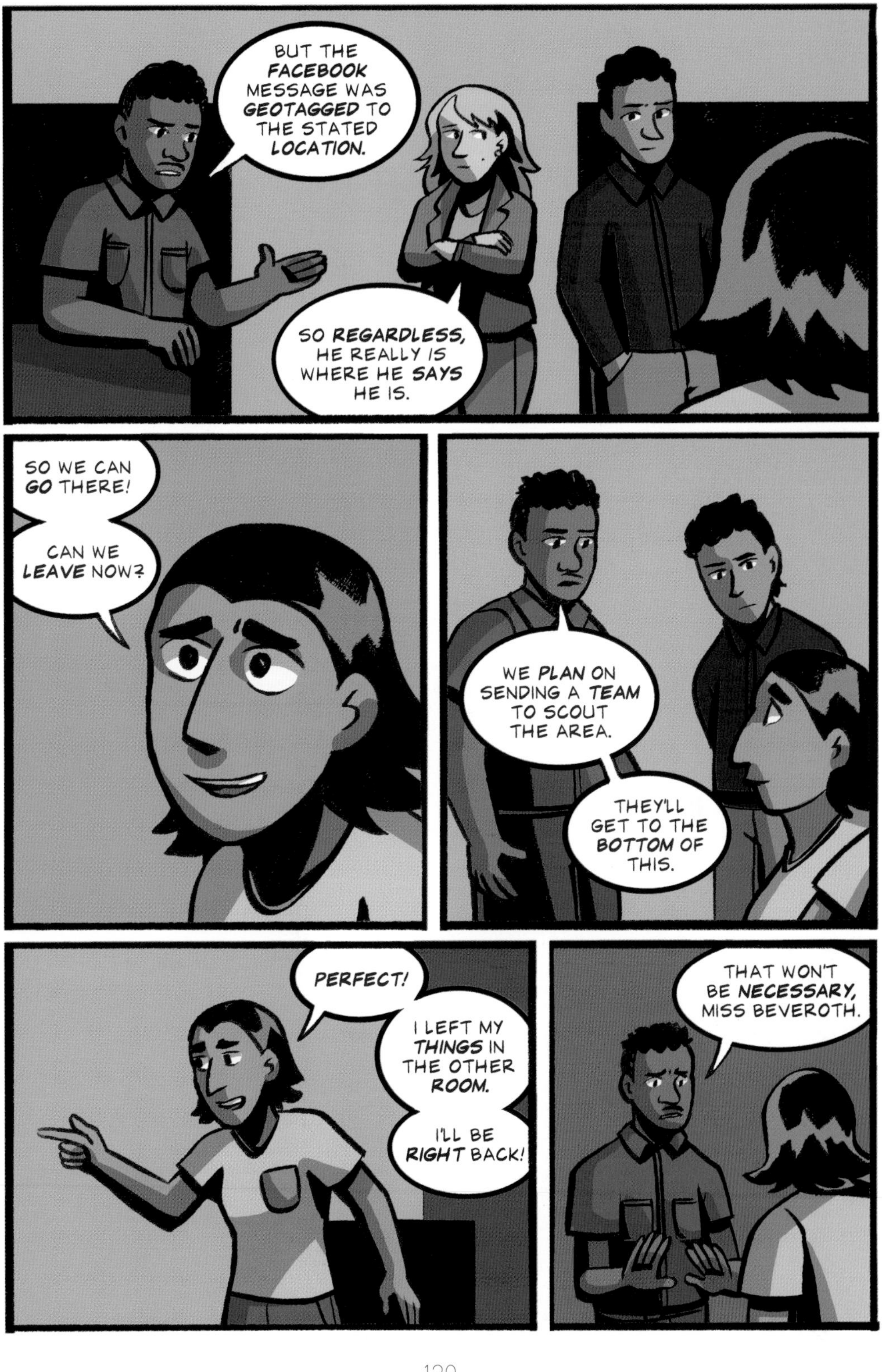
BUT THE FACEBOOK MESSAGE WAS GEOTAGGED TO THE STATED LOCATION.
SO REGARDLESS, HE REALLY IS WHERE HE SAYS HE IS.
SO WE CAN GO THERE!
CAN WE LEAVE NOW?
WE PLAN ON SENDING A TEAM TO SCOUT THE AREA.
THEY'LL GET TO THE BOTTOM OF THIS.
PERFECT!
I LEFT MY THINGS IN THE OTHER ROOM.
I'LL BE RIGHT BACK!
THAT WON'T BE NECESSARY, MISS BEVEROTH.

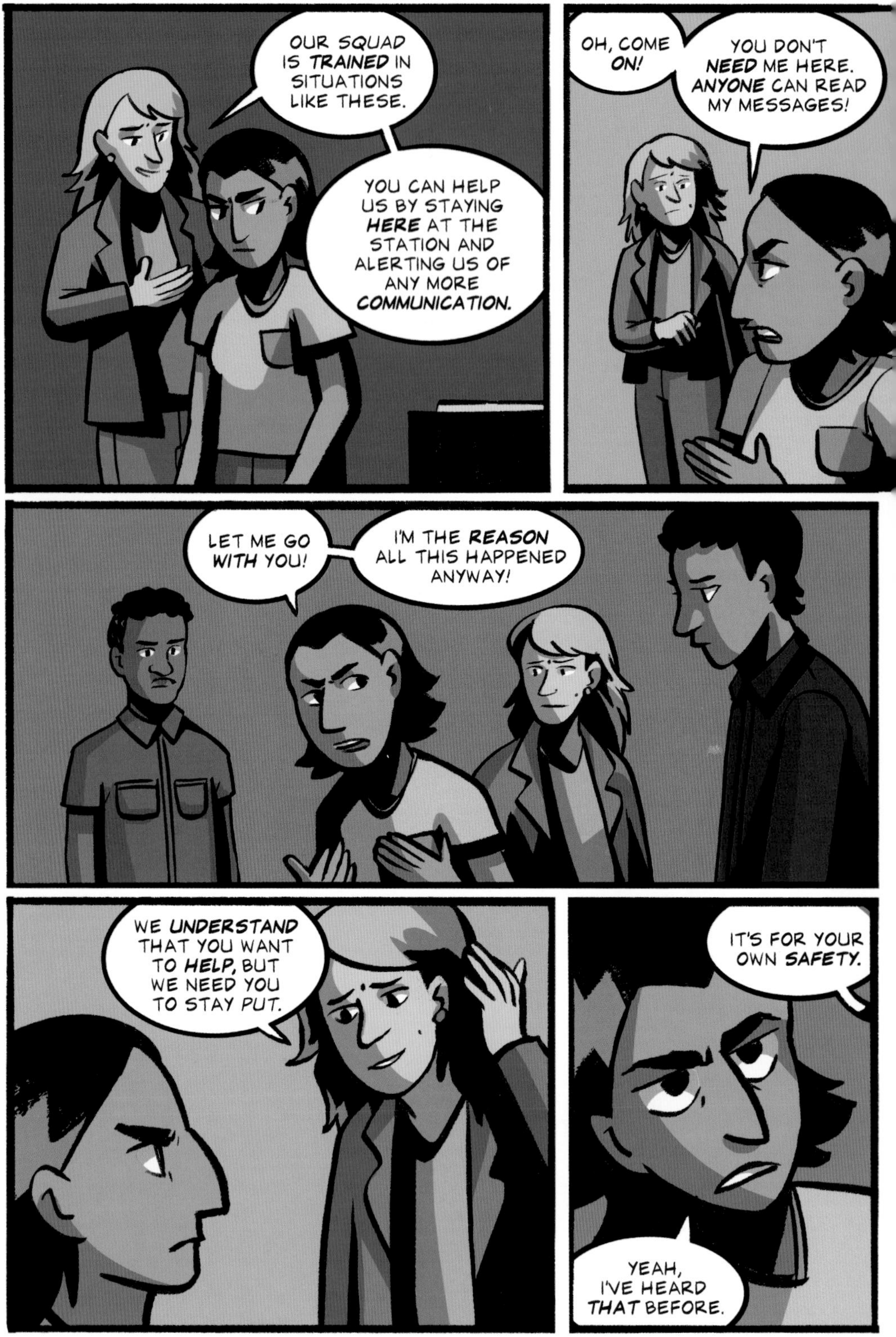
OUR SQUAD IS TRAINED IN SITUATIONS LIKE THESE.
YOU CAN HELP US BY STAYING HERE AT THE STATION AND ALERTING US OF ANY MORE COMMUNICATION.
OH, COME ON!
YOU DON'T NEED ME HERE. ANYONE CAN READ MY MESSAGES!
LET ME GO WITH YOU!
I'M THE REASON ALL THIS HAPPENED ANYWAY!
WE UNDERSTAND THAT YOU WANT TO HELP, BUT WE NEED YOU TO STAY PUT.
IT'S FOR YOUR OWN SAFETY.
YEAH, I'VE HEARD THAT BEFORE.

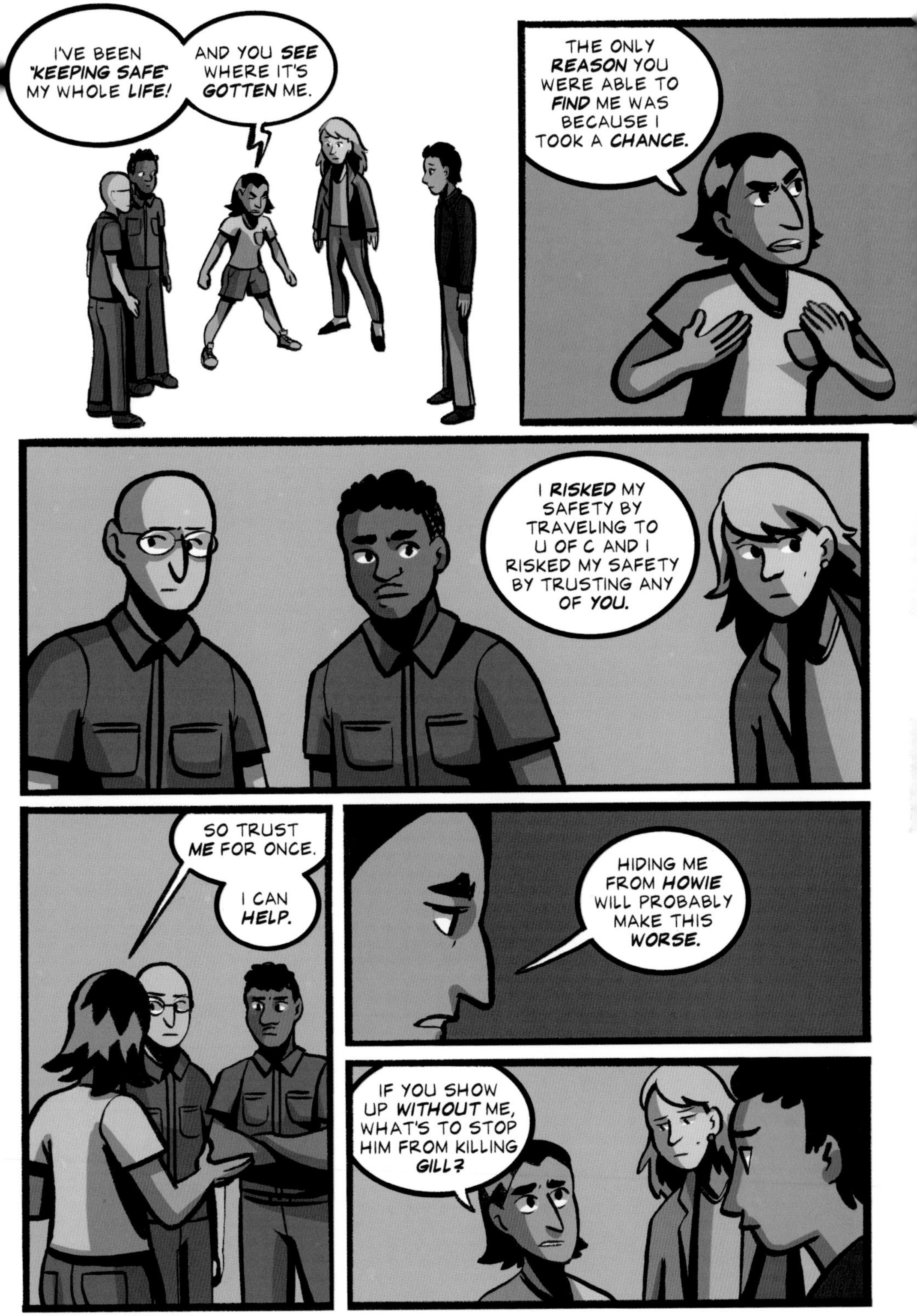
I'VE BEEN "KEEPING SAFE" MY WHOLE LIFE!
AND YOU SEE WHERE IT'S GOTTEN ME.
THE ONLY REASON YOU WERE ABLE TO FIND ME WAS BECAUSE I TOOK A CHANCE.
I RISKED MY SAFETY BY TRAVELING TO U OF C AND I RISKED MY SAFETY BY TRUSTING ANY OF YOU.
SO TRUST ME FOR ONCE.
I CAN HELP.
HIDING ME FROM HOWIE WILL PROBABLY MAKE THIS WORSE.
IF YOU SHOW UP WITHOUT ME, WHAT'S TO STOP HIM FROM KILLING GILL?

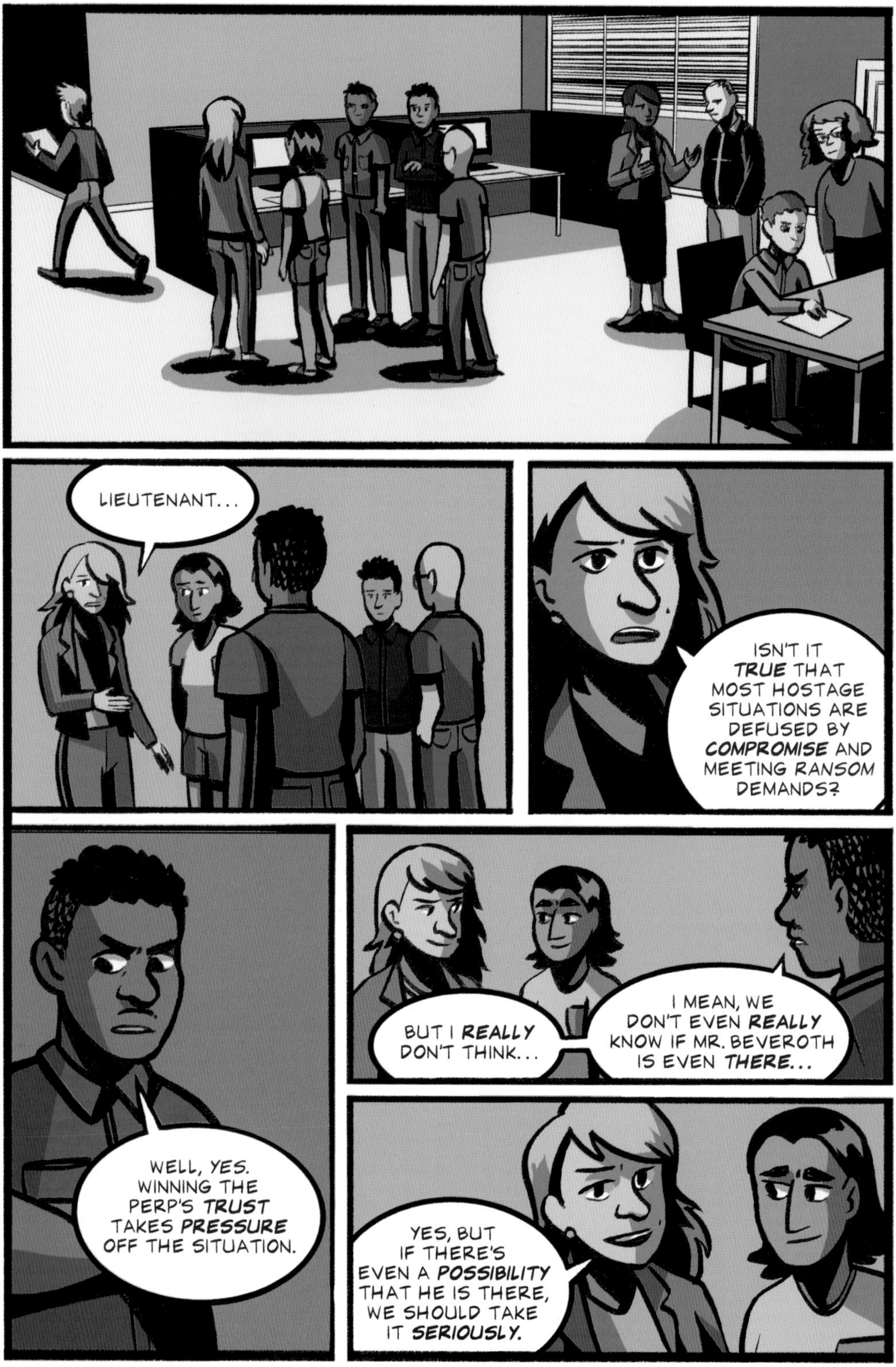
LIEUTENANT...
ISN'T IT TRUE THAT MOST HOSTAGE SITUATIONS ARE DEFUSED BY COMPROMISE AND MEETING RANSOM DEMANDS?
WELL, YES. WINNING THE PERP'S TRUST TAKES PRESSURE OFF THE SITUATION.
BUT I REALLY DON'T THINK...
I MEAN, WE DON'T EVEN REALLY KNOW IF MR. BEVEROTH IS EVEN THERE...
YES, BUT IF THERE'S EVEN A POSSIBILITY THAT HE IS THERE, WE SHOULD TAKE IT SERIOUSLY.

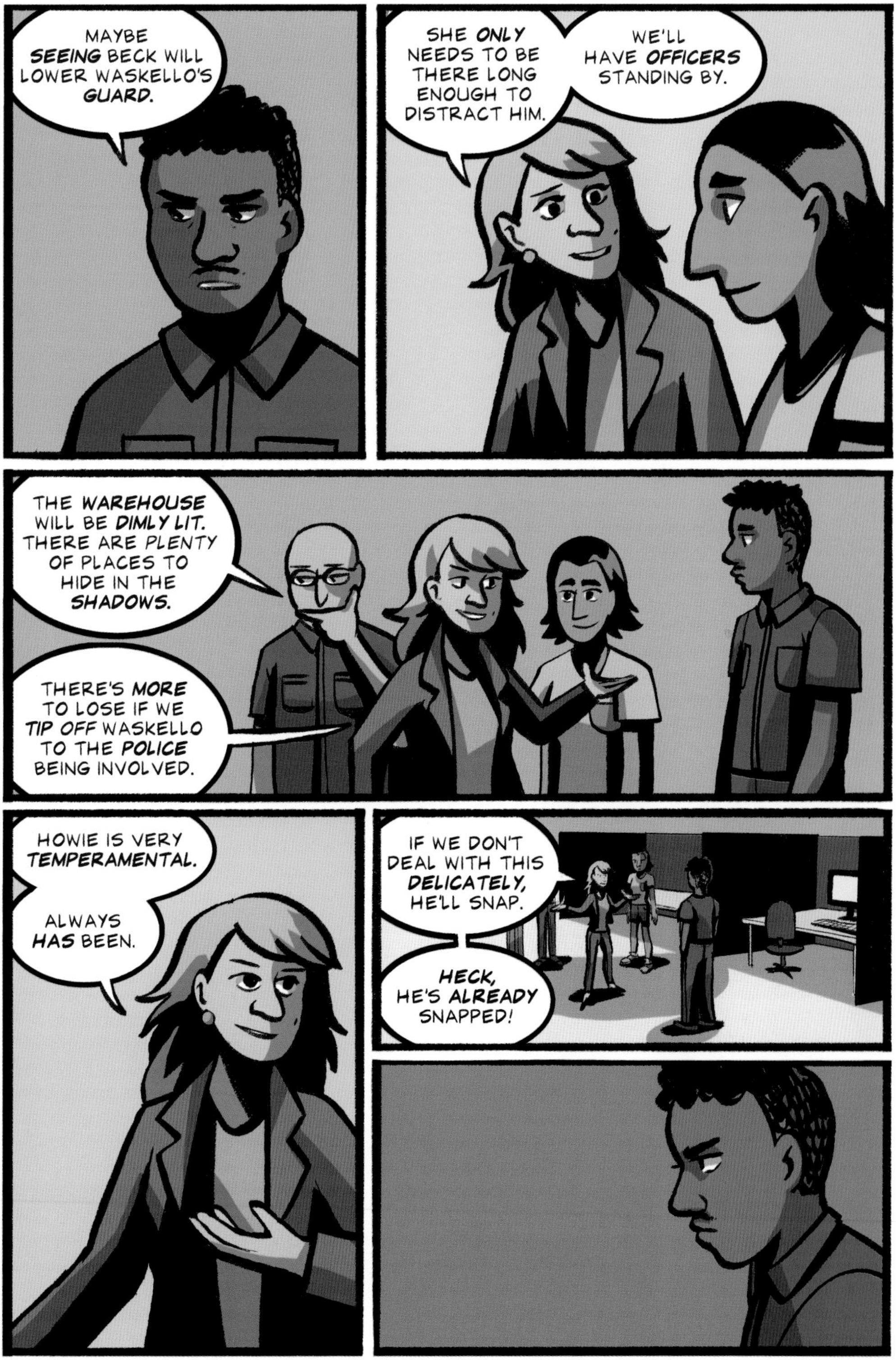
MAYBE SEEING BECK WILL LOWER WASKELLO'S GUARD.
SHE ONLY NEEDS TO BE THERE LONG ENOUGH TO DISTRACT HIM.
WE'LL HAVE OFFICERS STANDING BY.
THE WAREHOUSE WILL BE DIMLY LIT. THERE ARE PLENTY OF PLACES TO HIDE IN THE SHADOWS.
THERE'S MORE TO LOSE IF WE TIP OFF WASKELLO TO THE POLICE BEING INVOLVED.
HOWIE IS VERY TEMPERAMENTAL.
ALWAYS HAS BEEN.
IF WE DON'T DEAL WITH THIS DELICATELY, HE'LL SNAP.
HECK, HE'S ALREADY SNAPPED!

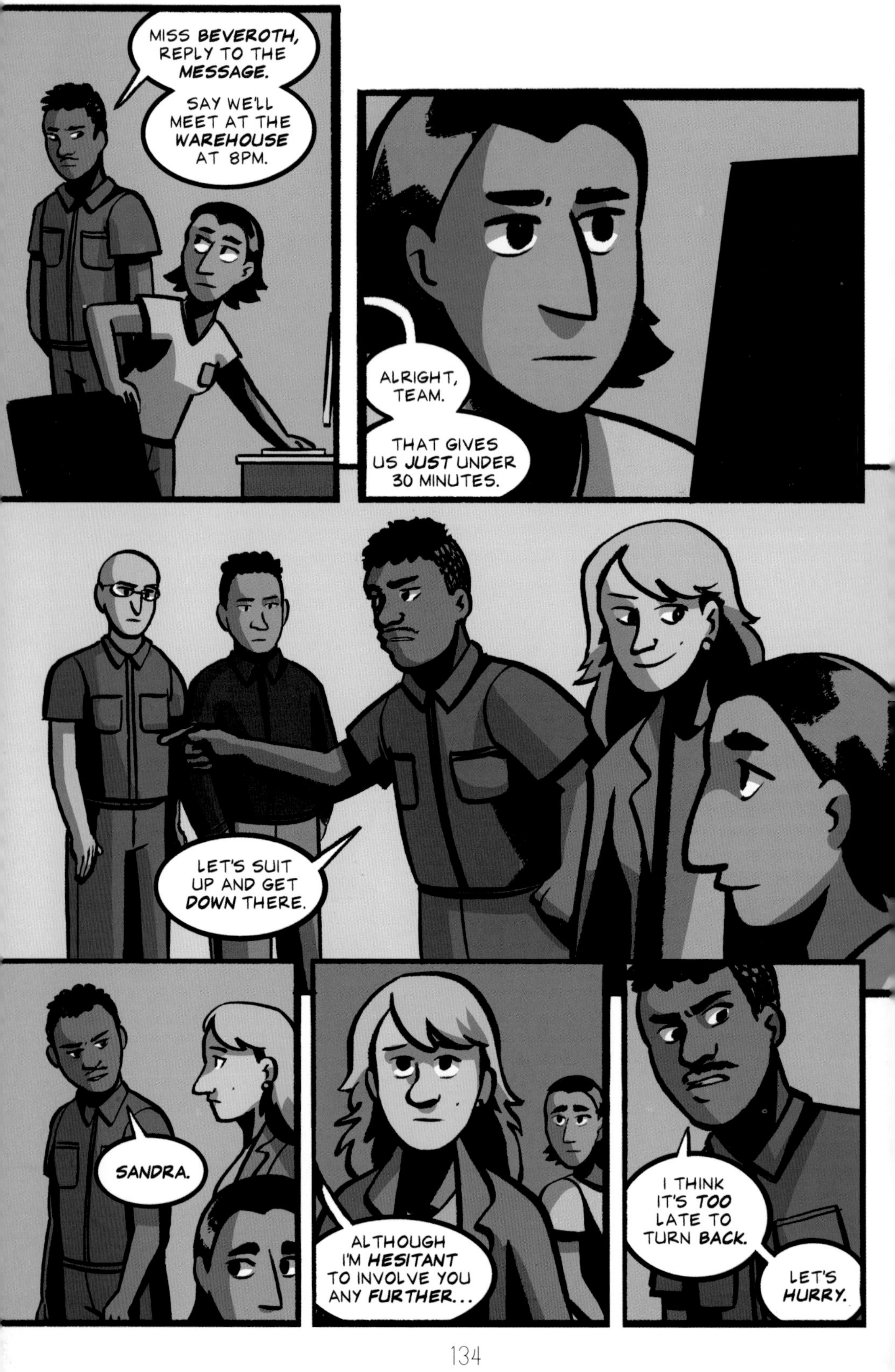
MISS BEVEROTH, REPLY TO THE MESSAGE.
SAY WE'LL MEET AT THE WAREHOUSE AT 8PM.
ALRIGHT, TEAM.
THAT GIVES US JUST UNDER 30 MINUTES.
LET'S SUIT UP AND GET DOWN THERE.
SANDRA.
ALTHOUGH I'M HESITANT TO INVOLVE YOU ANY FURTHER...
I THINK IT'S TOO LATE TO TURN BACK.
LET'S HURRY.

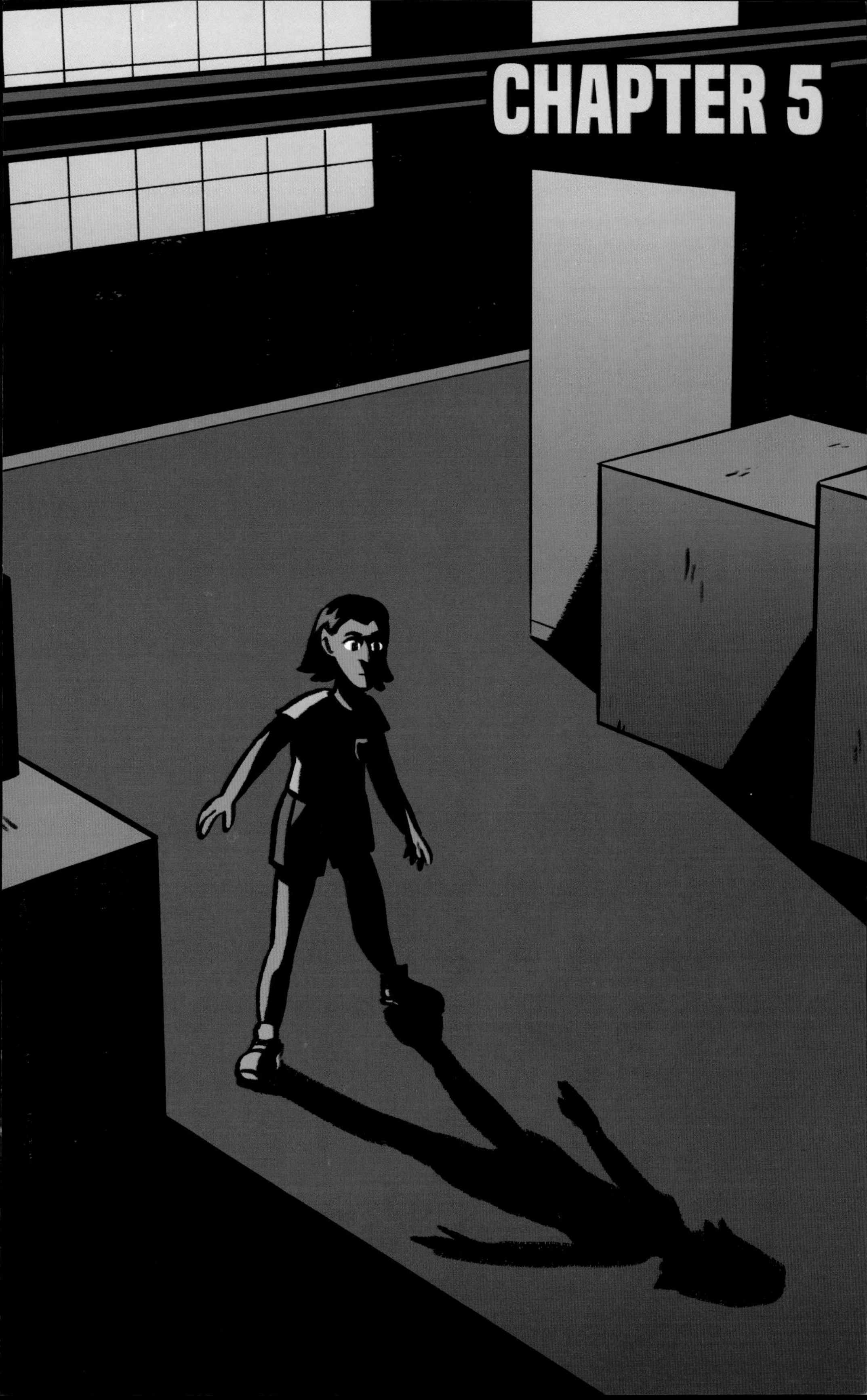
CHAPTER 5

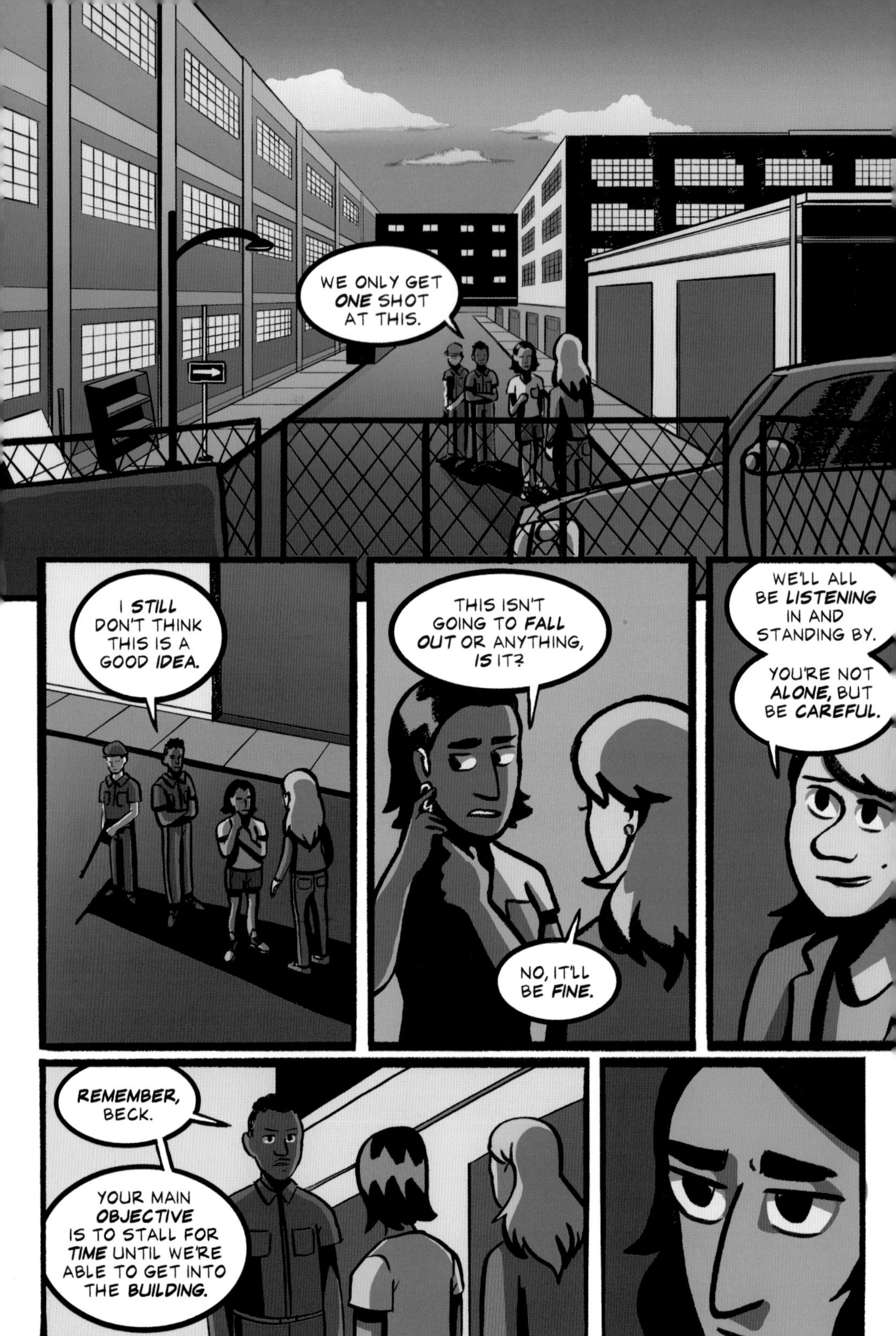
WE ONLY GET ONE SHOT AT THIS.
I STILL DON'T THINK THIS IS A GOOD IDEA.
THIS ISN'T GOING TO FALL OUT OR ANYTHING, IS IT?
NO, IT'LL BE FINE.
WE'LL ALL BE LISTENING IN AND STANDING BY.
YOU'RE NOT ALONE, BUT BE CAREFUL.
REMEMBER, BECK.
YOUR MAIN OBJECTIVE IS TO STALL FOR TIME UNTIL WE'RE ABLE TO GET INTO THE BUILDING.

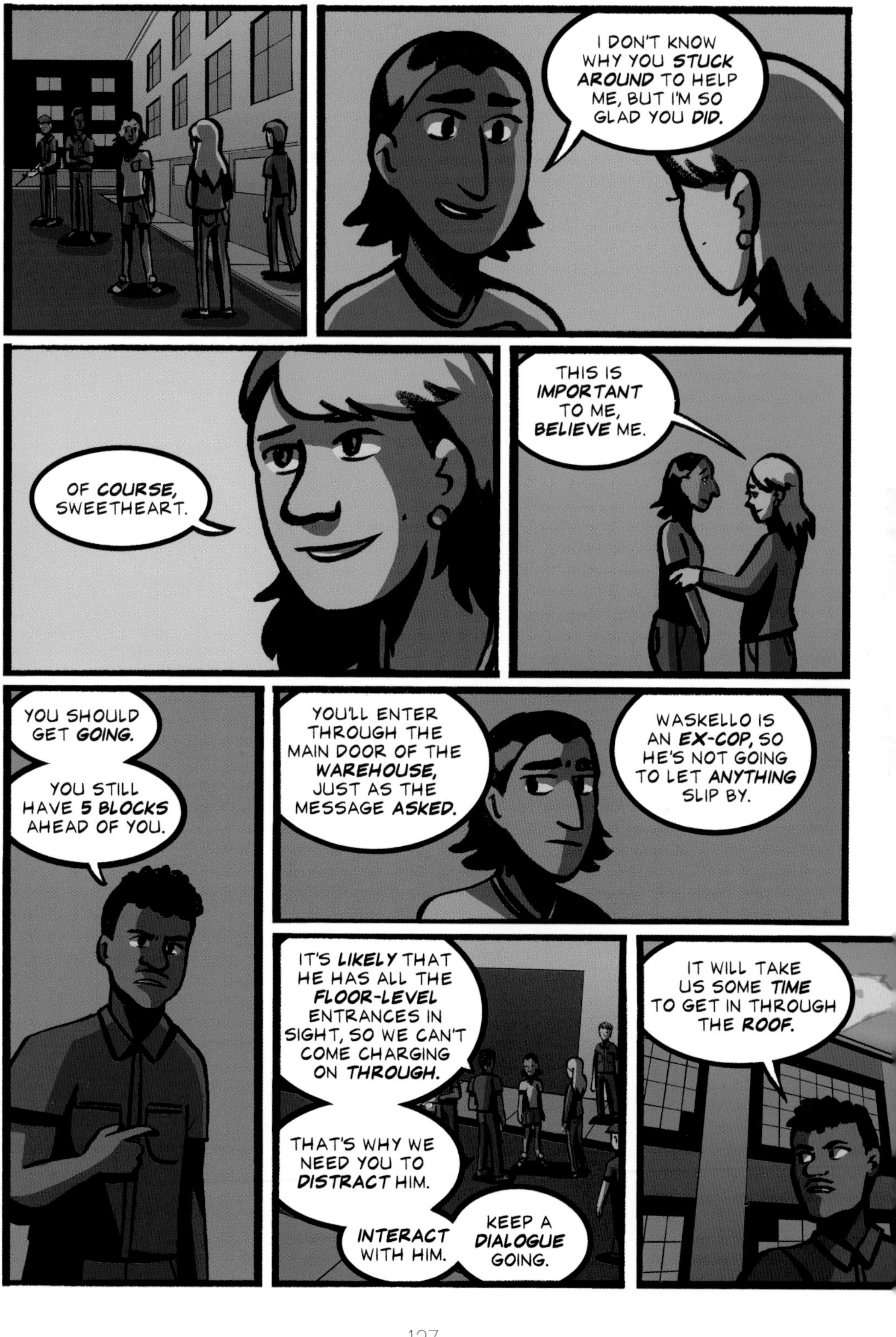
I DON'T KNOW WHY YOU STUCK AROUND TO HELP ME, BUT I'M SO GLAD YOU DID.
OF COURSE, SWEETHEART.
THIS IS IMPORTANT TO ME, BELIEVE ME.
YOU SHOULD GET GOING.
YOU STILL HAVE 5 BLOCKS AHEAD OF YOU.
YOU'LL ENTER THROUGH THE MAIN DOOR OF THE WAREHOUSE, JUST AS THE MESSAGE ASKED.
WASKELLO IS AN EX-COP, SO HE'S NOT GOING TO LET ANYTHING SLIP BY.
IT'S LIKELY THAT HE HAS ALL THE FLOOR-LEVEL ENTRANCES IN SIGHT, SO WE CAN'T COME CHARGING ON THROUGH.
THAT'S WHY WE NEED YOU TO DISTRACT HIM.
INTERACT WITH HIM.
KEEP A DIALOGUE GOING.
IT WILL TAKE US SOME TIME TO GET IN THROUGH THE ROOF.

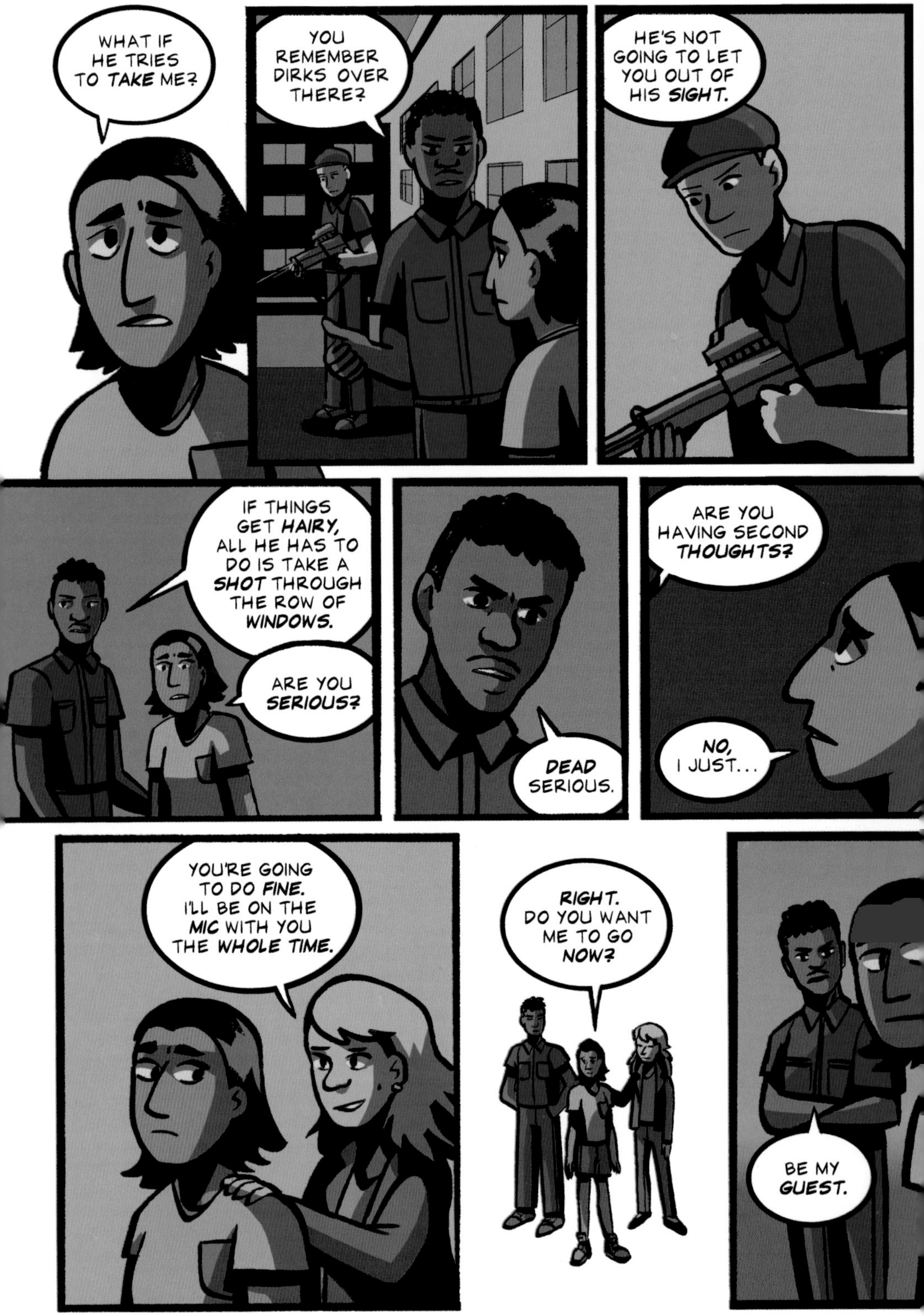

WHAT IF HE TRIES TO TAKE ME?
YOU REMEMBER DIRKS OVER THERE?
HE'S NOT GOING TO LET YOU OUT OF HIS SIGHT.
IF THINGS GET HAIRY, ALL HE HAS TO DO IS TAKE A SHOT THROUGH THE ROW OF WINDOWS.
ARE YOU SERIOUS?
DEAD SERIOUS.
ARE YOU HAVING SECOND THOUGHTS?
NO, I JUST...
YOU'RE GOING TO DO FINE. I'LL BE ON THE MIC WITH YOU THE WHOLE TIME.
RIGHT. DO YOU WANT ME TO GO NOW?
BE MY GUEST.

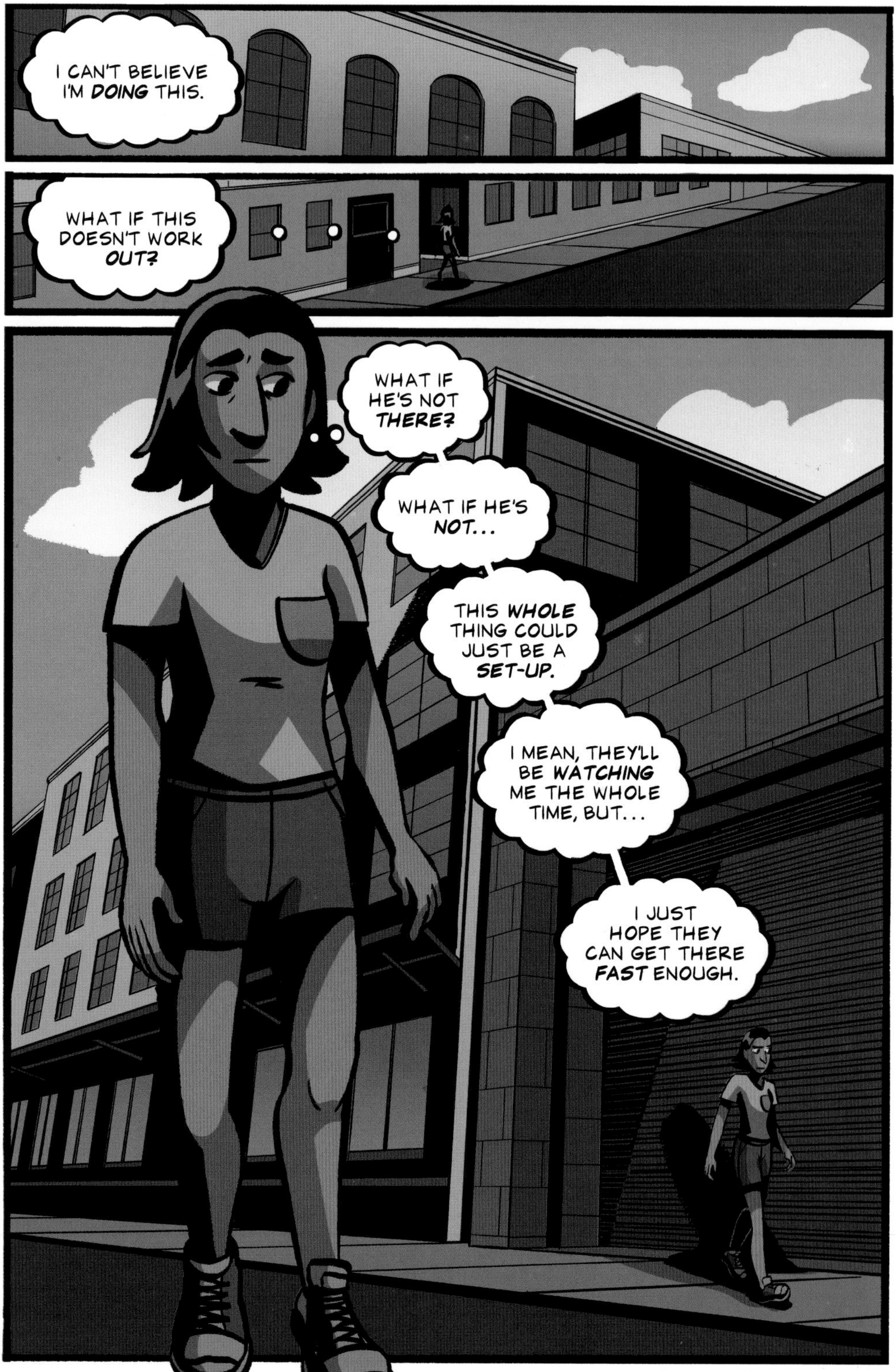
I CAN'T BELIEVE I'M DOING THIS.
WHAT IF THIS DOESN'T WORK OUT?
WHAT IF HE'S NOT THERE?
WHAT IF HE'S NOT...
THIS WHOLE THING COULD JUST BE A SET-UP.
I MEAN, THEY'LL BE WATCHING ME THE WHOLE TIME, BUT...
I JUST HOPE THEY CAN GET THERE FAST ENOUGH.

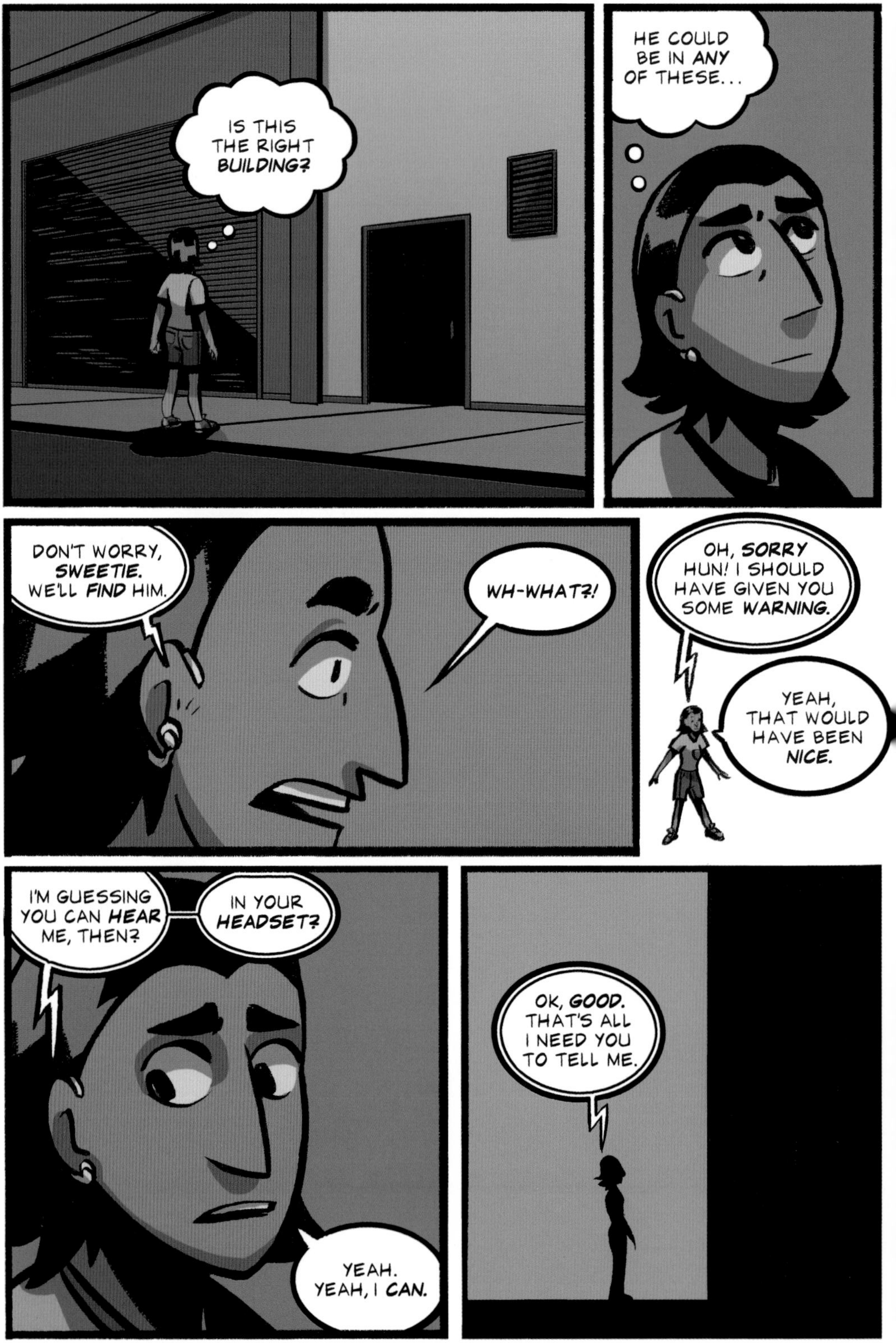
IS THIS THE RIGHT BUILDING?
HE COULD BE IN ANY OF THESE...
DON'T WORRY, SWEETIE. WE'LL FIND HIM.
WH-WHAT?!
OH, SORRY HUN! I SHOULD HAVE GIVEN YOU SOME WARNING.
YEAH, THAT WOULD HAVE BEEN NICE.
I'M GUESSING YOU CAN HEAR ME, THEN?
IN YOUR HEADSET?
YEAH. YEAH, I CAN.
OK, GOOD. THAT'S ALL I NEED YOU TO TELL ME.

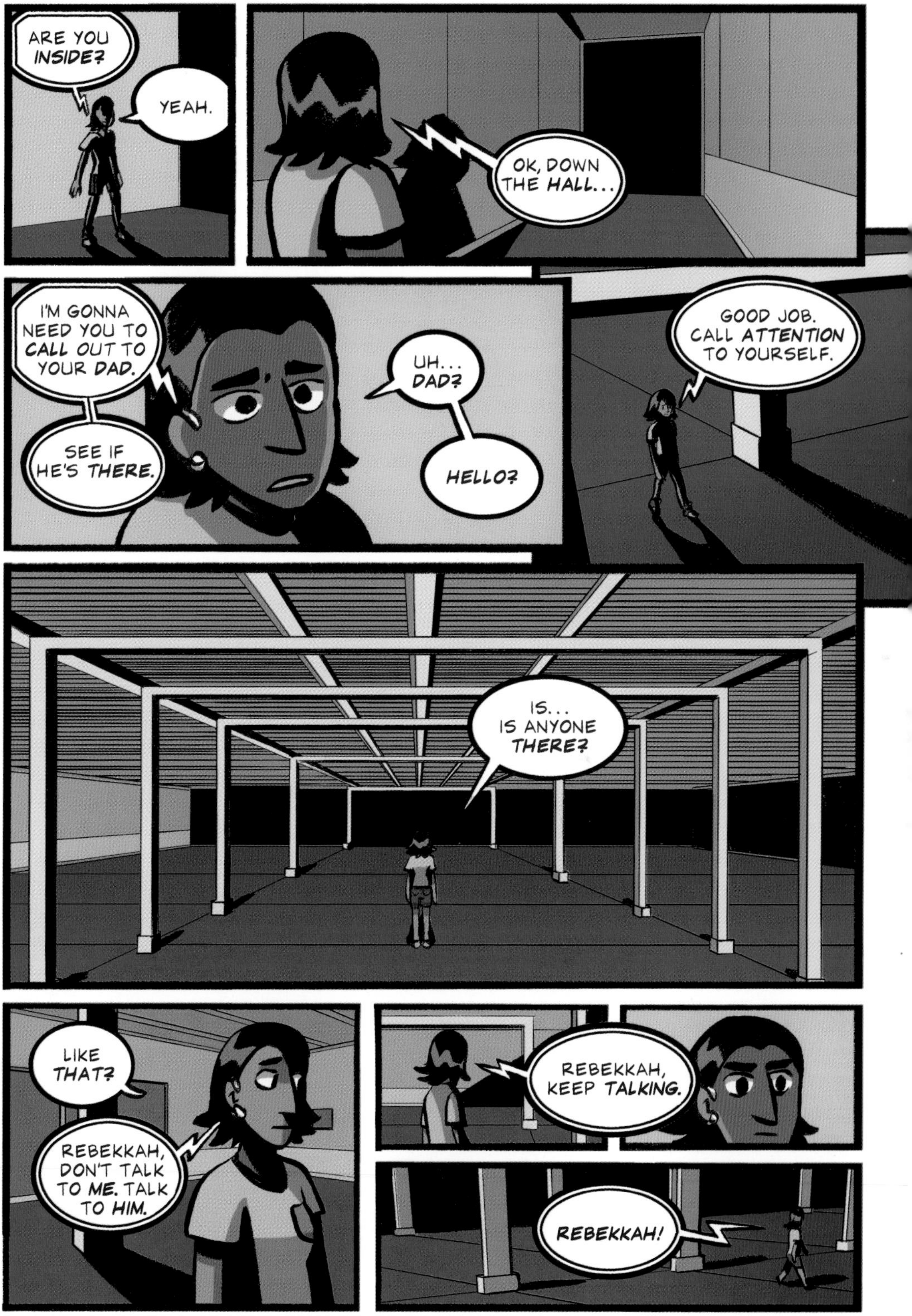
ARE YOU INSIDE?
YEAH.
OK, DOWN THE HALL...
I'M GONNA NEED YOU TO CALL OUT TO YOUR DAD.
SEE IF HE'S THERE.
UH... DAD?
HELLO?
GOOD JOB. CALL ATTENTION TO YOURSELF.
IS... IS ANYONE THERE?
LIKE THAT?
REBEKKAH, DON'T TALK TO ME. TALK TO HIM.
REBEKKAH, KEEP TALKING.
REBEKKAH!

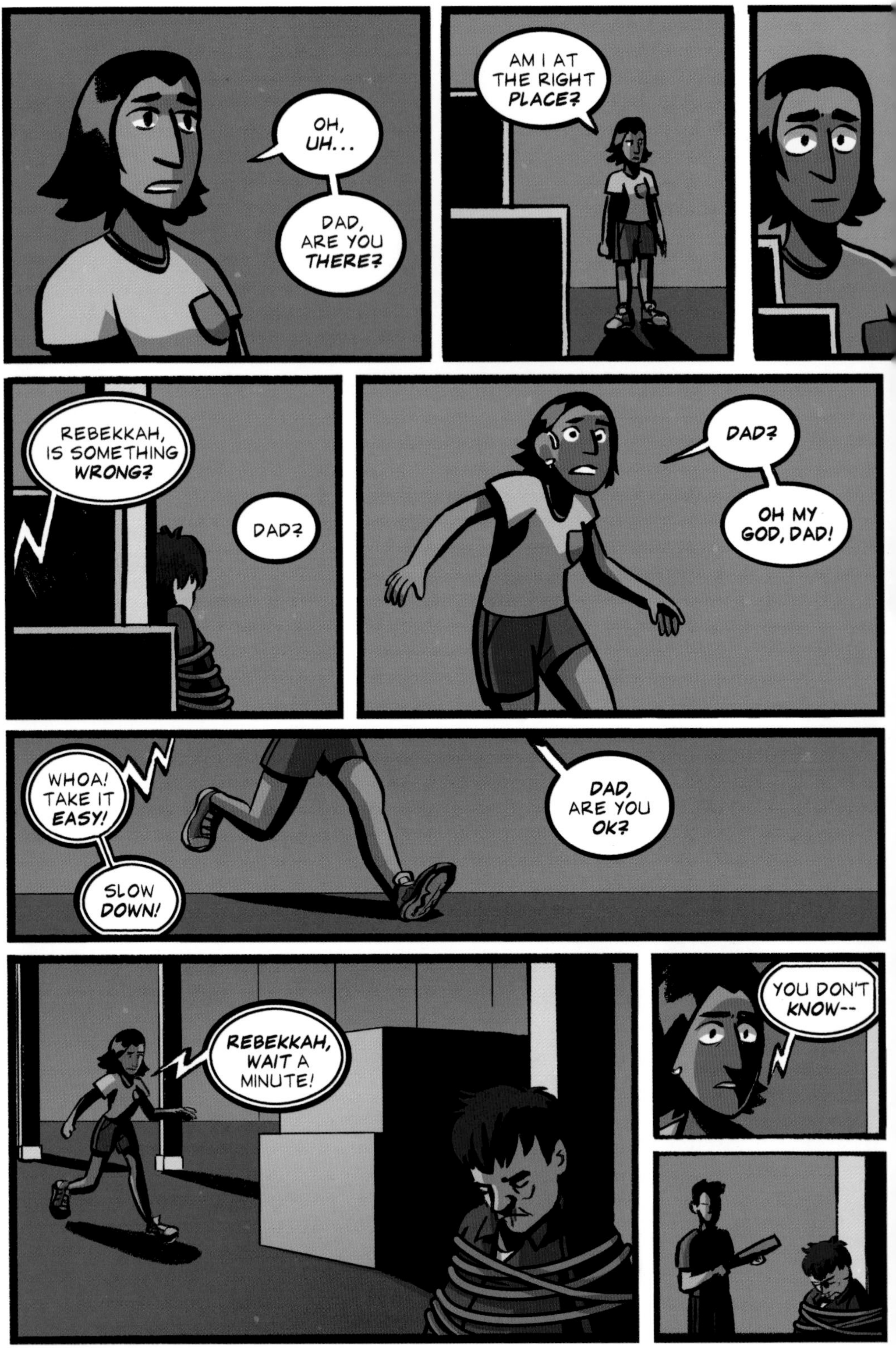
OH, UH...
DAD, ARE YOU THERE?
AM I AT THE RIGHT PLACE?
REBEKKAH, IS SOMETHING WRONG?
DAD?
DAD?
OH MY GOD, DAD!
WHOA! TAKE IT EASY!
SLOW DOWN!
DAD, ARE YOU OK?
REBEKKAH, WAIT A MINUTE!
YOU DON'T KNOW--

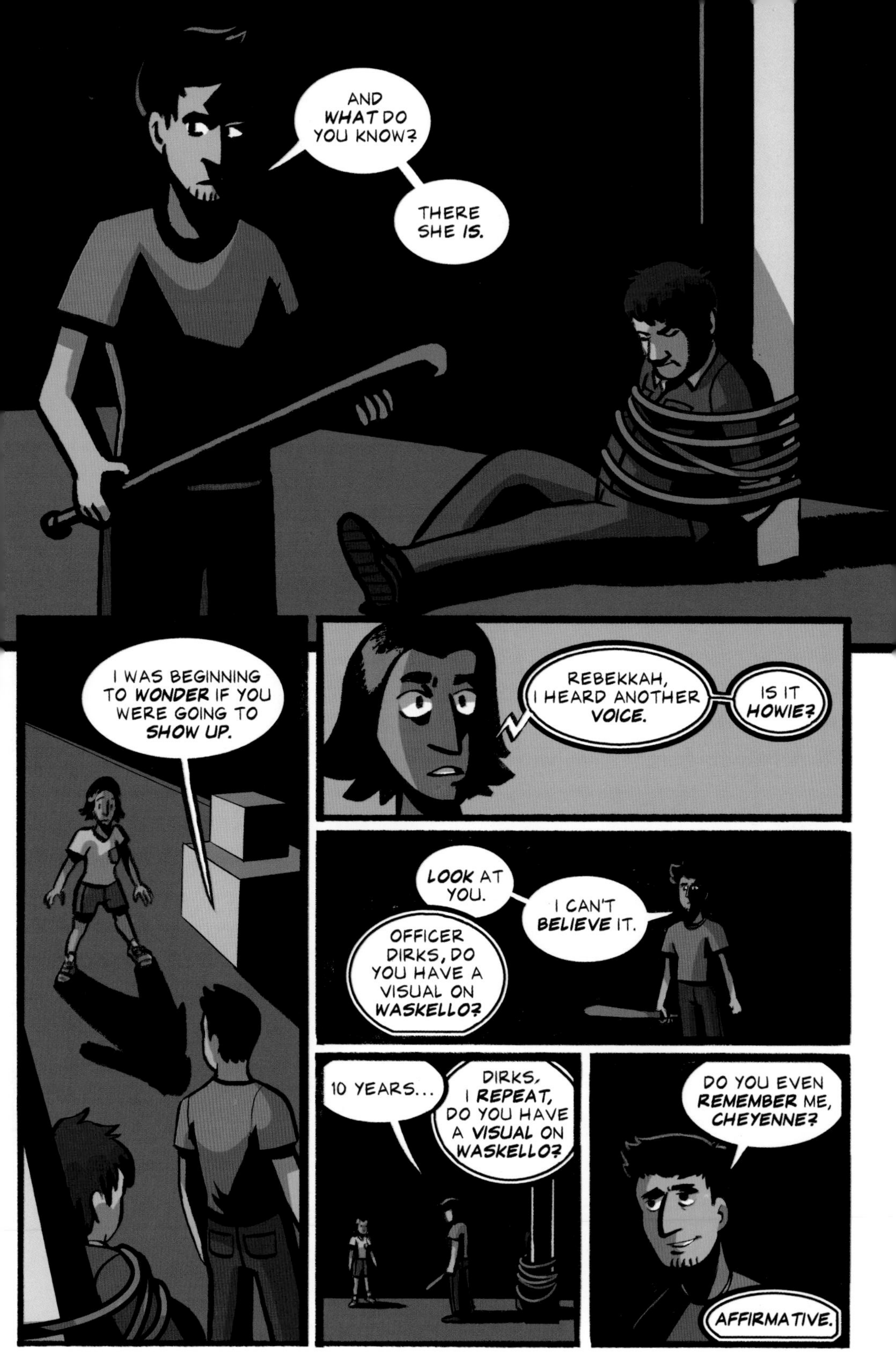
AND WHAT DO YOU KNOW?
THERE SHE IS.
I WAS BEGINNING TO WONDER IF YOU WERE GOING TO SHOW UP.
REBEKKAH, I HEARD ANOTHER VOICE.
IS IT HOWIE?
LOOK AT YOU.
I CAN'T BELIEVE IT.
OFFICER DIRKS, DO YOU HAVE A VISUAL ON WASKELLO?
10 YEARS...
DIRKS, I REPEAT, DO YOU HAVE A VISUAL ON WASKELLO?
DO YOU EVEN REMEMBER ME, CHEYENNE?
AFFIRMATIVE.

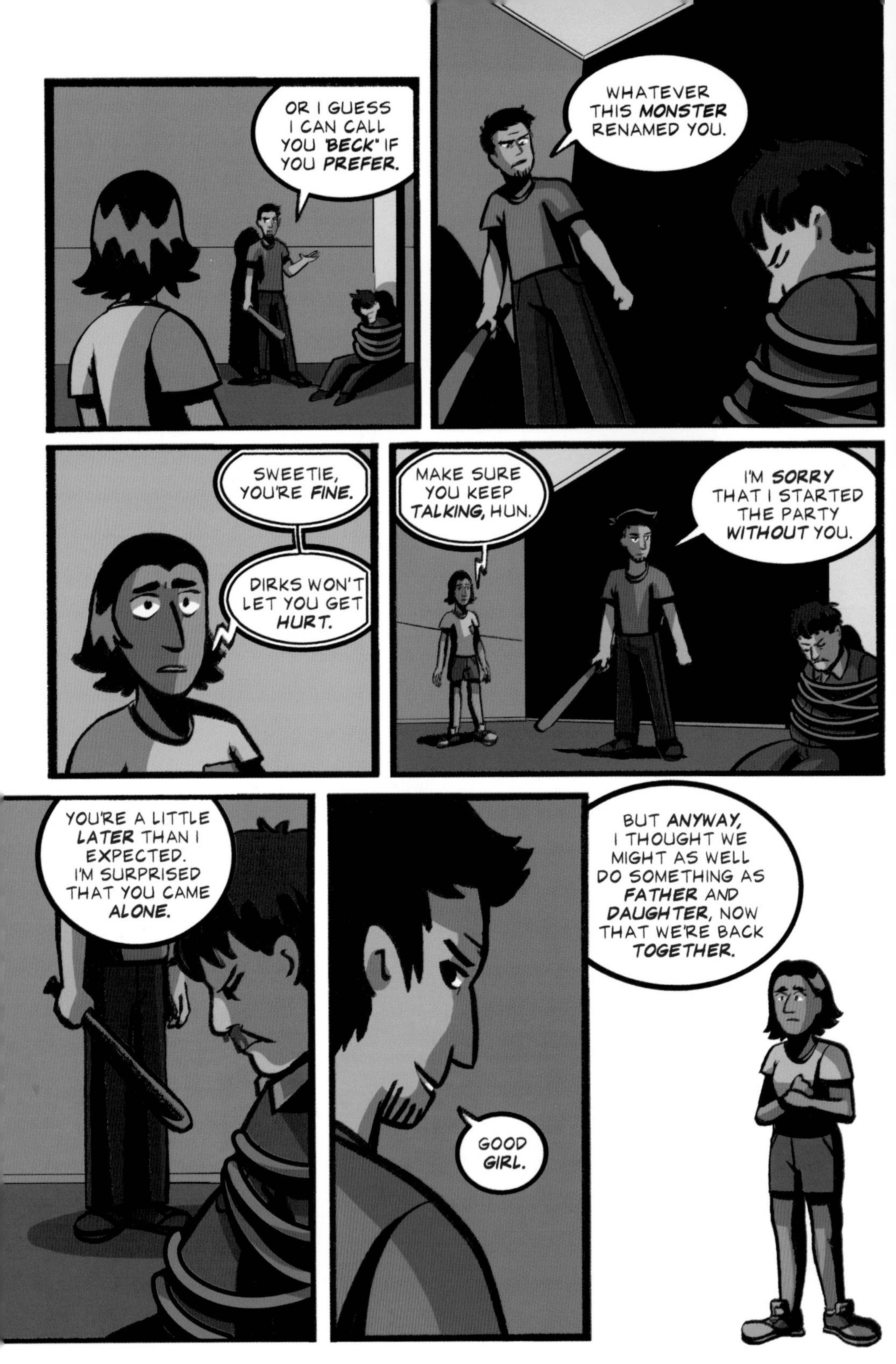
OR I GUESS I CAN CALL YOU "BECK" IF YOU PREFER.
WHATEVER THIS MONSTER RENAMED YOU.
SWEETIE, YOU'RE FINE.
DIRKS WON'T LET YOU GET HURT.
MAKE SURE YOU KEEP TALKING, HUN.
I'M SORRY THAT I STARTED THE PARTY WITHOUT YOU.
YOU'RE A LITTLE LATER THAN I EXPECTED. I'M SURPRISED THAT YOU CAME ALONE.
GOOD GIRL.
BUT ANYWAY, I THOUGHT WE MIGHT AS WELL DO SOMETHING AS FATHER AND DAUGHTER, NOW THAT WE'RE BACK TOGETHER.

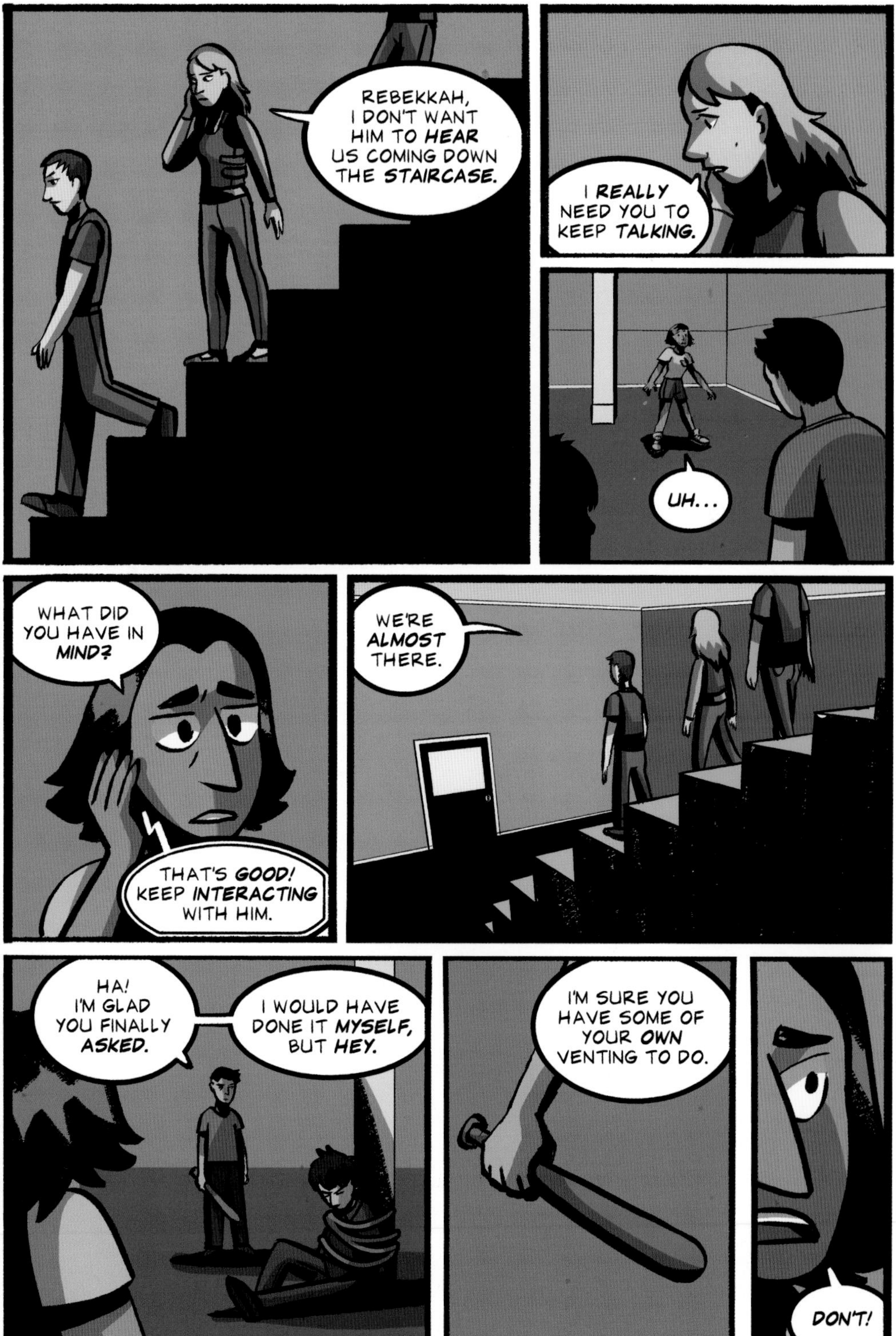
REBEKKAH, I DON'T WANT HIM TO HEAR US COMING DOWN THE STAIRCASE.
I REALLY NEED YOU TO KEEP TALKING.
UH...
WHAT DID YOU HAVE IN MIND?
THAT'S GOOD! KEEP INTERACTING WITH HIM.
WE'RE ALMOST THERE.
HA! I'M GLAD YOU FINALLY ASKED.
I WOULD HAVE DONE IT MYSELF, BUT HEY.
I'M SURE YOU HAVE SOME OF YOUR OWN VENTING TO DO.
DON'T!

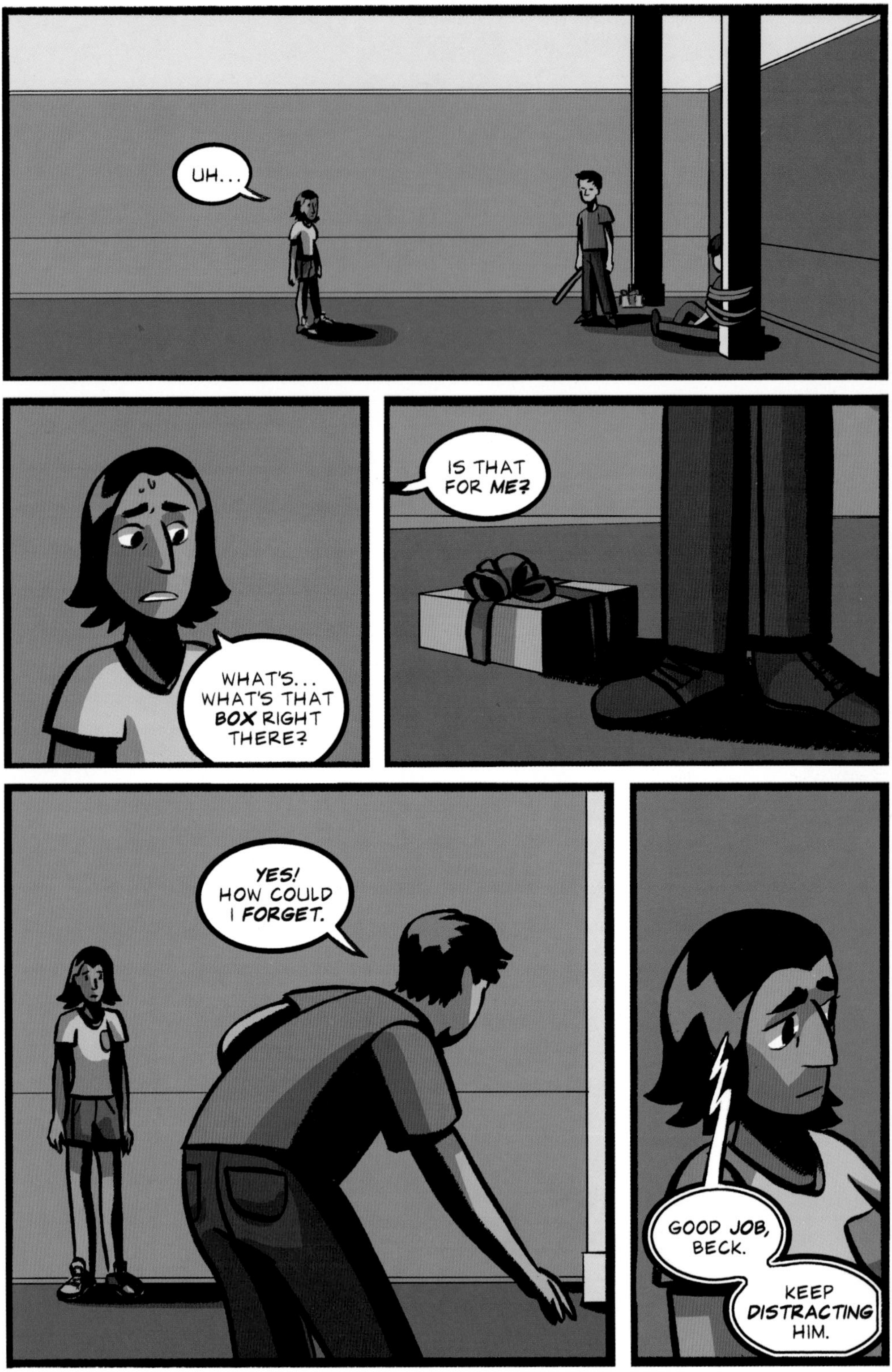
UH...
WHAT'S... WHAT'S THAT **BOX** RIGHT THERE?
IS THAT FOR **ME?**
YES! HOW COULD I **FORGET.**
GOOD **JOB**, BECK.
KEEP **DISTRACTING** HIM.

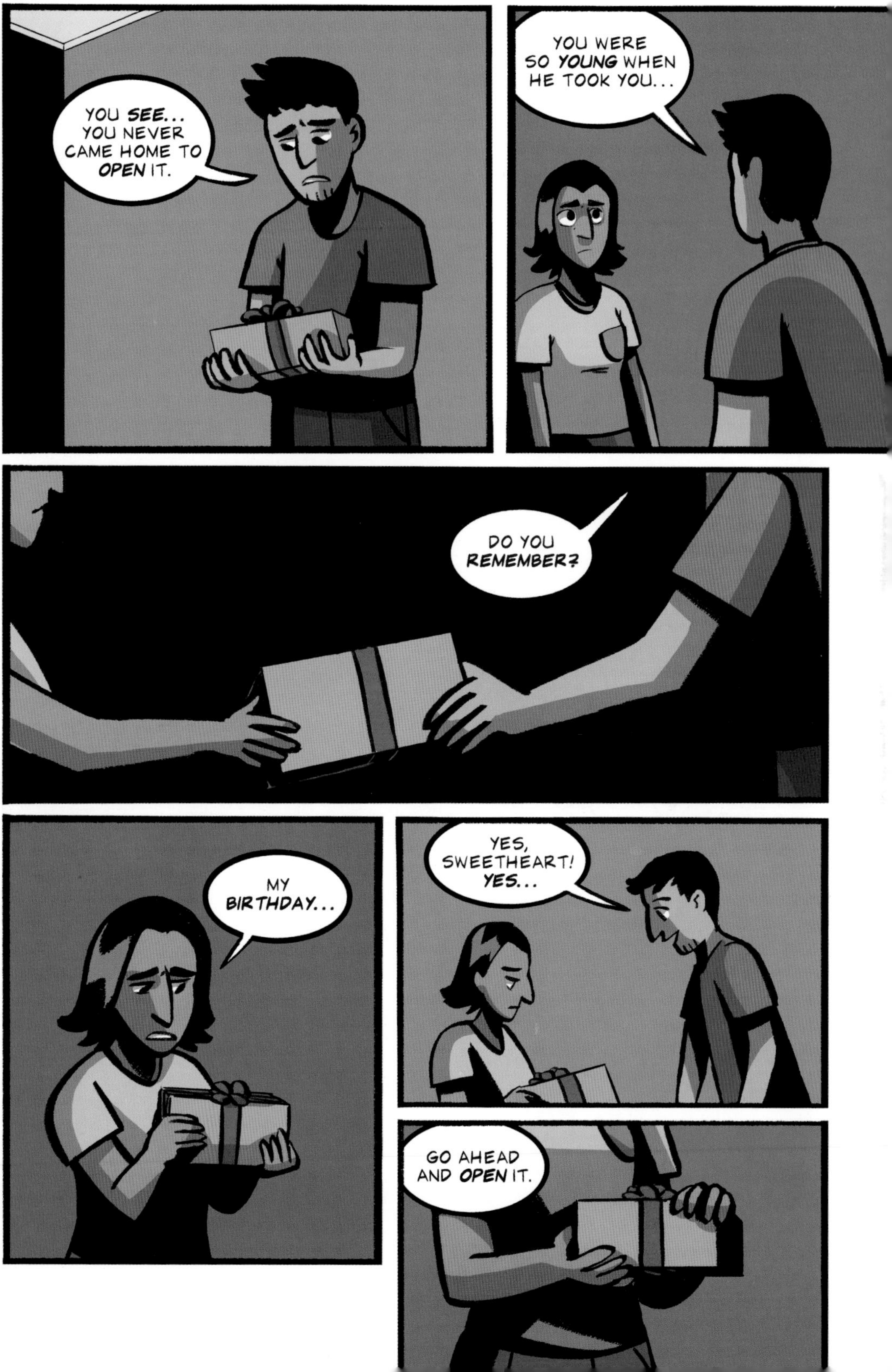
YOU **SEE...** YOU NEVER CAME HOME TO **OPEN** IT.
YOU WERE SO **YOUNG** WHEN HE TOOK YOU...
DO YOU **REMEMBER?**
MY **BIRTHDAY...**
YES, SWEETHEART! **YES...**
GO AHEAD AND **OPEN** IT.

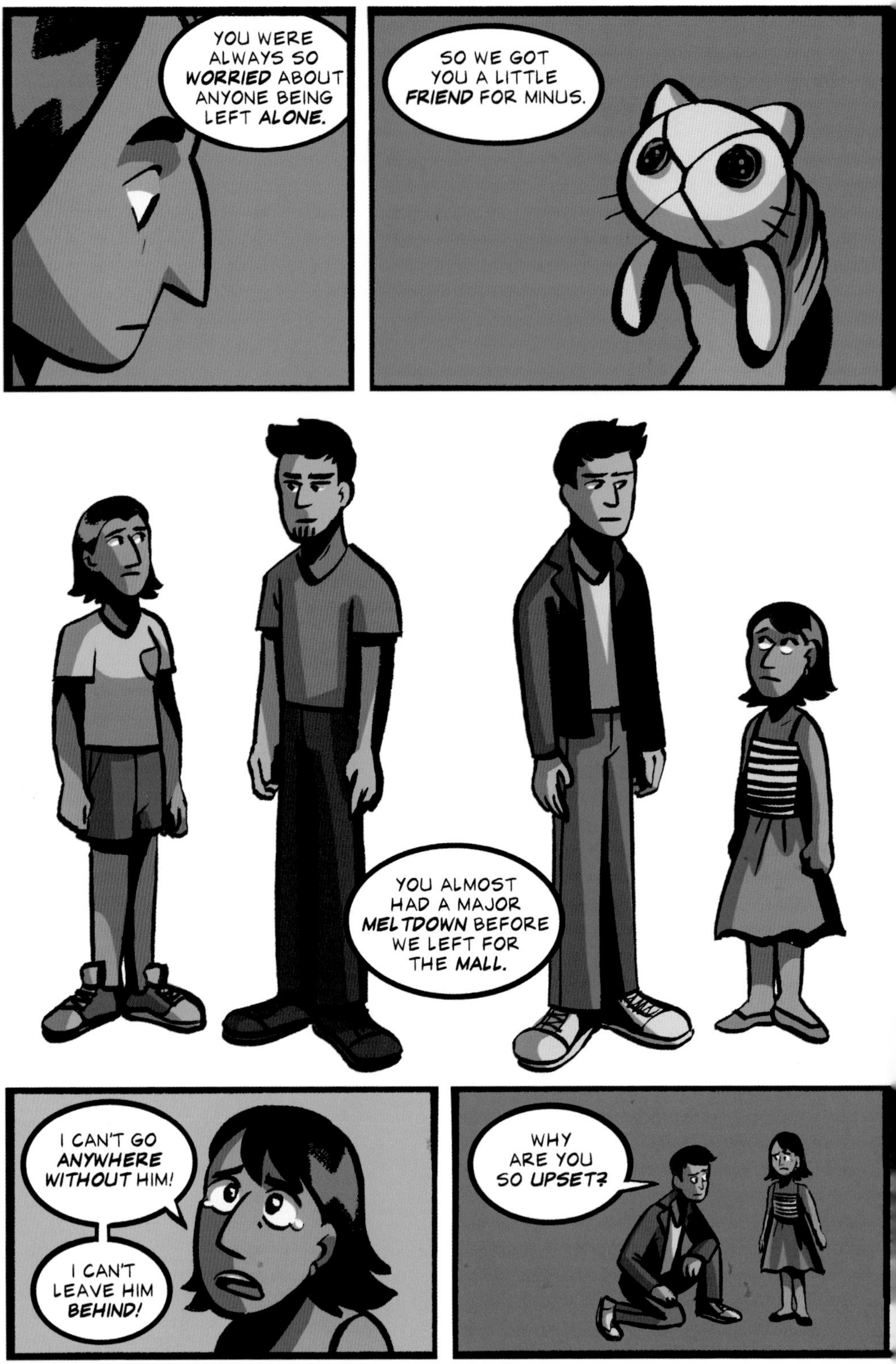
YOU WERE ALWAYS SO WORRIED ABOUT ANYONE BEING LEFT ALONE.
SO WE GOT YOU A LITTLE FRIEND FOR MINUS.
YOU ALMOST HAD A MAJOR MELTDOWN BEFORE WE LEFT FOR THE MALL.
I CAN'T GO ANYWHERE WITHOUT HIM!
I CAN'T LEAVE HIM BEHIND!
WHY ARE YOU SO UPSET?

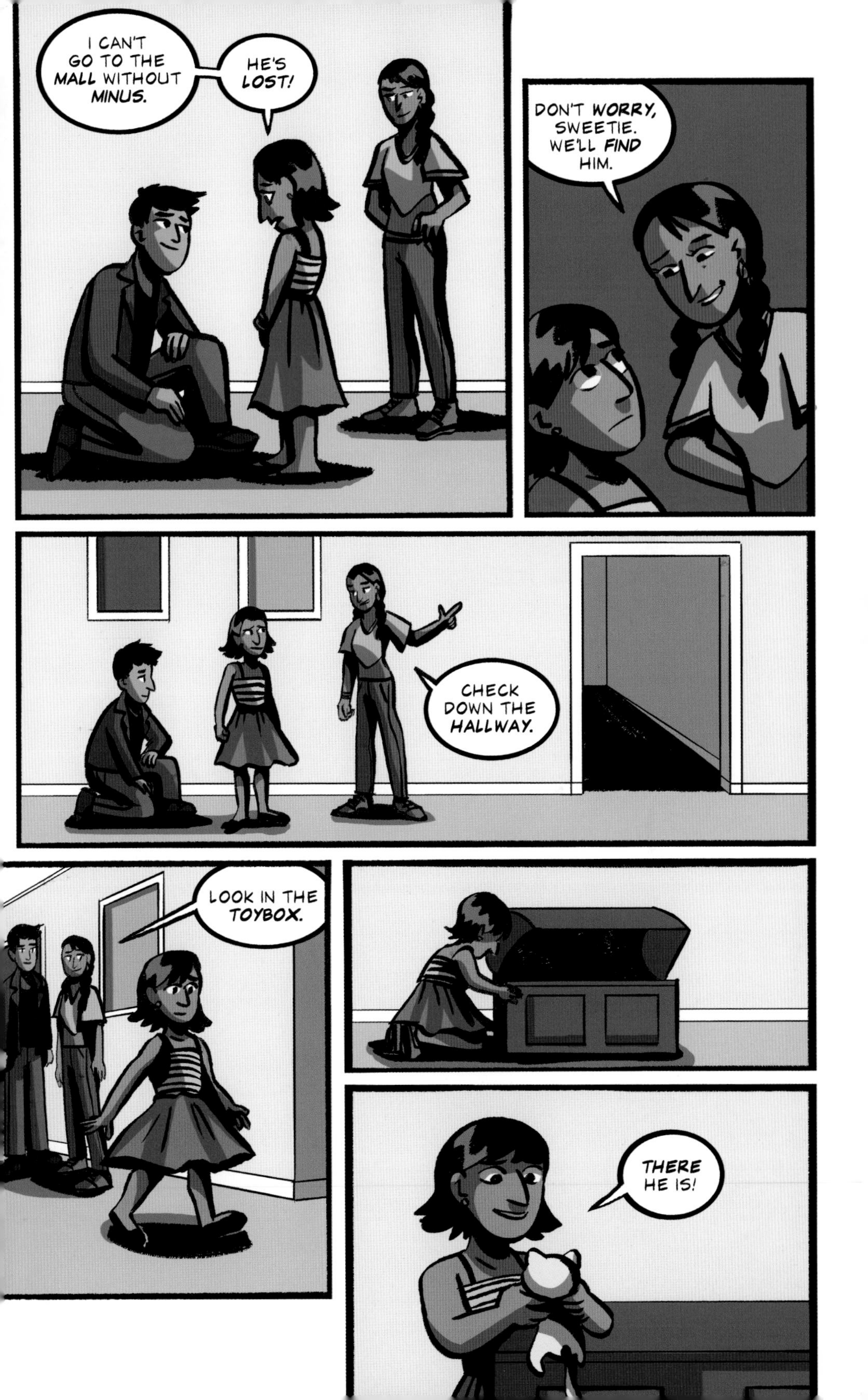
I CAN'T GO TO THE MALL WITHOUT MINUS.
HE'S LOST!
DON'T WORRY, SWEETIE. WE'LL FIND HIM.
CHECK DOWN THE HALLWAY.
LOOK IN THE TOYBOX.
THERE HE IS!

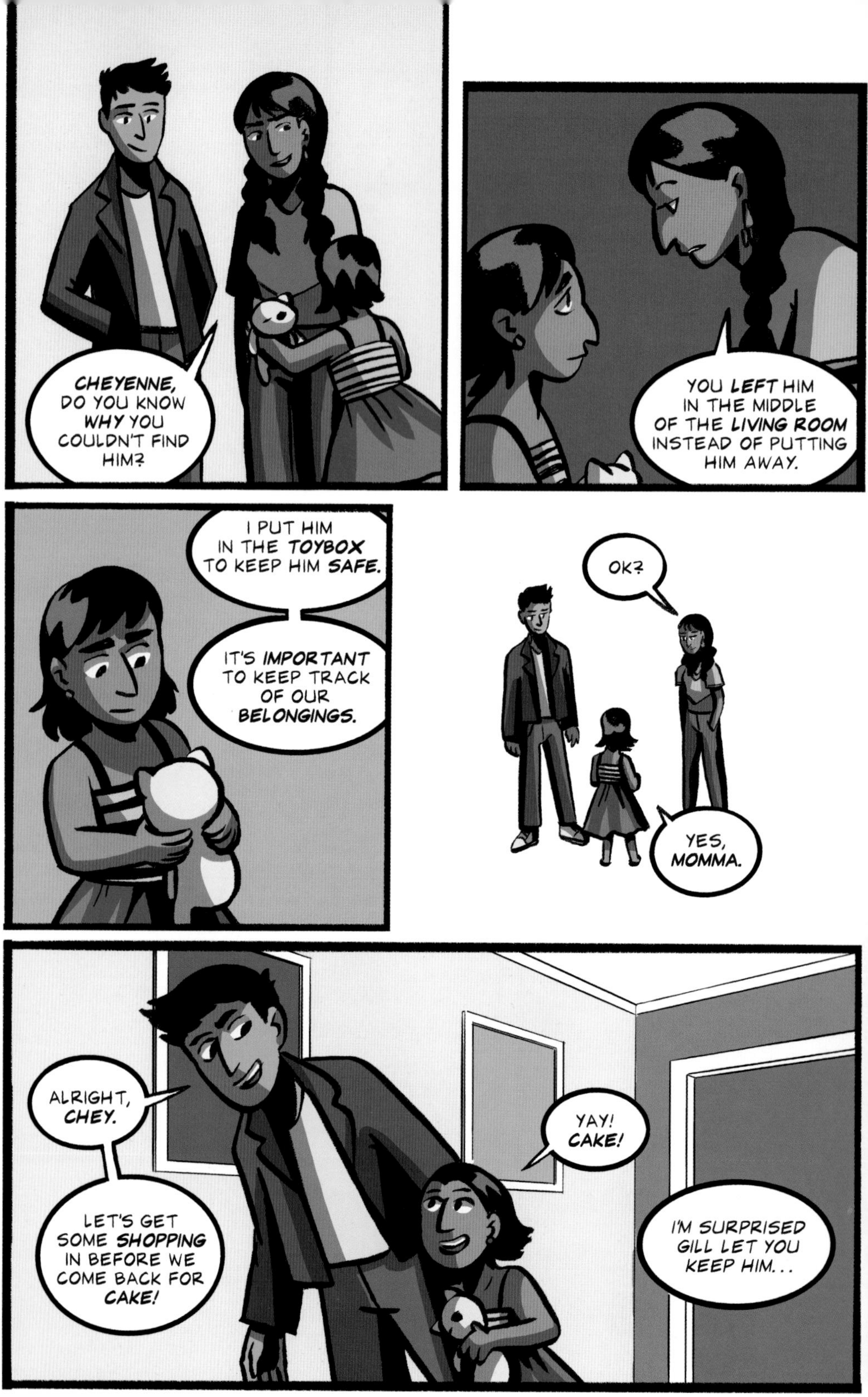
CHEYENNE, DO YOU KNOW WHY YOU COULDN'T FIND HIM?
YOU LEFT HIM IN THE MIDDLE OF THE LIVING ROOM INSTEAD OF PUTTING HIM AWAY.
I PUT HIM IN THE TOYBOX TO KEEP HIM SAFE.
IT'S IMPORTANT TO KEEP TRACK OF OUR BELONGINGS.
OK?
YES, MOMMA.
ALRIGHT, CHEY.
LET'S GET SOME SHOPPING IN BEFORE WE COME BACK FOR CAKE!
YAY! CAKE!
I'M SURPRISED GILL LET YOU KEEP HIM...

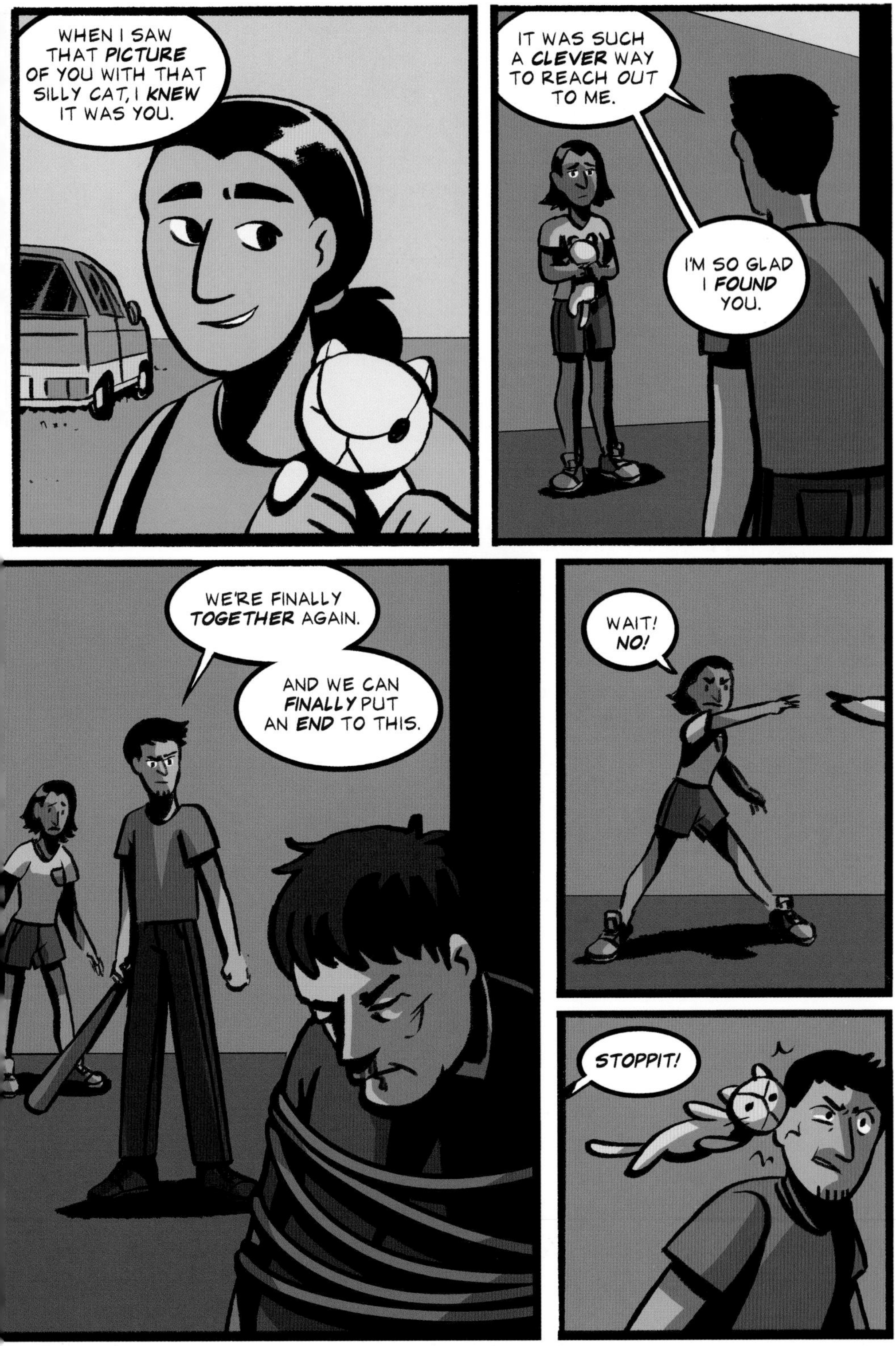

WHEN I SAW THAT **PICTURE** OF YOU WITH THAT SILLY CAT, I **KNEW** IT WAS YOU.
IT WAS SUCH A **CLEVER** WAY TO REACH OUT TO ME.
I'M SO GLAD I **FOUND** YOU.
WE'RE FINALLY **TOGETHER** AGAIN.
AND WE CAN **FINALLY** PUT AN **END** TO THIS.
WAIT! **NO!**
STOPPIT!

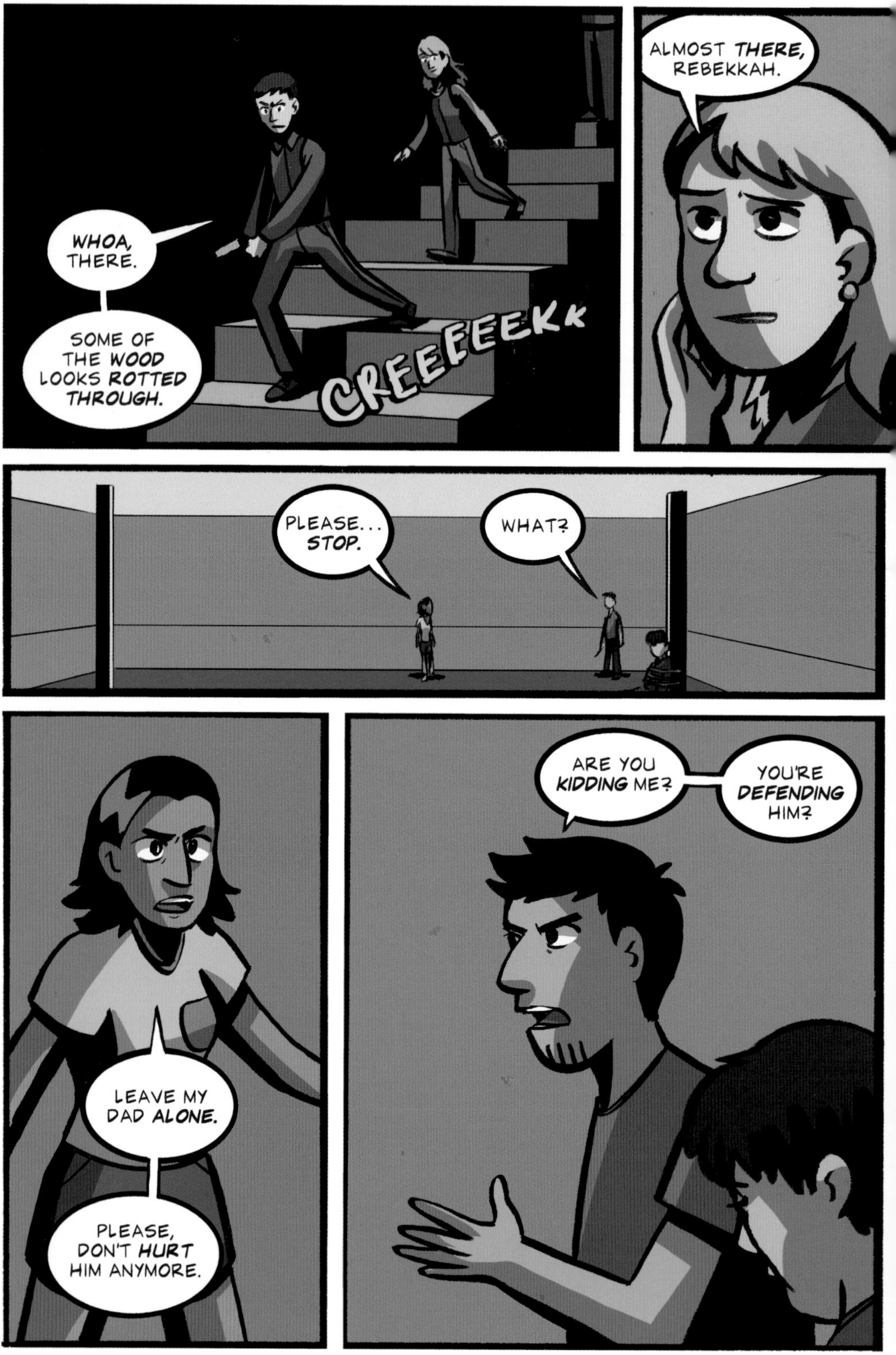
WHOA, THERE.
SOME OF THE WOOD LOOKS ROTTED THROUGH.
CREEEEEKK
ALMOST THERE, REBEKKAH.
PLEASE... STOP.
WHAT?
LEAVE MY DAD ALONE.
PLEASE, DON'T HURT HIM ANYMORE.
ARE YOU KIDDING ME?
YOU'RE DEFENDING HIM?

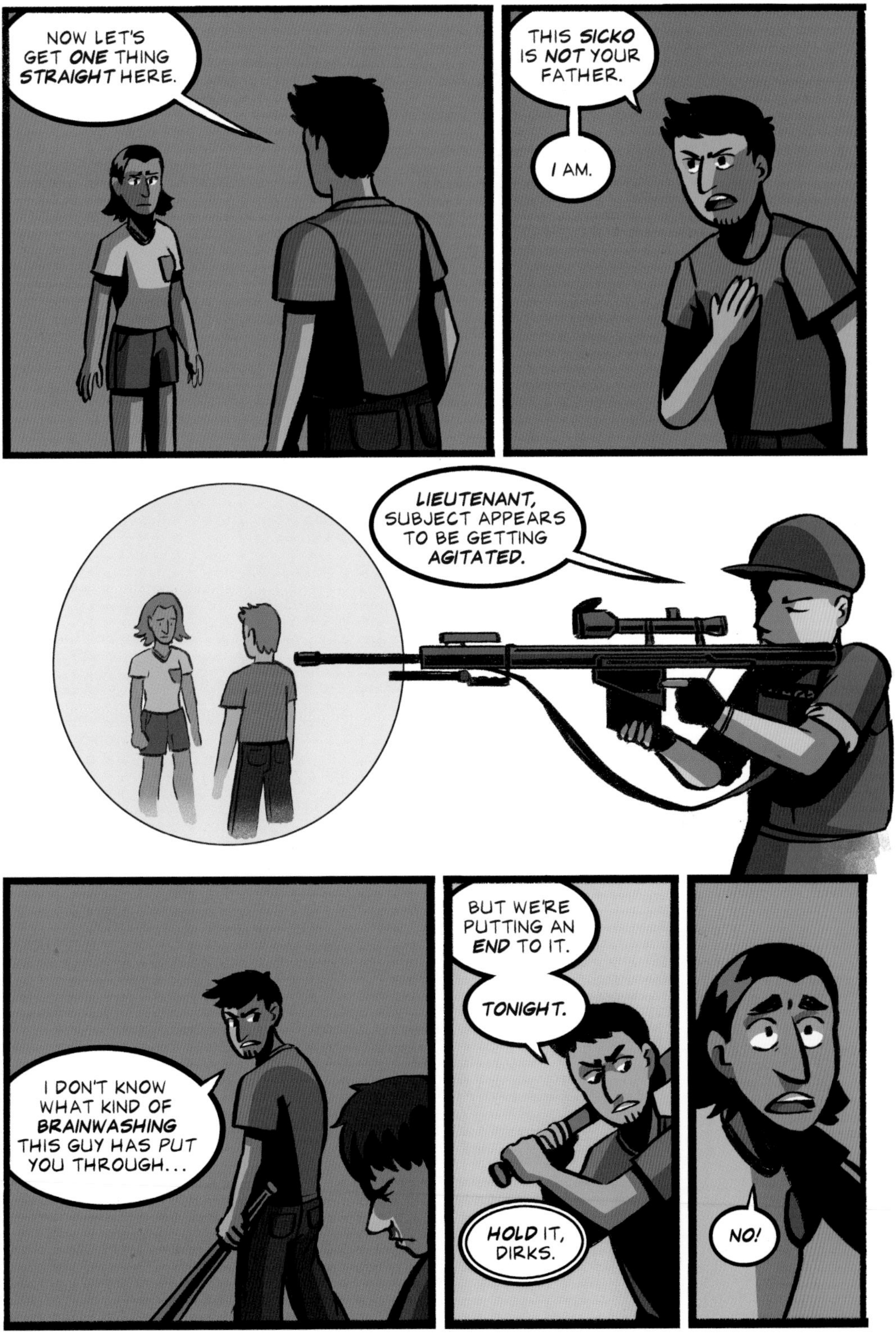
NOW LET'S GET **ONE** THING **STRAIGHT** HERE.
THIS **SICKO** IS **NOT** YOUR FATHER.
I AM.
LIEUTENANT, SUBJECT APPEARS TO BE GETTING **AGITATED.**
I DON'T KNOW WHAT KIND OF **BRAINWASHING** THIS GUY HAS PUT YOU THROUGH...
BUT WE'RE PUTTING AN **END** TO IT.
TONIGHT.
HOLD IT, DIRKS.
NO!

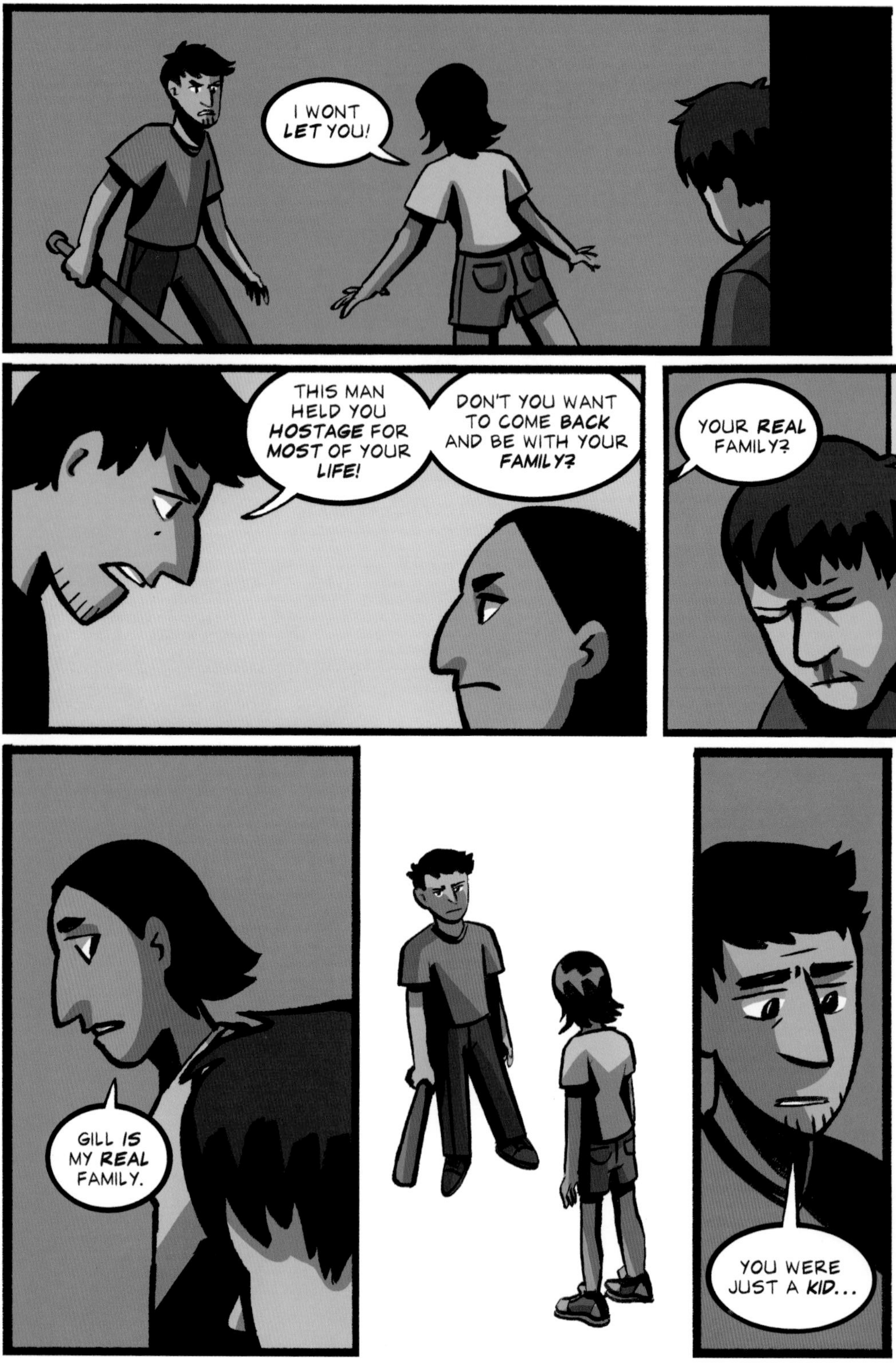
I WONT LET YOU!
THIS MAN HELD YOU HOSTAGE FOR MOST OF YOUR LIFE!
DON'T YOU WANT TO COME BACK AND BE WITH YOUR FAMILY?
YOUR REAL FAMILY?
GILL IS MY REAL FAMILY.
YOU WERE JUST A KID...

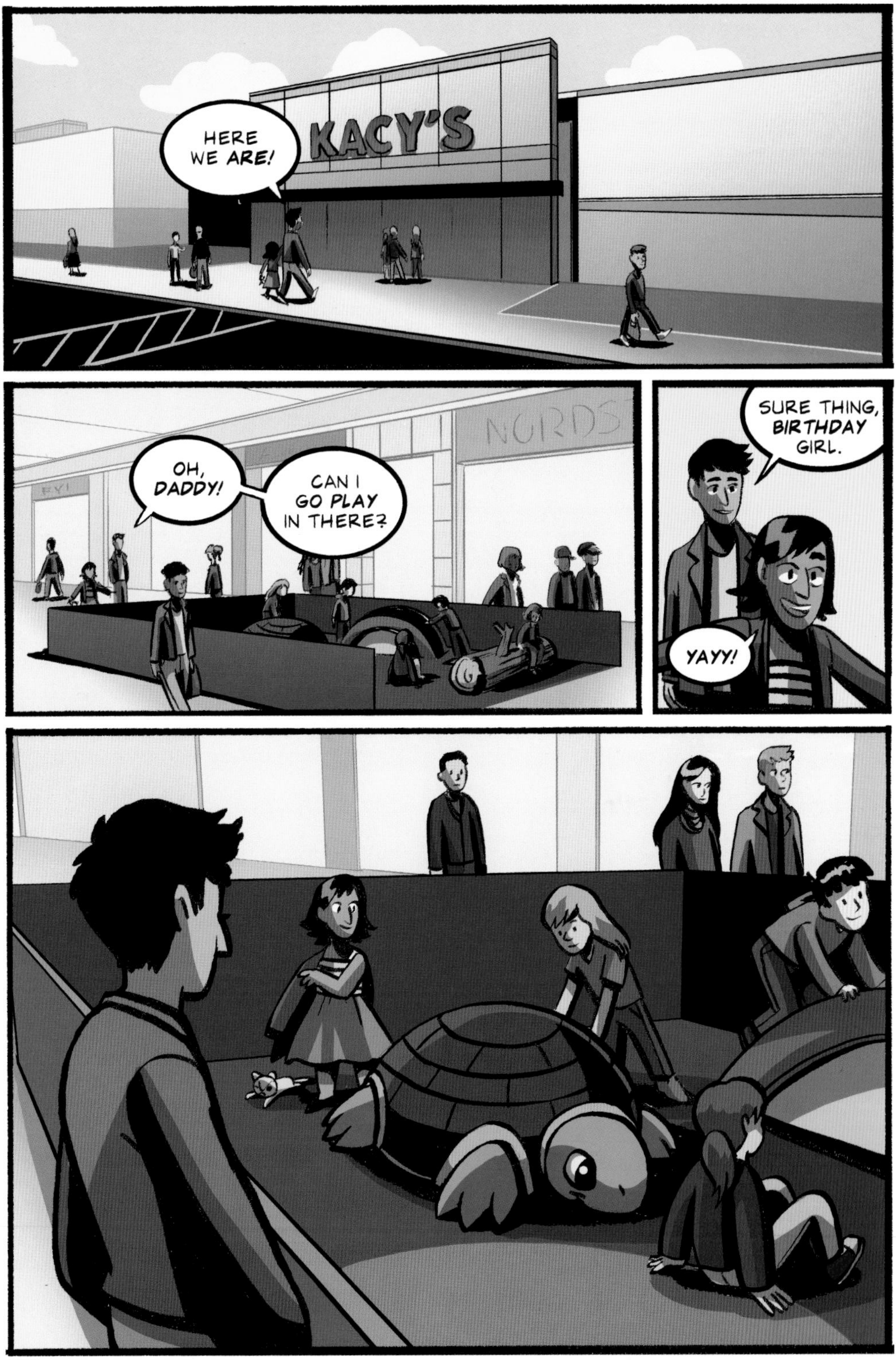
KACY'S
HERE WE ARE!
OH, DADDY!
CAN I GO PLAY IN THERE?
SURE THING, BIRTHDAY GIRL.
YAYY!

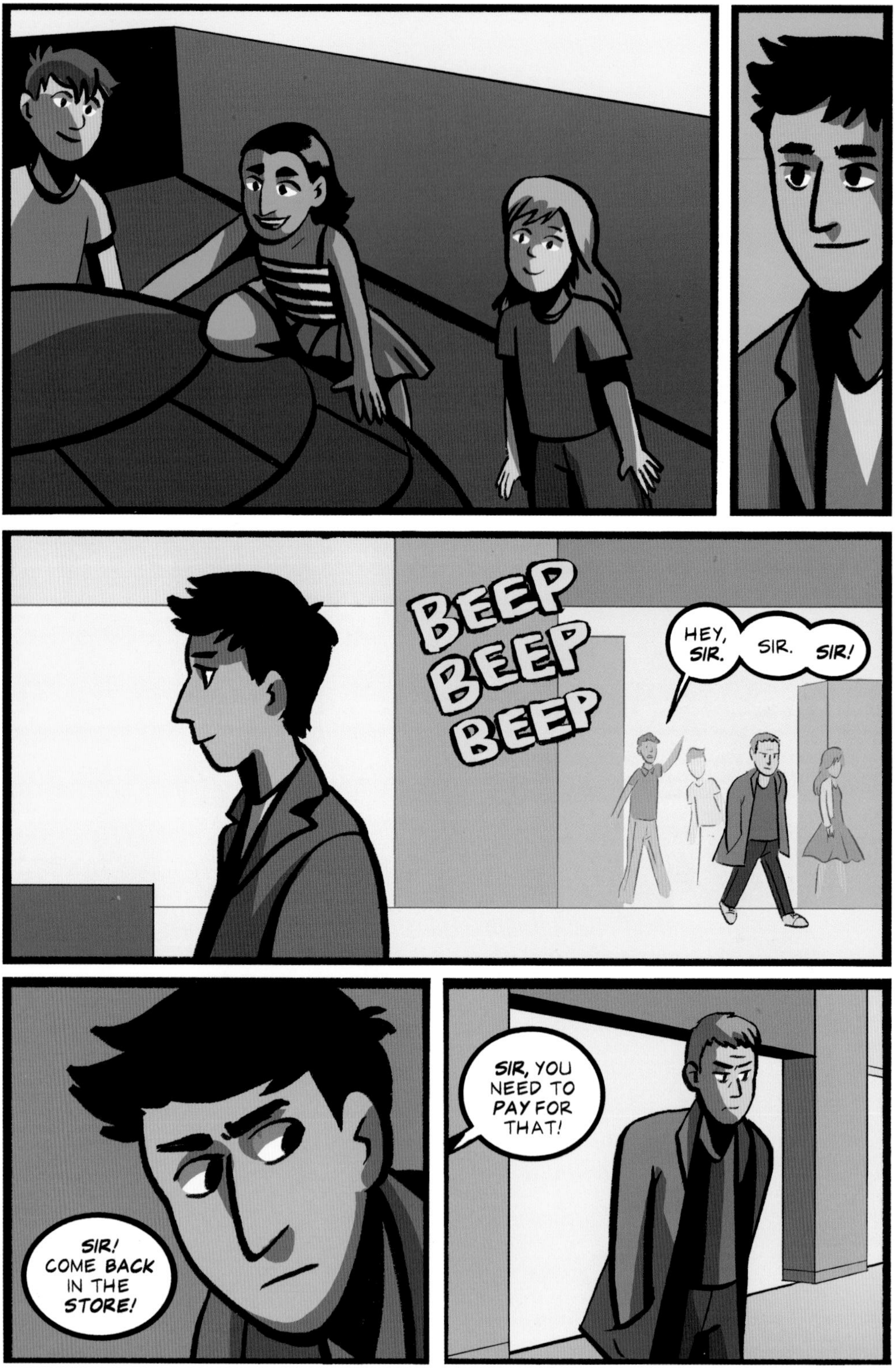
BEEP
BEEP
BEEP
HEY, SIR.
SIR.
SIR!
SIR! COME BACK IN THE STORE!
SIR, YOU NEED TO PAY FOR THAT!

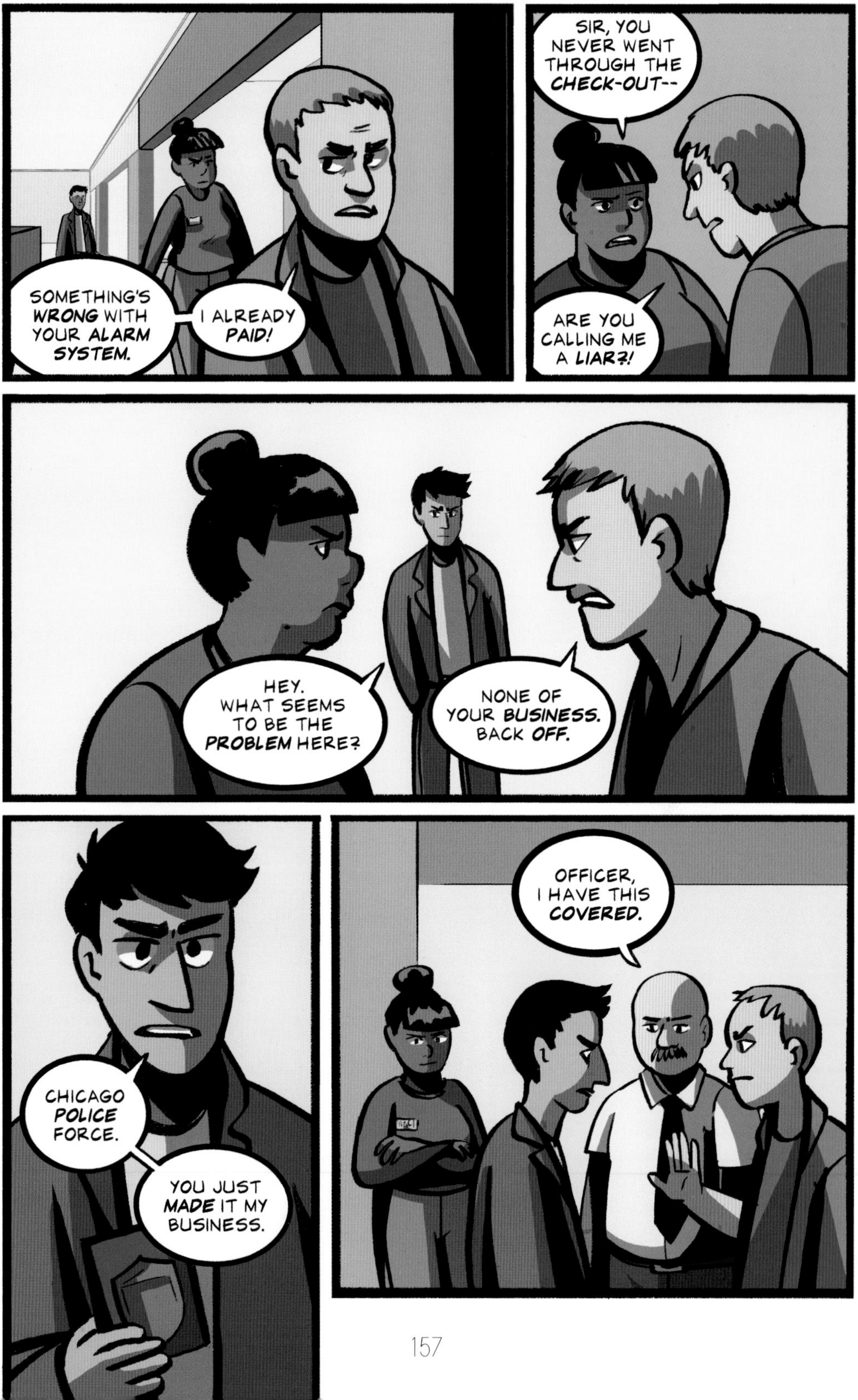
SOMETHING'S WRONG WITH YOUR ALARM SYSTEM.
I ALREADY PAID!
SIR, YOU NEVER WENT THROUGH THE CHECK-OUT--
ARE YOU CALLING ME A LIAR?!
HEY. WHAT SEEMS TO BE THE PROBLEM HERE?
NONE OF YOUR BUSINESS. BACK OFF.
CHICAGO POLICE FORCE.
YOU JUST MADE IT MY BUSINESS.
OFFICER, I HAVE THIS COVERED.

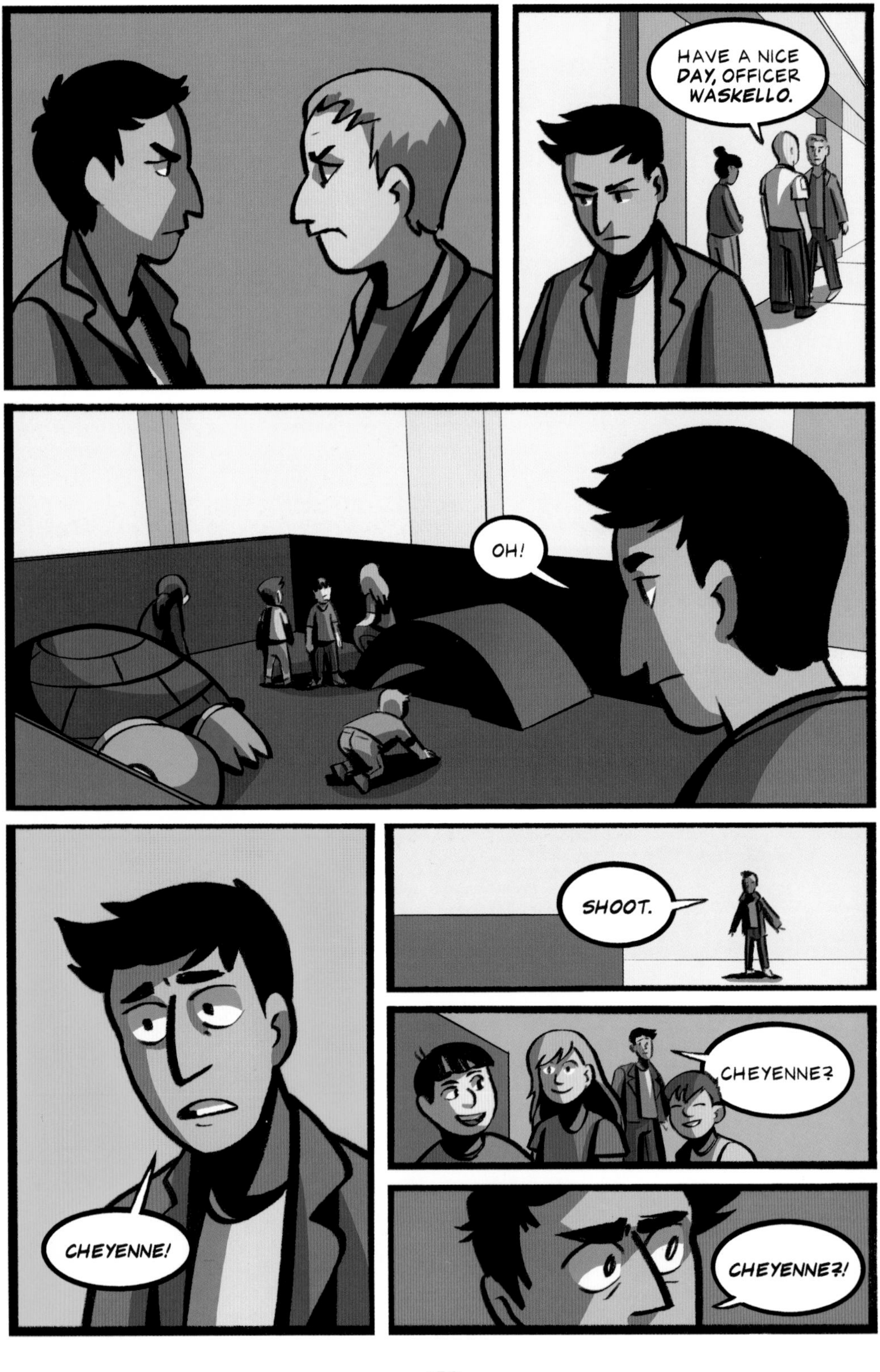
HAVE A NICE DAY, OFFICER WASKELLO.
OH!
CHEYENNE!
SHOOT.
CHEYENNE?
CHEYENNE?!

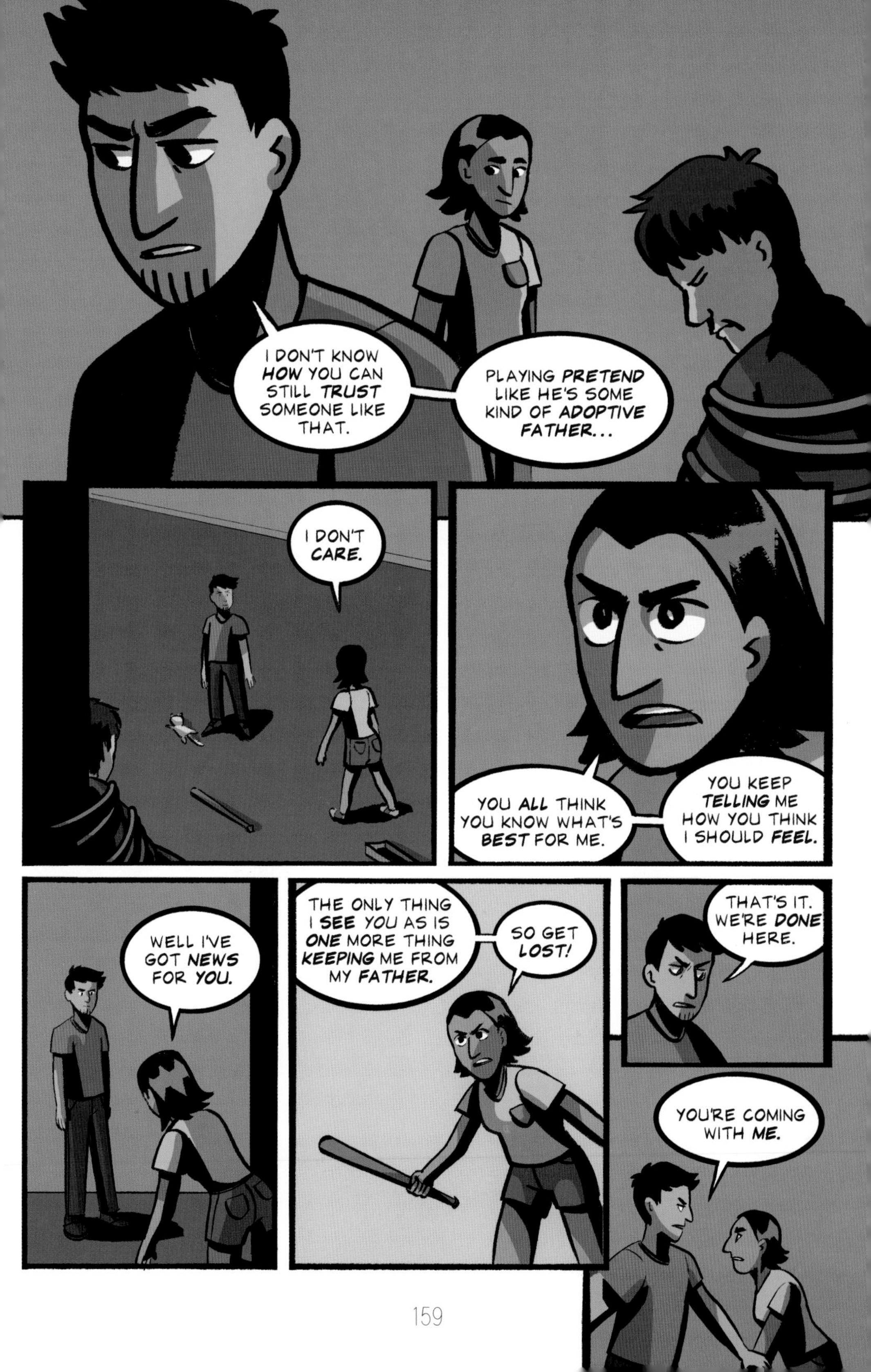
I DON'T KNOW HOW YOU CAN STILL TRUST SOMEONE LIKE THAT.
PLAYING PRETEND LIKE HE'S SOME KIND OF ADOPTIVE FATHER...
I DON'T CARE.
YOU ALL THINK YOU KNOW WHAT'S BEST FOR ME.
YOU KEEP TELLING ME HOW YOU THINK I SHOULD FEEL.
WELL I'VE GOT NEWS FOR YOU.
THE ONLY THING I SEE YOU AS IS ONE MORE THING KEEPING ME FROM MY FATHER.
SO GET LOST!
THAT'S IT. WE'RE DONE HERE.
YOU'RE COMING WITH ME.

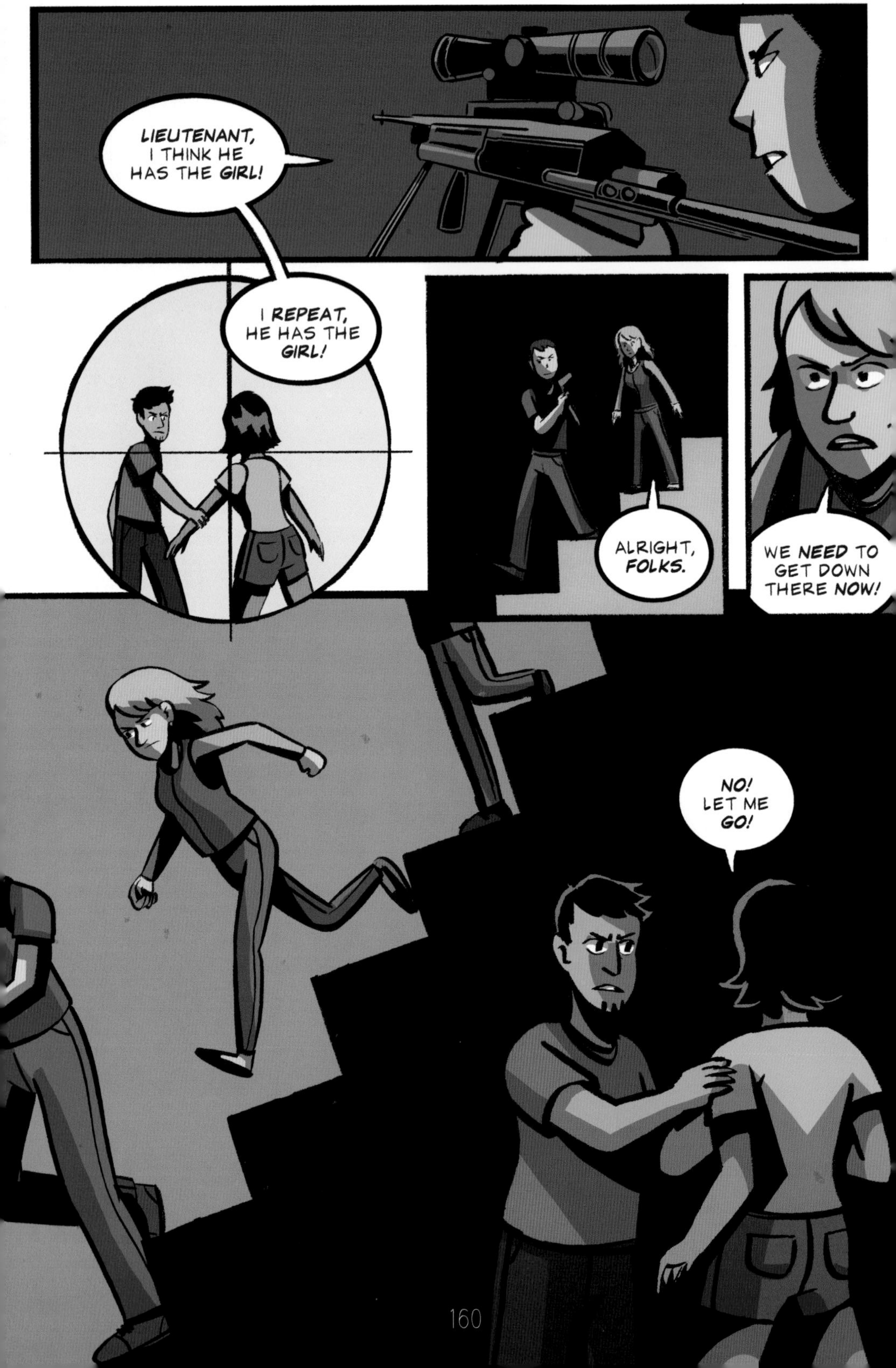
LIEUTENANT, I THINK HE HAS THE GIRL!
I REPEAT, HE HAS THE GIRL!
ALRIGHT, FOLKS.
WE NEED TO GET DOWN THERE NOW!
NO! LET ME GO!

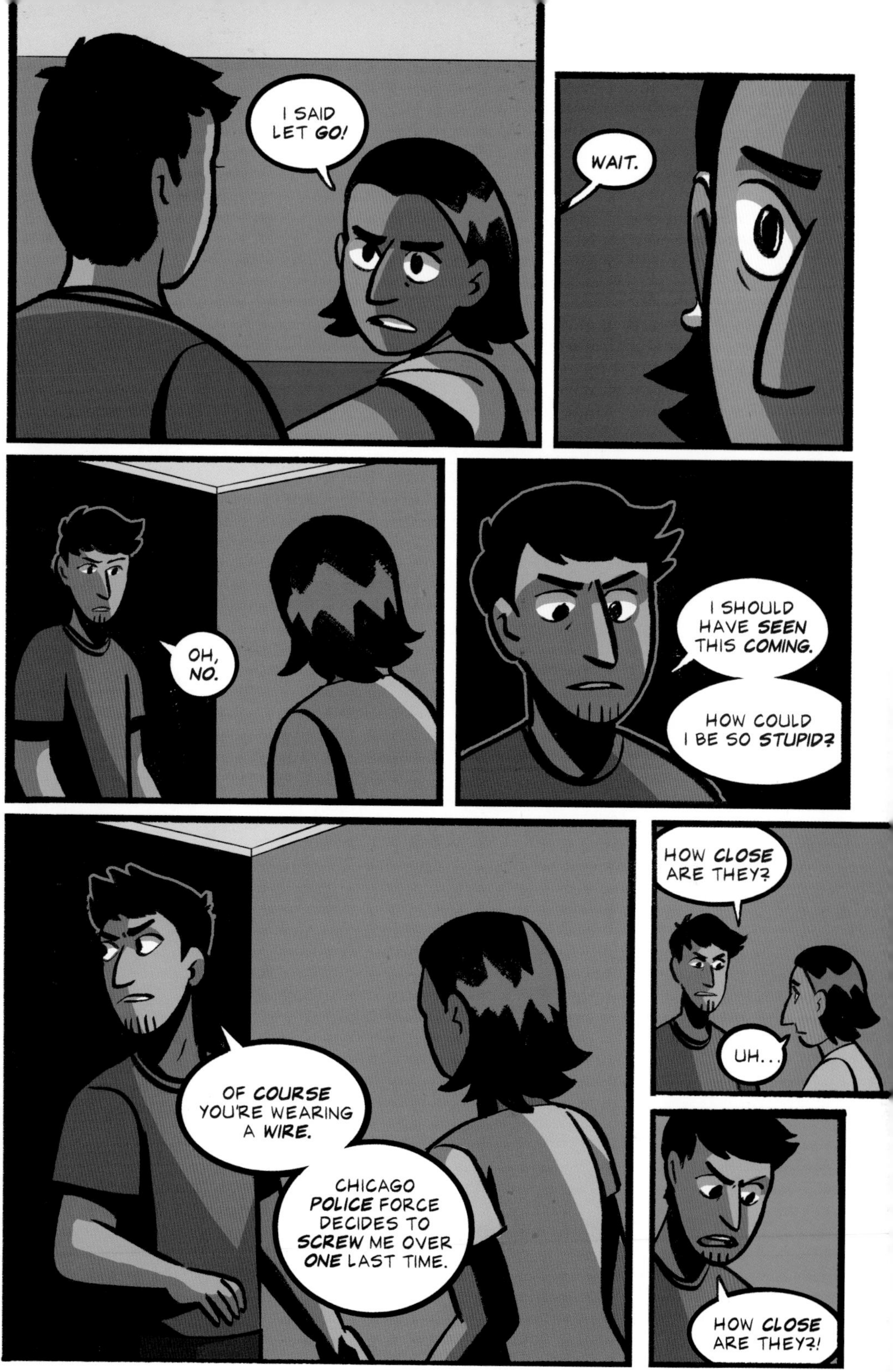
I SAID LET GO!
WAIT.
OH, NO.
I SHOULD HAVE SEEN THIS COMING.
HOW COULD I BE SO STUPID?
OF COURSE YOU'RE WEARING A WIRE.
CHICAGO POLICE FORCE DECIDES TO SCREW ME OVER ONE LAST TIME.
HOW CLOSE ARE THEY?
UH...
HOW CLOSE ARE THEY?!

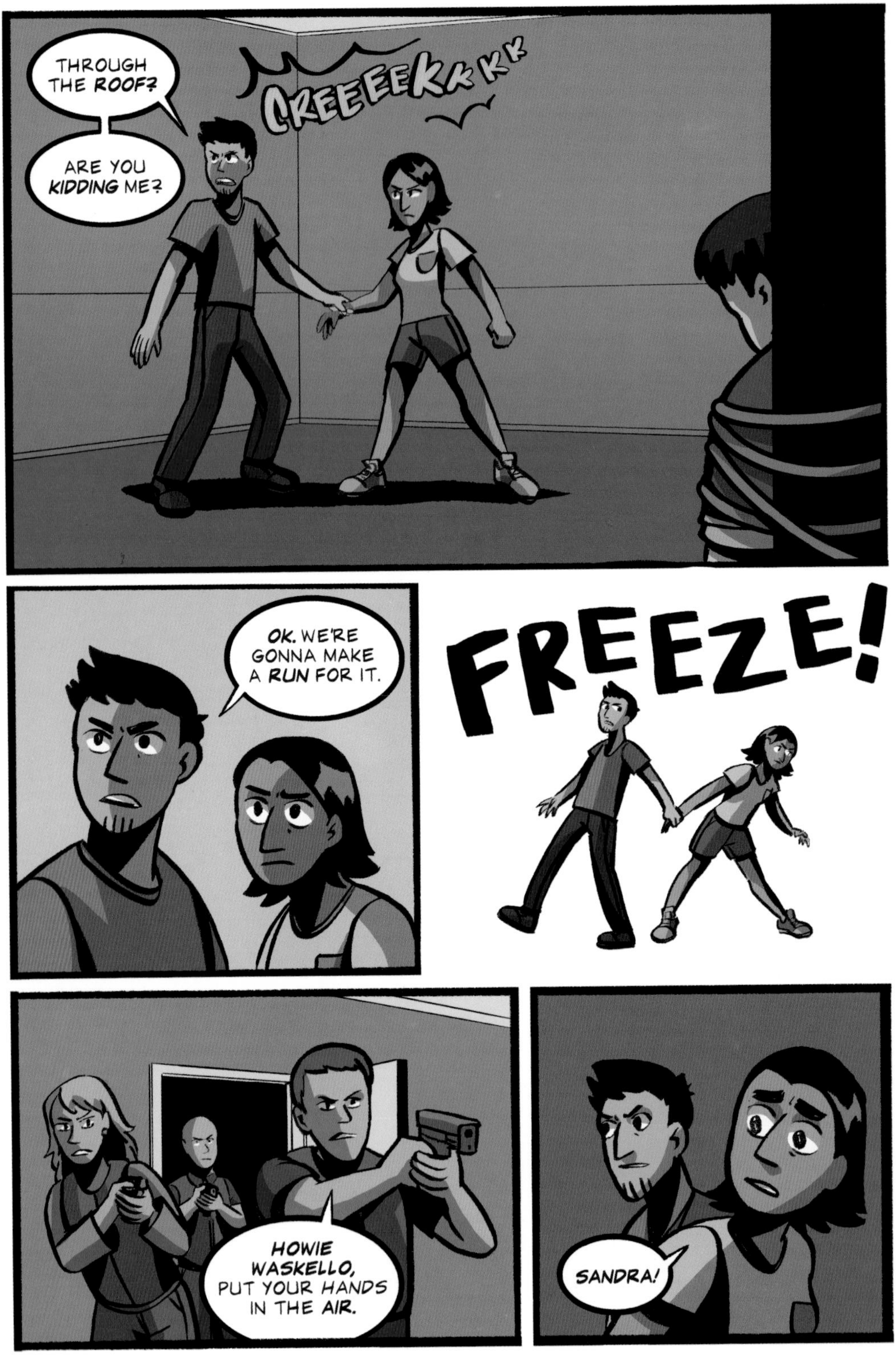
THROUGH THE ROOF?
ARE YOU KIDDING ME?
CREEEEKKKK
OK. WE'RE GONNA MAKE A RUN FOR IT.
FREEZE!
HOWIE WASKELLO, PUT YOUR HANDS IN THE AIR.
SANDRA!

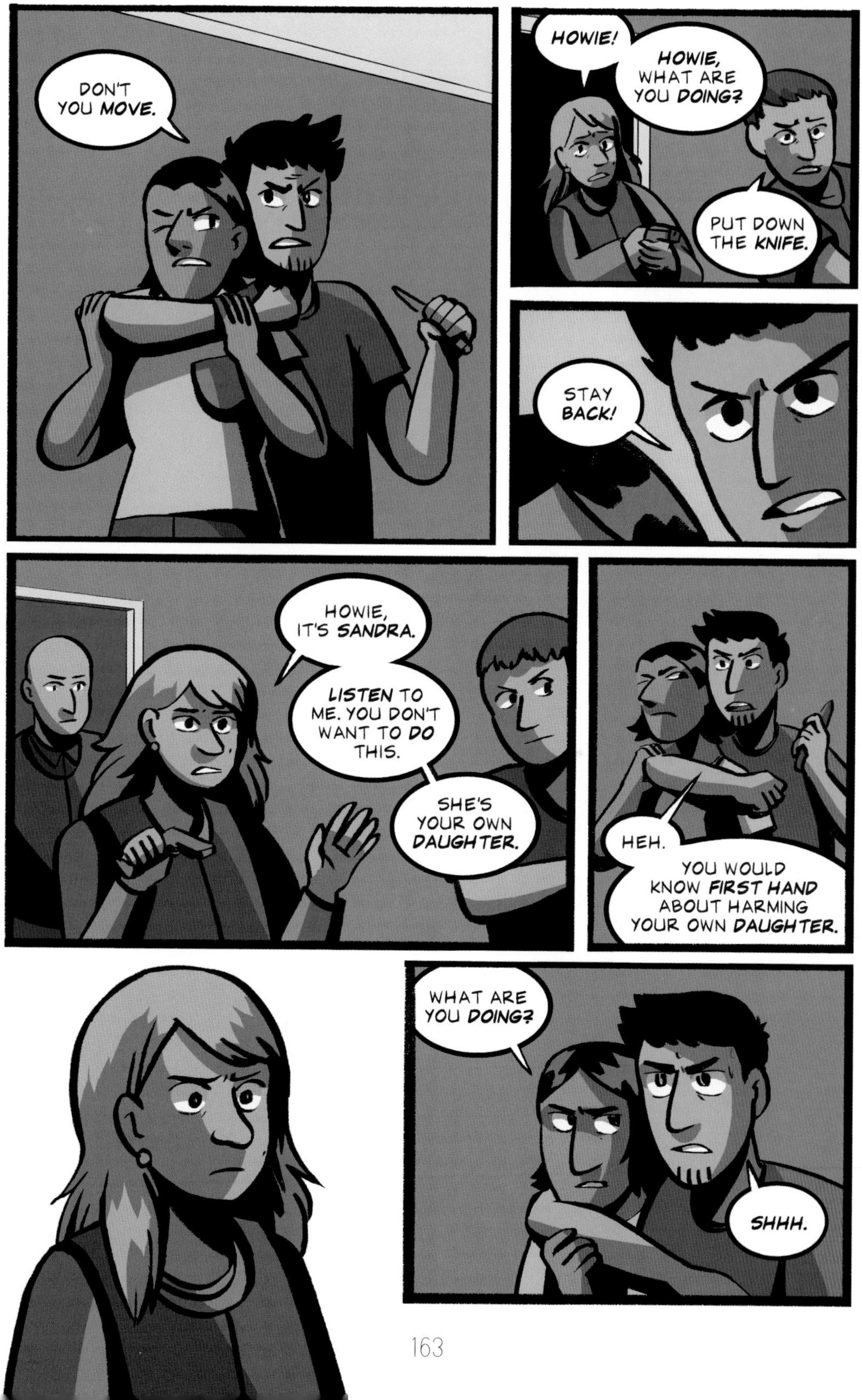
DON'T YOU MOVE.
HOWIE!
HOWIE, WHAT ARE YOU DOING?
PUT DOWN THE KNIFE.
STAY BACK!
HOWIE, IT'S SANDRA.
LISTEN TO ME. YOU DON'T WANT TO DO THIS.
SHE'S YOUR OWN DAUGHTER.
HEH.
YOU WOULD KNOW FIRST HAND ABOUT HARMING YOUR OWN DAUGHTER.
WHAT ARE YOU DOING?
SHHH.

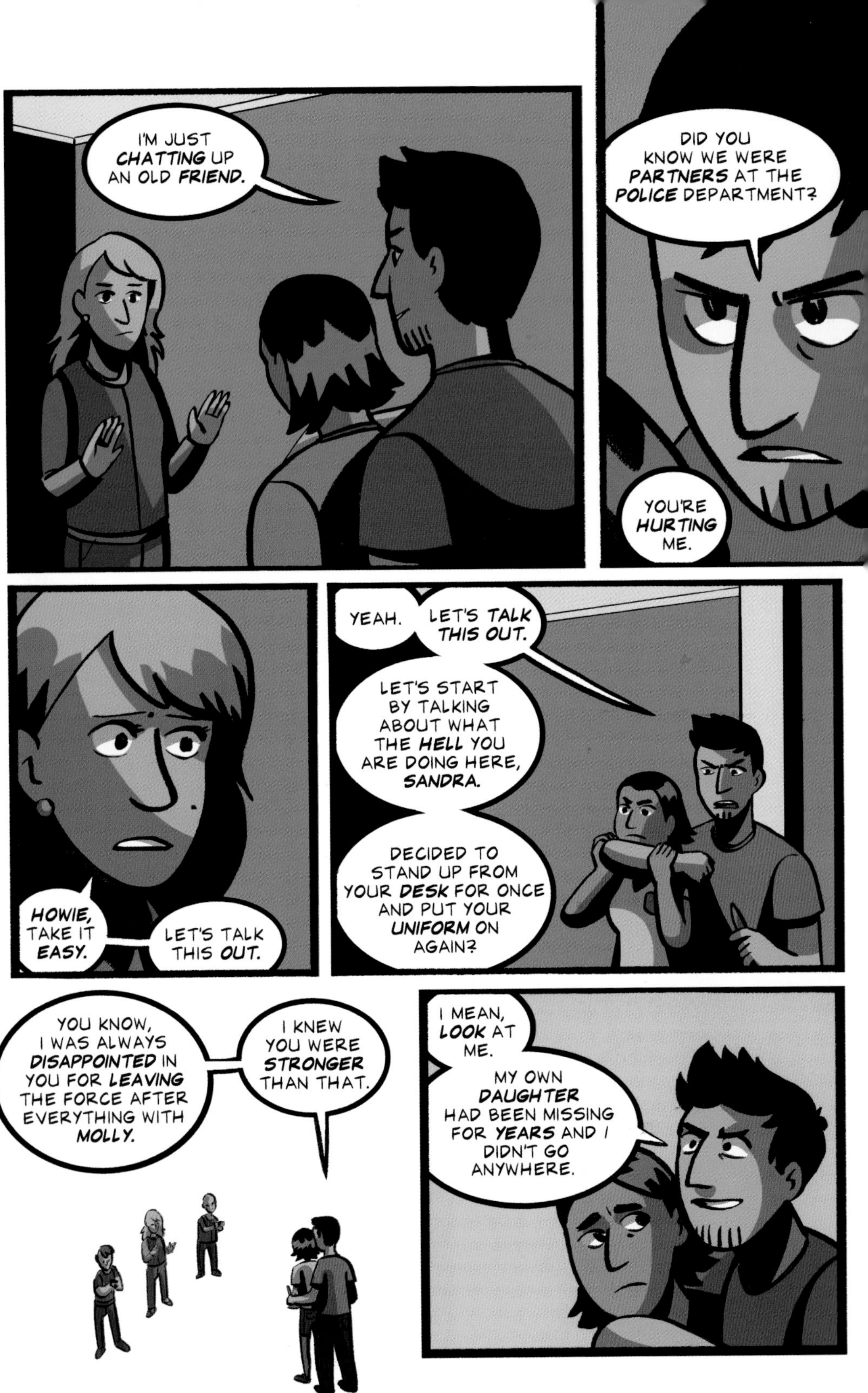
I'M JUST CHATTING UP AN OLD FRIEND.
DID YOU KNOW WE WERE PARTNERS AT THE POLICE DEPARTMENT?
YOU'RE HURTING ME.
HOWIE, TAKE IT EASY.
LET'S TALK THIS OUT.
YEAH.
LET'S TALK THIS OUT.
LET'S START BY TALKING ABOUT WHAT THE HELL YOU ARE DOING HERE, SANDRA.
DECIDED TO STAND UP FROM YOUR DESK FOR ONCE AND PUT YOUR UNIFORM ON AGAIN?
YOU KNOW, I WAS ALWAYS DISAPPOINTED IN YOU FOR LEAVING THE FORCE AFTER EVERYTHING WITH MOLLY.
I KNEW YOU WERE STRONGER THAN THAT.
I MEAN, LOOK AT ME.
MY OWN DAUGHTER HAD BEEN MISSING FOR YEARS AND I DIDN'T GO ANYWHERE.

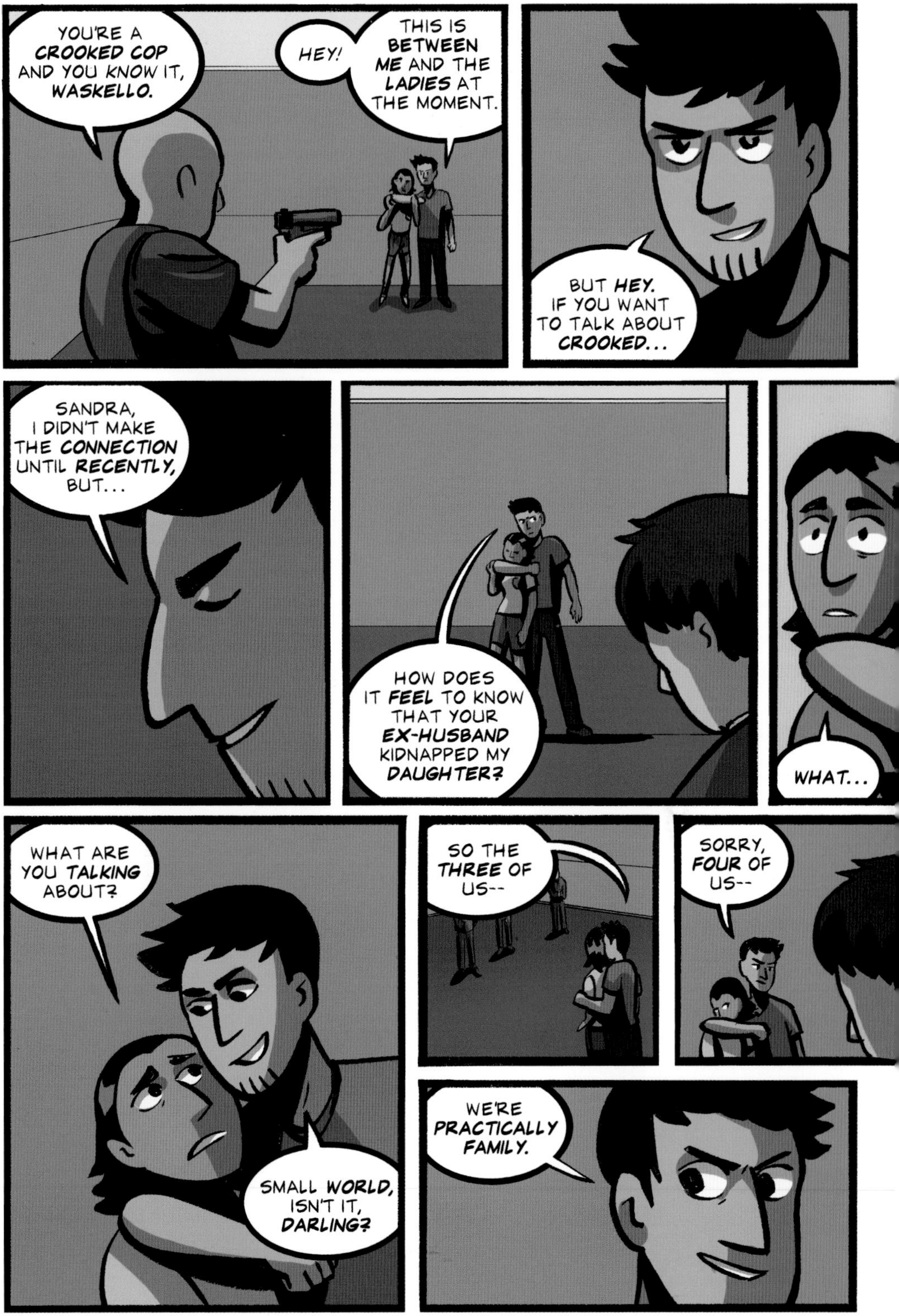
YOU'RE A CROOKED COP AND YOU KNOW IT, WASKELLO.
HEY!
THIS IS BETWEEN ME AND THE LADIES AT THE MOMENT.
BUT HEY. IF YOU WANT TO TALK ABOUT CROOKED...
SANDRA, I DIDN'T MAKE THE CONNECTION UNTIL RECENTLY, BUT...
HOW DOES IT FEEL TO KNOW THAT YOUR EX-HUSBAND KIDNAPPED MY DAUGHTER?
WHAT...
WHAT ARE YOU TALKING ABOUT?
SMALL WORLD, ISN'T IT, DARLING?
SO THE THREE OF US--
SORRY, FOUR OF US--
WE'RE PRACTICALLY FAMILY.

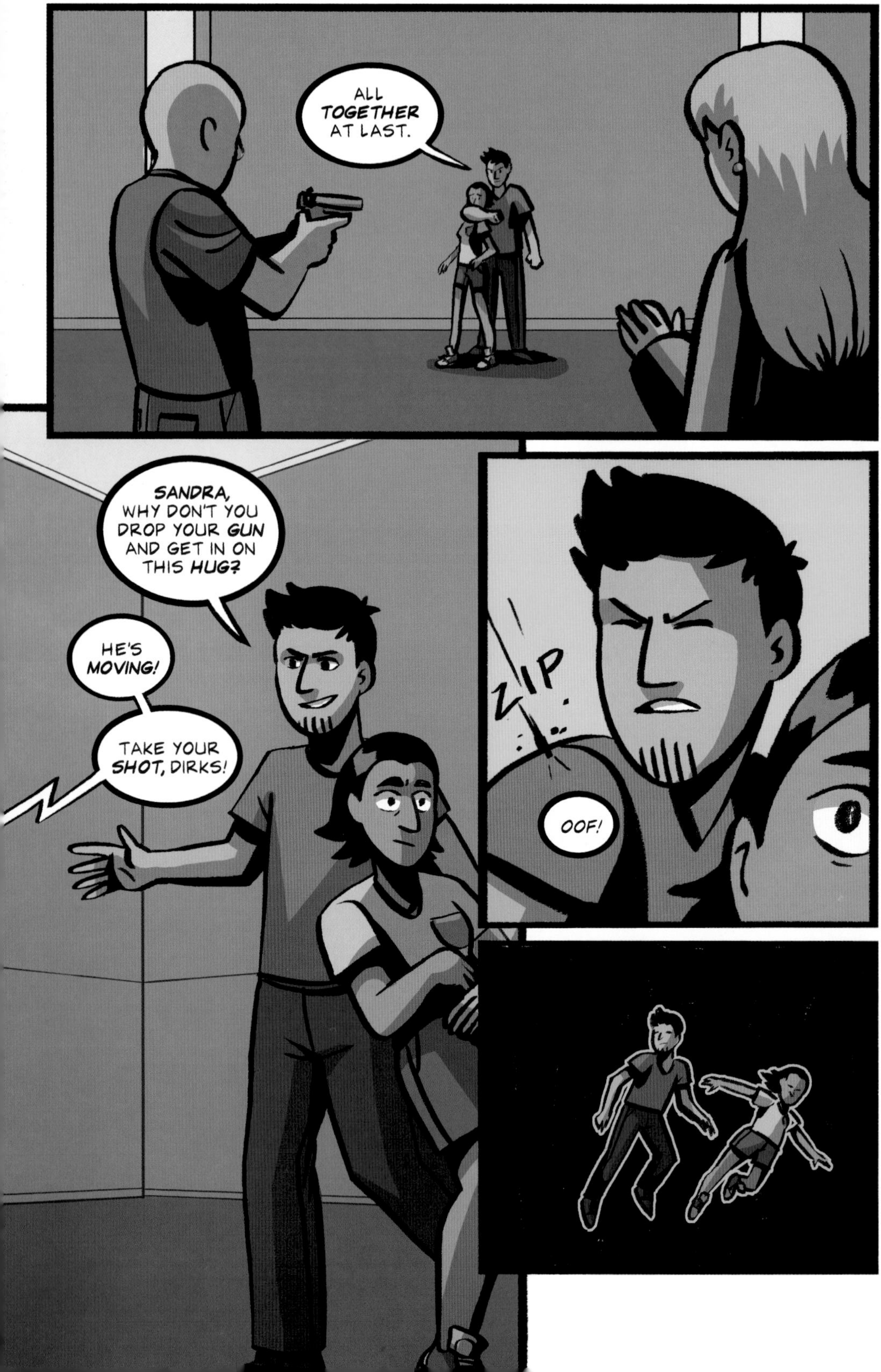
ALL TOGETHER AT LAST.
SANDRA, WHY DON'T YOU DROP YOUR GUN AND GET IN ON THIS HUG?
HE'S MOVING!
TAKE YOUR SHOT, DIRKS!
ZIP
OOF!

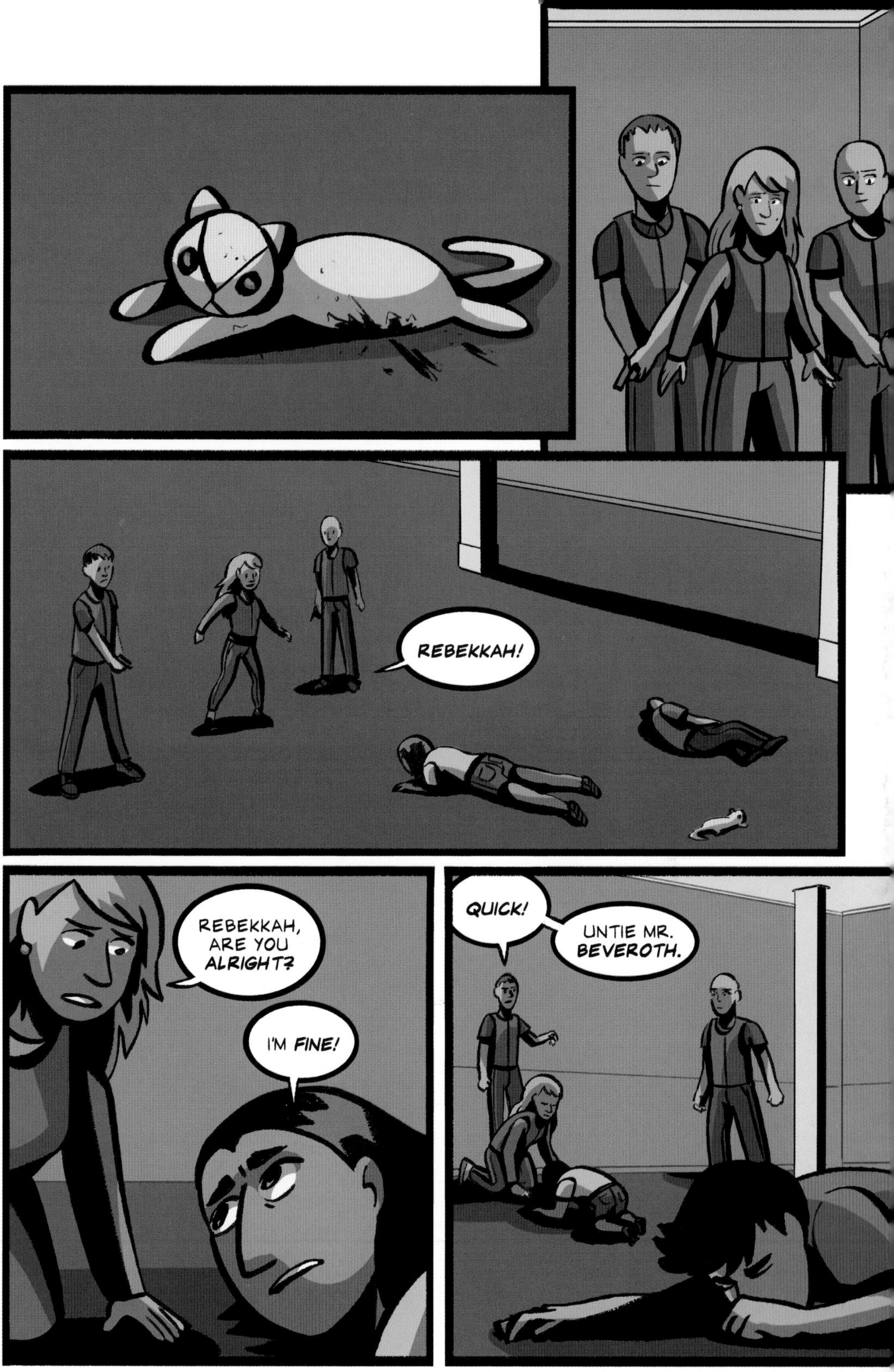
REBEKKAH!
REBEKKAH, ARE YOU ALRIGHT?
I'M FINE!
QUICK!
UNTIE MR. BEVEROTH.

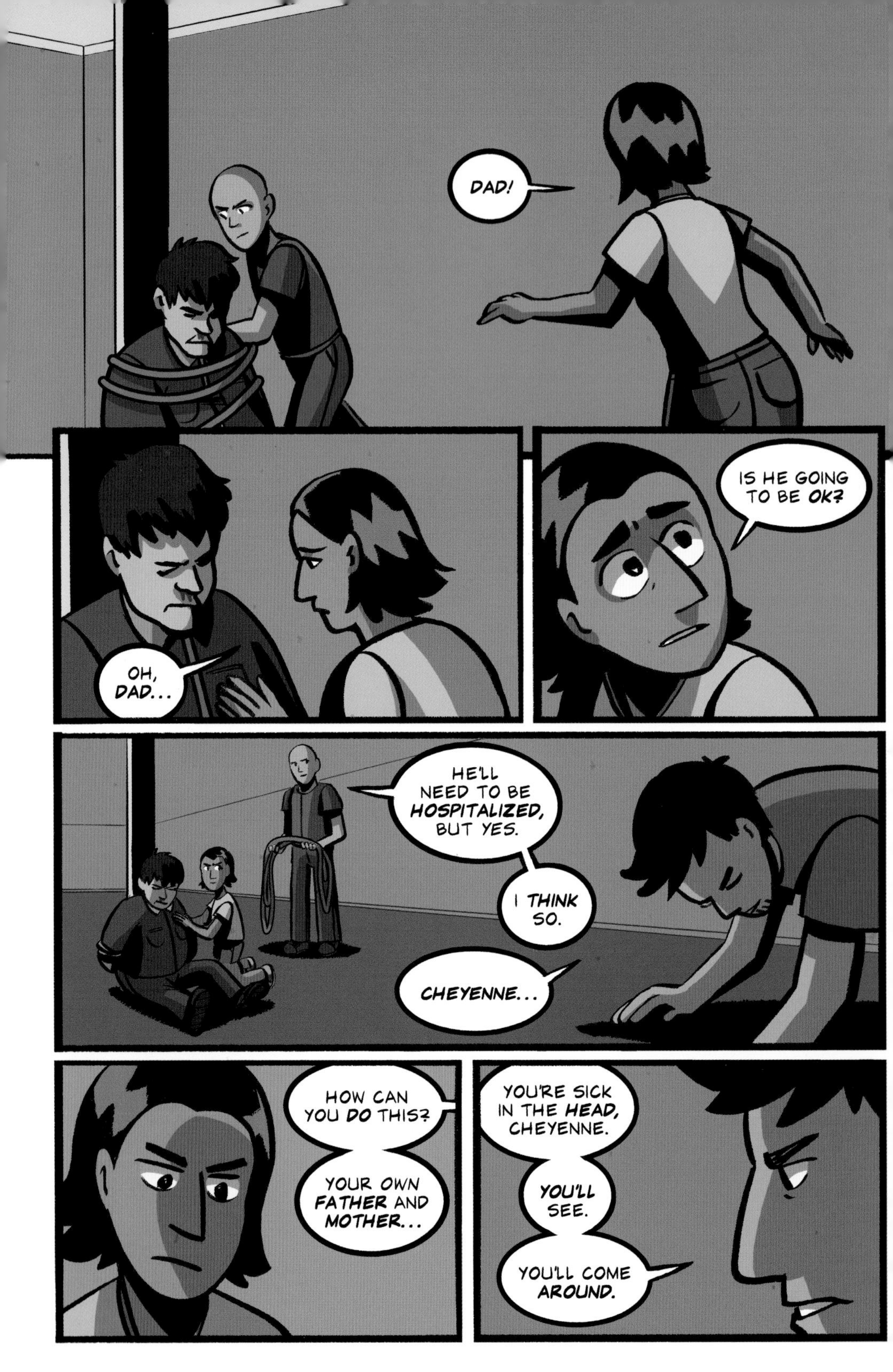
DAD!
OH, DAD...
IS HE GOING TO BE OK?
HE'LL NEED TO BE HOSPITALIZED, BUT YES.
I THINK SO.
CHEYENNE...
HOW CAN YOU DO THIS?
YOUR OWN FATHER AND MOTHER...
YOU'RE SICK IN THE HEAD, CHEYENNE.
YOU'LL SEE.
YOU'LL COME AROUND.

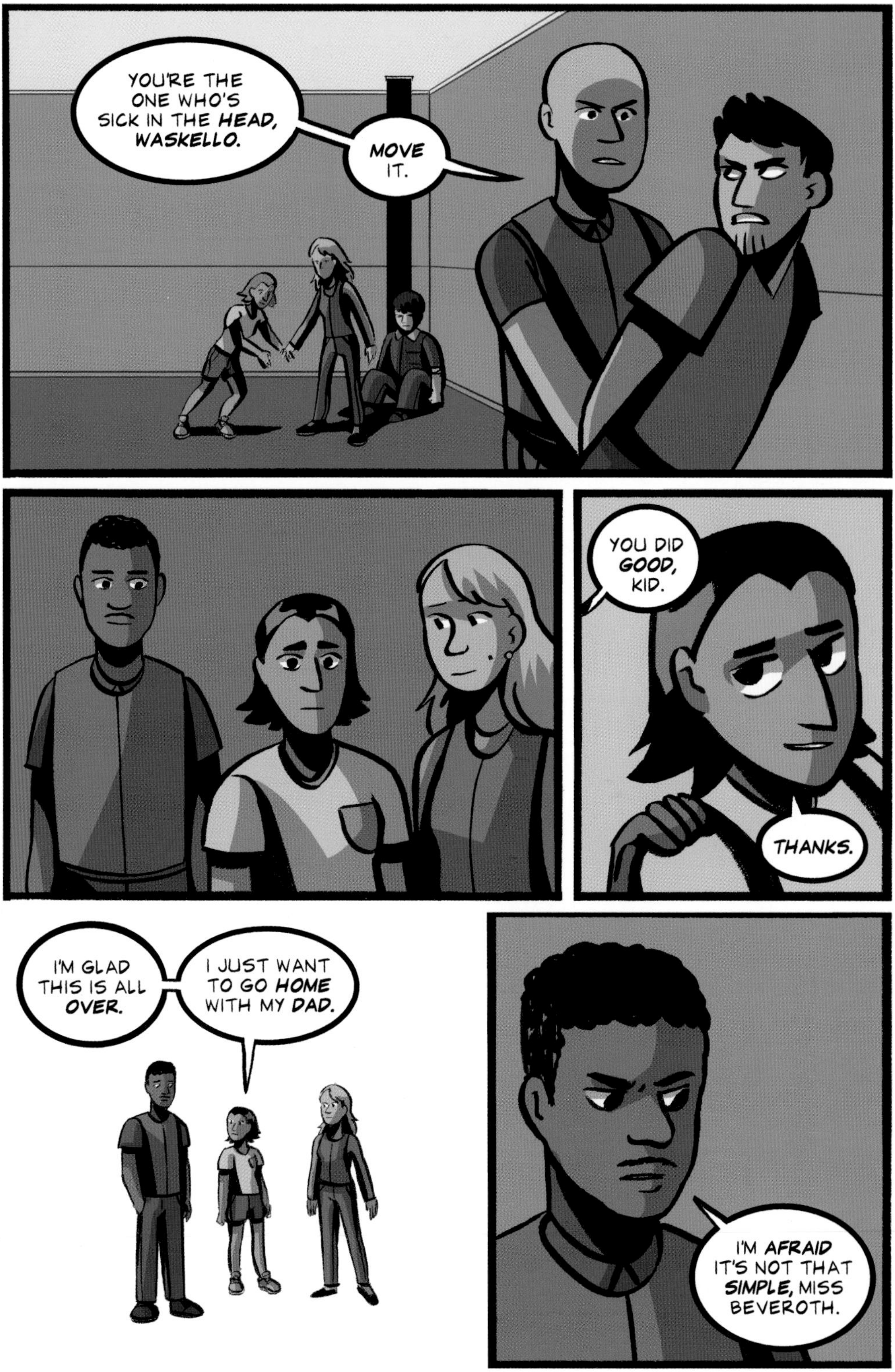
YOU'RE THE ONE WHO'S SICK IN THE HEAD, WASKELLO.
MOVE IT.
YOU DID GOOD, KID.
THANKS.
I'M GLAD THIS IS ALL OVER.
I JUST WANT TO GO HOME WITH MY DAD.
I'M AFRAID IT'S NOT THAT SIMPLE, MISS BEVEROTH.

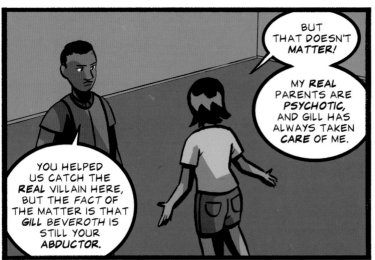

BUT THAT DOESN'T **MATTER!**

MY **REAL** PARENTS ARE **PSYCHOTIC**, AND GILL HAS ALWAYS TAKEN **CARE** OF ME.

YOU HELPED US CATCH THE **REAL** VILLAIN HERE, BUT THE **FACT** OF THE MATTER IS THAT **GILL** BEVEROTH IS STILL YOUR **ABDUCTOR.**

YOU CAN'T ACTUALLY **FORCE** ME TO **LIVE** WITH THEM, **CAN** YOU?

HOLD ON, **HOLD** ON.

WE HAVE A **LOT** TO **SORT** THROUGH BEFORE WE MAKE ANY **DECISIONS.**

WHAT I **DO** KNOW IS THAT **HOWIE** AND **GILL** WILL BE BEHIND **BARS** FROM NOW ON.

YOU, HOWEVER, ARE ATTENDING **COLLEGE** IN THE FALL. SO THAT MEANS--

BECK...

DAD?

DAD! YOU'RE AWAKE!

DAD?

...BECK, I'M SO *SORRY*...

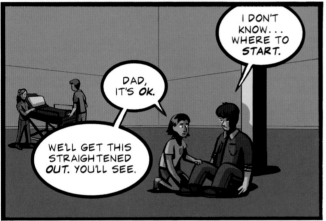

DAD, IT'S *OK*.

I DON'T KNOW... WHERE TO *START*.

WE'LL GET THIS STRAIGHTENED OUT. YOU'LL SEE.

MISS *BEVEROTH*, STEP ASIDE, PLEASE.

HE NEEDS *IMMEDIATE* MEDICAL TREATMENT.

I CAN'T JUST GO *WITH HIM?*

YOU SHOULD GET SOME *REST*, MISS.

I'LL BE THERE *FIRST* THING IN THE *MORNING*.

I *PROMISE*.

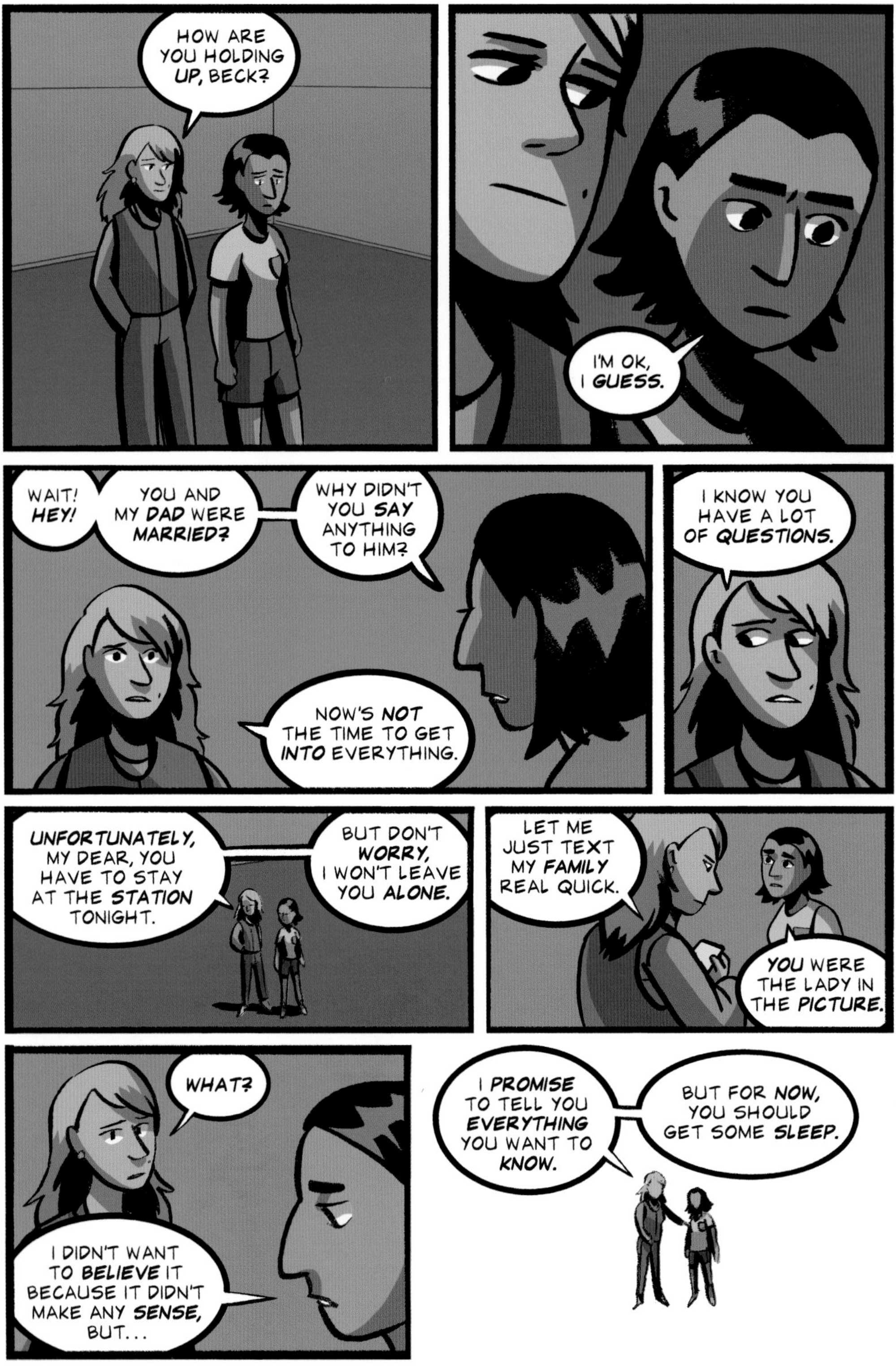
HOW ARE YOU HOLDING UP, BECK?
I'M OK, I GUESS.
WAIT! HEY!
YOU AND MY DAD WERE MARRIED?
WHY DIDN'T YOU SAY ANYTHING TO HIM?
NOW'S NOT THE TIME TO GET INTO EVERYTHING.
I KNOW YOU HAVE A LOT OF QUESTIONS.
UNFORTUNATELY, MY DEAR, YOU HAVE TO STAY AT THE STATION TONIGHT.
BUT DON'T WORRY, I WON'T LEAVE YOU ALONE.
LET ME JUST TEXT MY FAMILY REAL QUICK.
YOU WERE THE LADY IN THE PICTURE.
WHAT?
I DIDN'T WANT TO BELIEVE IT BECAUSE IT DIDN'T MAKE ANY SENSE, BUT...
I PROMISE TO TELL YOU EVERYTHING YOU WANT TO KNOW.
BUT FOR NOW, YOU SHOULD GET SOME SLEEP.

CHAPTER 6

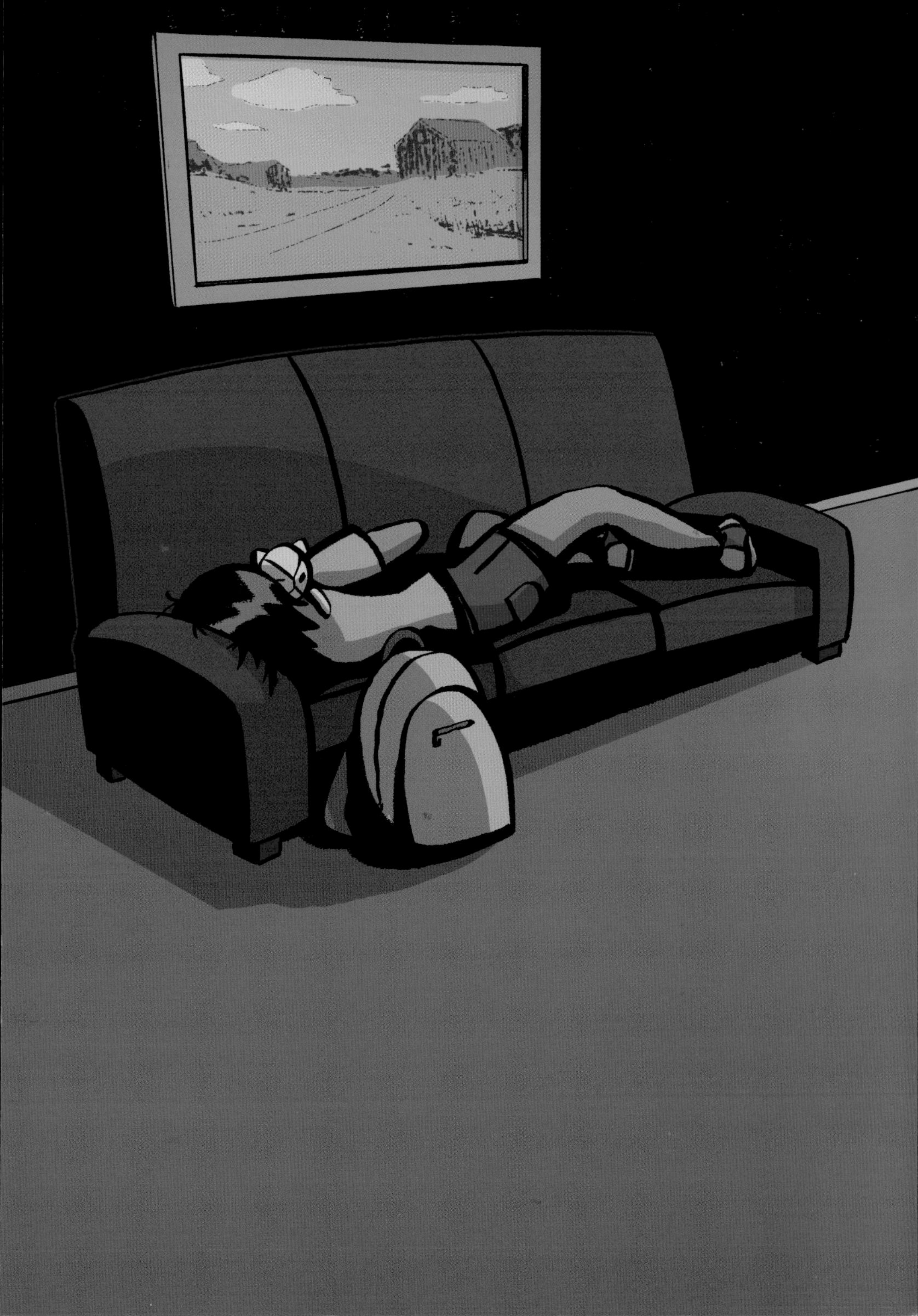

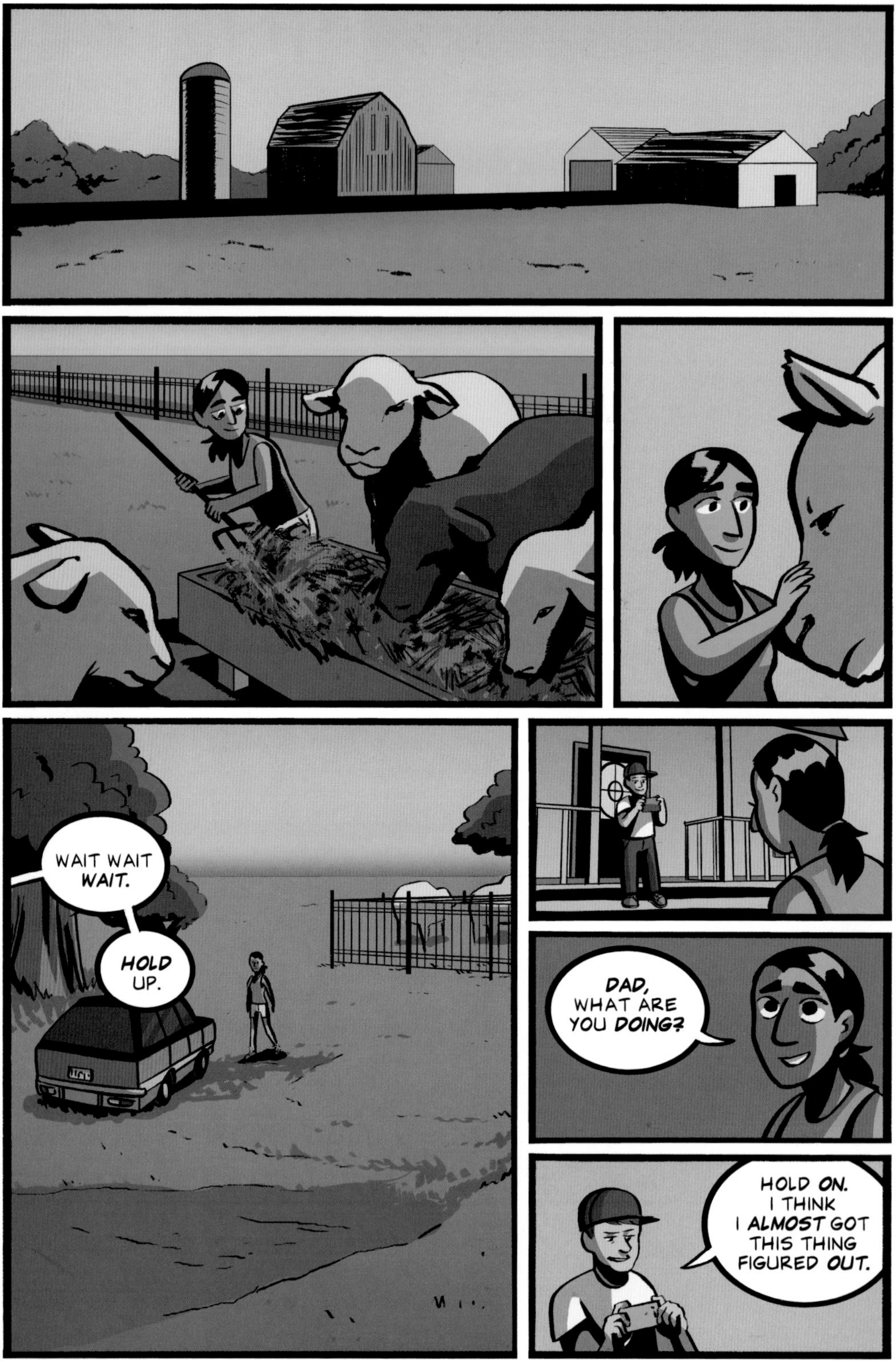
WAIT WAIT WAIT.
HOLD UP.
DAD, WHAT ARE YOU DOING?
HOLD ON. I THINK I ALMOST GOT THIS THING FIGURED OUT.

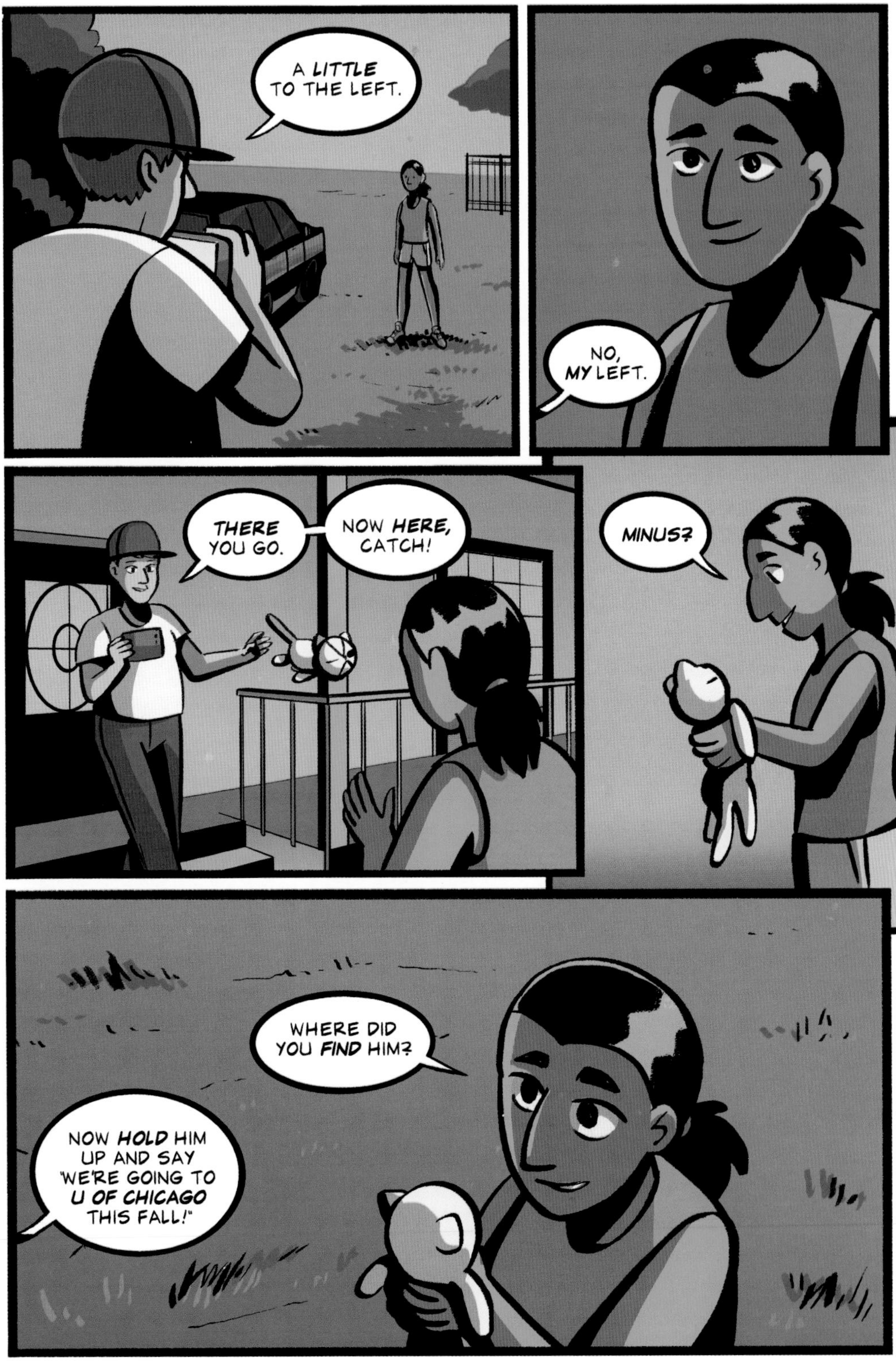
A LITTLE TO THE LEFT.
NO, MY LEFT.
THERE YOU GO.
NOW HERE, CATCH!
MINUS?
WHERE DID YOU FIND HIM?
NOW HOLD HIM UP AND SAY 'WE'RE GOING TO U OF CHICAGO THIS FALL!'

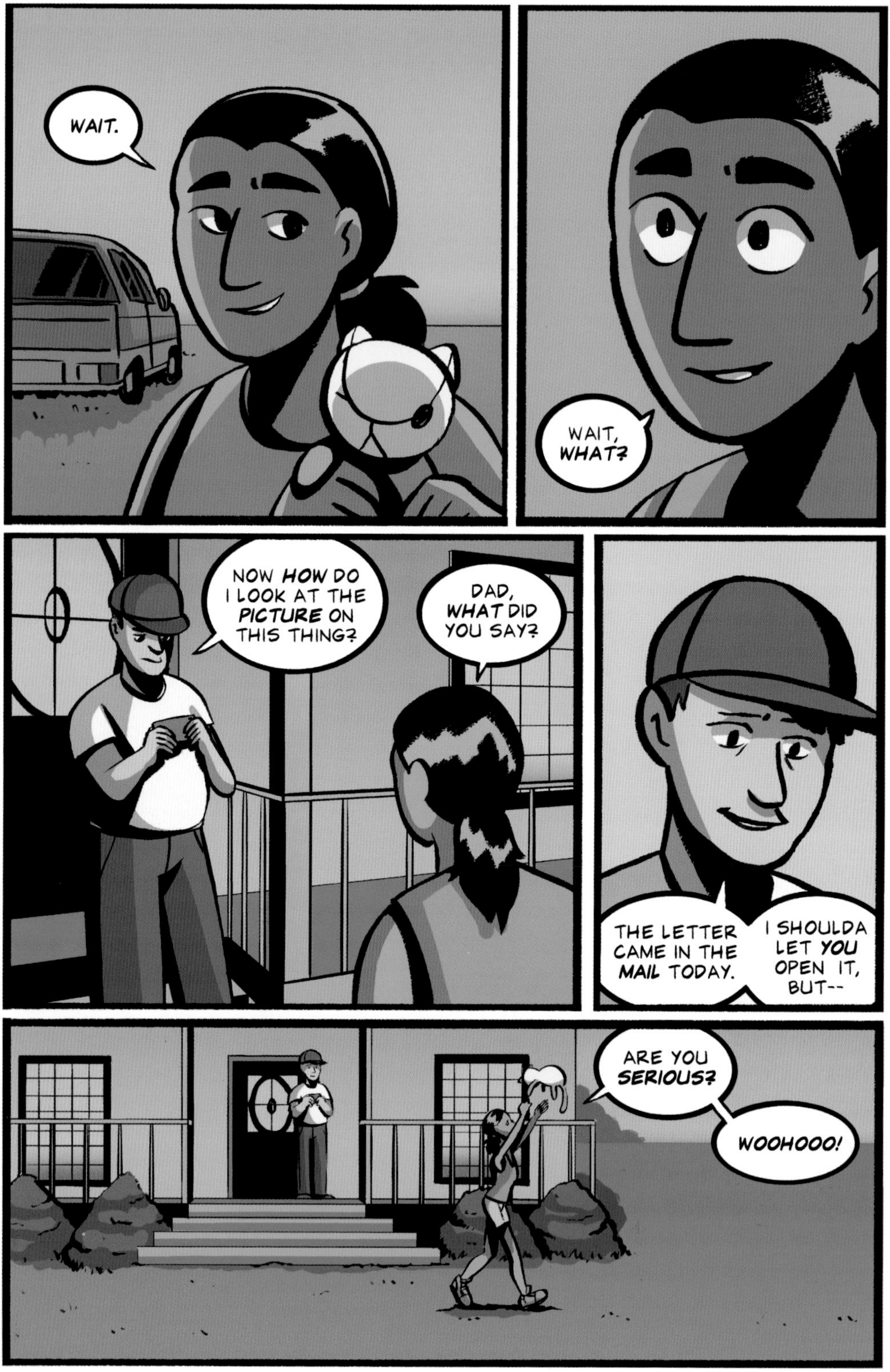
WAIT.
WAIT, WHAT?
NOW HOW DO I LOOK AT THE PICTURE ON THIS THING?
DAD, WHAT DID YOU SAY?
THE LETTER CAME IN THE MAIL TODAY.
I SHOULDA LET YOU OPEN IT, BUT--
ARE YOU SERIOUS?
WOOHOOO!

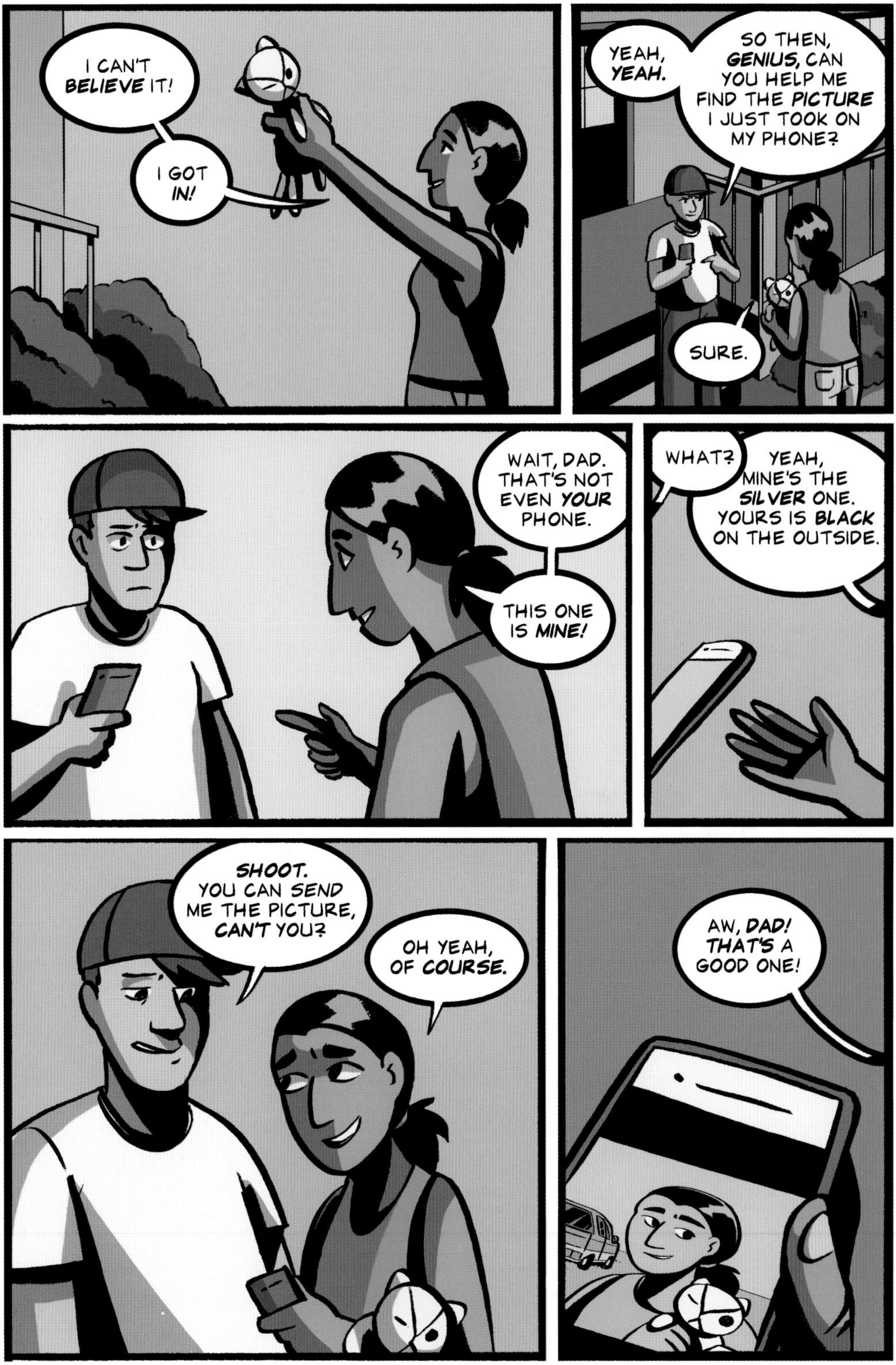
I CAN'T BELIEVE IT!
I GOT IN!
YEAH, YEAH.
SO THEN, GENIUS, CAN YOU HELP ME FIND THE PICTURE I JUST TOOK ON MY PHONE?
SURE.
WAIT, DAD. THAT'S NOT EVEN YOUR PHONE.
THIS ONE IS MINE!
WHAT?
YEAH, MINE'S THE SILVER ONE. YOURS IS BLACK ON THE OUTSIDE.
SHOOT. YOU CAN SEND ME THE PICTURE, CAN'T YOU?
OH YEAH, OF COURSE.
AW, DAD! THAT'S A GOOD ONE!

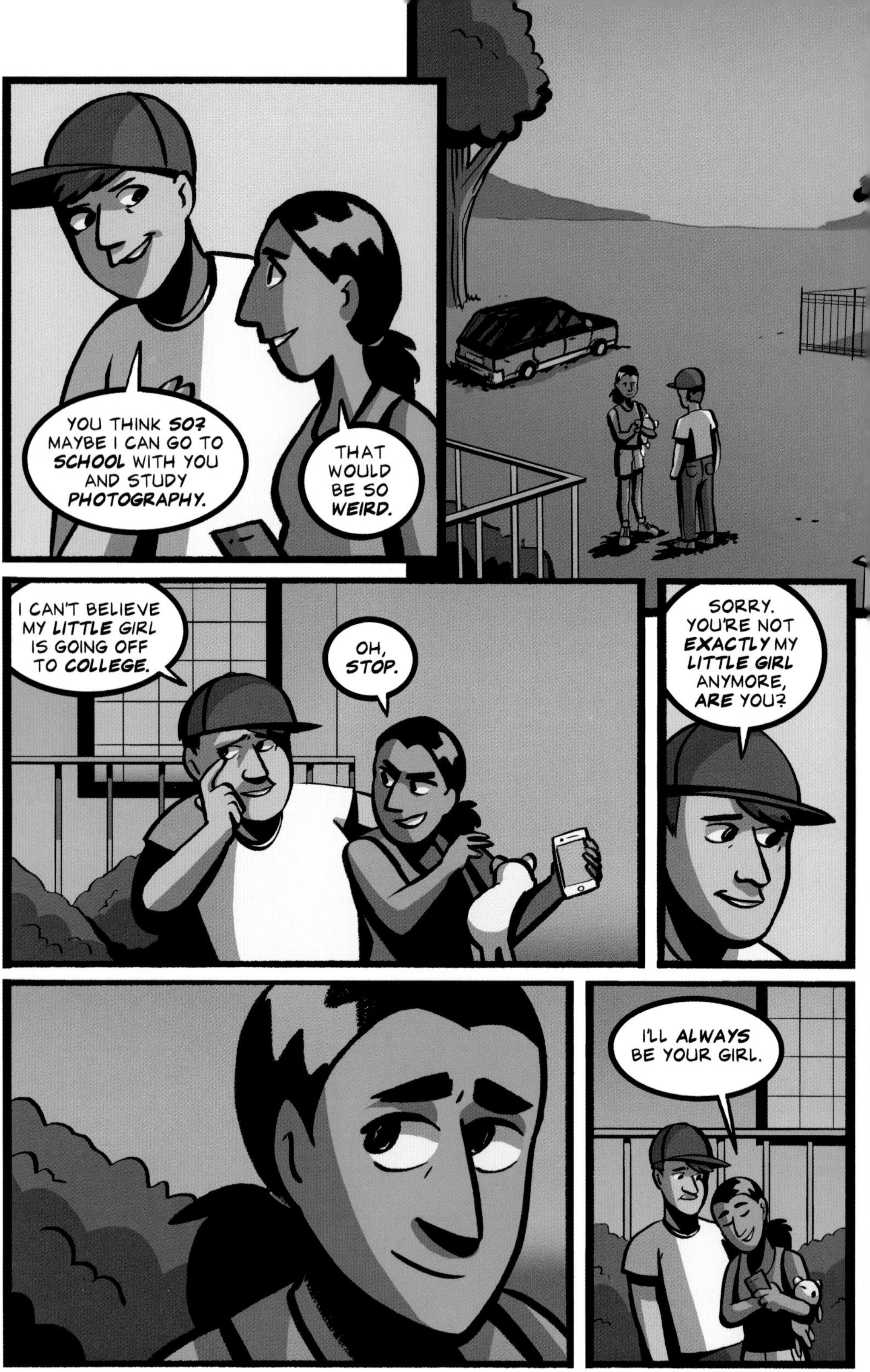
YOU THINK SO? MAYBE I CAN GO TO SCHOOL WITH YOU AND STUDY PHOTOGRAPHY.
THAT WOULD BE SO WEIRD.
I CAN'T BELIEVE MY LITTLE GIRL IS GOING OFF TO COLLEGE.
OH, STOP.
SORRY. YOU'RE NOT EXACTLY MY LITTLE GIRL ANYMORE, ARE YOU?
I'LL ALWAYS BE YOUR GIRL.

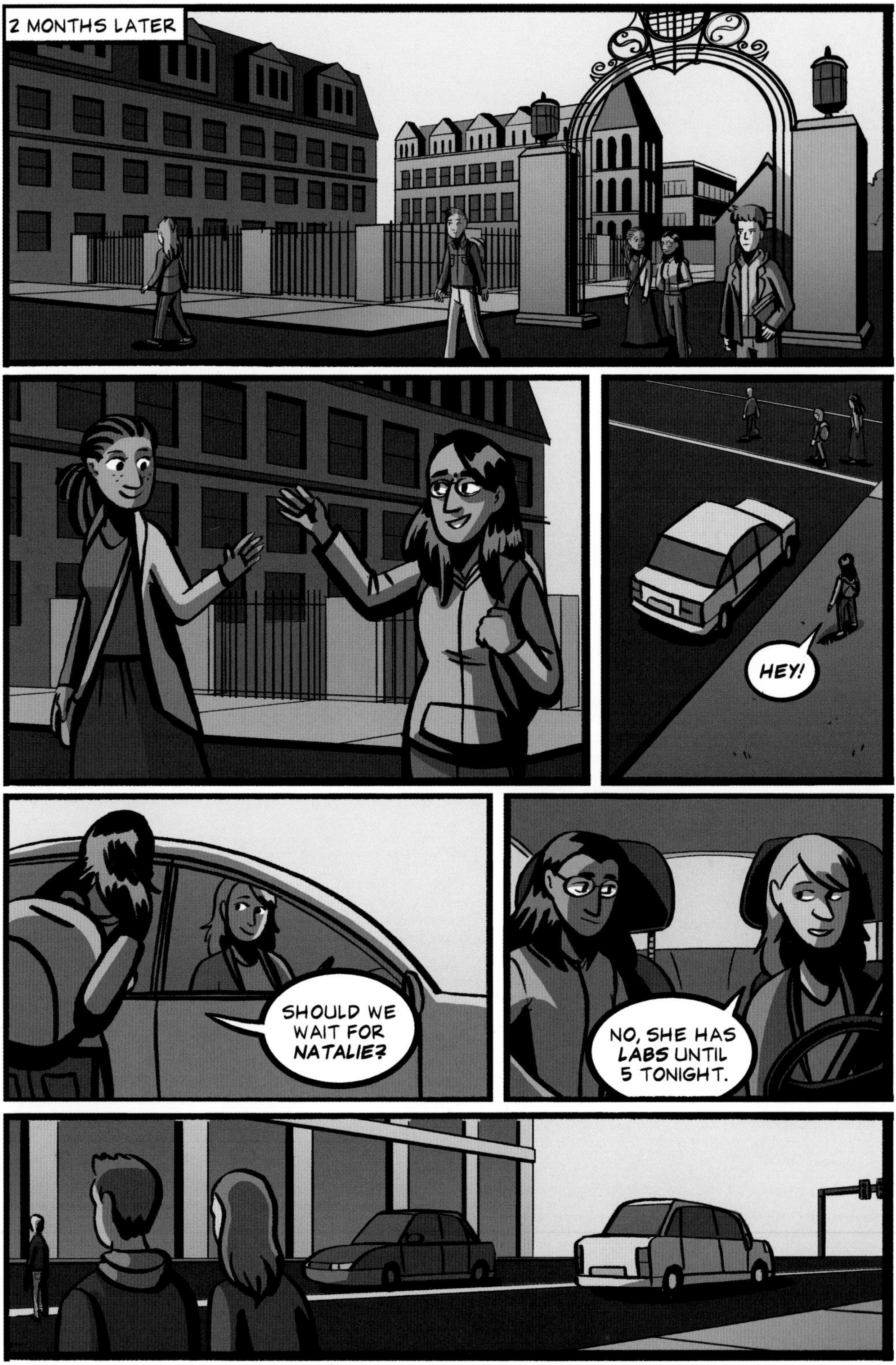
2 MONTHS LATER
HEY!
SHOULD WE WAIT FOR NATALIE?
NO, SHE HAS LABS UNTIL 5 TONIGHT.

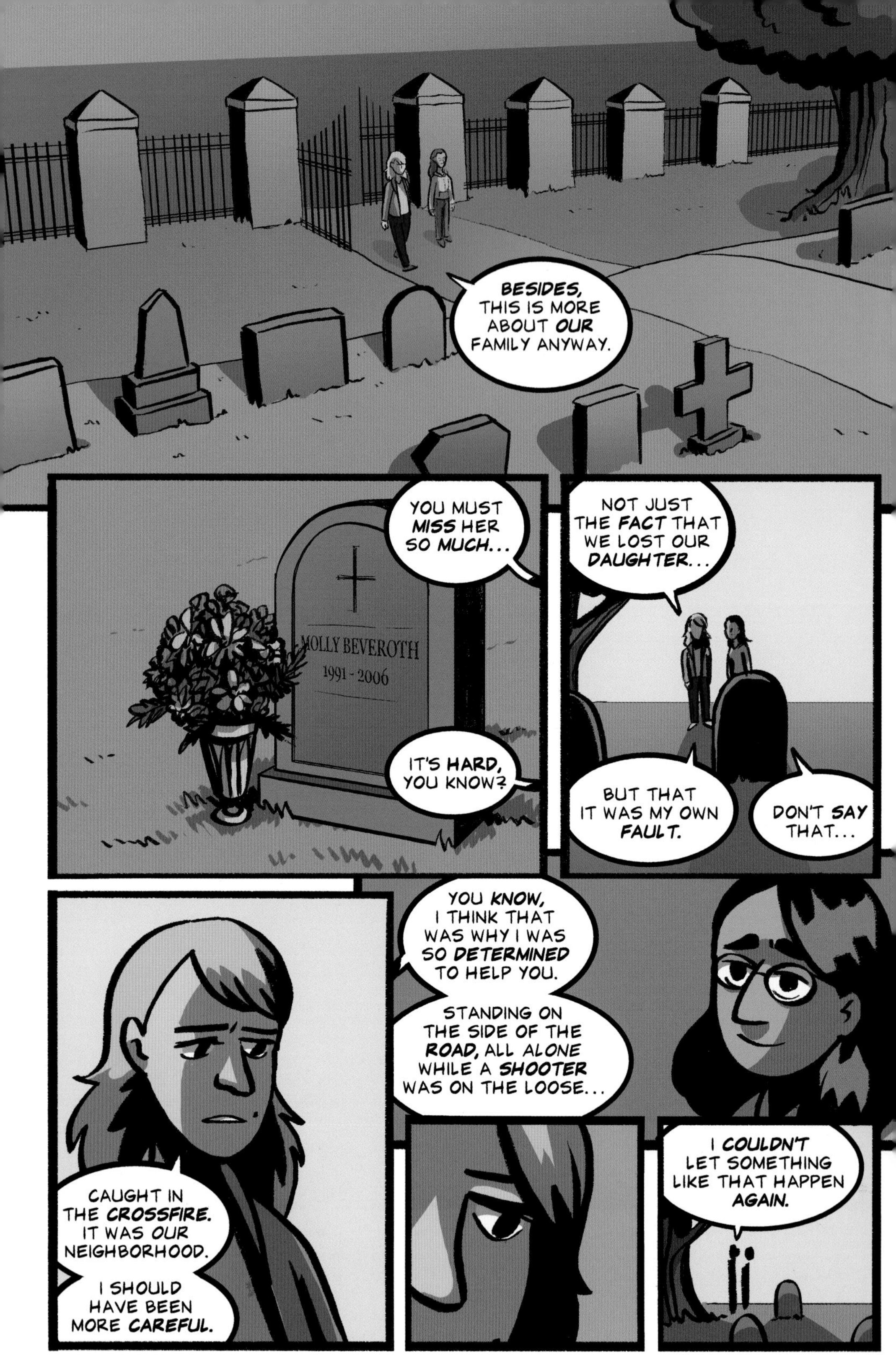
BESIDES, THIS IS MORE ABOUT OUR FAMILY ANYWAY.
YOU MUST MISS HER SO MUCH...
MOLLY BEVEROTH
1991 - 2006
IT'S HARD, YOU KNOW?
NOT JUST THE FACT THAT WE LOST OUR DAUGHTER...
BUT THAT IT WAS MY OWN FAULT.
DON'T SAY THAT...
CAUGHT IN THE CROSSFIRE. IT WAS OUR NEIGHBORHOOD.
I SHOULD HAVE BEEN MORE CAREFUL.
YOU KNOW, I THINK THAT WAS WHY I WAS SO DETERMINED TO HELP YOU.
STANDING ON THE SIDE OF THE ROAD, ALL ALONE WHILE A SHOOTER WAS ON THE LOOSE...
I COULDN'T LET SOMETHING LIKE THAT HAPPEN AGAIN.

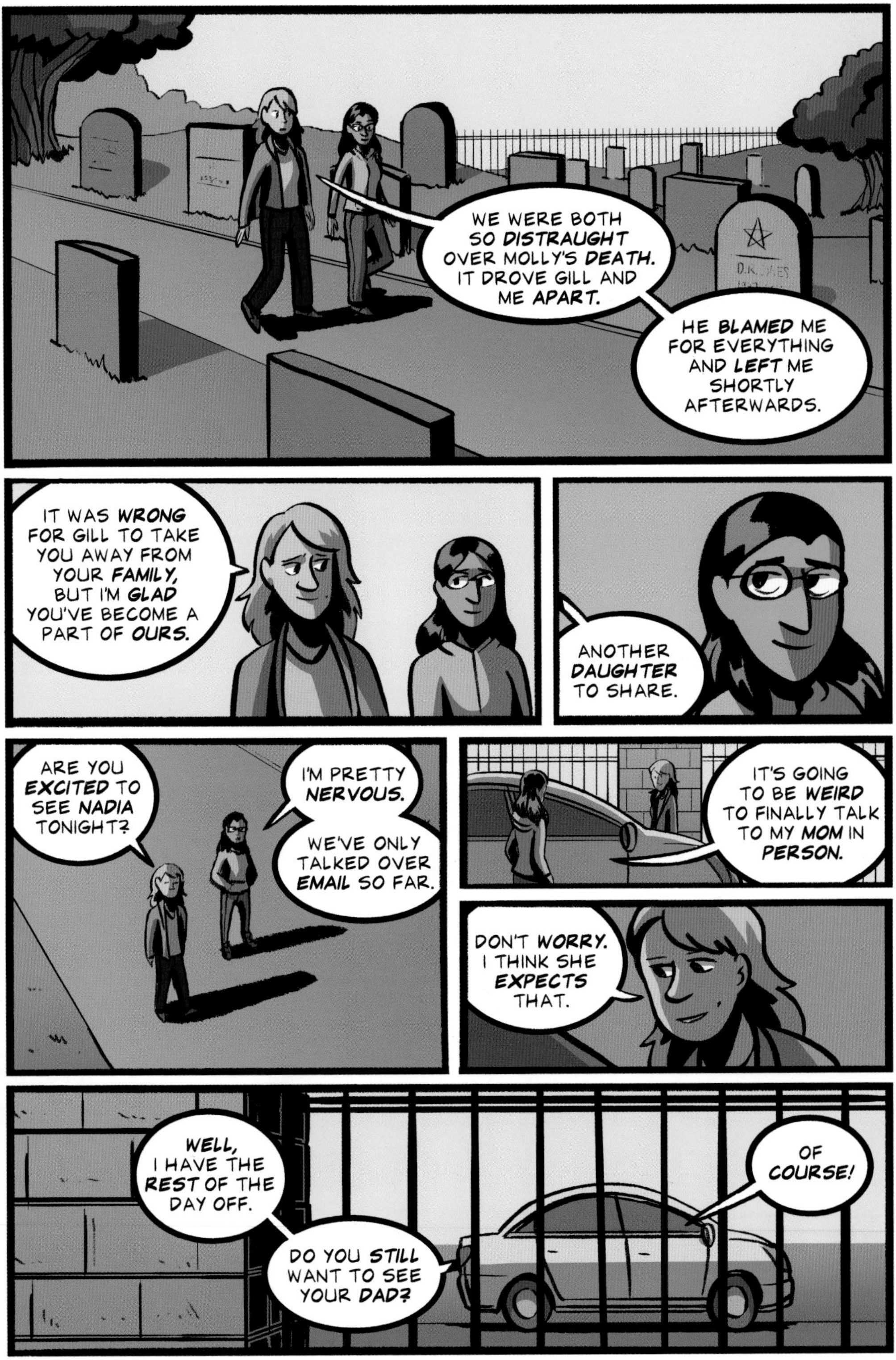
WE WERE BOTH SO DISTRAUGHT OVER MOLLY'S DEATH. IT DROVE GILL AND ME APART.
HE BLAMED ME FOR EVERYTHING AND LEFT ME SHORTLY AFTERWARDS.
IT WAS WRONG FOR GILL TO TAKE YOU AWAY FROM YOUR FAMILY, BUT I'M GLAD YOU'VE BECOME A PART OF OURS.
ANOTHER DAUGHTER TO SHARE.
ARE YOU EXCITED TO SEE NADIA TONIGHT?
I'M PRETTY NERVOUS.
WE'VE ONLY TALKED OVER EMAIL SO FAR.
IT'S GOING TO BE WEIRD TO FINALLY TALK TO MY MOM IN PERSON.
DON'T WORRY. I THINK SHE EXPECTS THAT.
WELL, I HAVE THE REST OF THE DAY OFF.
DO YOU STILL WANT TO SEE YOUR DAD?
OF COURSE!

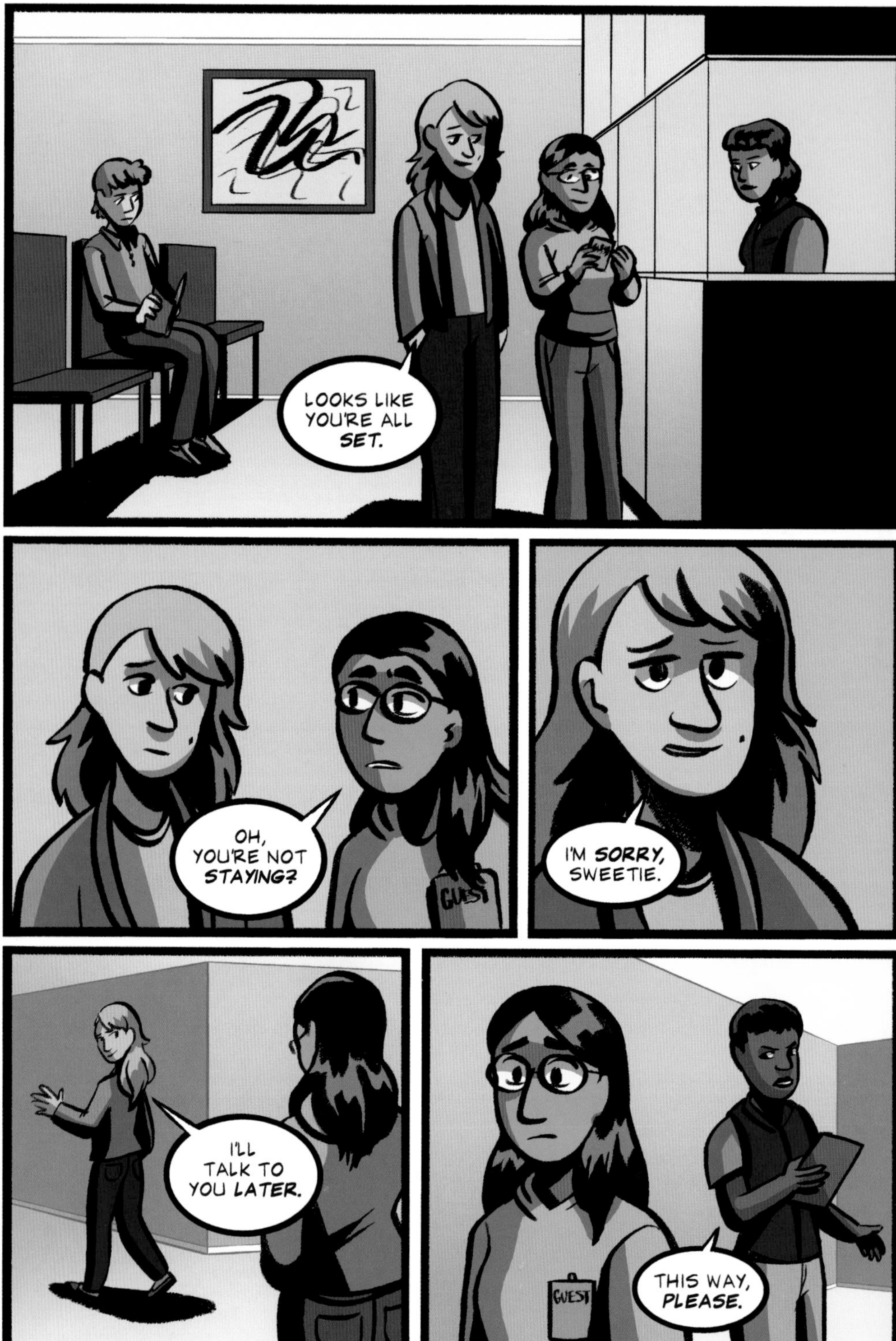
LOOKS LIKE YOU'RE ALL SET.
OH, YOU'RE NOT STAYING?
I'M SORRY, SWEETIE.
I'LL TALK TO YOU LATER.
THIS WAY, PLEASE.

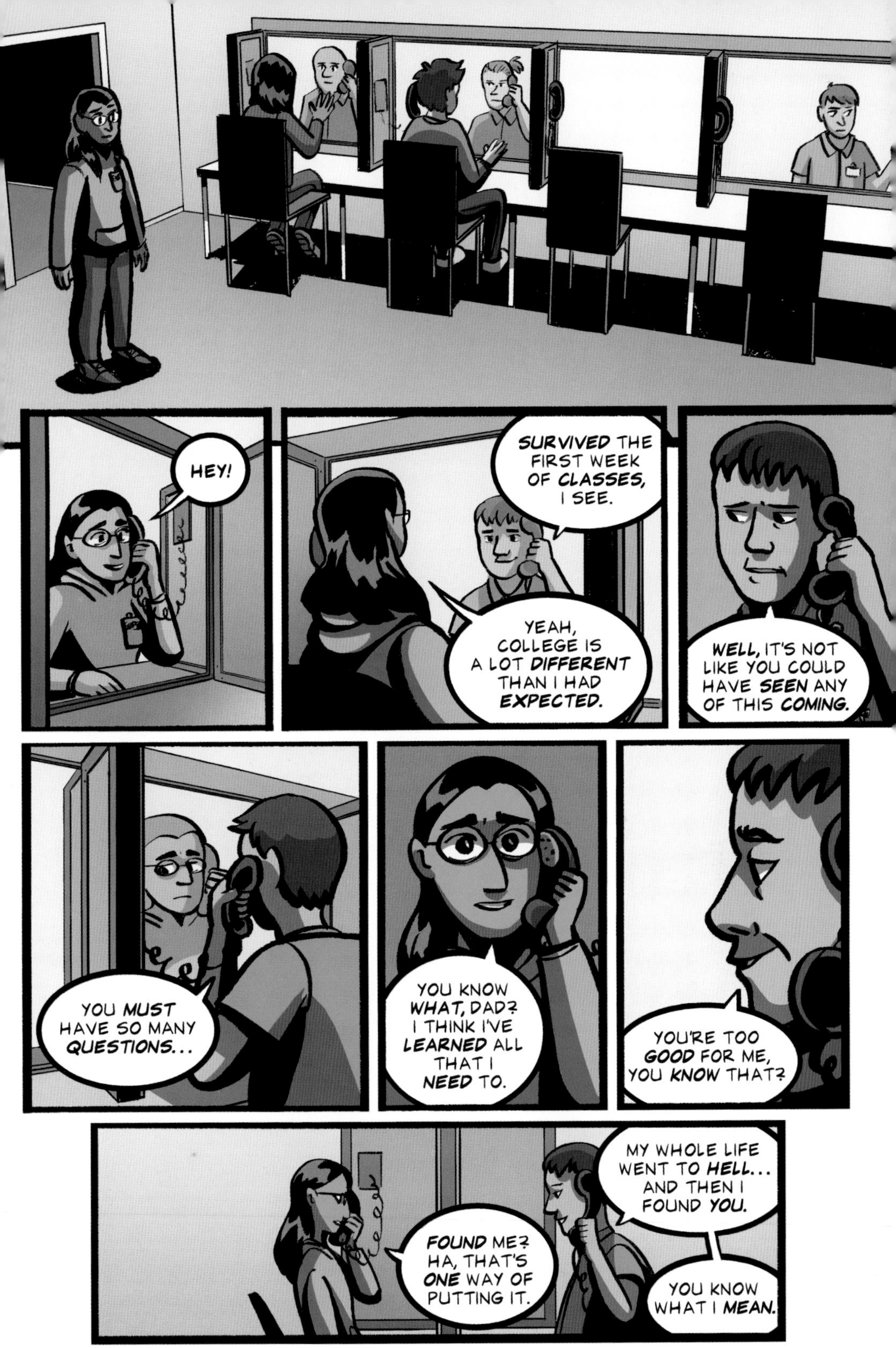
HEY!
SURVIVED THE FIRST WEEK OF CLASSES, I SEE.
YEAH, COLLEGE IS A LOT DIFFERENT THAN I HAD EXPECTED.
WELL, IT'S NOT LIKE YOU COULD HAVE SEEN ANY OF THIS COMING.
YOU MUST HAVE SO MANY QUESTIONS...
YOU KNOW WHAT, DAD? I THINK I'VE LEARNED ALL THAT I NEED TO.
YOU'RE TOO GOOD FOR ME, YOU KNOW THAT?
MY WHOLE LIFE WENT TO HELL... AND THEN I FOUND YOU.
FOUND ME? HA, THAT'S ONE WAY OF PUTTING IT.
YOU KNOW WHAT I MEAN.

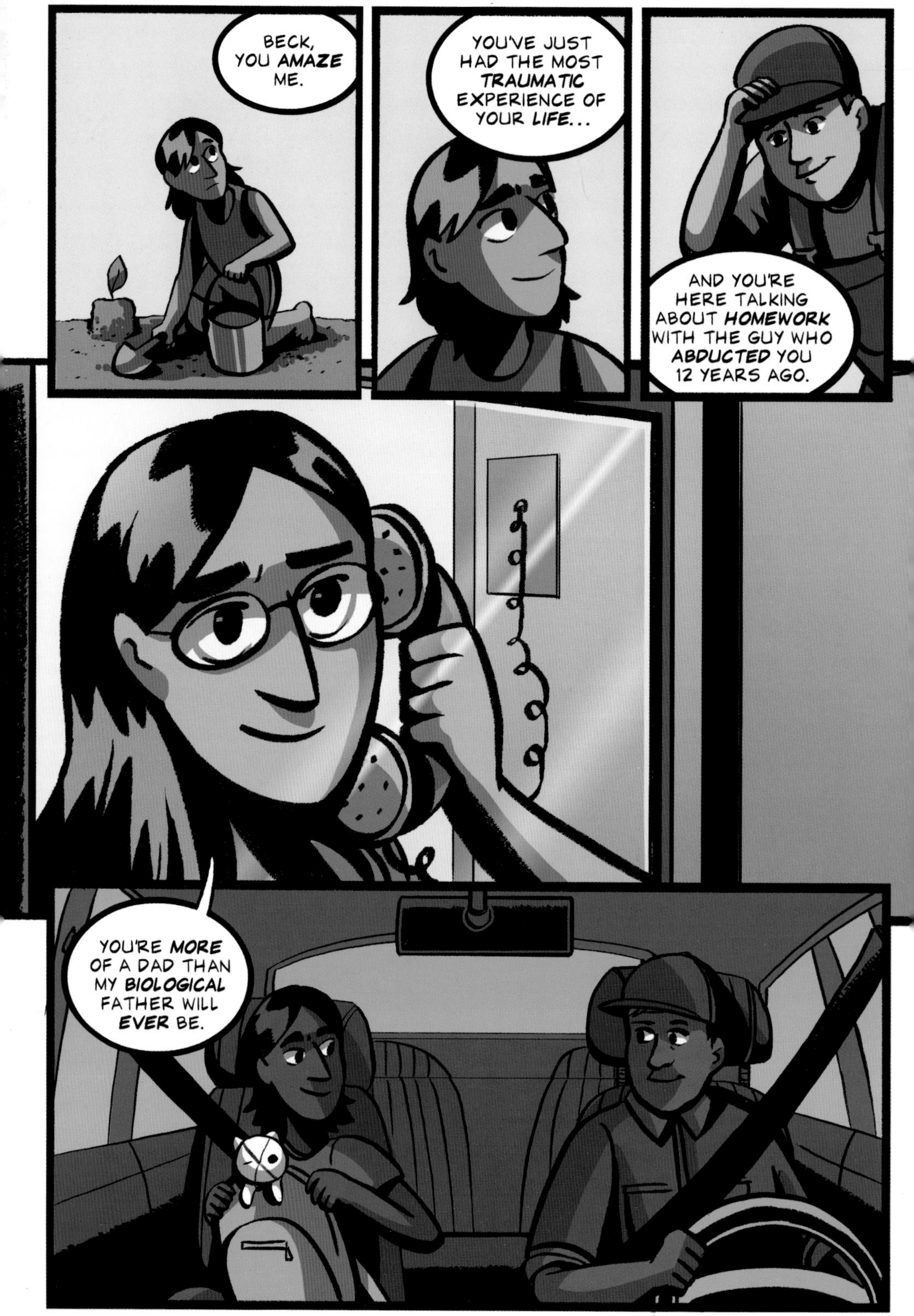
BECK, YOU AMAZE ME.
YOU'VE JUST HAD THE MOST TRAUMATIC EXPERIENCE OF YOUR LIFE...
AND YOU'RE HERE TALKING ABOUT HOMEWORK WITH THE GUY WHO ABDUCTED YOU 12 YEARS AGO.
YOU'RE MORE OF A DAD THAN MY BIOLOGICAL FATHER WILL EVER BE.